ARCHIE COMIC PUBLICATIONS,

CHAIRMAN AND CO-PUBLISHER
MICHAEL I. SILBERKLEIT

PRESIDENT AND CO-PUBLISHER
RICHARD H. GOLDWATER

VP/MANAGING EDITOR
VICTOR GORELICK

VP/DIRECTOR OF CIRCULATION
FRED MAUSSER

EDITOR
NELSON RIBEIRO

CONTRIBUTING EDITOR
MIKE PELLERITO

ART DIRECTOR
JOE PEP

SCRIPT
MELANIE J. MORGAN

PENCILS
STEVEN BUTLER

INKING
AL MILGROM

COLORS
STEPHANIE VOZZO

LETTERS
JOHN WORKMAN

BETTY AND VERONICA IN BAD BOY TROUBLE, Volume 1, 2007. Printed in Canada. Published by Archie Comic Publications, Inc., 325 Fayette Avenue, Mamaroneck, New York 10543-2318.

ISBN-13: 978-1-879794-25-2
ISBN-10: 1-879794-25-X

www.archiecomics.com

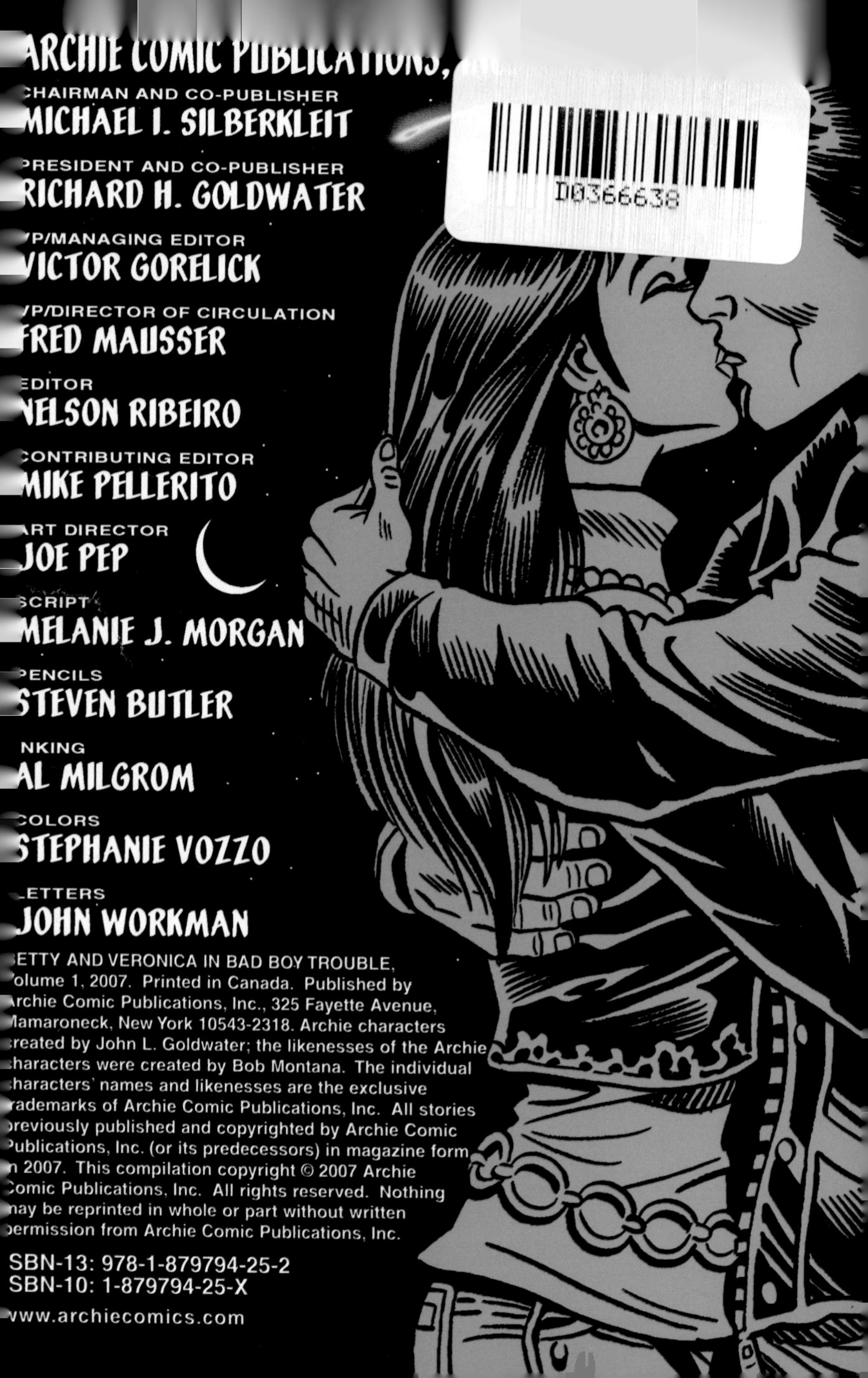

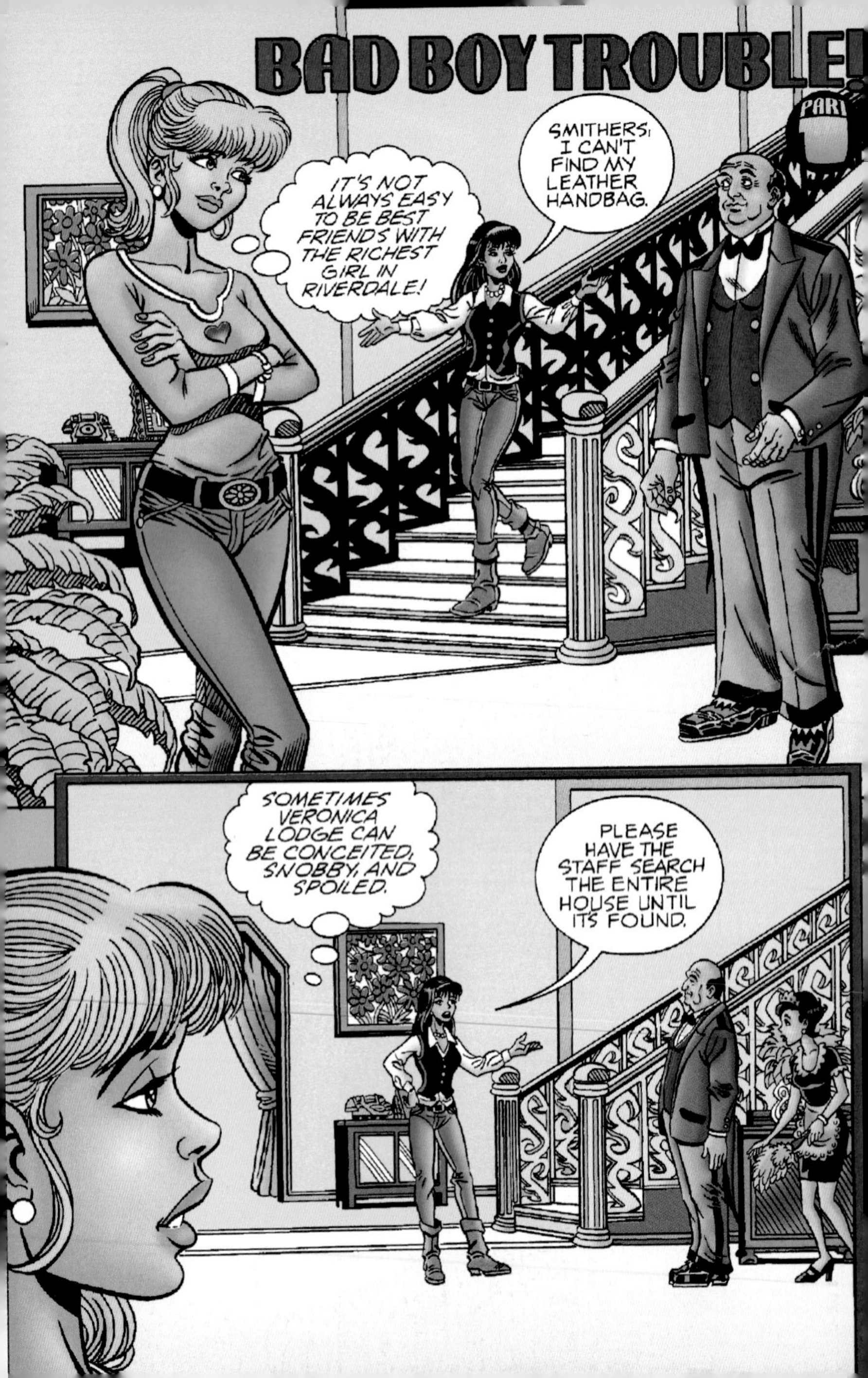
BAD BOY TROUBLE!
PART 1
IT'S NOT ALWAYS EASY TO BE BEST FRIENDS WITH THE RICHEST GIRL IN RIVERDALE!
SMITHERS: I CAN'T FIND MY LEATHER HANDBAG.
SOMETIMES VERONICA LODGE CAN BE CONCEITED, SNOBBY, AND SPOILED.
PLEASE HAVE THE STAFF SEARCH THE ENTIRE HOUSE UNTIL IT'S FOUND.

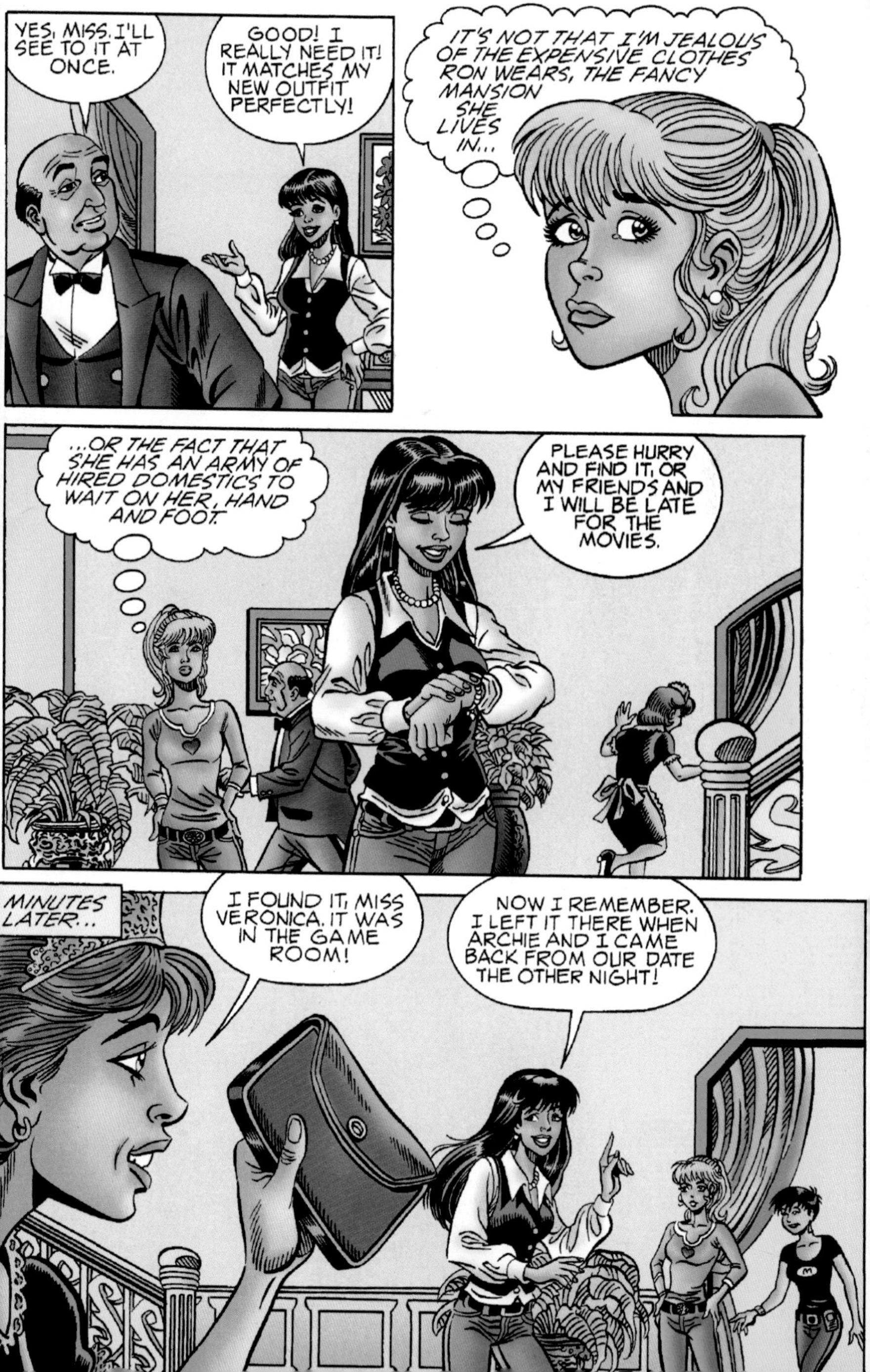
YES, MISS. I'LL SEE TO IT AT ONCE.
GOOD! I REALLY NEED IT! IT MATCHES MY NEW OUTFIT PERFECTLY!
IT'S NOT THAT I'M JEALOUS OF THE EXPENSIVE CLOTHES RON WEARS, THE FANCY MANSION SHE LIVES IN...
...OR THE FACT THAT SHE HAS AN ARMY OF HIRED DOMESTICS TO WAIT ON HER, HAND AND FOOT.
PLEASE HURRY AND FIND IT, OR MY FRIENDS AND I WILL BE LATE FOR THE MOVIES.
MINUTES LATER...
I FOUND IT, MISS VERONICA. IT WAS IN THE GAME ROOM!
NOW I REMEMBER. I LEFT IT THERE WHEN ARCHIE AND I CAME BACK FROM OUR DATE THE OTHER NIGHT!

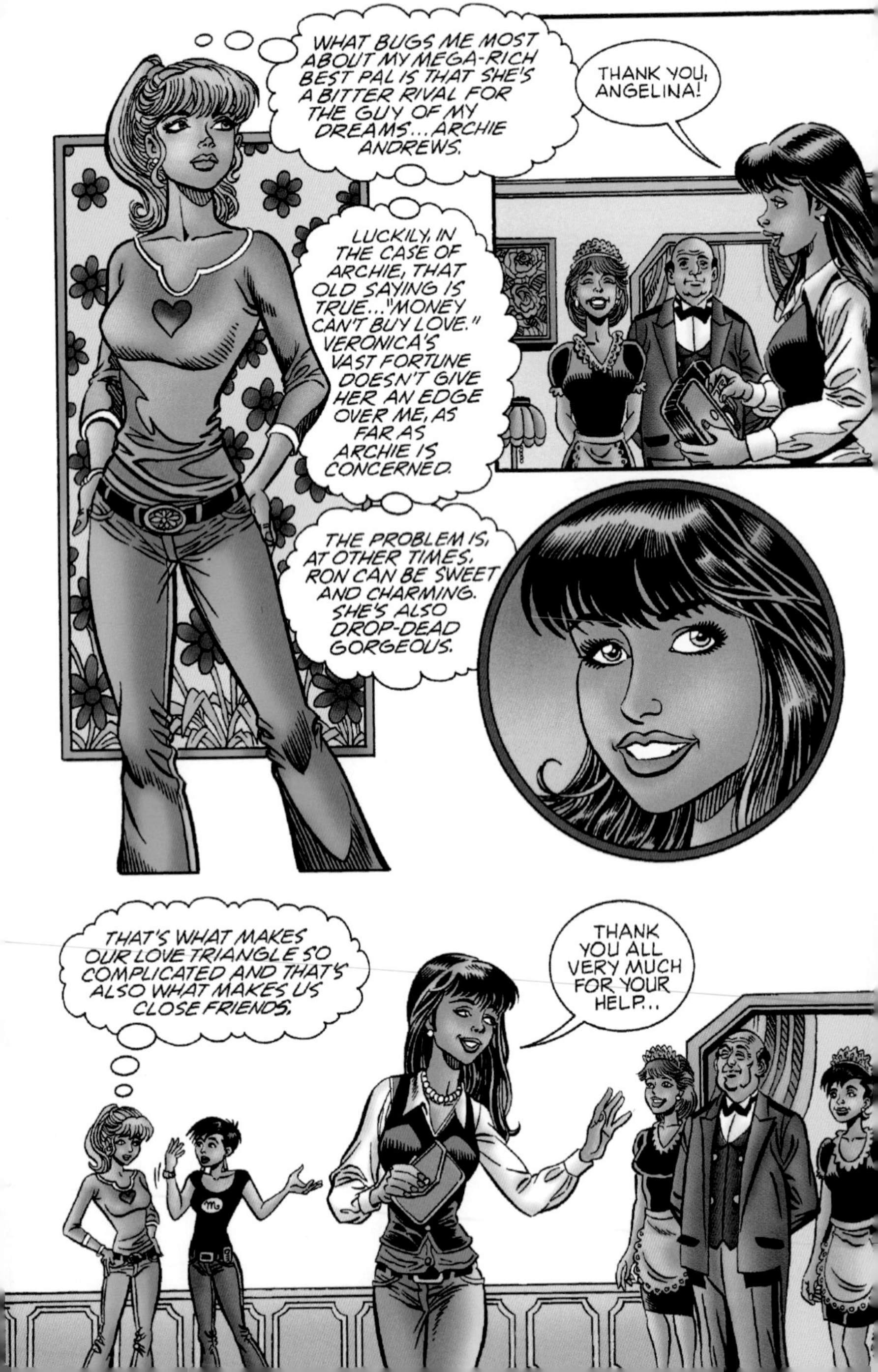
WHAT BUGS ME MOST ABOUT MY MEGA-RICH BEST PAL IS THAT SHE'S A BITTER RIVAL FOR THE GUY OF MY DREAMS... ARCHIE ANDREWS.
THANK YOU, ANGELINA!
LUCKILY, IN THE CASE OF ARCHIE, THAT OLD SAYING IS TRUE..."MONEY CAN'T BUY LOVE." VERONICA'S VAST FORTUNE DOESN'T GIVE HER AN EDGE OVER ME, AS FAR AS ARCHIE IS CONCERNED.
THE PROBLEM IS, AT OTHER TIMES, RON CAN BE SWEET AND CHARMING. SHE'S ALSO DROP-DEAD GORGEOUS.
THAT'S WHAT MAKES OUR LOVE TRIANGLE SO COMPLICATED AND THAT'S ALSO WHAT MAKES US CLOSE FRIENDS.
THANK YOU ALL VERY MUCH FOR YOUR HELP...

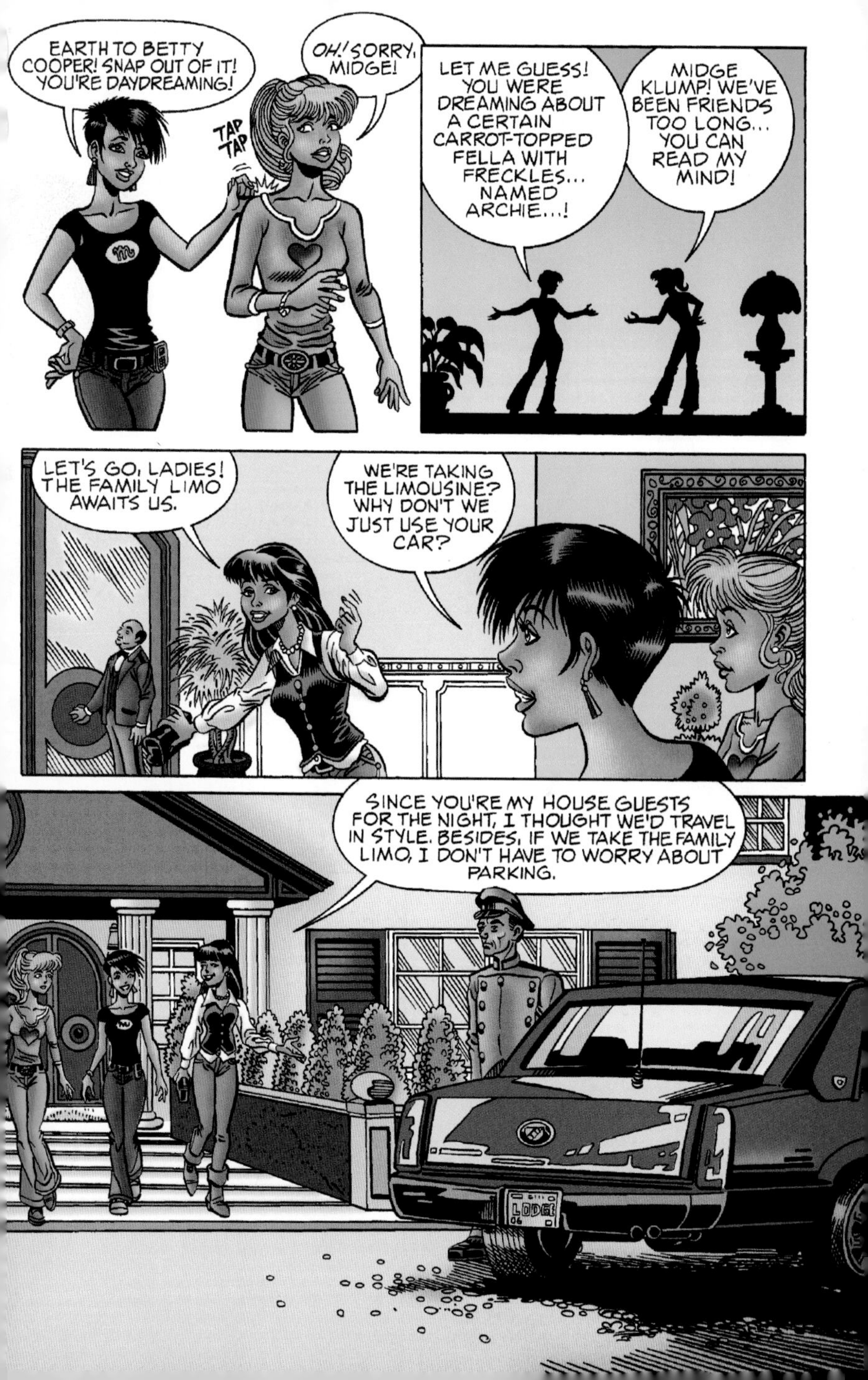
EARTH TO BETTY COOPER! SNAP OUT OF IT! YOU'RE DAYDREAMING!
OH! SORRY, MIDGE!
TAP TAP
LET ME GUESS! YOU WERE DREAMING ABOUT A CERTAIN CARROT-TOPPED FELLA WITH FRECKLES... NAMED ARCHIE...!
MIDGE KLUMP! WE'VE BEEN FRIENDS TOO LONG... YOU CAN READ MY MIND!
LET'S GO, LADIES! THE FAMILY LIMO AWAITS US.
WE'RE TAKING THE LIMOUSINE? WHY DON'T WE JUST USE YOUR CAR?
SINCE YOU'RE MY HOUSE GUESTS FOR THE NIGHT, I THOUGHT WE'D TRAVEL IN STYLE. BESIDES, IF WE TAKE THE FAMILY LIMO, I DON'T HAVE TO WORRY ABOUT PARKING.
LODGE

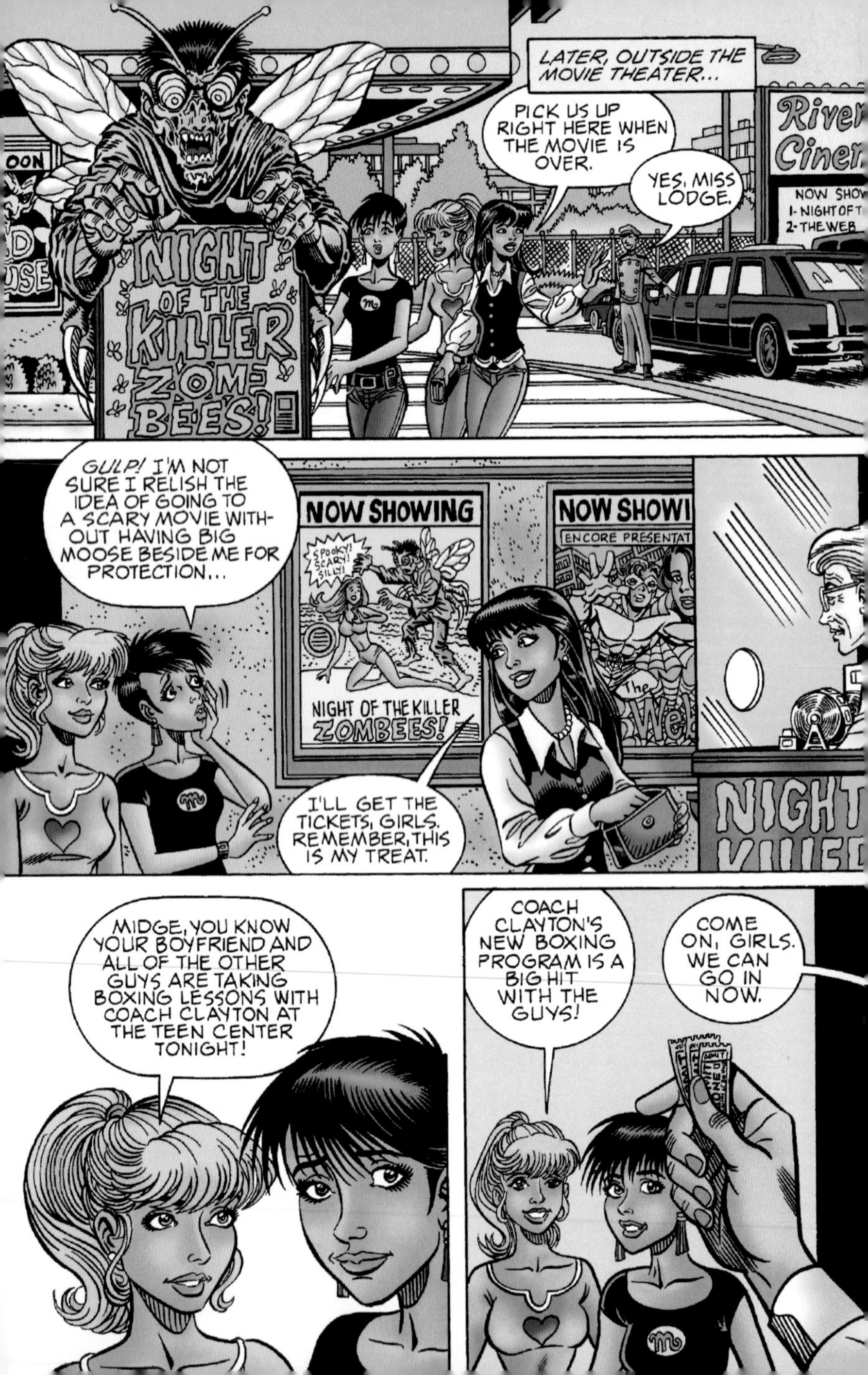

LATER, OUTSIDE THE MOVIE THEATER...
NIGHT OF THE KILLER ZOM-BEES!
River Cinema
NOW SHOW
1- NIGHT OF T
2- THE WEB
PICK US UP RIGHT HERE WHEN THE MOVIE IS OVER.
YES, MISS LODGE.
GULP! I'M NOT SURE I RELISH THE IDEA OF GOING TO A SCARY MOVIE WITH-OUT HAVING BIG MOOSE BESIDE ME FOR PROTECTION...
NOW SHOWING
SPOOKY! SCARY! SILLY!
NIGHT OF THE KILLER ZOMBEES!
NOW SHOWI
ENCORE PRESENTAT
I'LL GET THE TICKETS, GIRLS. REMEMBER, THIS IS MY TREAT.
MIDGE, YOU KNOW YOUR BOYFRIEND AND ALL OF THE OTHER GUYS ARE TAKING BOXING LESSONS WITH COACH CLAYTON AT THE TEEN CENTER TONIGHT!
COACH CLAYTON'S NEW BOXING PROGRAM IS A BIG HIT WITH THE GUYS!
COME ON, GIRLS. WE CAN GO IN NOW.

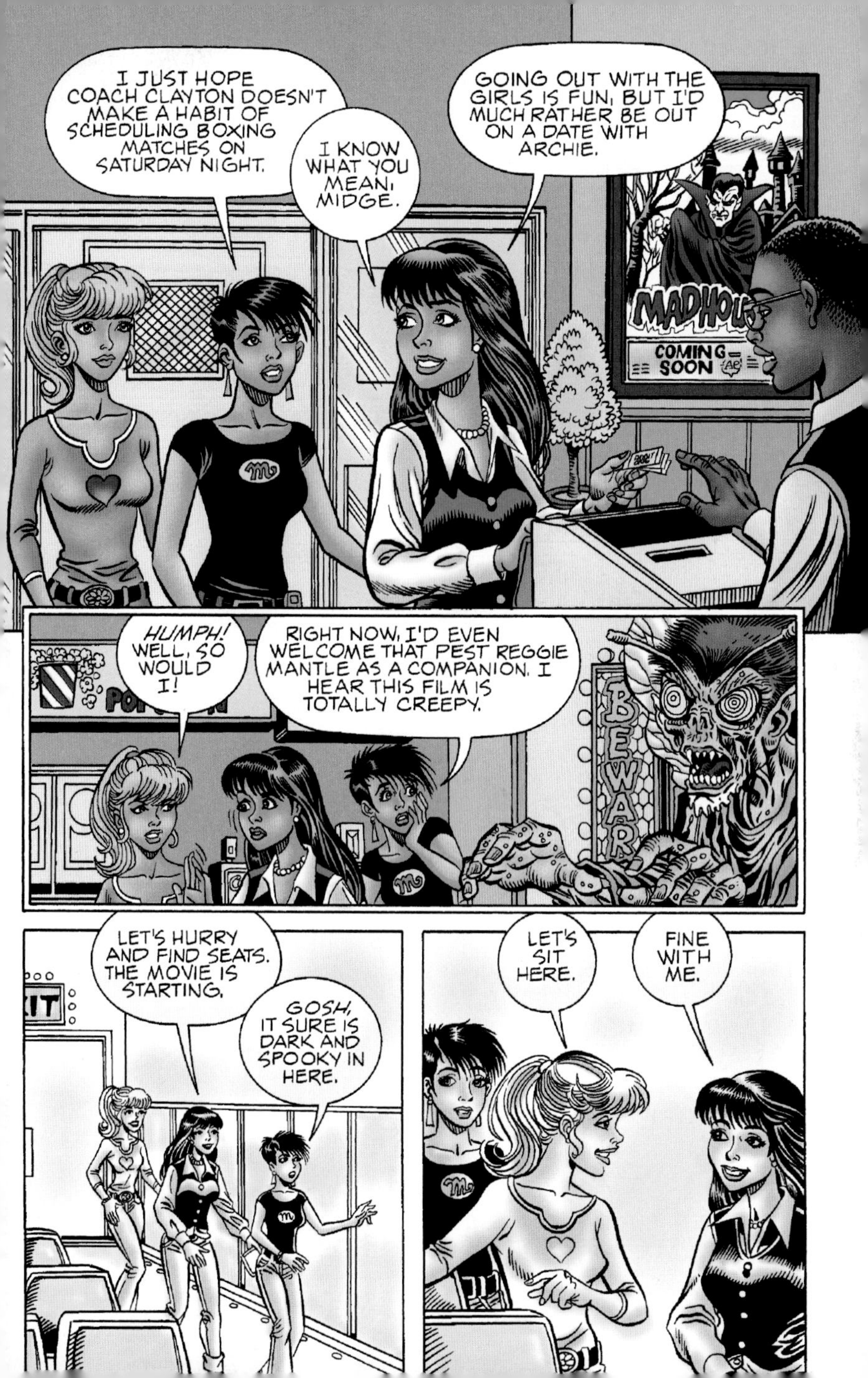
I JUST HOPE COACH CLAYTON DOESN'T MAKE A HABIT OF SCHEDULING BOXING MATCHES ON SATURDAY NIGHT.
I KNOW WHAT YOU MEAN, MIDGE.
GOING OUT WITH THE GIRLS IS FUN, BUT I'D MUCH RATHER BE OUT ON A DATE WITH ARCHIE.
MADHOUS
COMING SOON
HUMPH! WELL, SO WOULD I!
RIGHT NOW, I'D EVEN WELCOME THAT PEST REGGIE MANTLE AS A COMPANION. I HEAR THIS FILM IS TOTALLY CREEPY.
BEWAR
LET'S HURRY AND FIND SEATS. THE MOVIE IS STARTING.
GOSH, IT SURE IS DARK AND SPOOKY IN HERE.
LET'S SIT HERE.
FINE WITH ME.

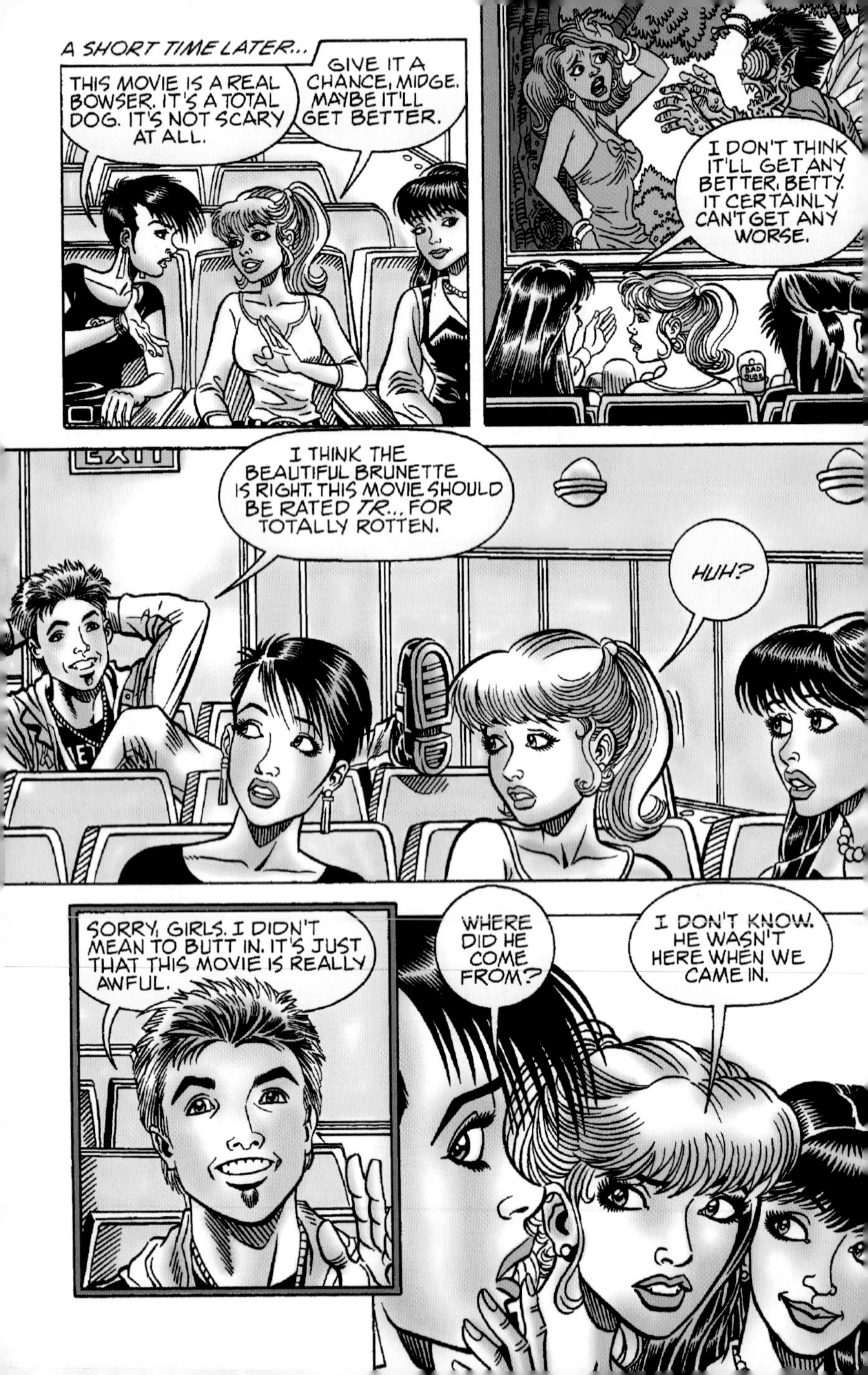
A SHORT TIME LATER...
THIS MOVIE IS A REAL BOWSER. IT'S A TOTAL DOG. IT'S NOT SCARY AT ALL.
GIVE IT A CHANCE, MIDGE. MAYBE IT'LL GET BETTER.
I DON'T THINK IT'LL GET ANY BETTER, BETTY. IT CERTAINLY CAN'T GET ANY WORSE.
BAD DUDE
EXIT
I THINK THE BEAUTIFUL BRUNETTE IS RIGHT. THIS MOVIE SHOULD BE RATED *TR*... FOR TOTALLY ROTTEN.
HUH?
SORRY, GIRLS. I DIDN'T MEAN TO BUTT IN. IT'S JUST THAT THIS MOVIE IS REALLY AWFUL.
WHERE DID HE COME FROM?
I DON'T KNOW. HE WASN'T HERE WHEN WE CAME IN.

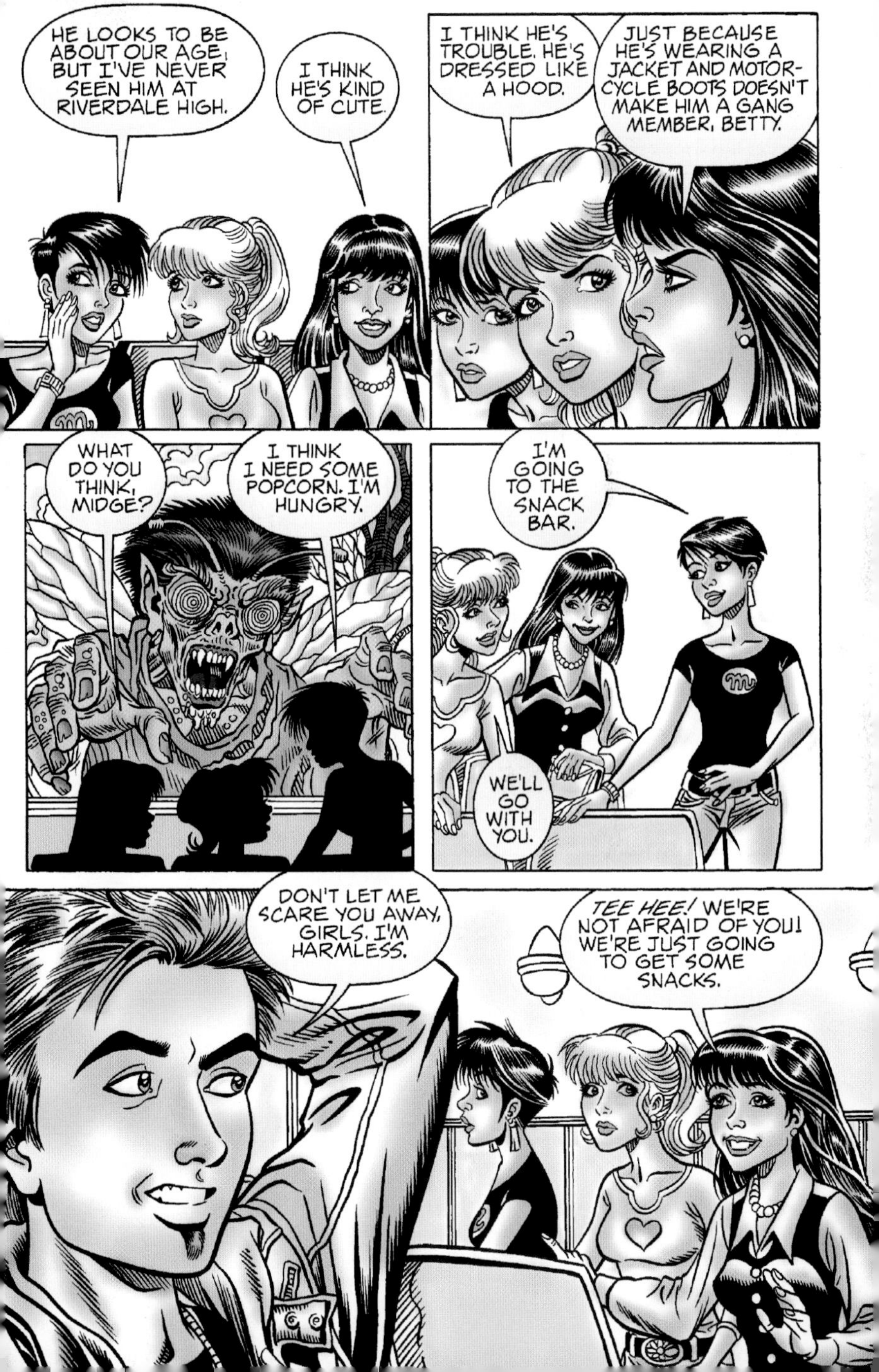
HE LOOKS TO BE ABOUT OUR AGE, BUT I'VE NEVER SEEN HIM AT RIVERDALE HIGH.
I THINK HE'S KIND OF CUTE.
I THINK HE'S TROUBLE. HE'S DRESSED LIKE A HOOD.
JUST BECAUSE HE'S WEARING A JACKET AND MOTOR-CYCLE BOOTS DOESN'T MAKE HIM A GANG MEMBER, BETTY.
WHAT DO YOU THINK, MIDGE?
I THINK I NEED SOME POPCORN. I'M HUNGRY.
I'M GOING TO THE SNACK BAR.
WE'LL GO WITH YOU.
DON'T LET ME SCARE YOU AWAY, GIRLS. I'M HARMLESS.
TEE HEE! WE'RE NOT AFRAID OF YOU! WE'RE JUST GOING TO GET SOME SNACKS.

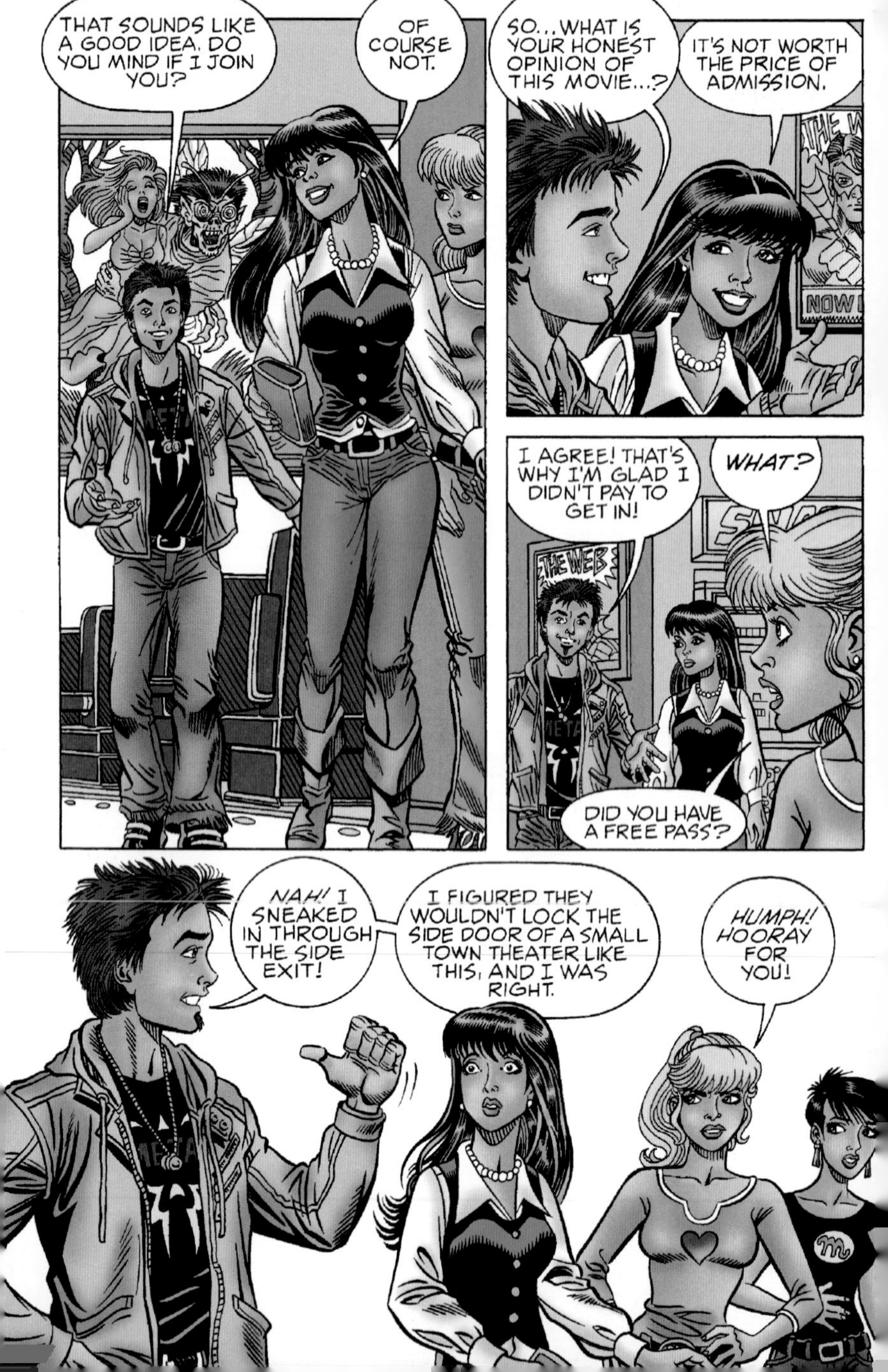
THAT SOUNDS LIKE A GOOD IDEA. DO YOU MIND IF I JOIN YOU?
OF COURSE NOT.
SO... WHAT IS YOUR HONEST OPINION OF THIS MOVIE...?
IT'S NOT WORTH THE PRICE OF ADMISSION.
I AGREE! THAT'S WHY I'M GLAD I DIDN'T PAY TO GET IN!
WHAT?
THE WEB
DID YOU HAVE A FREE PASS?
NAH! I SNEAKED IN THROUGH THE SIDE EXIT!
I FIGURED THEY WOULDN'T LOCK THE SIDE DOOR OF A SMALL TOWN THEATER LIKE THIS, AND I WAS RIGHT.
HUMPH! HOORAY FOR YOU!

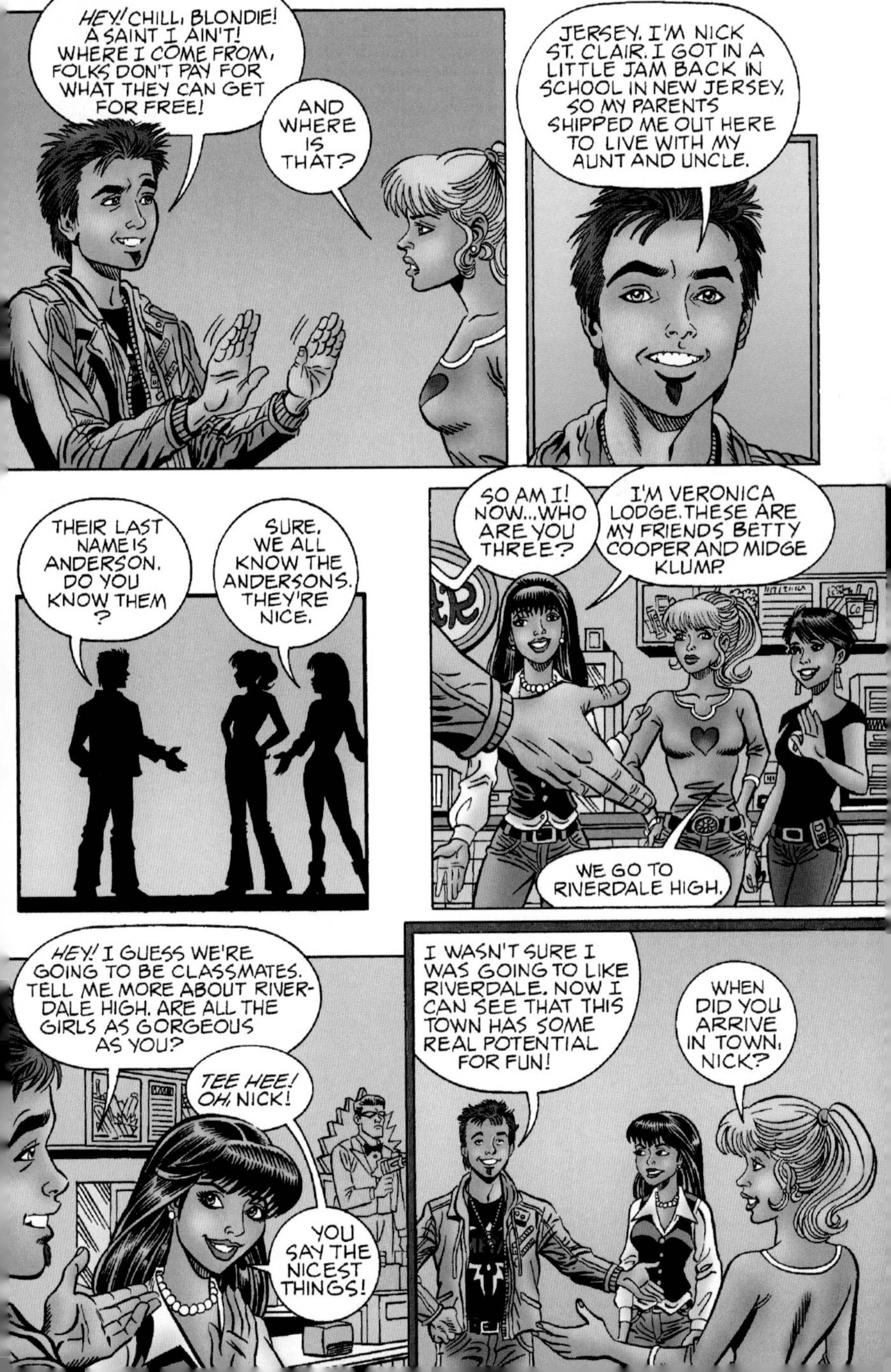
HEY! CHILL, BLONDIE! A SAINT I AIN'T! WHERE I COME FROM, FOLKS DON'T PAY FOR WHAT THEY CAN GET FOR FREE!
AND WHERE IS THAT?
JERSEY. I'M NICK ST. CLAIR. I GOT IN A LITTLE JAM BACK IN SCHOOL IN NEW JERSEY, SO MY PARENTS SHIPPED ME OUT HERE TO LIVE WITH MY AUNT AND UNCLE.
THEIR LAST NAME IS ANDERSON. DO YOU KNOW THEM?
SURE, WE ALL KNOW THE ANDERSONS. THEY'RE NICE.
SO AM I! NOW...WHO ARE YOU THREE?
I'M VERONICA LODGE. THESE ARE MY FRIENDS BETTY COOPER AND MIDGE KLUMP.
WE GO TO RIVERDALE HIGH.
HEY! I GUESS WE'RE GOING TO BE CLASSMATES. TELL ME MORE ABOUT RIVER-DALE HIGH. ARE ALL THE GIRLS AS GORGEOUS AS YOU?
TEE HEE! OH, NICK!
YOU SAY THE NICEST THINGS!
I WASN'T SURE I WAS GOING TO LIKE RIVERDALE. NOW I CAN SEE THAT THIS TOWN HAS SOME REAL POTENTIAL FOR FUN!
WHEN DID YOU ARRIVE IN TOWN, NICK?

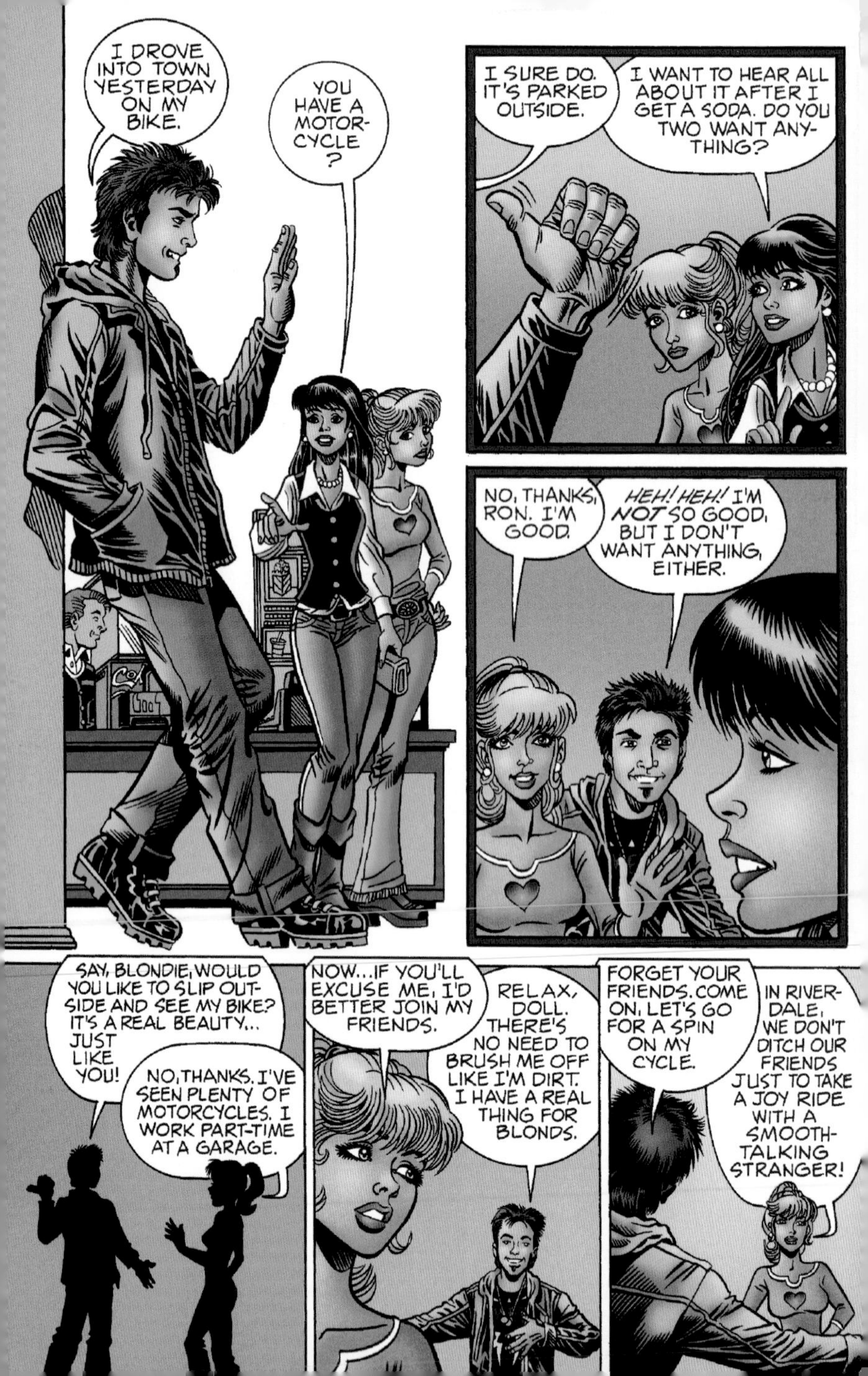
I DROVE INTO TOWN YESTERDAY ON MY BIKE.
YOU HAVE A MOTOR-CYCLE?
I SURE DO. IT'S PARKED OUTSIDE.
I WANT TO HEAR ALL ABOUT IT AFTER I GET A SODA. DO YOU TWO WANT ANY-THING?
NO, THANKS, RON. I'M GOOD.
HEH! HEH! I'M NOT SO GOOD, BUT I DON'T WANT ANYTHING, EITHER.
SAY, BLONDIE, WOULD YOU LIKE TO SLIP OUT-SIDE AND SEE MY BIKE? IT'S A REAL BEAUTY... JUST LIKE YOU!
NO, THANKS. I'VE SEEN PLENTY OF MOTORCYCLES. I WORK PART-TIME AT A GARAGE.
NOW...IF YOU'LL EXCUSE ME, I'D BETTER JOIN MY FRIENDS.
RELAX, DOLL. THERE'S NO NEED TO BRUSH ME OFF LIKE I'M DIRT. I HAVE A REAL THING FOR BLONDS.
FORGET YOUR FRIENDS. COME ON, LET'S GO FOR A SPIN ON MY CYCLE.
IN RIVER-DALE, WE DON'T DITCH OUR FRIENDS JUST TO TAKE A JOY RIDE WITH A SMOOTH-TALKING STRANGER!

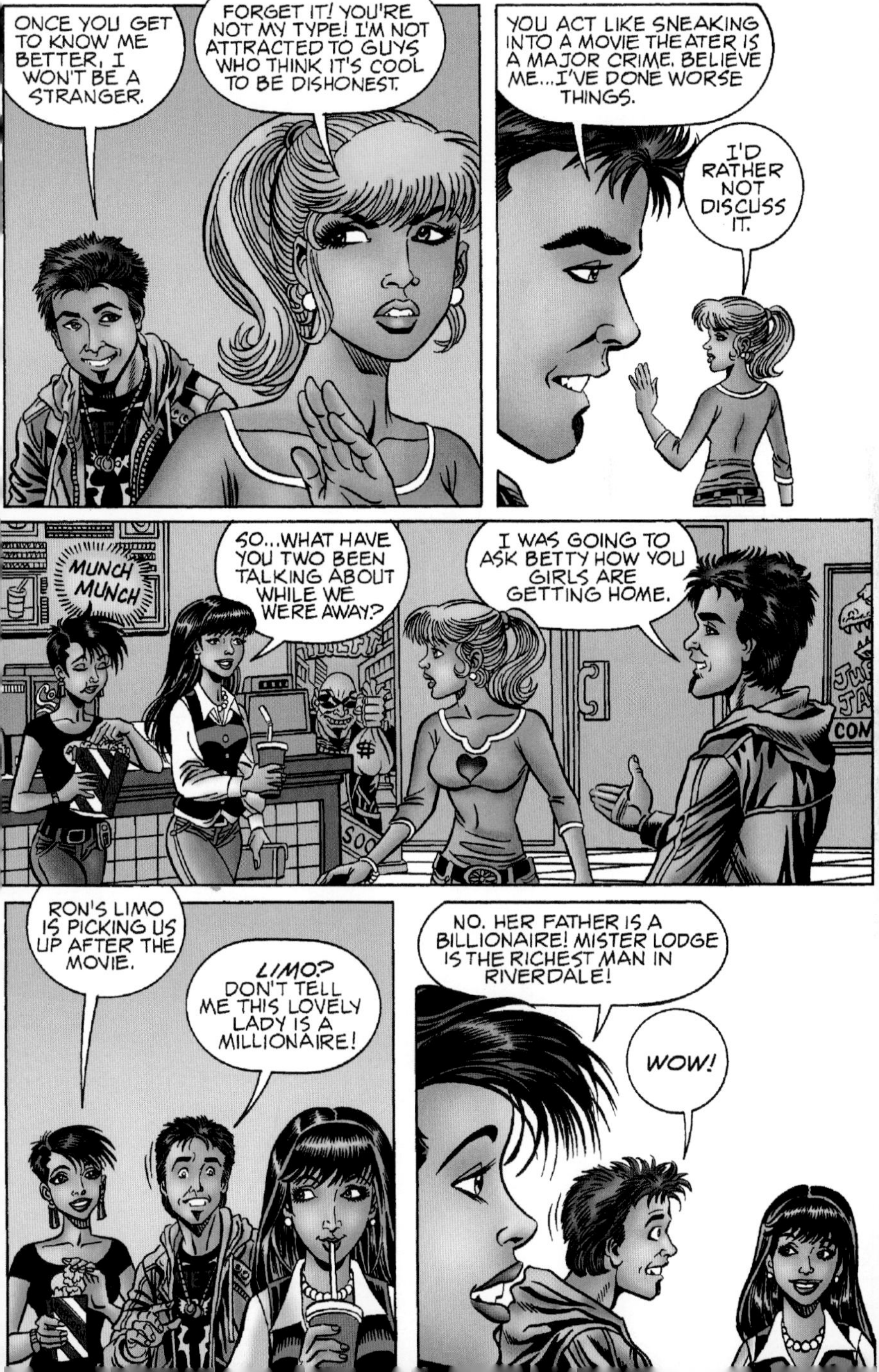
ONCE YOU GET TO KNOW ME BETTER, I WON'T BE A STRANGER.
FORGET IT! YOU'RE NOT MY TYPE! I'M NOT ATTRACTED TO GUYS WHO THINK IT'S COOL TO BE DISHONEST.
YOU ACT LIKE SNEAKING INTO A MOVIE THEATER IS A MAJOR CRIME. BELIEVE ME...I'VE DONE WORSE THINGS.
I'D RATHER NOT DISCUSS IT.
MUNCH MUNCH
SO...WHAT HAVE YOU TWO BEEN TALKING ABOUT WHILE WE WERE AWAY?
I WAS GOING TO ASK BETTY HOW YOU GIRLS ARE GETTING HOME.
RON'S LIMO IS PICKING US UP AFTER THE MOVIE.
LIMO? DON'T TELL ME THIS LOVELY LADY IS A MILLIONAIRE!
NO. HER FATHER IS A BILLIONAIRE! MISTER LODGE IS THE RICHEST MAN IN RIVERDALE!
WOW!

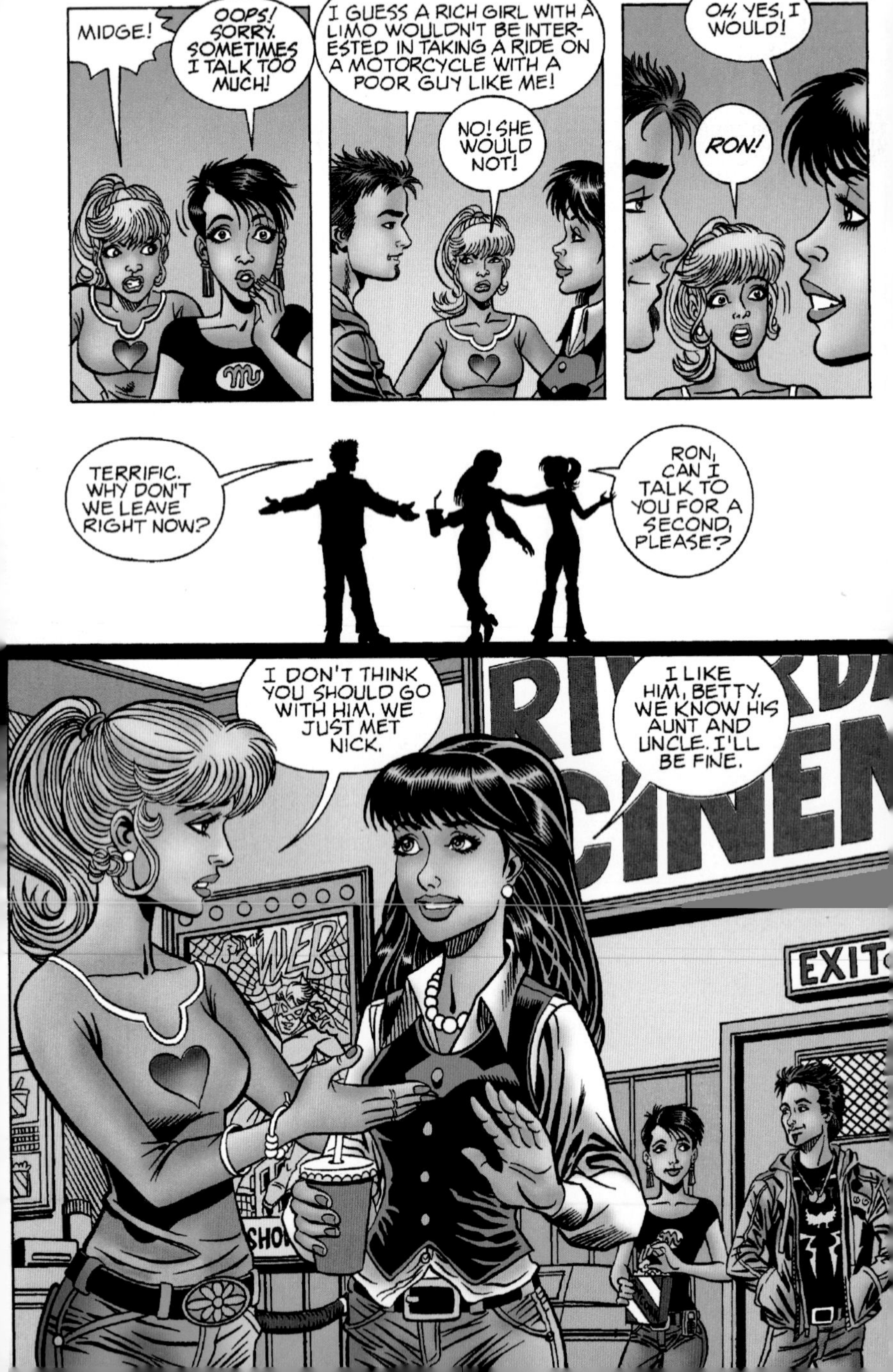
MIDGE!
OOPS! SORRY. SOMETIMES I TALK TOO MUCH!
I GUESS A RICH GIRL WITH A LIMO WOULDN'T BE INTER-ESTED IN TAKING A RIDE ON A MOTORCYCLE WITH A POOR GUY LIKE ME!
NO! SHE WOULD NOT!
OH, YES, I WOULD!
RON!
TERRIFIC. WHY DON'T WE LEAVE RIGHT NOW?
RON, CAN I TALK TO YOU FOR A SECOND, PLEASE?
I DON'T THINK YOU SHOULD GO WITH HIM. WE JUST MET NICK.
I LIKE HIM, BETTY. WE KNOW HIS AUNT AND UNCLE. I'LL BE FINE.
EXIT

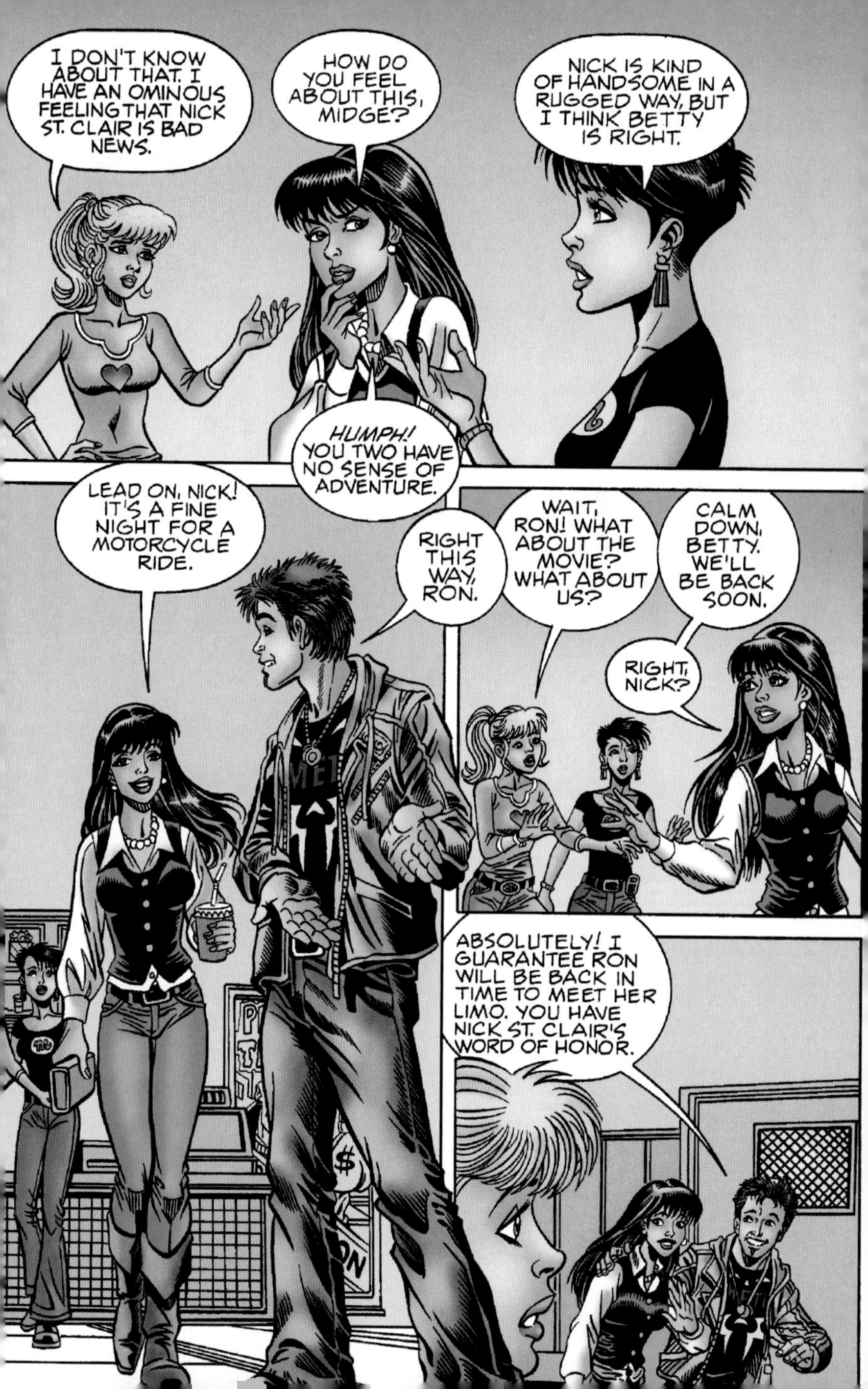
I DON'T KNOW ABOUT THAT. I HAVE AN OMINOUS FEELING THAT NICK ST. CLAIR IS BAD NEWS.
HOW DO YOU FEEL ABOUT THIS, MIDGE?
NICK IS KIND OF HANDSOME IN A RUGGED WAY, BUT I THINK BETTY IS RIGHT.
HUMPH! YOU TWO HAVE NO SENSE OF ADVENTURE.
LEAD ON, NICK! IT'S A FINE NIGHT FOR A MOTORCYCLE RIDE.
RIGHT THIS WAY, RON.
WAIT, RON! WHAT ABOUT THE MOVIE? WHAT ABOUT US?
CALM DOWN, BETTY. WE'LL BE BACK SOON.
RIGHT, NICK?
ABSOLUTELY! I GUARANTEE RON WILL BE BACK IN TIME TO MEET HER LIMO. YOU HAVE NICK ST. CLAIR'S WORD OF HONOR.

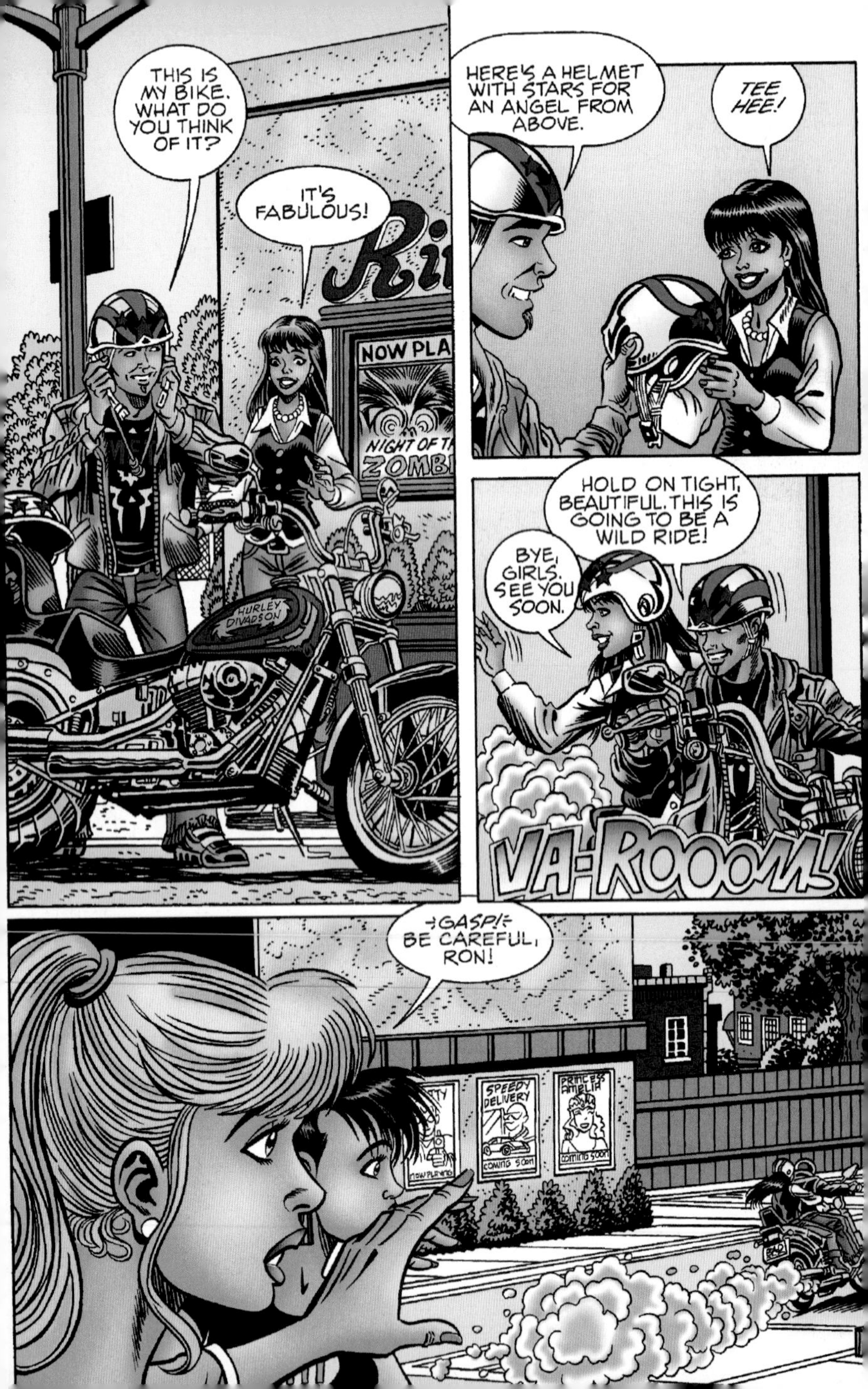
THIS IS MY BIKE. WHAT DO YOU THINK OF IT?
IT'S FABULOUS!
NOW PLA
NIGHT OF TH
ZOMBI
HURLEY DIVADSON
HERE'S A HELMET WITH STARS FOR AN ANGEL FROM ABOVE.
TEE HEE!
HOLD ON TIGHT, BEAUTIFUL. THIS IS GOING TO BE A WILD RIDE!
BYE, GIRLS. SEE YOU SOON.
VA-ROOOM!
GASP! BE CAREFUL, RON!
SPEEDY DELIVERY
COMING SOON
PRINCESS AMELIA
COMING SOON

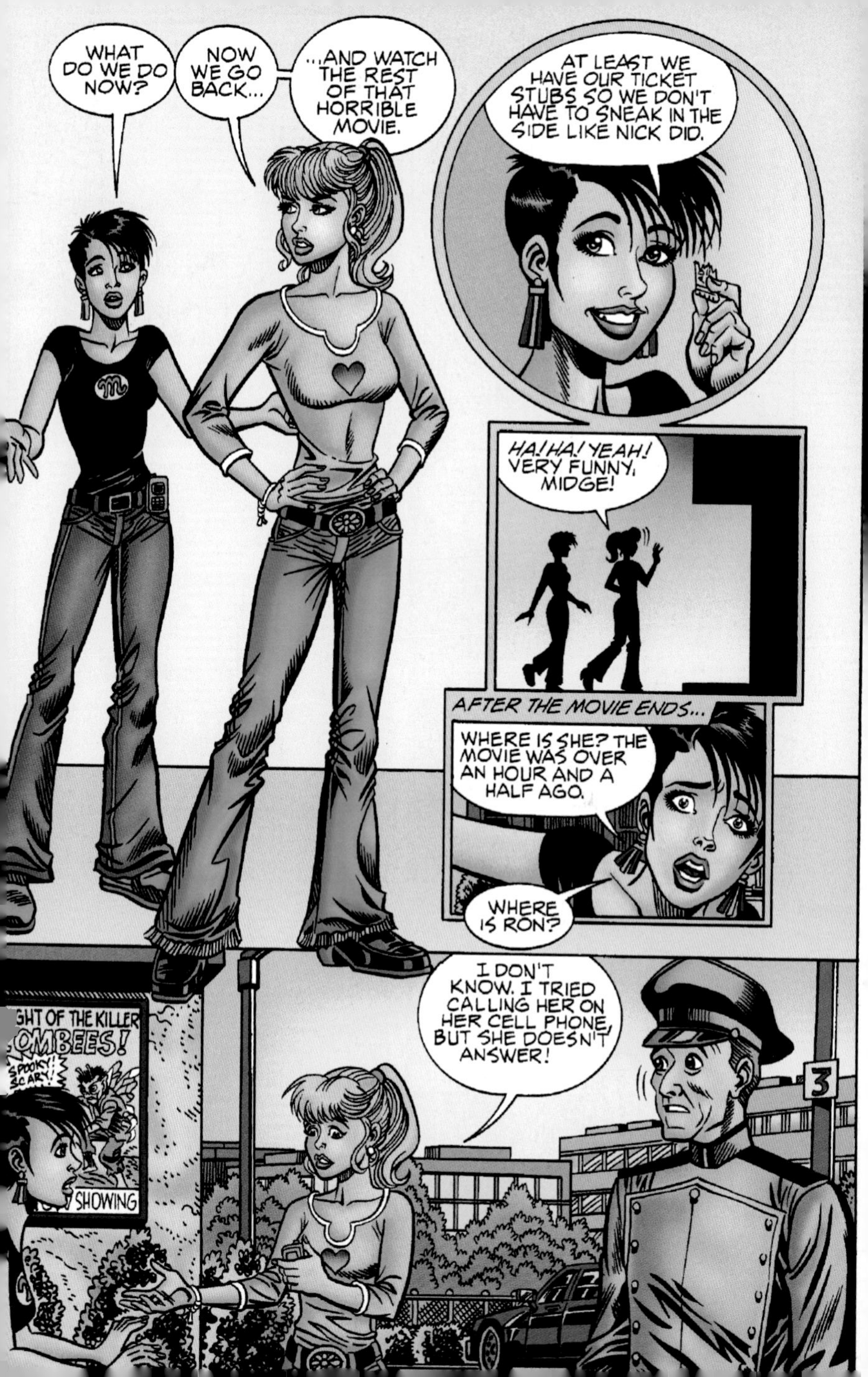
WHAT DO WE DO NOW?
NOW WE GO BACK...
...AND WATCH THE REST OF THAT HORRIBLE MOVIE.
AT LEAST WE HAVE OUR TICKET STUBS SO WE DON'T HAVE TO SNEAK IN THE SIDE LIKE NICK DID.
HA! HA! YEAH! VERY FUNNY, MIDGE!
AFTER THE MOVIE ENDS...
WHERE IS SHE? THE MOVIE WAS OVER AN HOUR AND A HALF AGO.
WHERE IS RON?
GHT OF THE KILLER
OMBEES!
SPOOKY! SCARY!
SHOWING
I DON'T KNOW. I TRIED CALLING HER ON HER CELL PHONE, BUT SHE DOESN'T ANSWER!
3

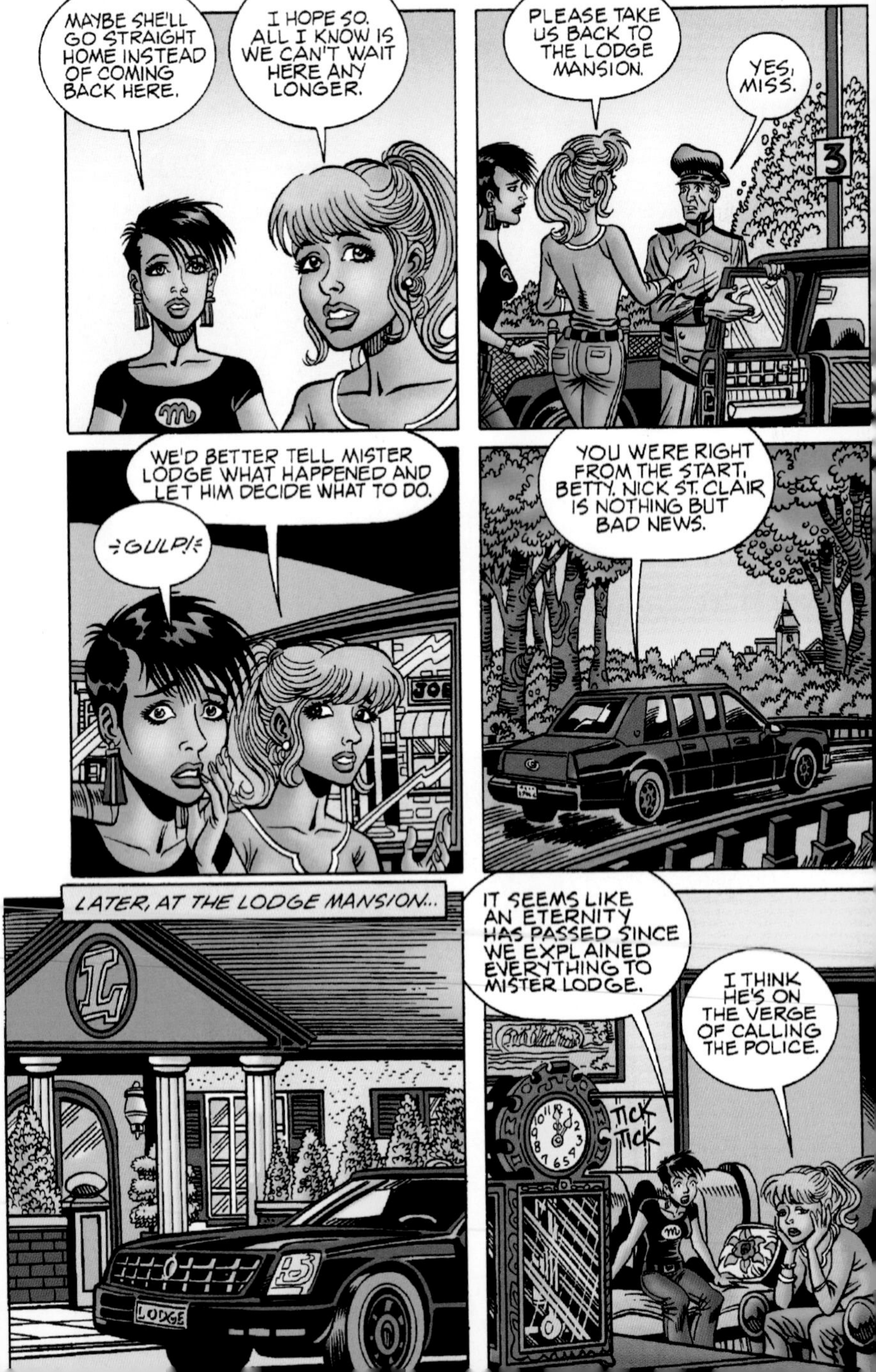
MAYBE SHE'LL GO STRAIGHT HOME INSTEAD OF COMING BACK HERE.
I HOPE SO. ALL I KNOW IS WE CAN'T WAIT HERE ANY LONGER.
PLEASE TAKE US BACK TO THE LODGE MANSION.
YES, MISS.
3
WE'D BETTER TELL MISTER LODGE WHAT HAPPENED AND LET HIM DECIDE WHAT TO DO.
GULP!
YOU WERE RIGHT FROM THE START, BETTY. NICK ST. CLAIR IS NOTHING BUT BAD NEWS.
LATER, AT THE LODGE MANSION...
LODGE
IT SEEMS LIKE AN ETERNITY HAS PASSED SINCE WE EXPLAINED EVERYTHING TO MISTER LODGE.
TICK TICK
I THINK HE'S ON THE VERGE OF CALLING THE POLICE.

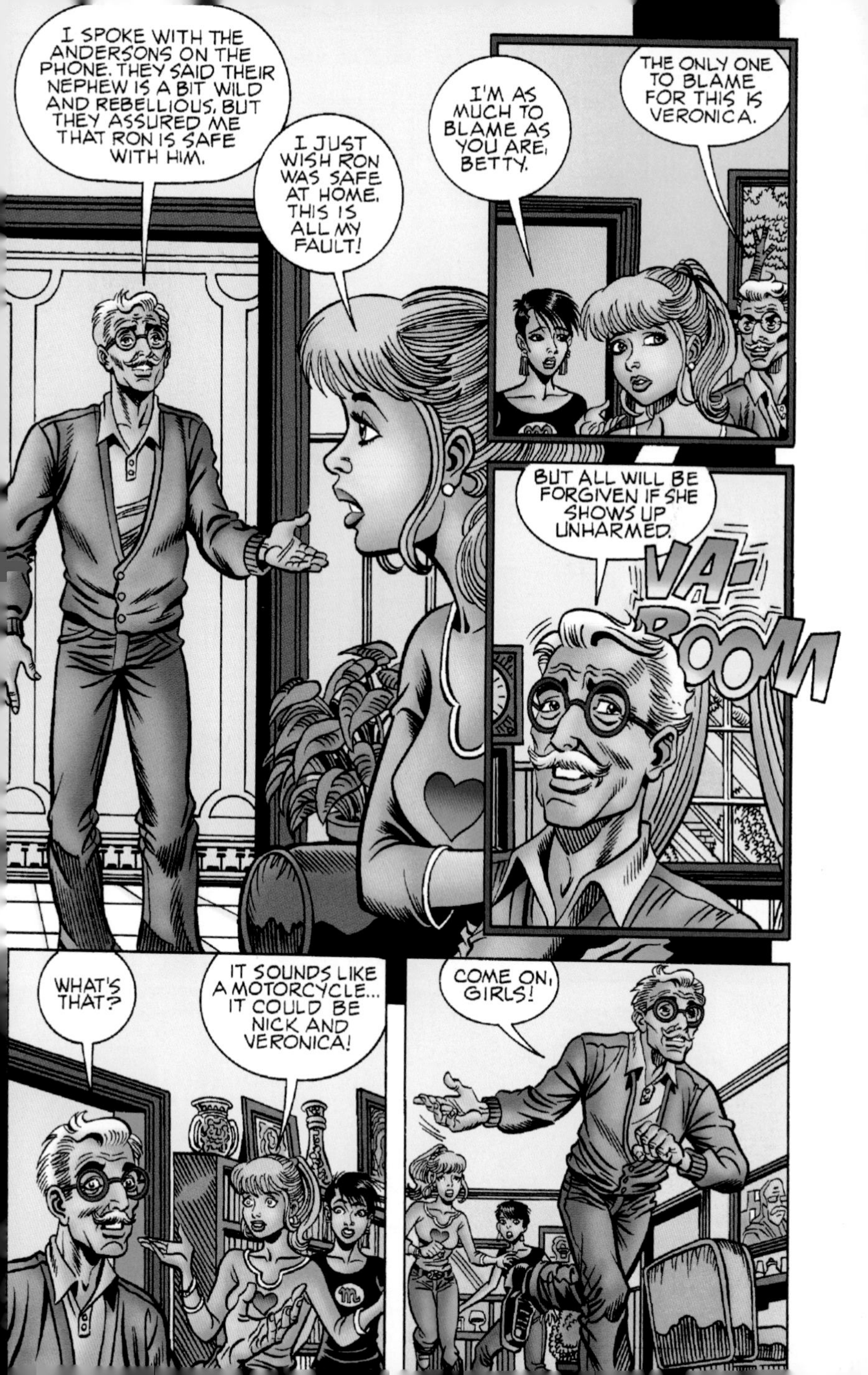
I SPOKE WITH THE ANDERSONS ON THE PHONE. THEY SAID THEIR NEPHEW IS A BIT WILD AND REBELLIOUS, BUT THEY ASSURED ME THAT RON IS SAFE WITH HIM.
I JUST WISH RON WAS SAFE AT HOME. THIS IS ALL MY FAULT!
I'M AS MUCH TO BLAME AS YOU ARE, BETTY.
THE ONLY ONE TO BLAME FOR THIS IS VERONICA.
BUT ALL WILL BE FORGIVEN IF SHE SHOWS UP UNHARMED.
VA-ROOM
WHAT'S THAT?
IT SOUNDS LIKE A MOTORCYCLE... IT COULD BE NICK AND VERONICA!
COME ON, GIRLS!

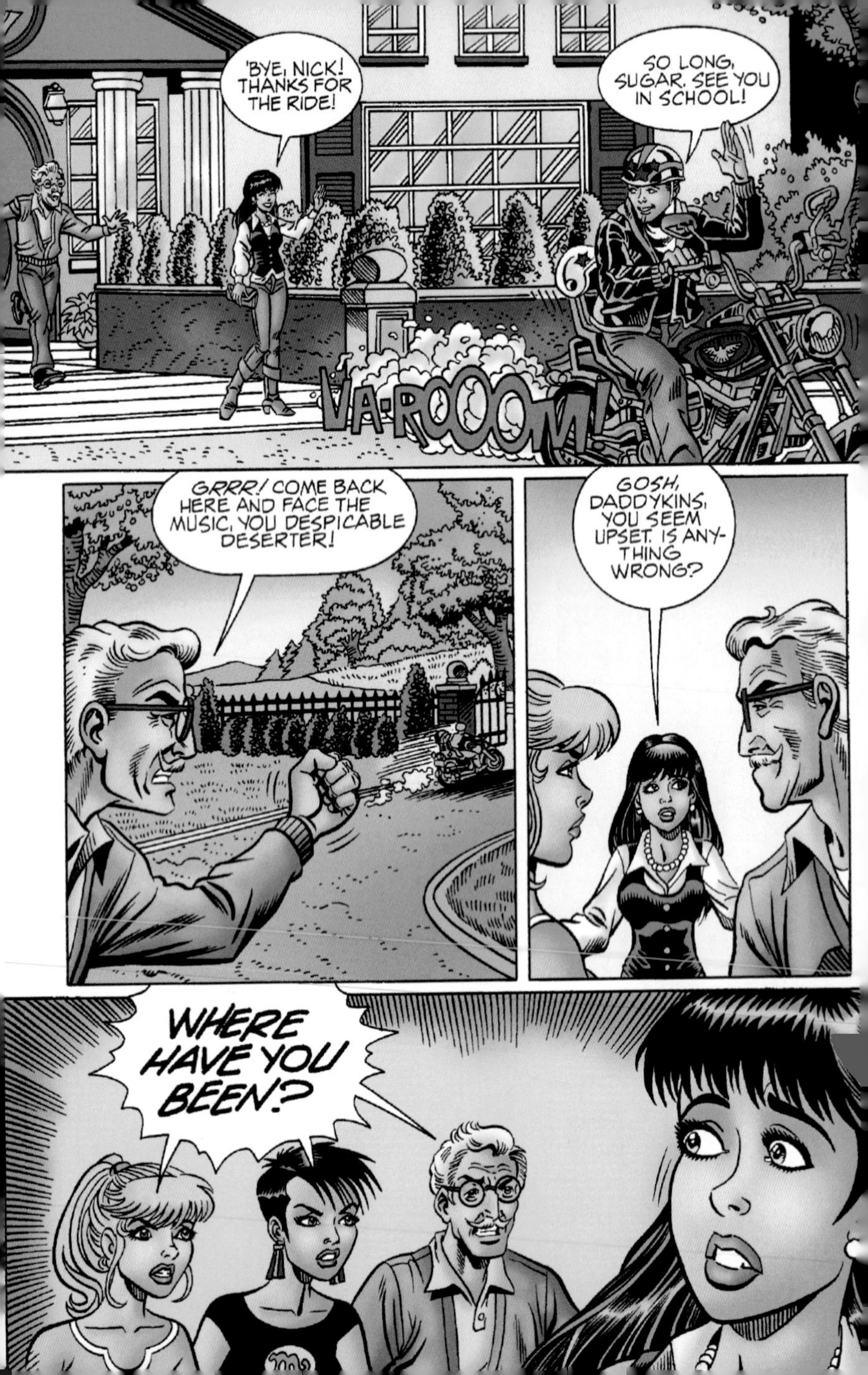
'BYE, NICK! THANKS FOR THE RIDE!
SO LONG, SUGAR. SEE YOU IN SCHOOL!
VA-ROOOOM!
GRRR! COME BACK HERE AND FACE THE MUSIC, YOU DESPICABLE DESERTER!
GOSH, DADDYKINS, YOU SEEM UPSET. IS ANYTHING WRONG?
WHERE HAVE YOU BEEN?

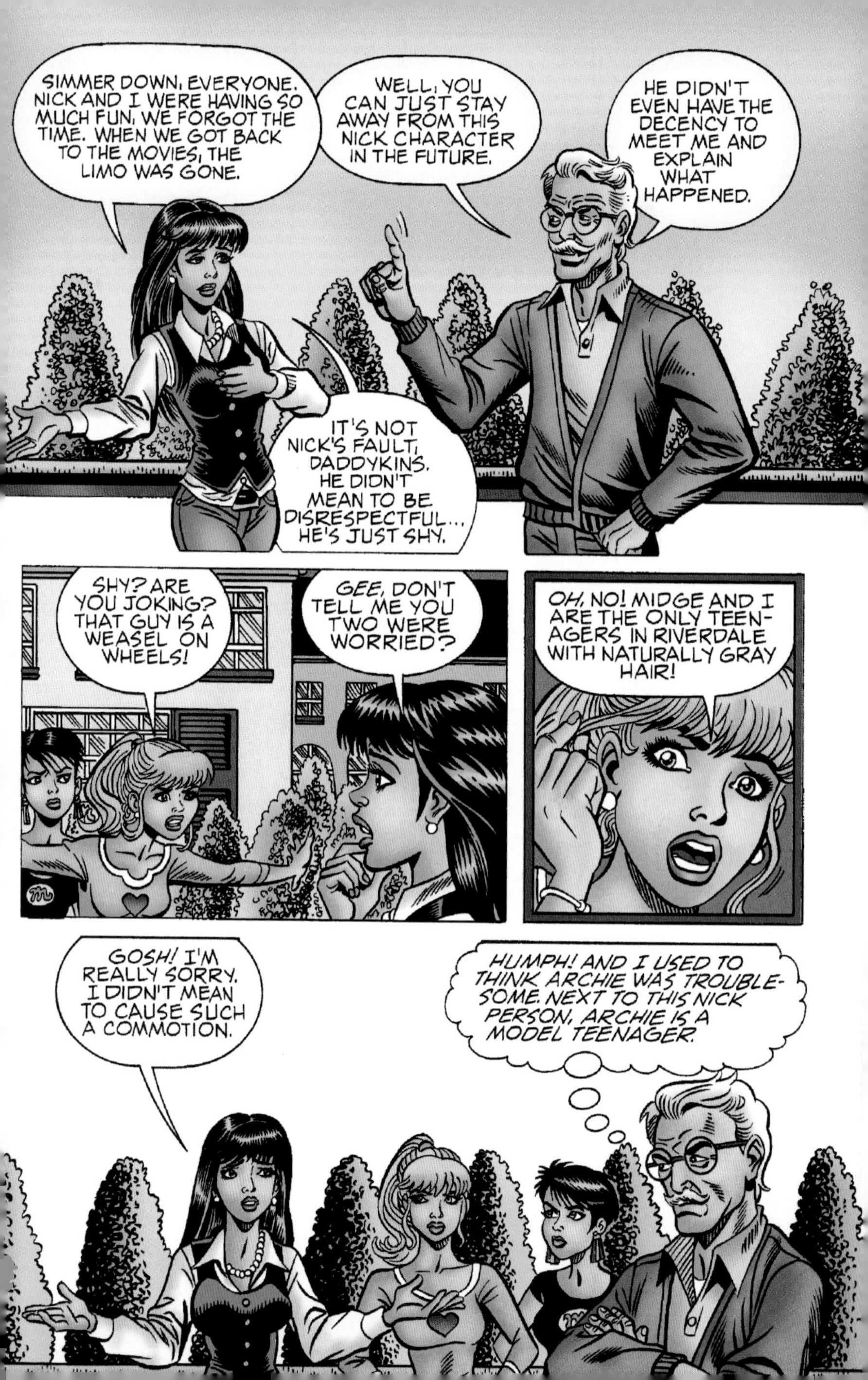

SIMMER DOWN, EVERYONE. NICK AND I WERE HAVING SO MUCH FUN, WE FORGOT THE TIME. WHEN WE GOT BACK TO THE MOVIES, THE LIMO WAS GONE.
WELL, YOU CAN JUST STAY AWAY FROM THIS NICK CHARACTER IN THE FUTURE.
HE DIDN'T EVEN HAVE THE DECENCY TO MEET ME AND EXPLAIN WHAT HAPPENED.
IT'S NOT NICK'S FAULT, DADDYKINS. HE DIDN'T MEAN TO BE DISRESPECTFUL... HE'S JUST SHY.
SHY? ARE YOU JOKING? THAT GUY IS A WEASEL ON WHEELS!
GEE, DON'T TELL ME YOU TWO WERE WORRIED?
OH, NO! MIDGE AND I ARE THE ONLY TEEN-AGERS IN RIVERDALE WITH NATURALLY GRAY HAIR!
GOSH! I'M REALLY SORRY. I DIDN'T MEAN TO CAUSE SUCH A COMMOTION.
HUMPH! AND I USED TO THINK ARCHIE WAS TROUBLE-SOME. NEXT TO THIS NICK PERSON, ARCHIE IS A MODEL TEENAGER.

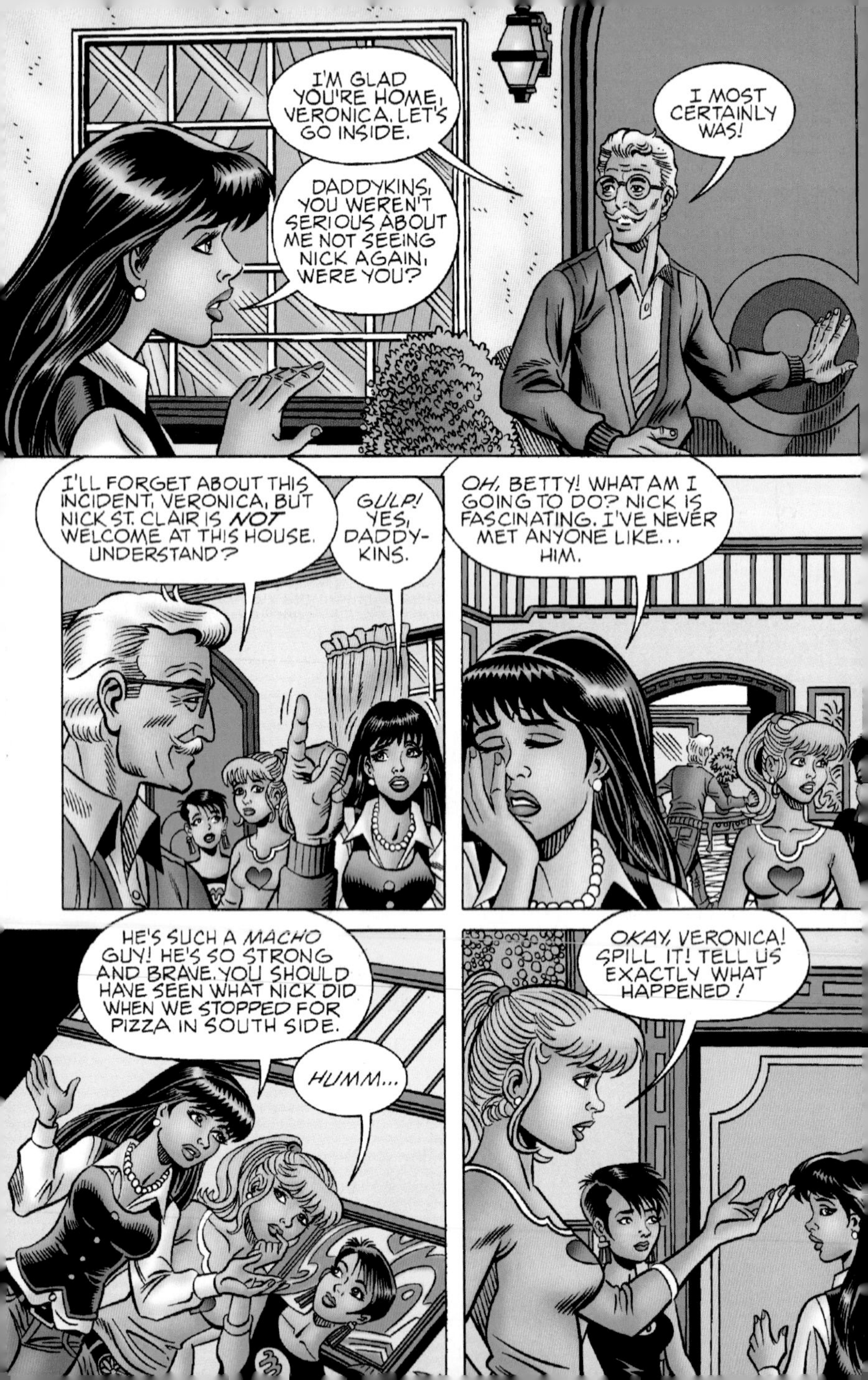
I'M GLAD YOU'RE HOME, VERONICA. LET'S GO INSIDE.
DADDYKINS, YOU WEREN'T SERIOUS ABOUT ME NOT SEEING NICK AGAIN, WERE YOU?
I MOST CERTAINLY WAS!
I'LL FORGET ABOUT THIS INCIDENT, VERONICA, BUT NICK ST. CLAIR IS *NOT* WELCOME AT THIS HOUSE. UNDERSTAND?
GULP! YES, DADDY-KINS.
OH, BETTY! WHAT AM I GOING TO DO? NICK IS FASCINATING. I'VE NEVER MET ANYONE LIKE... HIM.
HE'S SUCH A *MACHO* GUY! HE'S SO STRONG AND BRAVE. YOU SHOULD HAVE SEEN WHAT NICK DID WHEN WE STOPPED FOR PIZZA IN SOUTH SIDE.
HUMM...
OKAY, VERONICA! SPILL IT! TELL US EXACTLY WHAT HAPPENED!

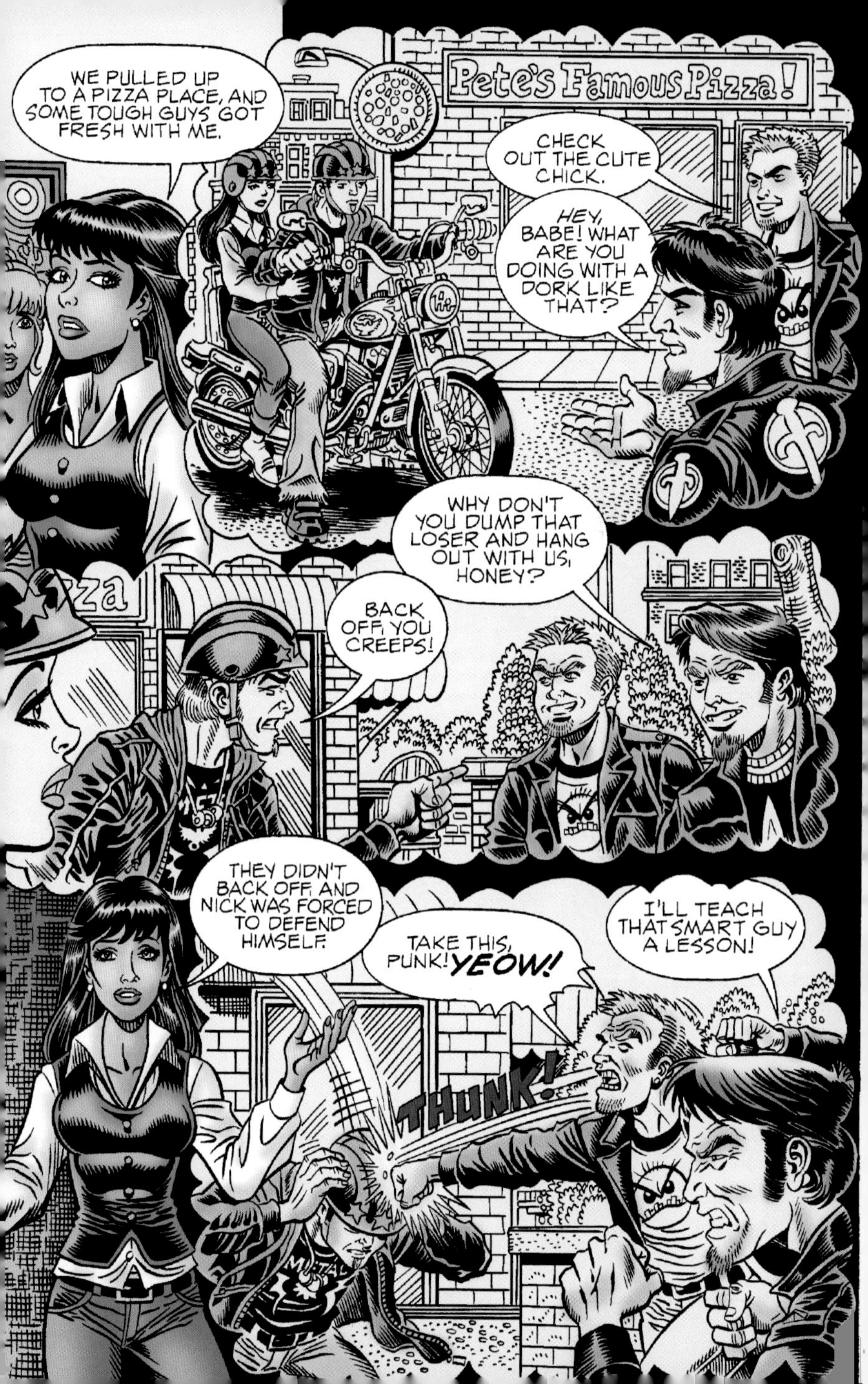
WE PULLED UP TO A PIZZA PLACE, AND SOME TOUGH GUYS GOT FRESH WITH ME.
Pete's Famous Pizza!
CHECK OUT THE CUTE CHICK.
HEY, BABE! WHAT ARE YOU DOING WITH A DORK LIKE THAT?
WHY DON'T YOU DUMP THAT LOSER AND HANG OUT WITH US, HONEY?
BACK OFF, YOU CREEPS!
THEY DIDN'T BACK OFF, AND NICK WAS FORCED TO DEFEND HIMSELF.
TAKE THIS, PUNK! YEOW!
I'LL TEACH THAT SMART GUY A LESSON!
THUNK!

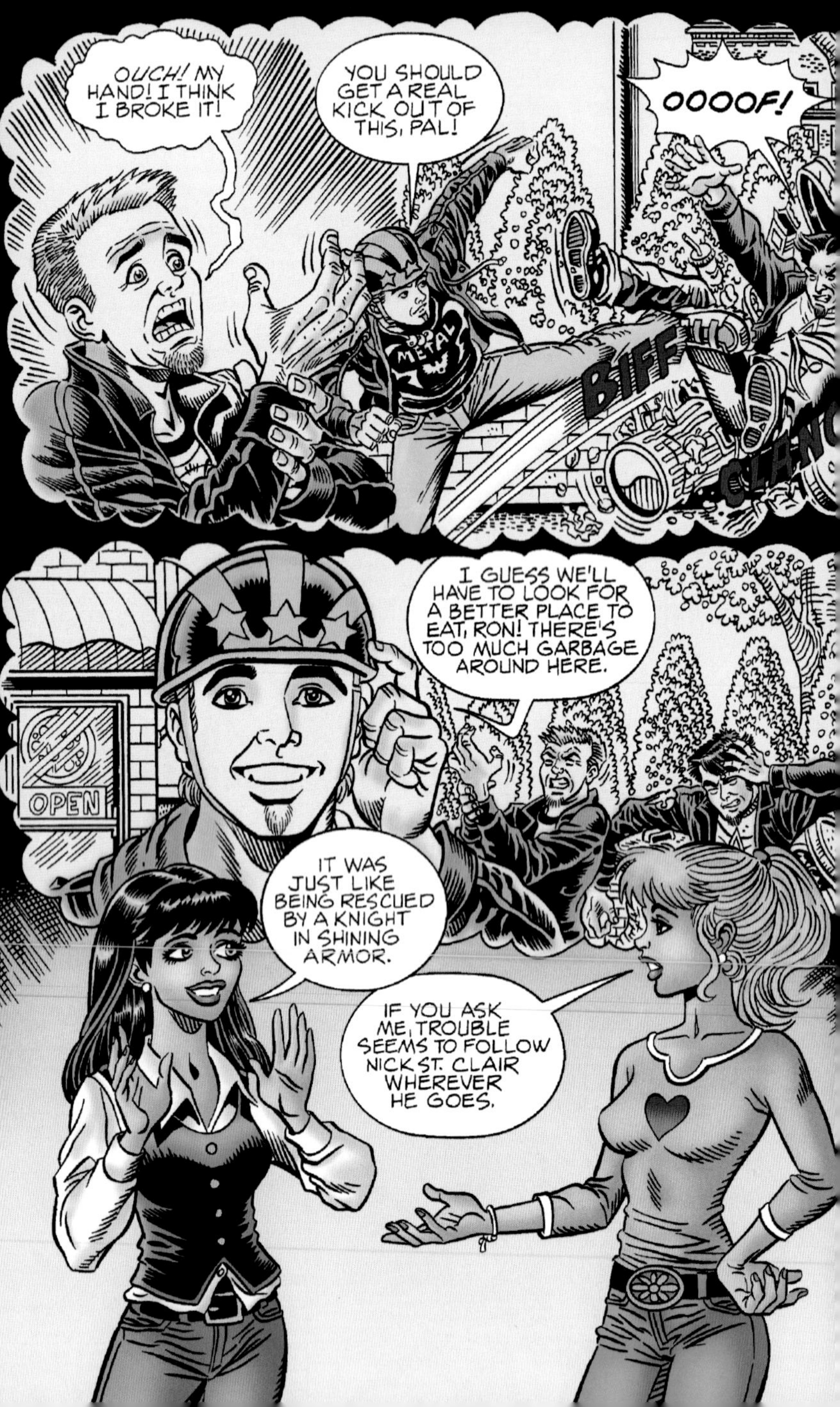
OUCH! MY HAND! I THINK I BROKE IT!
YOU SHOULD GET A REAL KICK OUT OF THIS, PAL!
OOOOF!
METAL
BIFF
I GUESS WE'LL HAVE TO LOOK FOR A BETTER PLACE TO EAT, RON! THERE'S TOO MUCH GARBAGE AROUND HERE.
OPEN
IT WAS JUST LIKE BEING RESCUED BY A KNIGHT IN SHINING ARMOR.
IF YOU ASK ME, TROUBLE SEEMS TO FOLLOW NICK ST. CLAIR WHEREVER HE GOES.

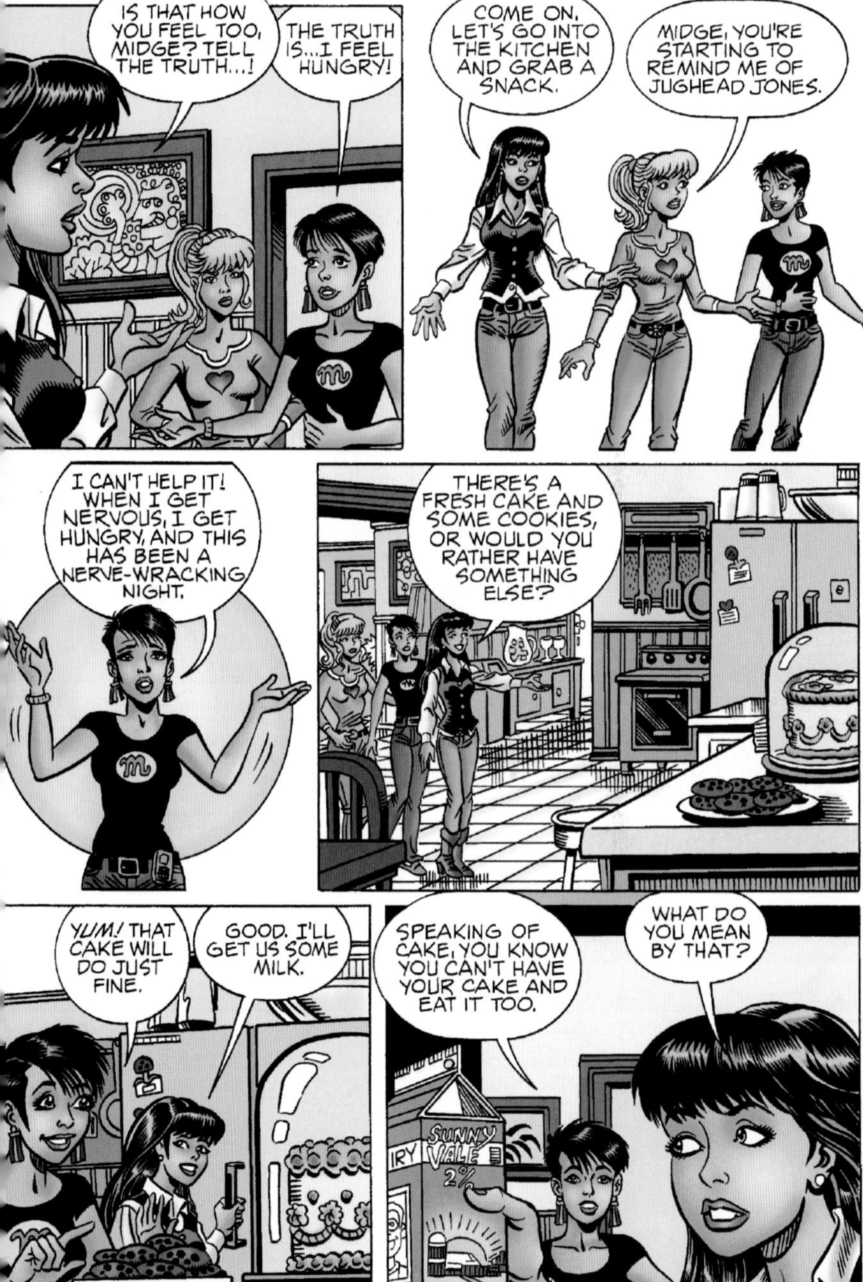
IS THAT HOW YOU FEEL TOO, MIDGE? TELL THE TRUTH...!
THE TRUTH IS...I FEEL HUNGRY!
COME ON. LET'S GO INTO THE KITCHEN AND GRAB A SNACK.
MIDGE, YOU'RE STARTING TO REMIND ME OF JUGHEAD JONES.
I CAN'T HELP IT! WHEN I GET NERVOUS, I GET HUNGRY, AND THIS HAS BEEN A NERVE-WRACKING NIGHT.
THERE'S A FRESH CAKE AND SOME COOKIES, OR WOULD YOU RATHER HAVE SOMETHING ELSE?
YUM! THAT CAKE WILL DO JUST FINE.
GOOD. I'LL GET US SOME MILK.
SPEAKING OF CAKE, YOU KNOW YOU CAN'T HAVE YOUR CAKE AND EAT IT TOO.
WHAT DO YOU MEAN BY THAT?
SUNNY VALE
2%

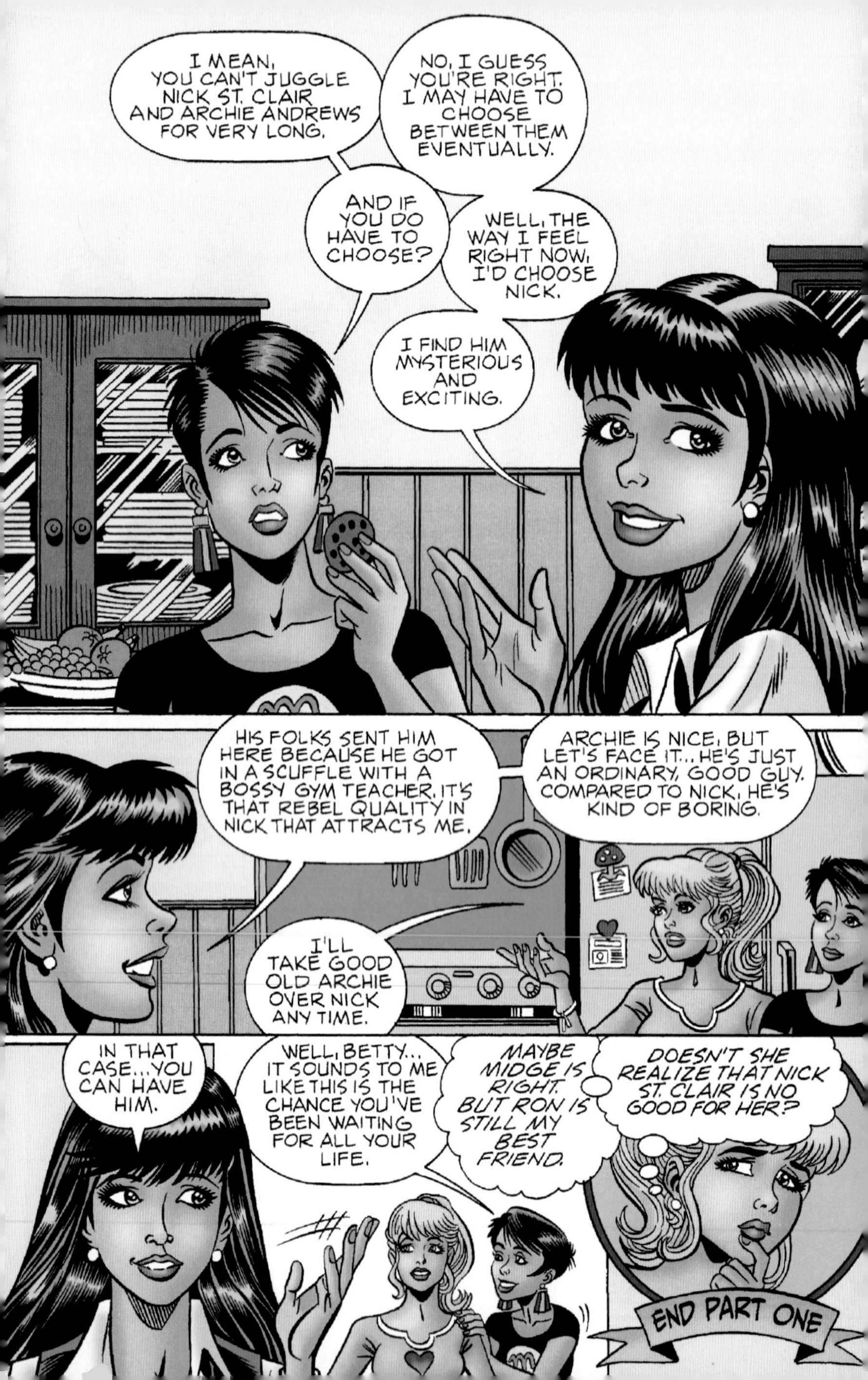
I MEAN, YOU CAN'T JUGGLE NICK ST. CLAIR AND ARCHIE ANDREWS FOR VERY LONG.
NO, I GUESS YOU'RE RIGHT. I MAY HAVE TO CHOOSE BETWEEN THEM EVENTUALLY.
AND IF YOU DO HAVE TO CHOOSE?
WELL, THE WAY I FEEL RIGHT NOW, I'D CHOOSE NICK.
I FIND HIM MYSTERIOUS AND EXCITING.
HIS FOLKS SENT HIM HERE BECAUSE HE GOT IN A SCUFFLE WITH A BOSSY GYM TEACHER. IT'S THAT REBEL QUALITY IN NICK THAT ATTRACTS ME.
ARCHIE IS NICE, BUT LET'S FACE IT... HE'S JUST AN ORDINARY, GOOD GUY. COMPARED TO NICK, HE'S KIND OF BORING.
I'LL TAKE GOOD OLD ARCHIE OVER NICK ANY TIME.
IN THAT CASE... YOU CAN HAVE HIM.
WELL, BETTY... IT SOUNDS TO ME LIKE THIS IS THE CHANCE YOU'VE BEEN WAITING FOR ALL YOUR LIFE.
MAYBE MIDGE IS RIGHT. BUT RON IS STILL MY BEST FRIEND.
DOESN'T SHE REALIZE THAT NICK ST. CLAIR IS NO GOOD FOR HER?
END PART ONE

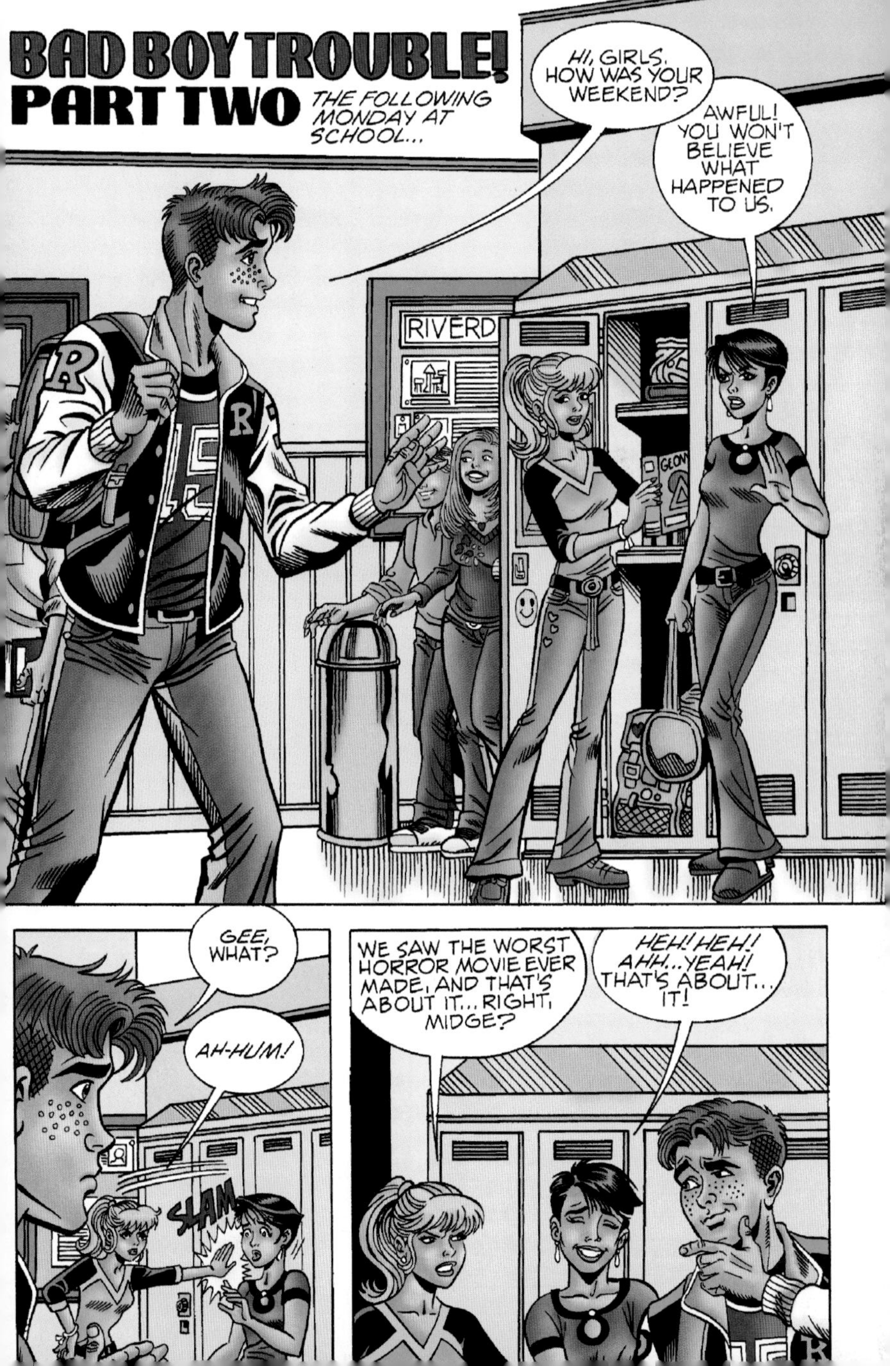
BAD BOY TROUBLE!
PART TWO
THE FOLLOWING MONDAY AT SCHOOL...
HI, GIRLS. HOW WAS YOUR WEEKEND?
AWFUL! YOU WON'T BELIEVE WHAT HAPPENED TO US.
RIVERD
GEE, WHAT?
AH-HUM!
SLAM
WE SAW THE WORST HORROR MOVIE EVER MADE, AND THAT'S ABOUT IT... RIGHT, MIDGE?
HEH! HEH! AHH...YEAH! THAT'S ABOUT... IT!

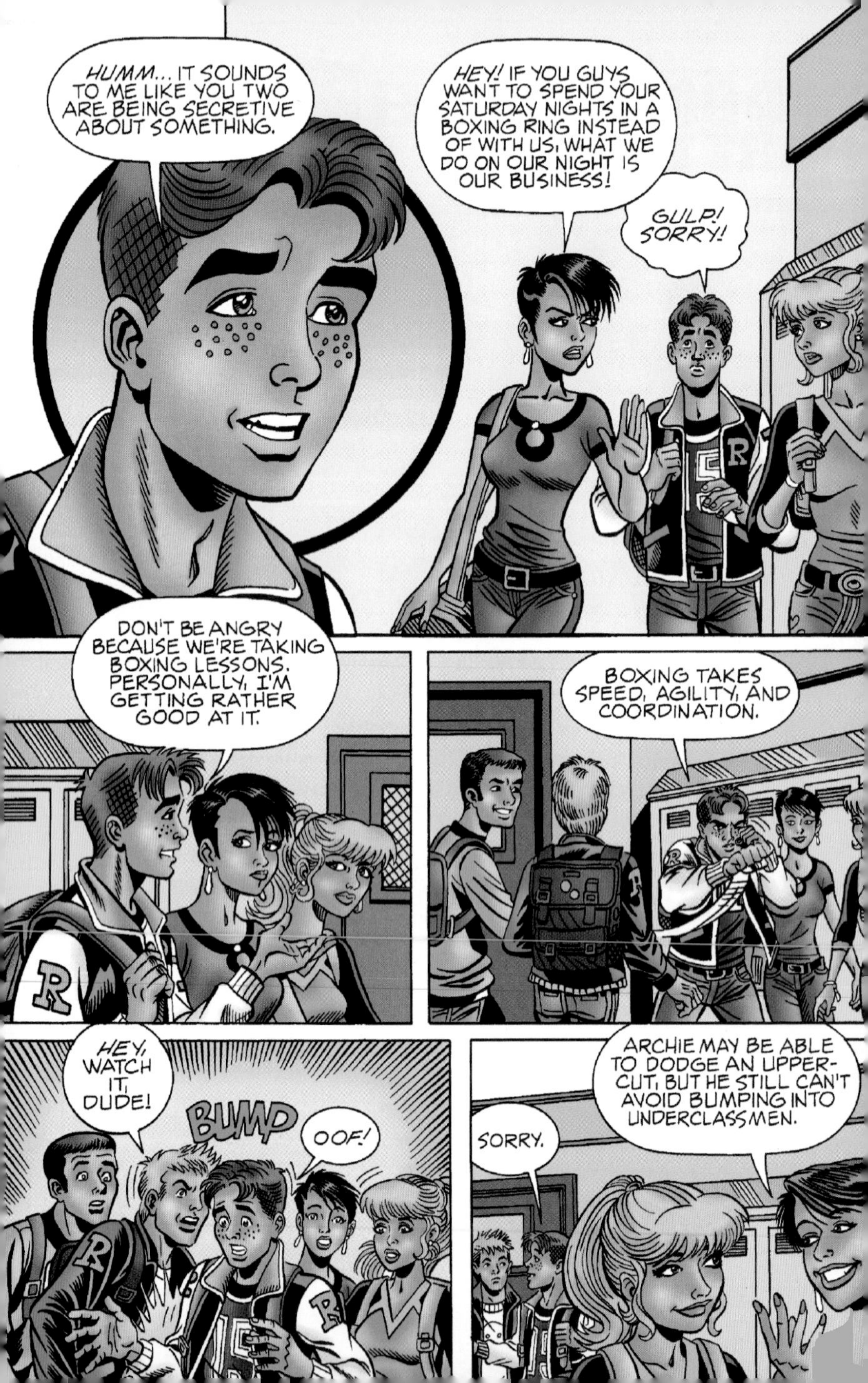
HUMM... IT SOUNDS TO ME LIKE YOU TWO ARE BEING SECRETIVE ABOUT SOMETHING.
HEY! IF YOU GUYS WANT TO SPEND YOUR SATURDAY NIGHTS IN A BOXING RING INSTEAD OF WITH US, WHAT WE DO ON OUR NIGHT IS OUR BUSINESS!
GULP! SORRY!
DON'T BE ANGRY BECAUSE WE'RE TAKING BOXING LESSONS. PERSONALLY, I'M GETTING RATHER GOOD AT IT.
BOXING TAKES SPEED, AGILITY, AND COORDINATION.
HEY, WATCH IT, DUDE!
BUMP
OOF!
SORRY.
ARCHIE MAY BE ABLE TO DODGE AN UPPER-CUT, BUT HE STILL CAN'T AVOID BUMPING INTO UNDERCLASSMEN.

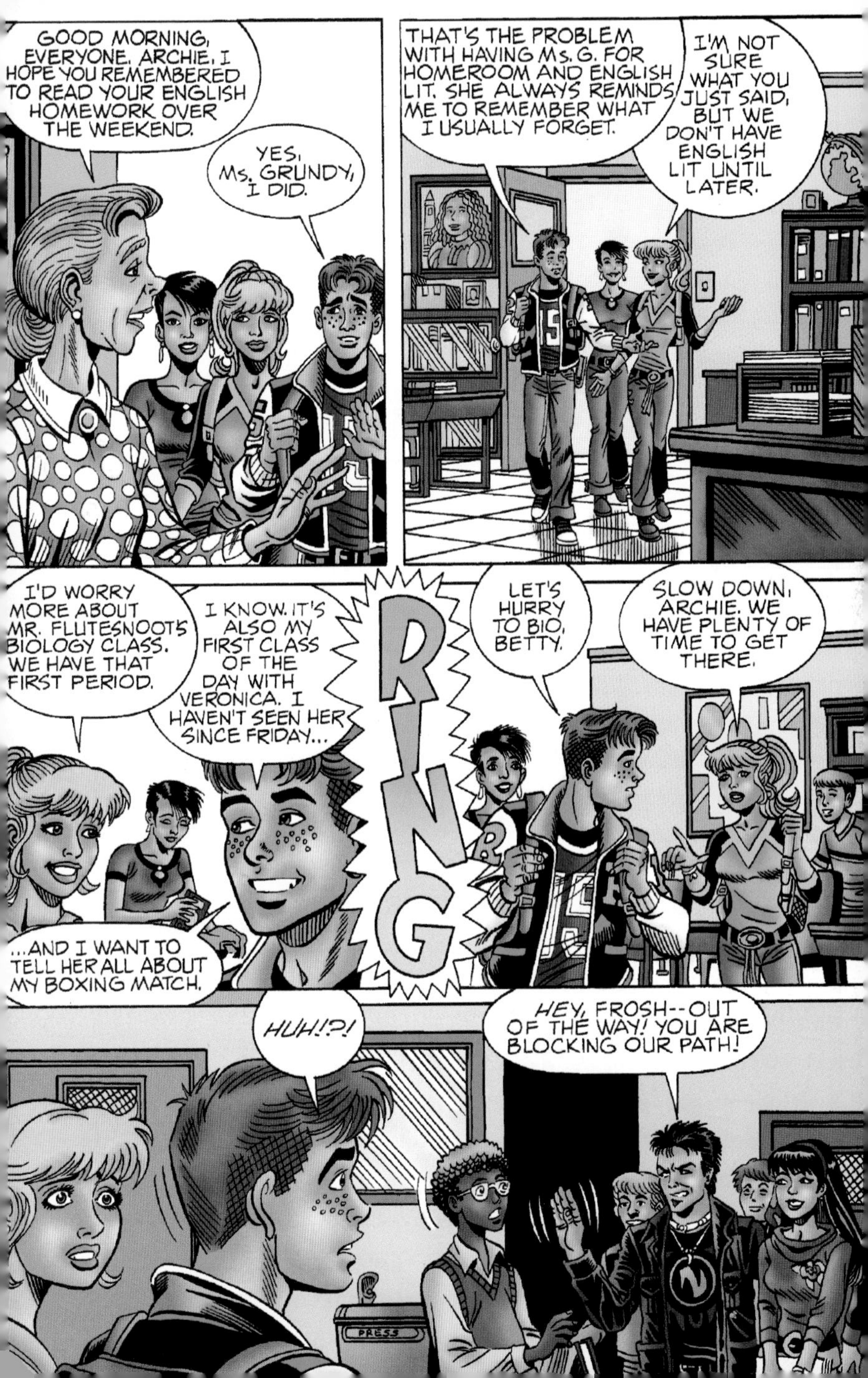
GOOD MORNING, EVERYONE. ARCHIE, I HOPE YOU REMEMBERED TO READ YOUR ENGLISH HOMEWORK OVER THE WEEKEND.
YES, Ms. GRUNDY, I DID.
THAT'S THE PROBLEM WITH HAVING Ms. G. FOR HOMEROOM AND ENGLISH LIT. SHE ALWAYS REMINDS ME TO REMEMBER WHAT I USUALLY FORGET.
I'M NOT SURE WHAT YOU JUST SAID, BUT WE DON'T HAVE ENGLISH LIT UNTIL LATER.
I'D WORRY MORE ABOUT MR. FLUTESNOOT'S BIOLOGY CLASS. WE HAVE THAT FIRST PERIOD.
I KNOW. IT'S ALSO MY FIRST CLASS OF THE DAY WITH VERONICA. I HAVEN'T SEEN HER SINCE FRIDAY...
...AND I WANT TO TELL HER ALL ABOUT MY BOXING MATCH.
RING
LET'S HURRY TO BIO, BETTY.
SLOW DOWN, ARCHIE. WE HAVE PLENTY OF TIME TO GET THERE.
HUH!?!
HEY, FROSH--OUT OF THE WAY! YOU ARE BLOCKING OUR PATH!
PRESS

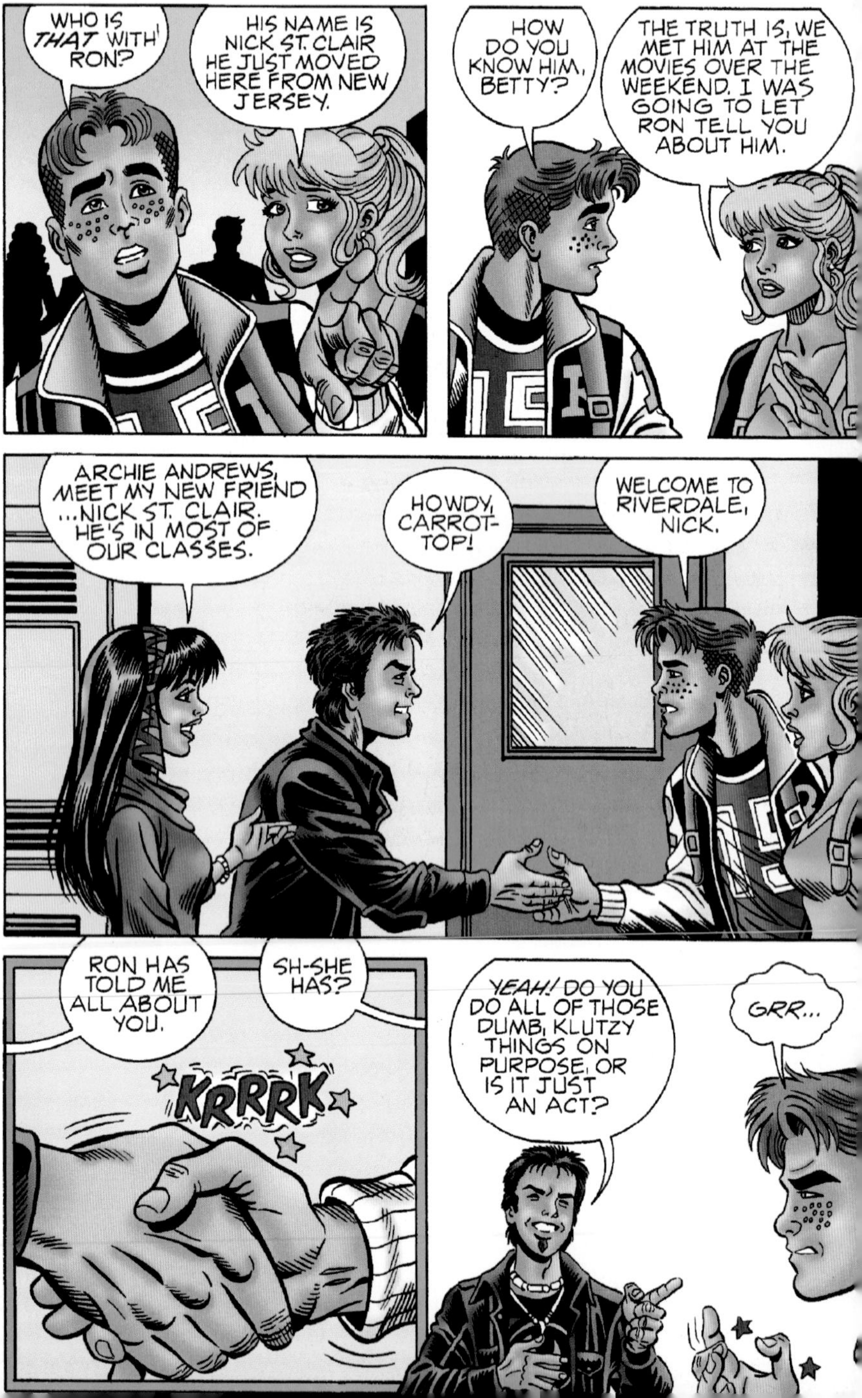
WHO IS *THAT* WITH RON?
HIS NAME IS NICK ST. CLAIR HE JUST MOVED HERE FROM NEW JERSEY.
HOW DO YOU KNOW HIM, BETTY?
THE TRUTH IS, WE MET HIM AT THE MOVIES OVER THE WEEKEND. I WAS GOING TO LET RON TELL YOU ABOUT HIM.
ARCHIE ANDREWS, MEET MY NEW FRIEND ...NICK ST. CLAIR. HE'S IN MOST OF OUR CLASSES.
HOWDY, CARROT-TOP!
WELCOME TO RIVERDALE, NICK.
RON HAS TOLD ME ALL ABOUT YOU.
SH-SHE HAS?
KRRRK
YEAH! DO YOU DO ALL OF THOSE DUMB, KLUTZY THINGS ON PURPOSE, OR IS IT JUST AN ACT?
GRR...

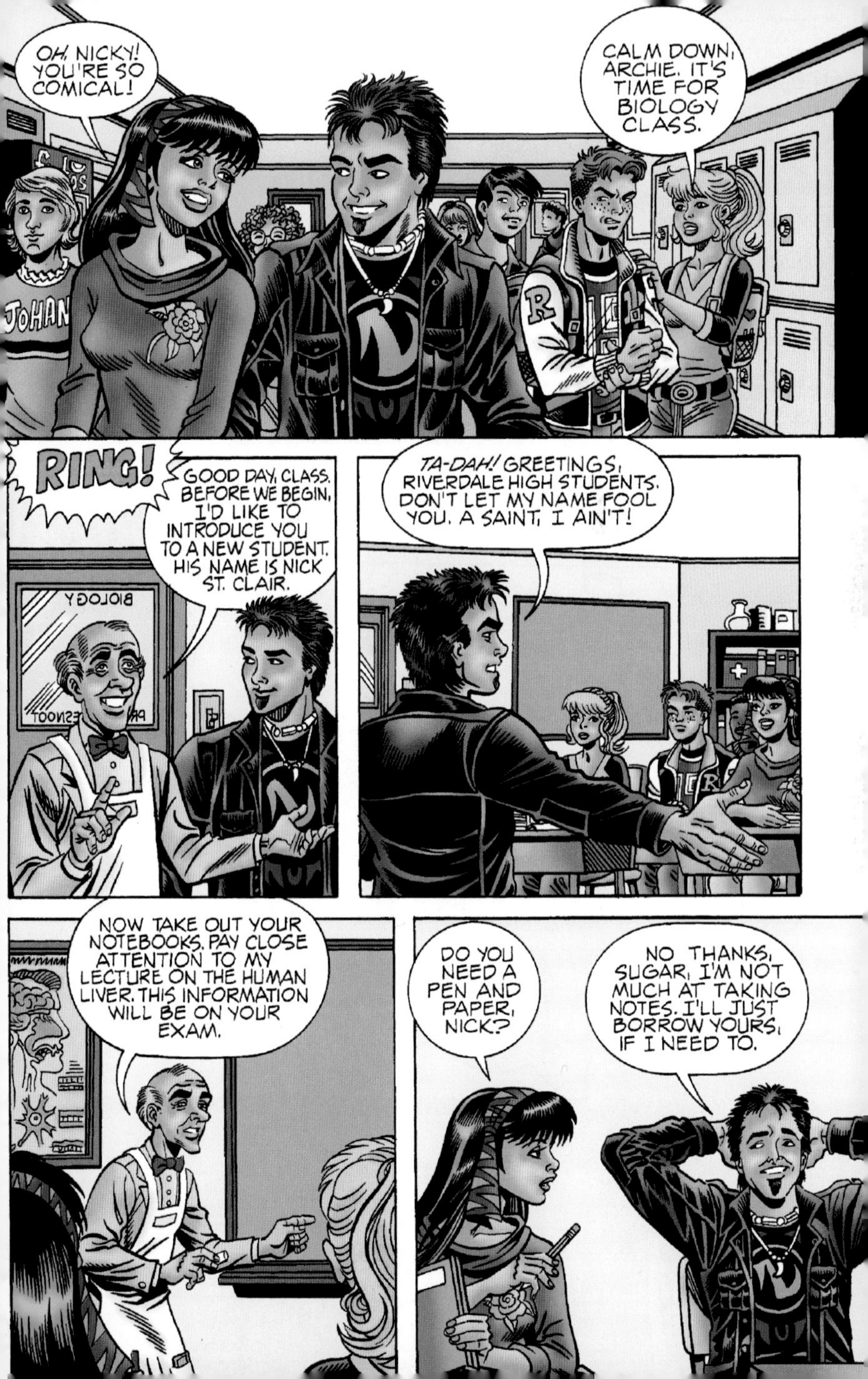

OH, NICKY! YOU'RE SO COMICAL!
CALM DOWN, ARCHIE. IT'S TIME FOR BIOLOGY CLASS.
JOHAN
RING!
GOOD DAY, CLASS. BEFORE WE BEGIN, I'D LIKE TO INTRODUCE YOU TO A NEW STUDENT. HIS NAME IS NICK ST. CLAIR.
BIOLOGY
TA-DAH! GREETINGS, RIVERDALE HIGH STUDENTS. DON'T LET MY NAME FOOL YOU. A SAINT, I AIN'T!
NOW TAKE OUT YOUR NOTEBOOKS. PAY CLOSE ATTENTION TO MY LECTURE ON THE HUMAN LIVER. THIS INFORMATION WILL BE ON YOUR EXAM.
DO YOU NEED A PEN AND PAPER, NICK?
NO THANKS, SUGAR, I'M NOT MUCH AT TAKING NOTES. I'LL JUST BORROW YOURS, IF I NEED TO.

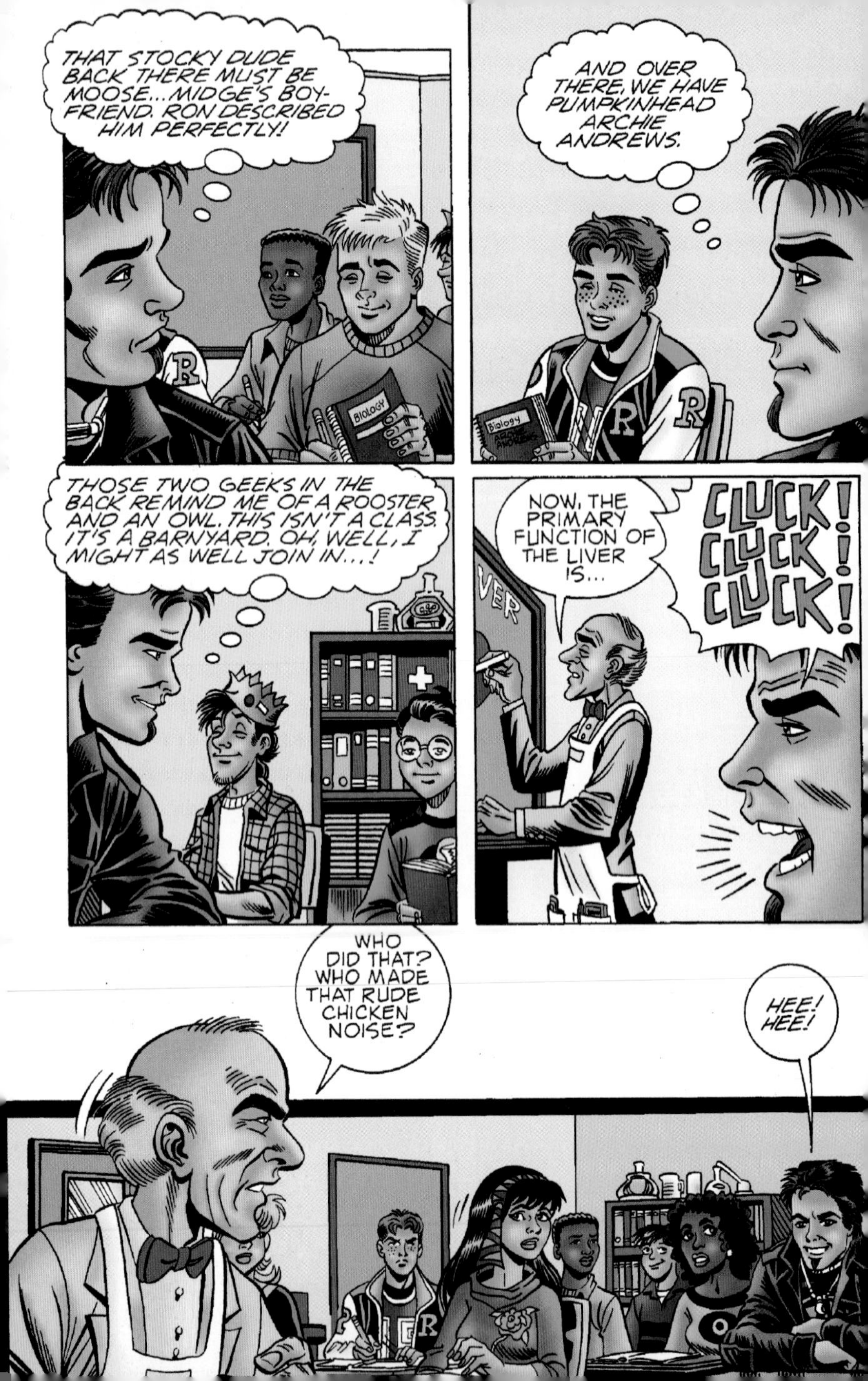

THAT STOCKY DUDE BACK THERE MUST BE MOOSE...MIDGE'S BOY-FRIEND. RON DESCRIBED HIM PERFECTLY!
BIOLOGY
AND OVER THERE, WE HAVE PUMPKINHEAD ARCHIE ANDREWS.
Biology
THOSE TWO GEEKS IN THE BACK REMIND ME OF A ROOSTER AND AN OWL. THIS ISN'T A CLASS. IT'S A BARNYARD. OH, WELL, I MIGHT AS WELL JOIN IN...!
NOW, THE PRIMARY FUNCTION OF THE LIVER IS...
CLUCK! CLUCK! CLUCK!
WHO DID THAT? WHO MADE THAT RUDE CHICKEN NOISE?
HEE! HEE!

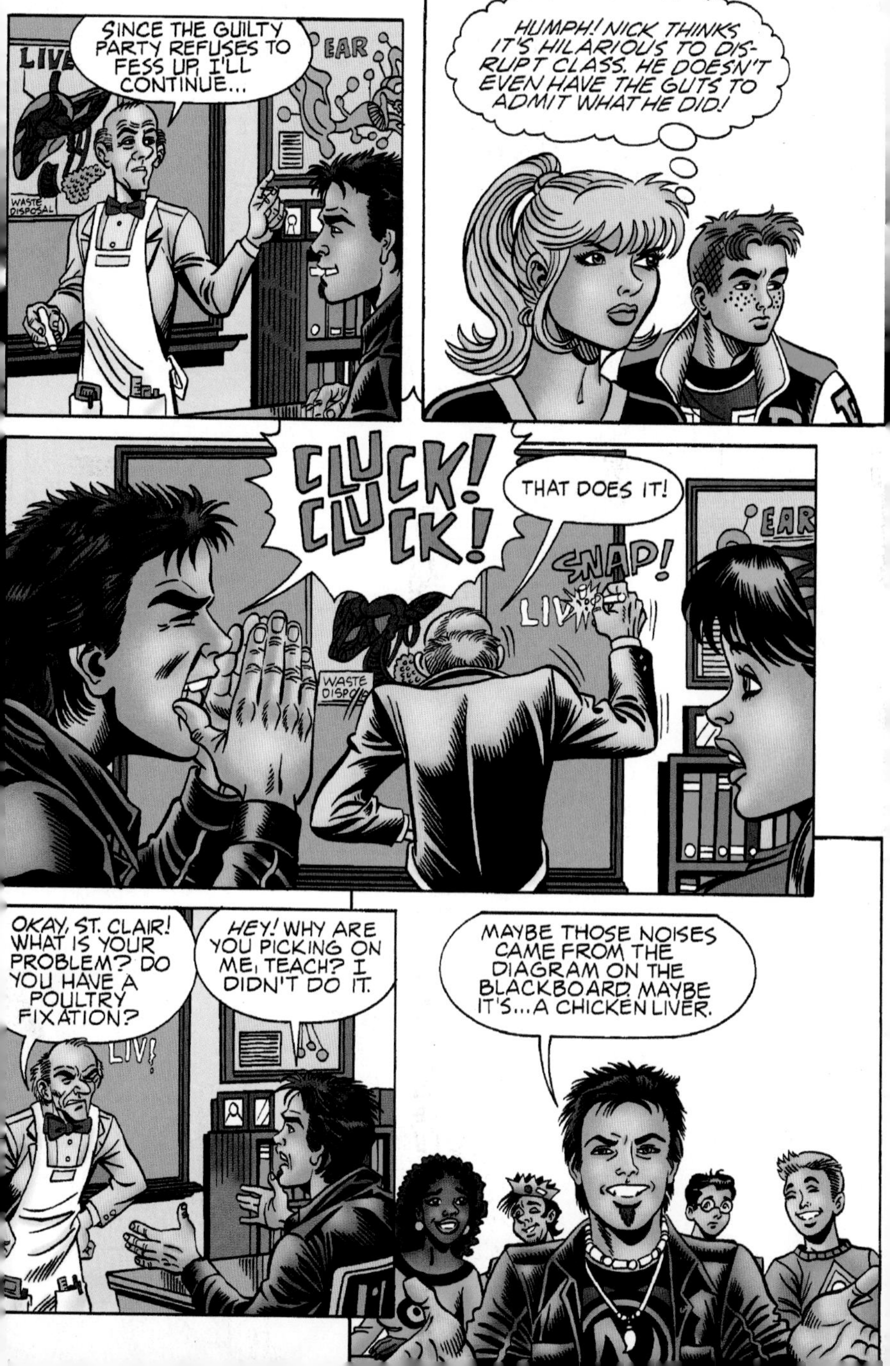

SINCE THE GUILTY PARTY REFUSES TO FESS UP, I'LL CONTINUE...
LIVE
EAR
WASTE DISPOSAL
HUMPH! NICK THINKS IT'S HILARIOUS TO DIS-RUPT CLASS. HE DOESN'T EVEN HAVE THE GUTS TO ADMIT WHAT HE DID!
CLUCK! CLUCK!
THAT DOES IT!
SNAP!
LIV
WASTE DISPO
OKAY, ST. CLAIR! WHAT IS YOUR PROBLEM? DO YOU HAVE A POULTRY FIXATION?
HEY! WHY ARE YOU PICKING ON ME, TEACH? I DIDN'T DO IT.
MAYBE THOSE NOISES CAME FROM THE DIAGRAM ON THE BLACKBOARD. MAYBE IT'S...A CHICKEN LIVER.

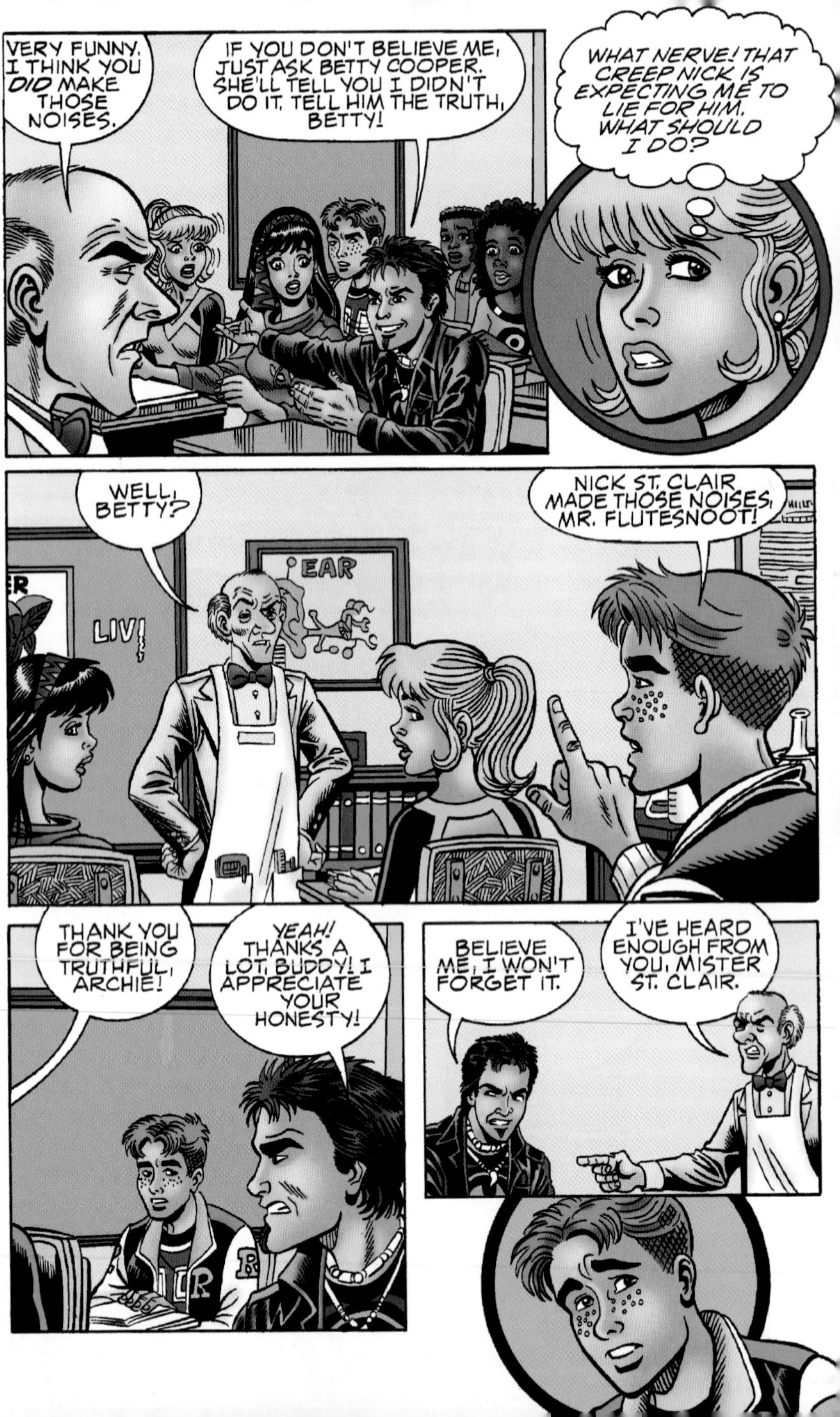
VERY FUNNY. I THINK YOU *DID* MAKE THOSE NOISES.
IF YOU DON'T BELIEVE ME, JUST ASK BETTY COOPER. SHE'LL TELL YOU I DIDN'T DO IT. TELL HIM THE TRUTH, BETTY!
WHAT NERVE! THAT CREEP NICK IS EXPECTING ME TO LIE FOR HIM. WHAT SHOULD I DO?
WELL, BETTY?
NICK ST. CLAIR MADE THOSE NOISES, MR. FLUTESNOOT!
EAR
LIV
THANK YOU FOR BEING TRUTHFUL, ARCHIE!
YEAH! THANKS A LOT, BUDDY! I APPRECIATE YOUR HONESTY!
BELIEVE ME, I WON'T FORGET IT.
I'VE HEARD ENOUGH FROM YOU, MISTER ST. CLAIR.

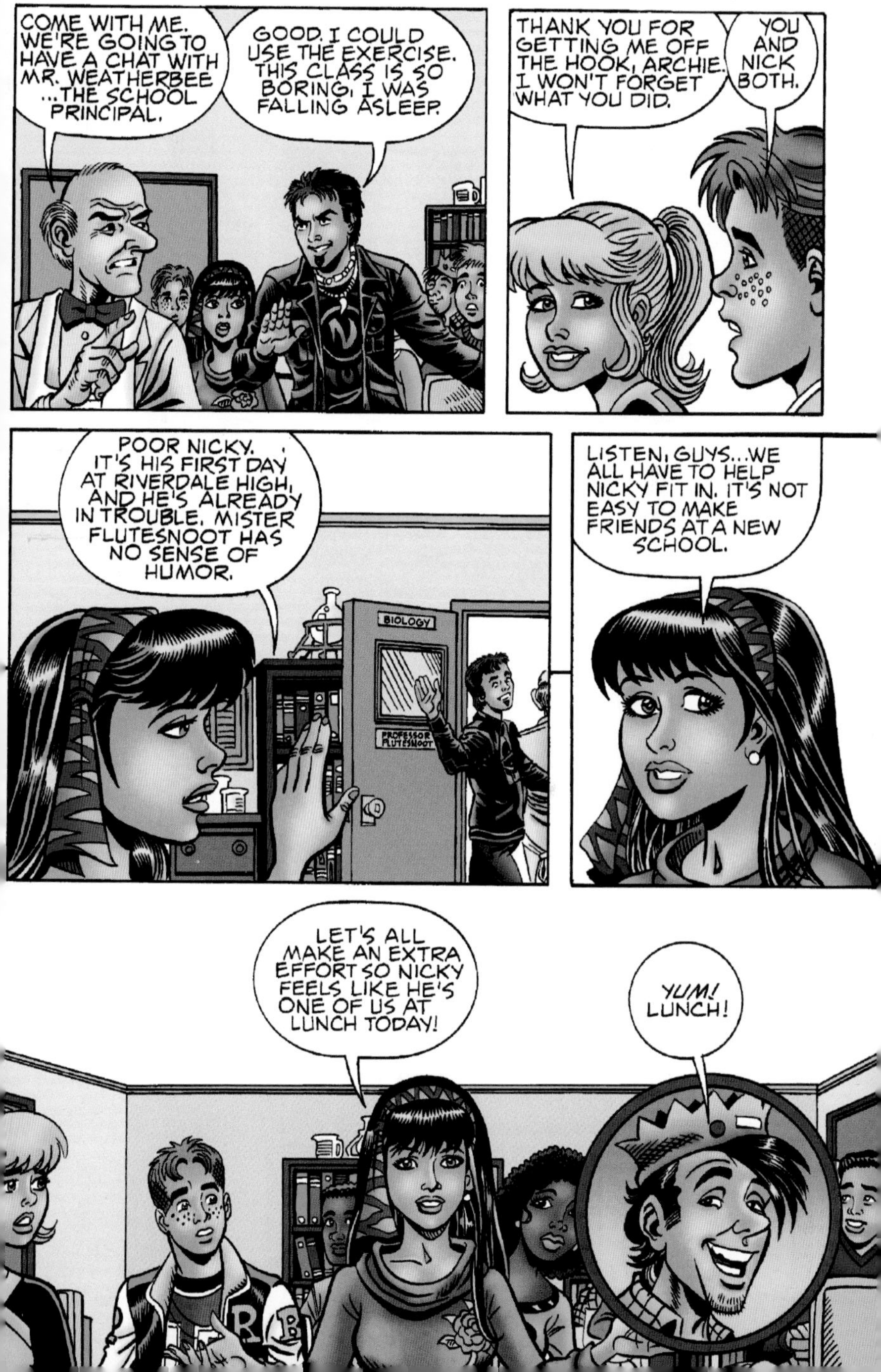
COME WITH ME. WE'RE GOING TO HAVE A CHAT WITH MR. WEATHERBEE ...THE SCHOOL PRINCIPAL.
GOOD. I COULD USE THE EXERCISE. THIS CLASS IS SO BORING, I WAS FALLING ASLEEP.
THANK YOU FOR GETTING ME OFF THE HOOK, ARCHIE. I WON'T FORGET WHAT YOU DID.
YOU AND NICK BOTH.
POOR NICKY. IT'S HIS FIRST DAY AT RIVERDALE HIGH, AND HE'S ALREADY IN TROUBLE. MISTER FLUTESNOOT HAS NO SENSE OF HUMOR.
BIOLOGY
PROFESSOR FLUTESNOOT
LISTEN, GUYS...WE ALL HAVE TO HELP NICKY FIT IN. IT'S NOT EASY TO MAKE FRIENDS AT A NEW SCHOOL.
LET'S ALL MAKE AN EXTRA EFFORT SO NICKY FEELS LIKE HE'S ONE OF US AT LUNCH TODAY!
YUM! LUNCH!

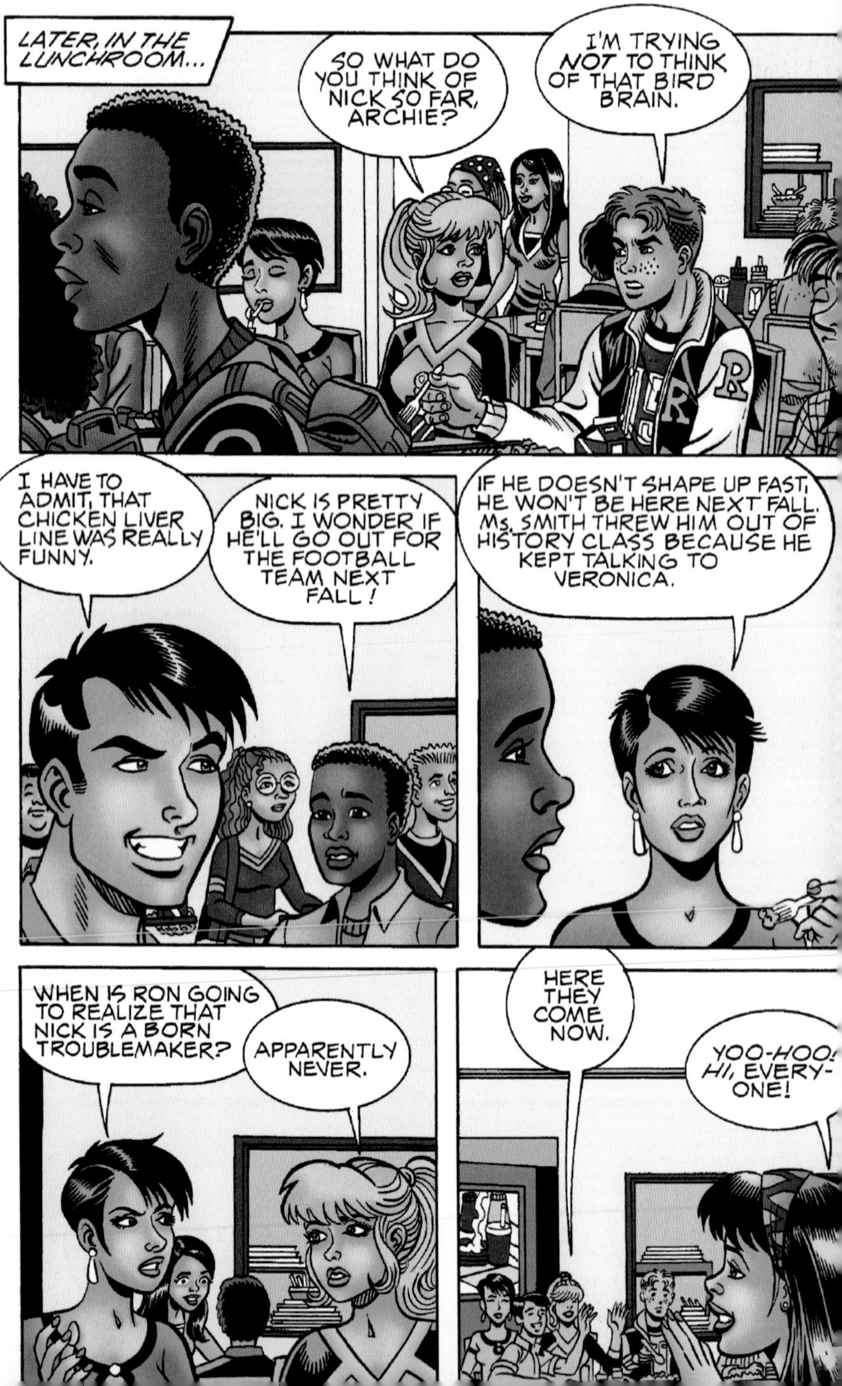
LATER, IN THE LUNCHROOM...
SO WHAT DO YOU THINK OF NICK SO FAR, ARCHIE?
I'M TRYING NOT TO THINK OF THAT BIRD BRAIN.
I HAVE TO ADMIT, THAT CHICKEN LIVER LINE WAS REALLY FUNNY.
NICK IS PRETTY BIG. I WONDER IF HE'LL GO OUT FOR THE FOOTBALL TEAM NEXT FALL!
IF HE DOESN'T SHAPE UP FAST, HE WON'T BE HERE NEXT FALL. Ms. SMITH THREW HIM OUT OF HISTORY CLASS BECAUSE HE KEPT TALKING TO VERONICA.
WHEN IS RON GOING TO REALIZE THAT NICK IS A BORN TROUBLEMAKER?
APPARENTLY NEVER.
HERE THEY COME NOW.
YOO-HOO! HI, EVERY-ONE!

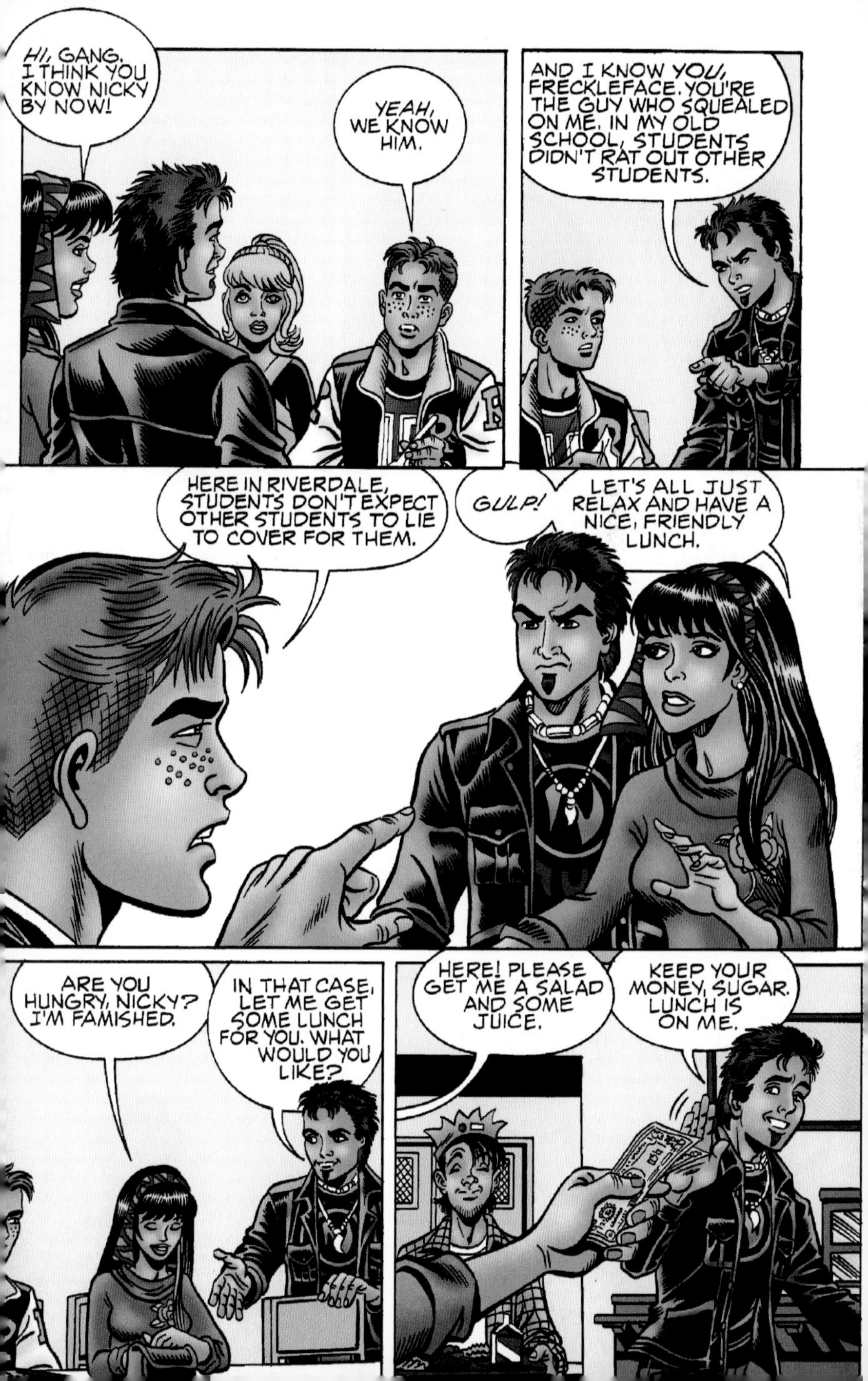

HI, GANG. I THINK YOU KNOW NICKY BY NOW!
YEAH, WE KNOW HIM.
AND I KNOW YOU, FRECKLEFACE. YOU'RE THE GUY WHO SQUEALED ON ME. IN MY OLD SCHOOL, STUDENTS DIDN'T RAT OUT OTHER STUDENTS.
HERE IN RIVERDALE, STUDENTS DON'T EXPECT OTHER STUDENTS TO LIE TO COVER FOR THEM.
GULP!
LET'S ALL JUST RELAX AND HAVE A NICE, FRIENDLY LUNCH.
ARE YOU HUNGRY, NICKY? I'M FAMISHED.
IN THAT CASE, LET ME GET SOME LUNCH FOR YOU. WHAT WOULD YOU LIKE?
HERE! PLEASE GET ME A SALAD AND SOME JUICE.
KEEP YOUR MONEY, SUGAR. LUNCH IS ON ME.

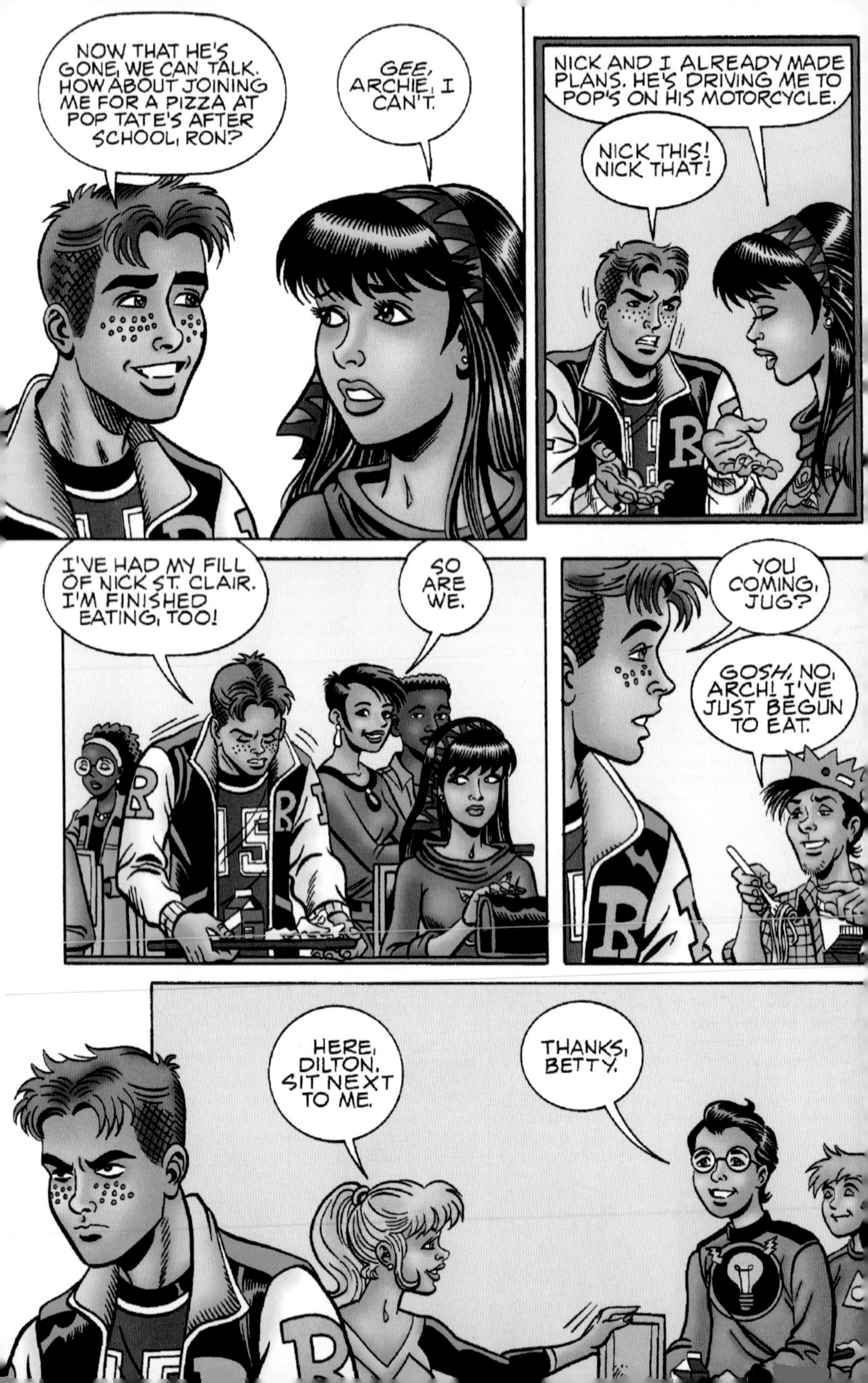
NOW THAT HE'S GONE, WE CAN TALK. HOW ABOUT JOINING ME FOR A PIZZA AT POP TATE'S AFTER SCHOOL, RON?
GEE, ARCHIE, I CAN'T.
NICK AND I ALREADY MADE PLANS. HE'S DRIVING ME TO POP'S ON HIS MOTORCYCLE.
NICK THIS! NICK THAT!
I'VE HAD MY FILL OF NICK ST. CLAIR. I'M FINISHED EATING, TOO!
SO ARE WE.
YOU COMING, JUG?
GOSH, NO, ARCH! I'VE JUST BEGUN TO EAT.
HERE, DILTON. SIT NEXT TO ME.
THANKS, BETTY.

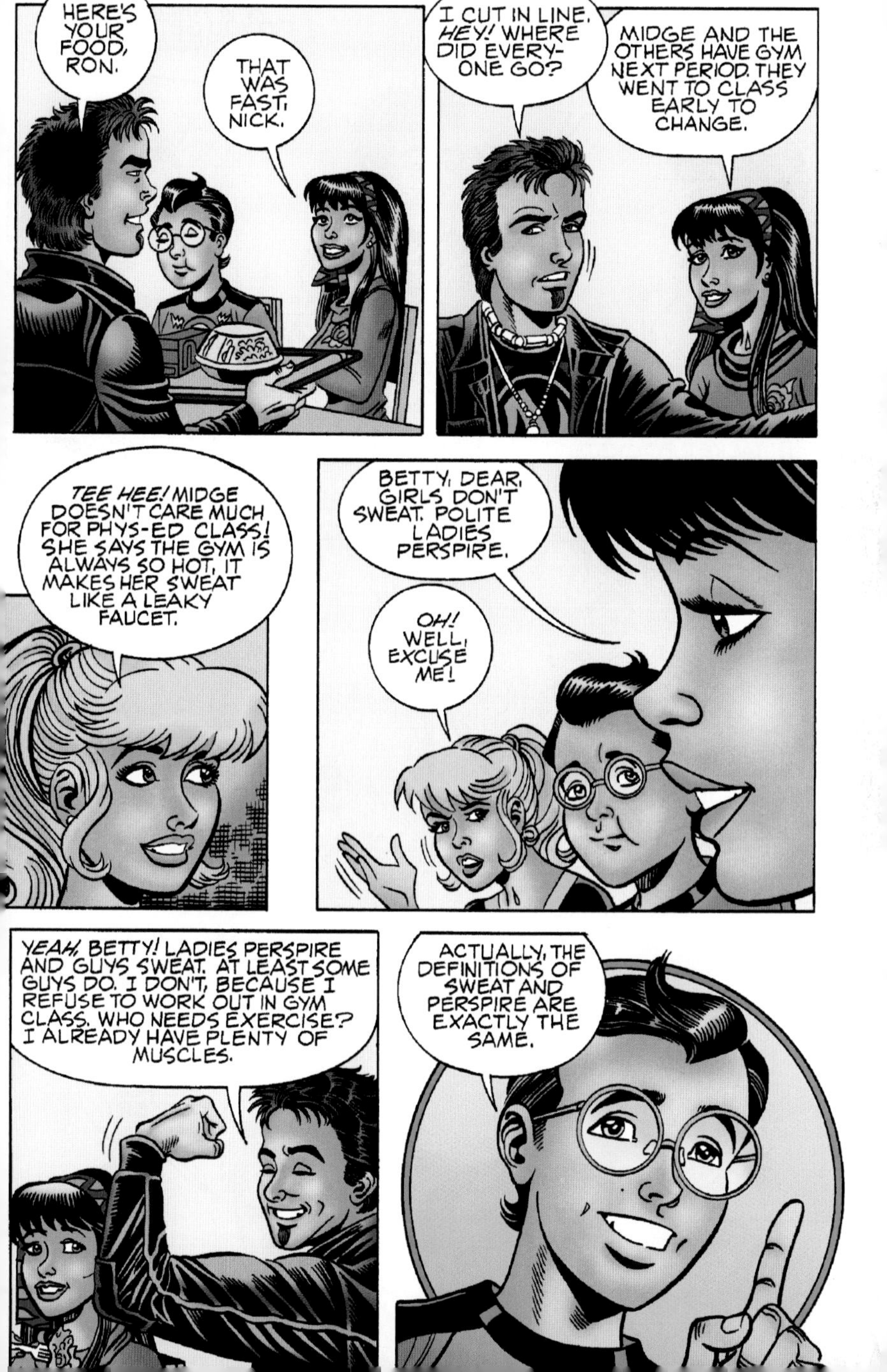
HERE'S YOUR FOOD, RON.
THAT WAS FAST, NICK.
I CUT IN LINE. HEY! WHERE DID EVERY-ONE GO?
MIDGE AND THE OTHERS HAVE GYM NEXT PERIOD. THEY WENT TO CLASS EARLY TO CHANGE.
TEE HEE! MIDGE DOESN'T CARE MUCH FOR PHYS-ED CLASS! SHE SAYS THE GYM IS ALWAYS SO HOT, IT MAKES HER SWEAT LIKE A LEAKY FAUCET.
BETTY, DEAR, GIRLS DON'T SWEAT. POLITE LADIES PERSPIRE.
OH! WELL, EXCUSE ME!
YEAH, BETTY! LADIES PERSPIRE AND GUYS SWEAT. AT LEAST SOME GUYS DO. I DON'T, BECAUSE I REFUSE TO WORK OUT IN GYM CLASS. WHO NEEDS EXERCISE? I ALREADY HAVE PLENTY OF MUSCLES.
ACTUALLY, THE DEFINITIONS OF SWEAT AND PERSPIRE ARE EXACTLY THE SAME.

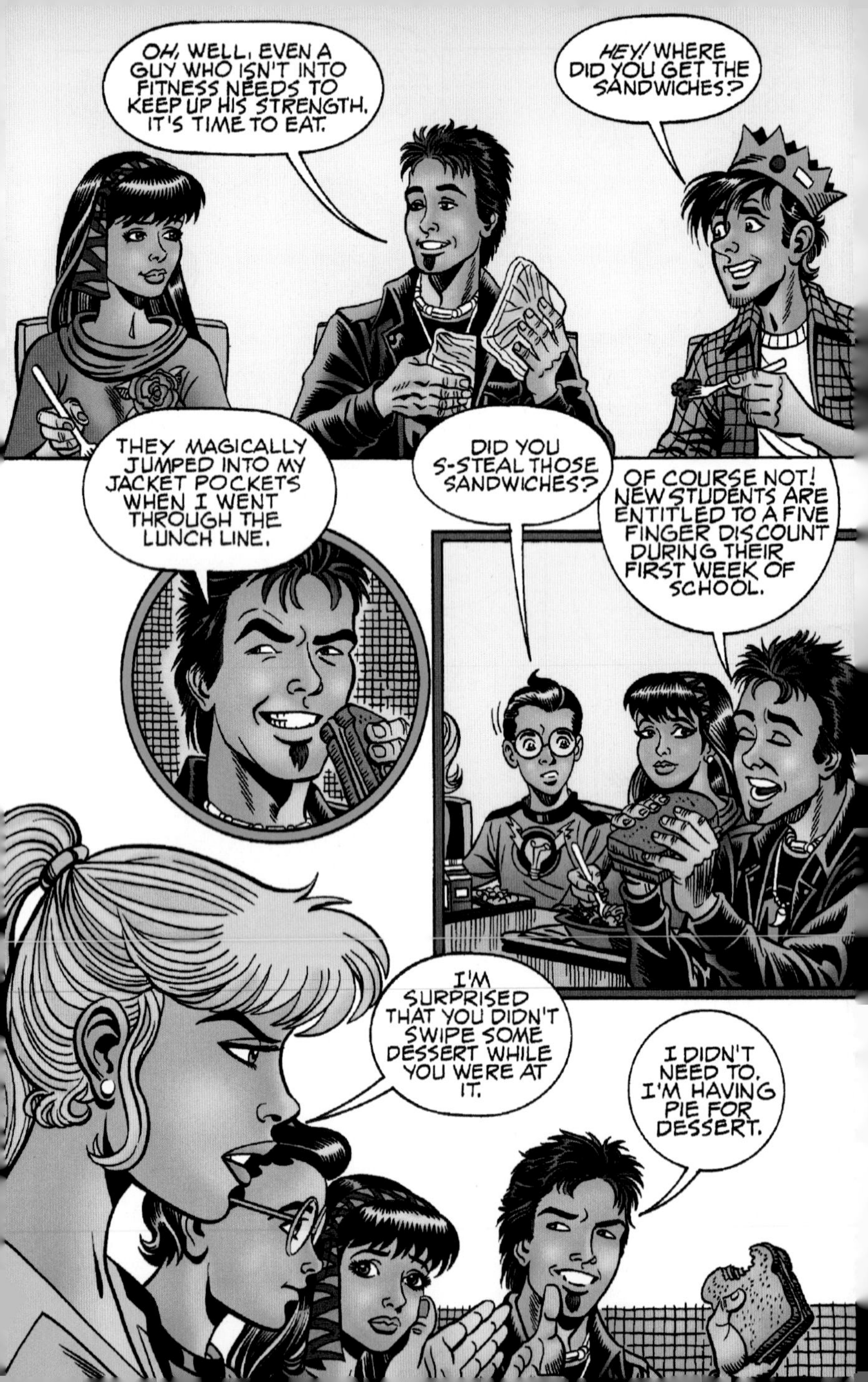
OH, WELL, EVEN A GUY WHO ISN'T INTO FITNESS NEEDS TO KEEP UP HIS STRENGTH. IT'S TIME TO EAT.
HEY! WHERE DID YOU GET THE SANDWICHES?
THEY MAGICALLY JUMPED INTO MY JACKET POCKETS WHEN I WENT THROUGH THE LUNCH LINE.
DID YOU S-STEAL THOSE SANDWICHES?
OF COURSE NOT! NEW STUDENTS ARE ENTITLED TO A FIVE FINGER DISCOUNT DURING THEIR FIRST WEEK OF SCHOOL.
I'M SURPRISED THAT YOU DIDN'T SWIPE SOME DESSERT WHILE YOU WERE AT IT.
I DIDN'T NEED TO. I'M HAVING PIE FOR DESSERT.

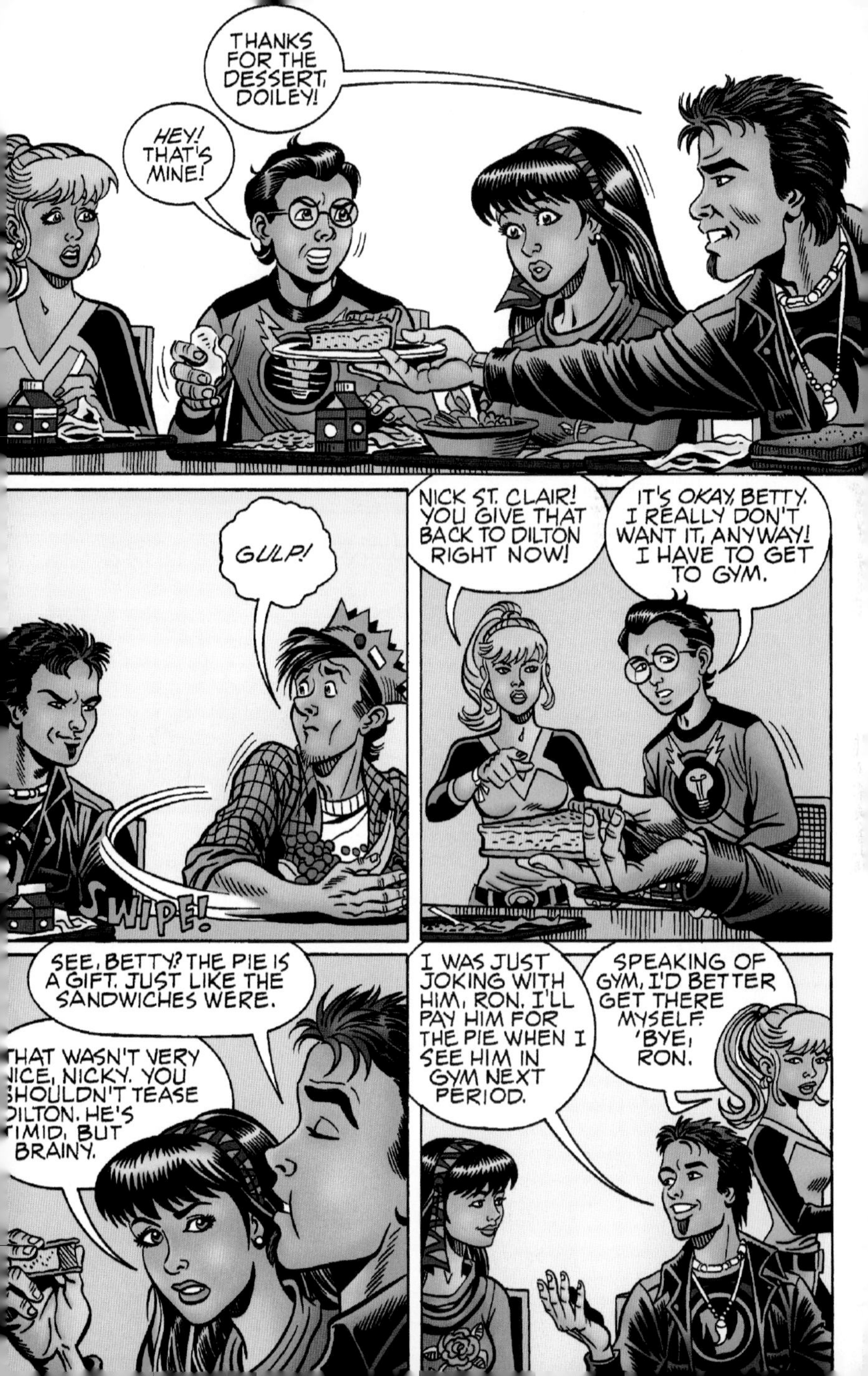
THANKS FOR THE DESSERT, DOILEY!
HEY! THAT'S MINE!
GULP!
SWIPE!
NICK ST. CLAIR! YOU GIVE THAT BACK TO DILTON RIGHT NOW!
IT'S OKAY, BETTY. I REALLY DON'T WANT IT, ANYWAY! I HAVE TO GET TO GYM.
SEE, BETTY? THE PIE IS A GIFT. JUST LIKE THE SANDWICHES WERE.
THAT WASN'T VERY NICE, NICKY. YOU SHOULDN'T TEASE DILTON. HE'S TIMID, BUT BRAINY.
I WAS JUST JOKING WITH HIM, RON. I'LL PAY HIM FOR THE PIE WHEN I SEE HIM IN GYM NEXT PERIOD.
SPEAKING OF GYM, I'D BETTER GET THERE MYSELF. 'BYE, RON.

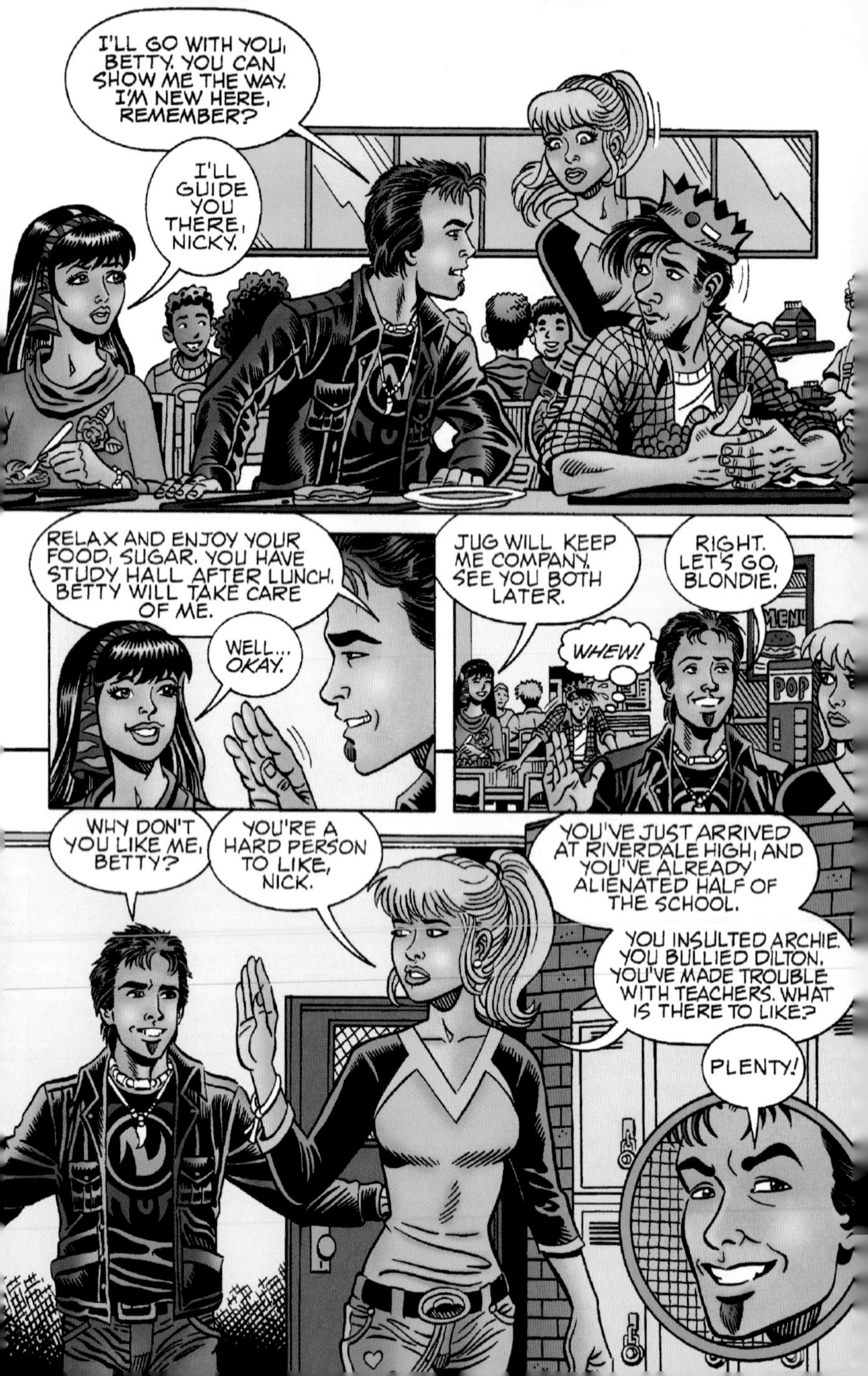
I'LL GO WITH YOU, BETTY. YOU CAN SHOW ME THE WAY. I'M NEW HERE, REMEMBER?
I'LL GUIDE YOU THERE, NICKY.
RELAX AND ENJOY YOUR FOOD, SUGAR. YOU HAVE STUDY HALL AFTER LUNCH. BETTY WILL TAKE CARE OF ME.
WELL... OKAY.
JUG WILL KEEP ME COMPANY. SEE YOU BOTH LATER.
RIGHT. LET'S GO, BLONDIE.
WHEW!
MENU
POP
WHY DON'T YOU LIKE ME, BETTY?
YOU'RE A HARD PERSON TO LIKE, NICK.
YOU'VE JUST ARRIVED AT RIVERDALE HIGH, AND YOU'VE ALREADY ALIENATED HALF OF THE SCHOOL.
YOU INSULTED ARCHIE. YOU BULLIED DILTON. YOU'VE MADE TROUBLE WITH TEACHERS. WHAT IS THERE TO LIKE?
PLENTY!

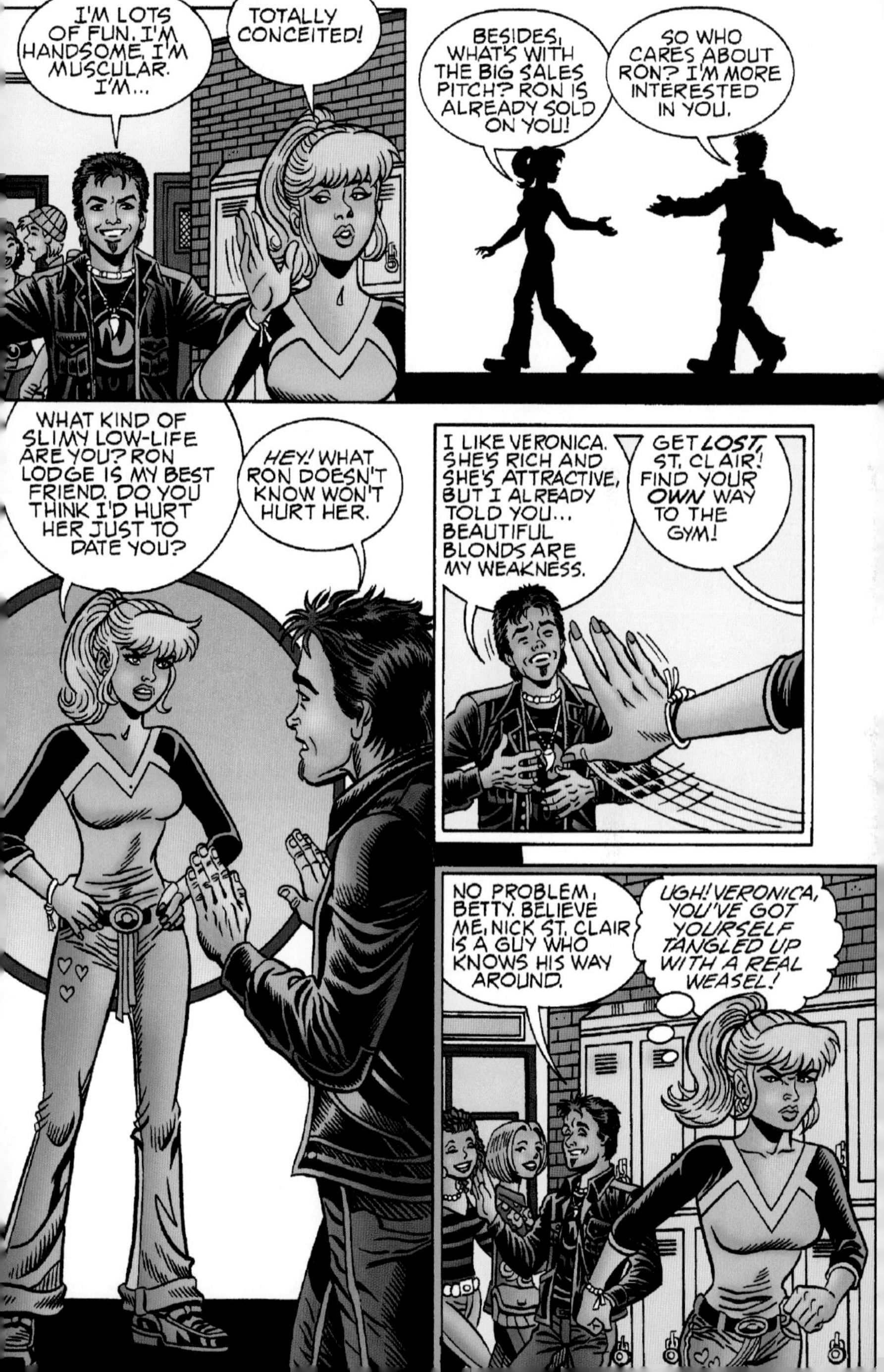

I'M LOTS OF FUN. I'M HANDSOME. I'M MUSCULAR. I'M...
TOTALLY CONCEITED!
BESIDES, WHAT'S WITH THE BIG SALES PITCH? RON IS ALREADY SOLD ON YOU!
SO WHO CARES ABOUT RON? I'M MORE INTERESTED IN YOU.
WHAT KIND OF SLIMY LOW-LIFE ARE YOU? RON LODGE IS MY BEST FRIEND. DO YOU THINK I'D HURT HER JUST TO DATE YOU?
HEY! WHAT RON DOESN'T KNOW WON'T HURT HER.
I LIKE VERONICA. SHE'S RICH AND SHE'S ATTRACTIVE, BUT I ALREADY TOLD YOU... BEAUTIFUL BLONDS ARE MY WEAKNESS.
GET LOST, ST. CLAIR! FIND YOUR OWN WAY TO THE GYM!
NO PROBLEM, BETTY. BELIEVE ME, NICK ST. CLAIR IS A GUY WHO KNOWS HIS WAY AROUND.
UGH! VERONICA, YOU'VE GOT YOURSELF TANGLED UP WITH A REAL WEASEL!

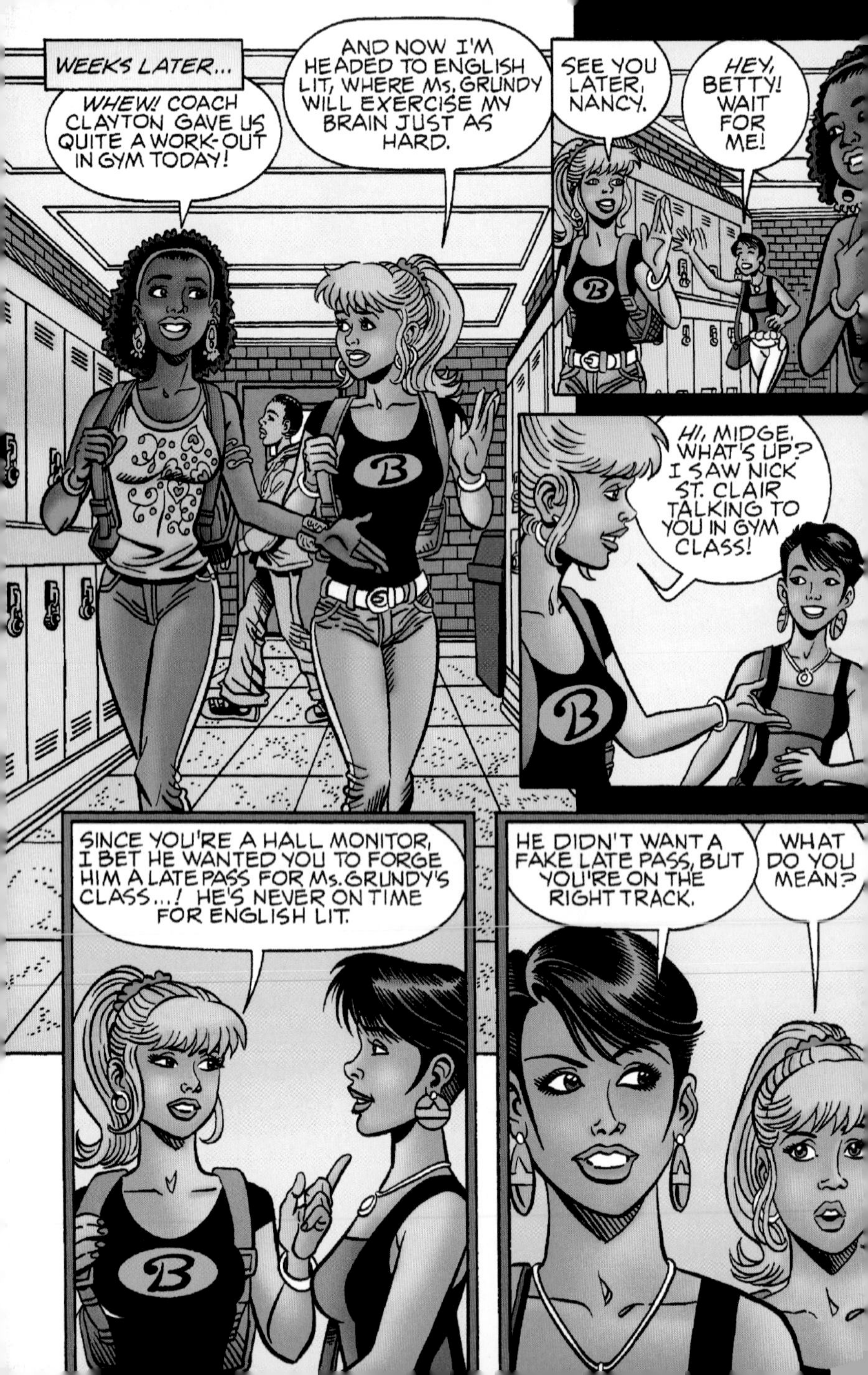
WEEKS LATER...
WHEW! COACH CLAYTON GAVE US QUITE A WORK-OUT IN GYM TODAY!
AND NOW I'M HEADED TO ENGLISH LIT, WHERE Ms. GRUNDY WILL EXERCISE MY BRAIN JUST AS HARD.
SEE YOU LATER, NANCY.
HEY, BETTY! WAIT FOR ME!
HI, MIDGE. WHAT'S UP? I SAW NICK ST. CLAIR TALKING TO YOU IN GYM CLASS!
SINCE YOU'RE A HALL MONITOR, I BET HE WANTED YOU TO FORGE HIM A LATE PASS FOR Ms. GRUNDY'S CLASS...! HE'S NEVER ON TIME FOR ENGLISH LIT.
HE DIDN'T WANT A FAKE LATE PASS, BUT YOU'RE ON THE RIGHT TRACK.
WHAT DO YOU MEAN?

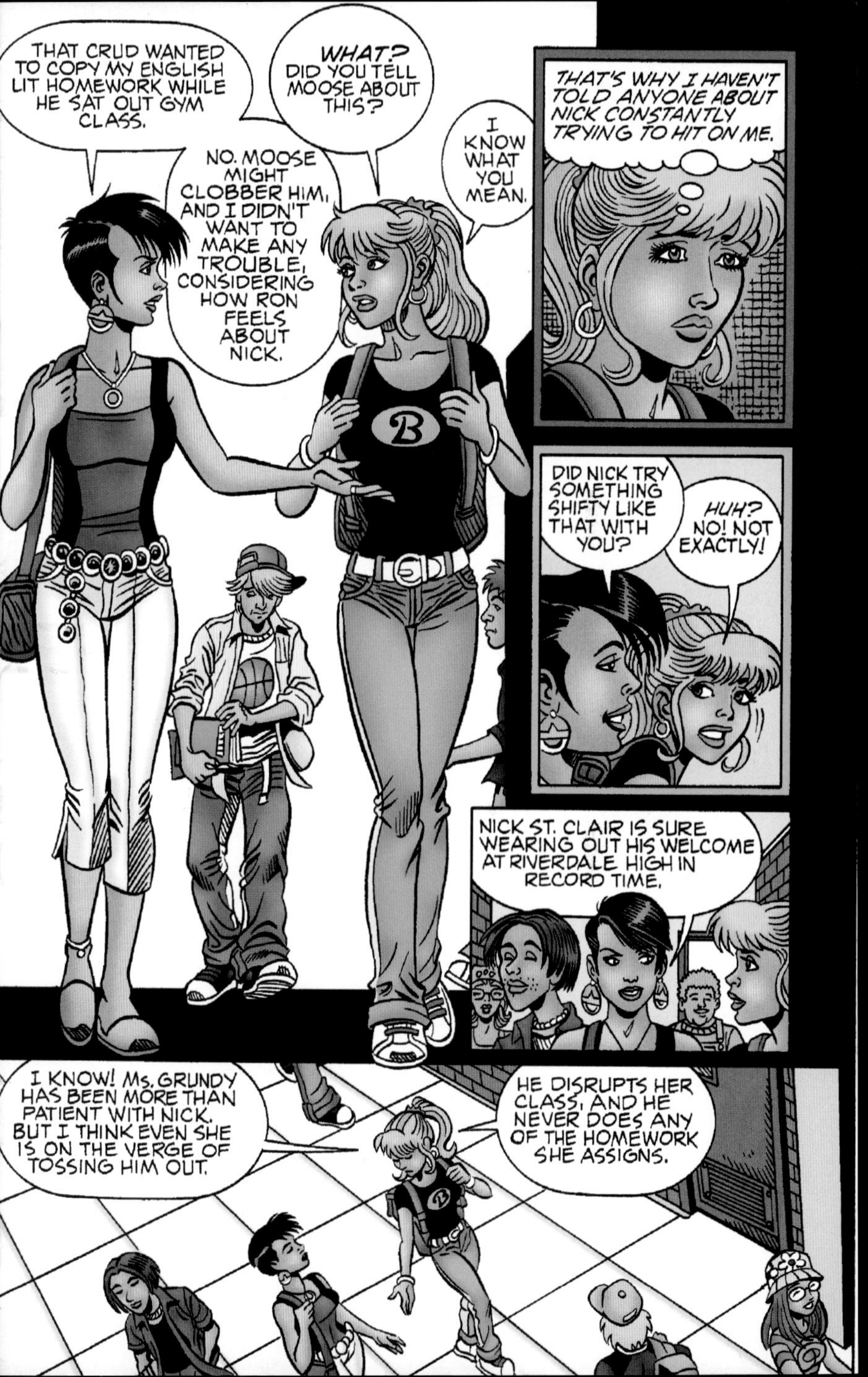
THAT CRUD WANTED TO COPY MY ENGLISH LIT HOMEWORK WHILE HE SAT OUT GYM CLASS.
WHAT? DID YOU TELL MOOSE ABOUT THIS?
NO. MOOSE MIGHT CLOBBER HIM, AND I DIDN'T WANT TO MAKE ANY TROUBLE, CONSIDERING HOW RON FEELS ABOUT NICK.
I KNOW WHAT YOU MEAN.
THAT'S WHY I HAVEN'T TOLD ANYONE ABOUT NICK CONSTANTLY TRYING TO HIT ON ME.
DID NICK TRY SOMETHING SHIFTY LIKE THAT WITH YOU?
HUH? NO! NOT EXACTLY!
NICK ST. CLAIR IS SURE WEARING OUT HIS WELCOME AT RIVERDALE HIGH IN RECORD TIME.
I KNOW! Ms. GRUNDY HAS BEEN MORE THAN PATIENT WITH NICK. BUT I THINK EVEN SHE IS ON THE VERGE OF TOSSING HIM OUT.
HE DISRUPTS HER CLASS, AND HE NEVER DOES ANY OF THE HOMEWORK SHE ASSIGNS.

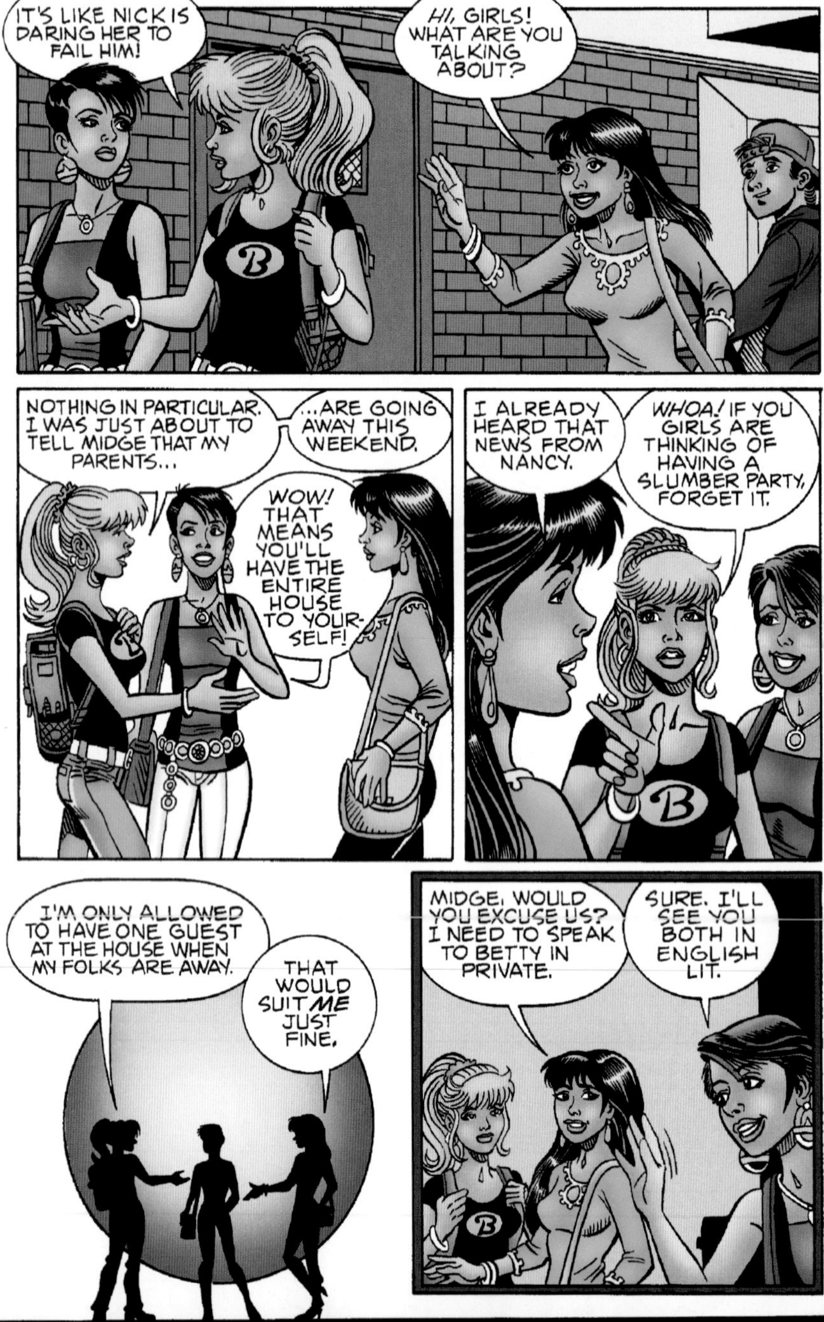
IT'S LIKE NICK IS DARING HER TO FAIL HIM!
HI, GIRLS! WHAT ARE YOU TALKING ABOUT?
NOTHING IN PARTICULAR. I WAS JUST ABOUT TO TELL MIDGE THAT MY PARENTS...
...ARE GOING AWAY THIS WEEKEND.
WOW! THAT MEANS YOU'LL HAVE THE ENTIRE HOUSE TO YOURSELF!
I ALREADY HEARD THAT NEWS FROM NANCY.
WHOA! IF YOU GIRLS ARE THINKING OF HAVING A SLUMBER PARTY, FORGET IT.
I'M ONLY ALLOWED TO HAVE ONE GUEST AT THE HOUSE WHEN MY FOLKS ARE AWAY.
THAT WOULD SUIT ME JUST FINE.
MIDGE, WOULD YOU EXCUSE US? I NEED TO SPEAK TO BETTY IN PRIVATE.
SURE. I'LL SEE YOU BOTH IN ENGLISH LIT.

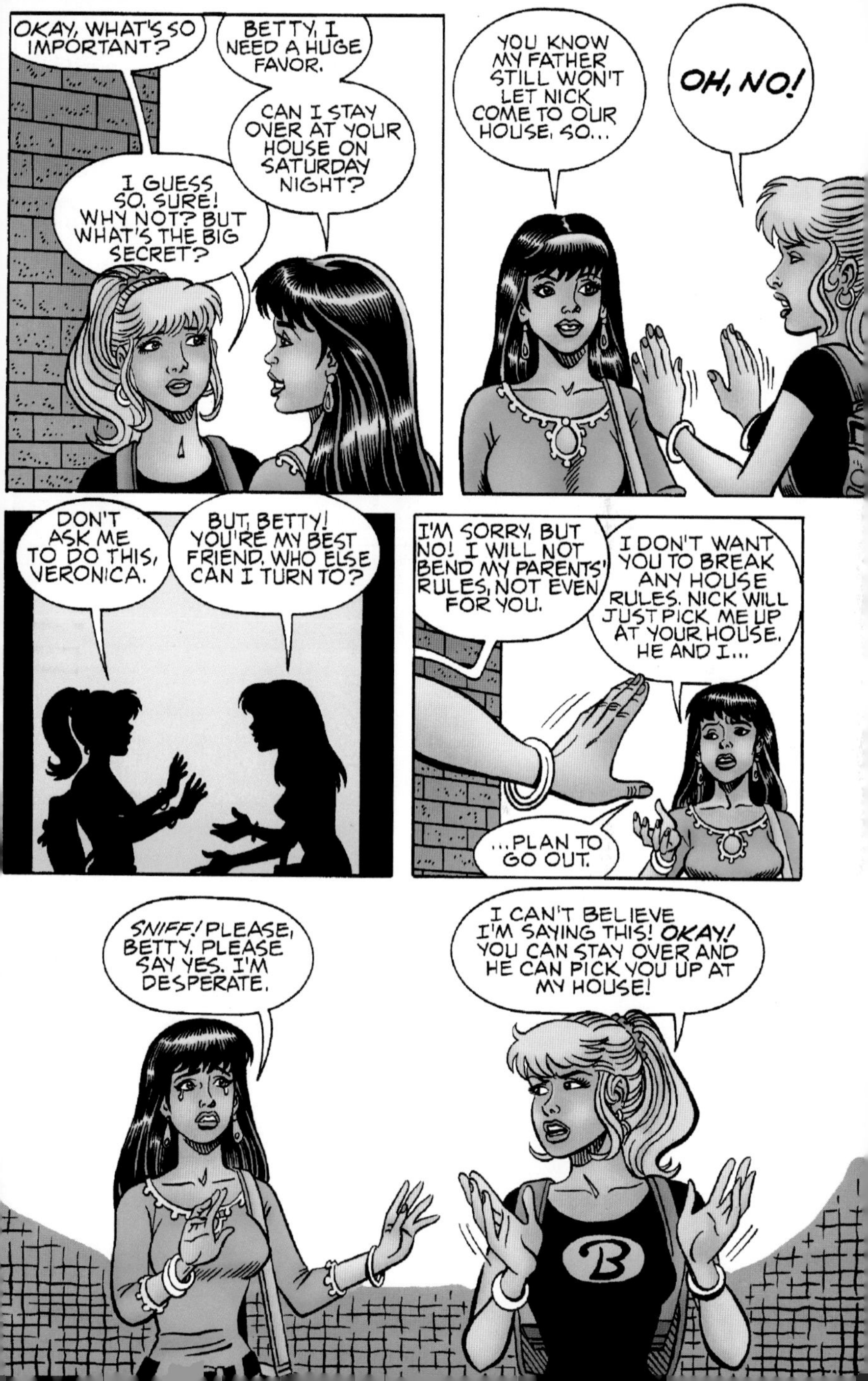
OKAY, WHAT'S SO IMPORTANT?
BETTY, I NEED A HUGE FAVOR.
CAN I STAY OVER AT YOUR HOUSE ON SATURDAY NIGHT?
I GUESS SO. SURE! WHY NOT? BUT WHAT'S THE BIG SECRET?
YOU KNOW MY FATHER STILL WON'T LET NICK COME TO OUR HOUSE, SO...
OH, NO!
DON'T ASK ME TO DO THIS, VERONICA.
BUT, BETTY! YOU'RE MY BEST FRIEND. WHO ELSE CAN I TURN TO?
I'M SORRY, BUT NO! I WILL NOT BEND MY PARENTS' RULES, NOT EVEN FOR YOU.
I DON'T WANT YOU TO BREAK ANY HOUSE RULES. NICK WILL JUST PICK ME UP AT YOUR HOUSE. HE AND I...
...PLAN TO GO OUT.
SNIFF! PLEASE, BETTY. PLEASE SAY YES. I'M DESPERATE.
I CAN'T BELIEVE I'M SAYING THIS! OKAY! YOU CAN STAY OVER AND HE CAN PICK YOU UP AT MY HOUSE!

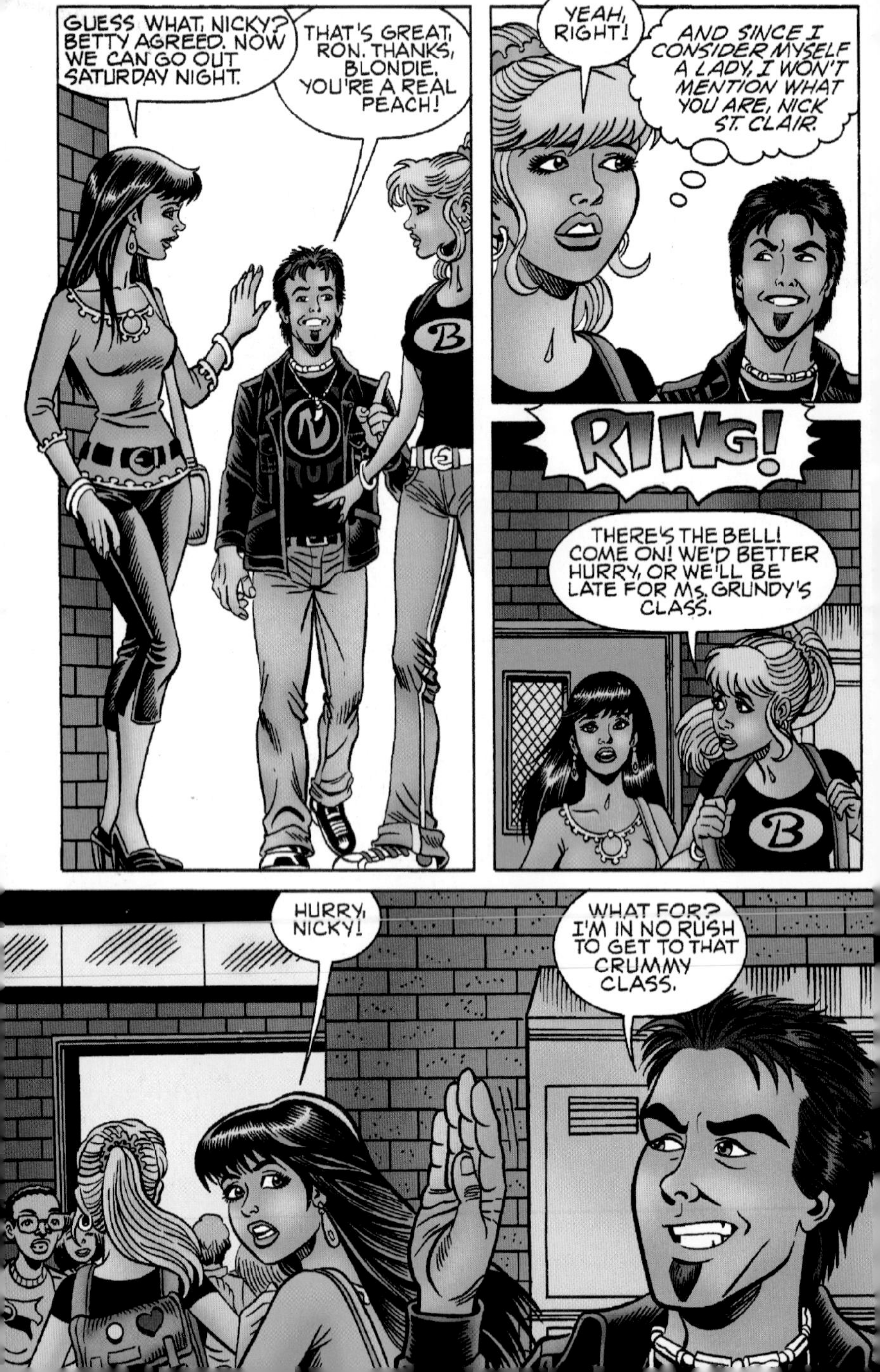
GUESS WHAT, NICKY? BETTY AGREED. NOW WE CAN GO OUT SATURDAY NIGHT.
THAT'S GREAT, RON. THANKS, BLONDIE. YOU'RE A REAL PEACH!
YEAH, RIGHT!
AND SINCE I CONSIDER MYSELF A LADY, I WON'T MENTION WHAT YOU ARE, NICK ST. CLAIR.
RING!
THERE'S THE BELL! COME ON! WE'D BETTER HURRY, OR WE'LL BE LATE FOR Ms. GRUNDY'S CLASS.
HURRY, NICKY!
WHAT FOR? I'M IN NO RUSH TO GET TO THAT CRUMMY CLASS.

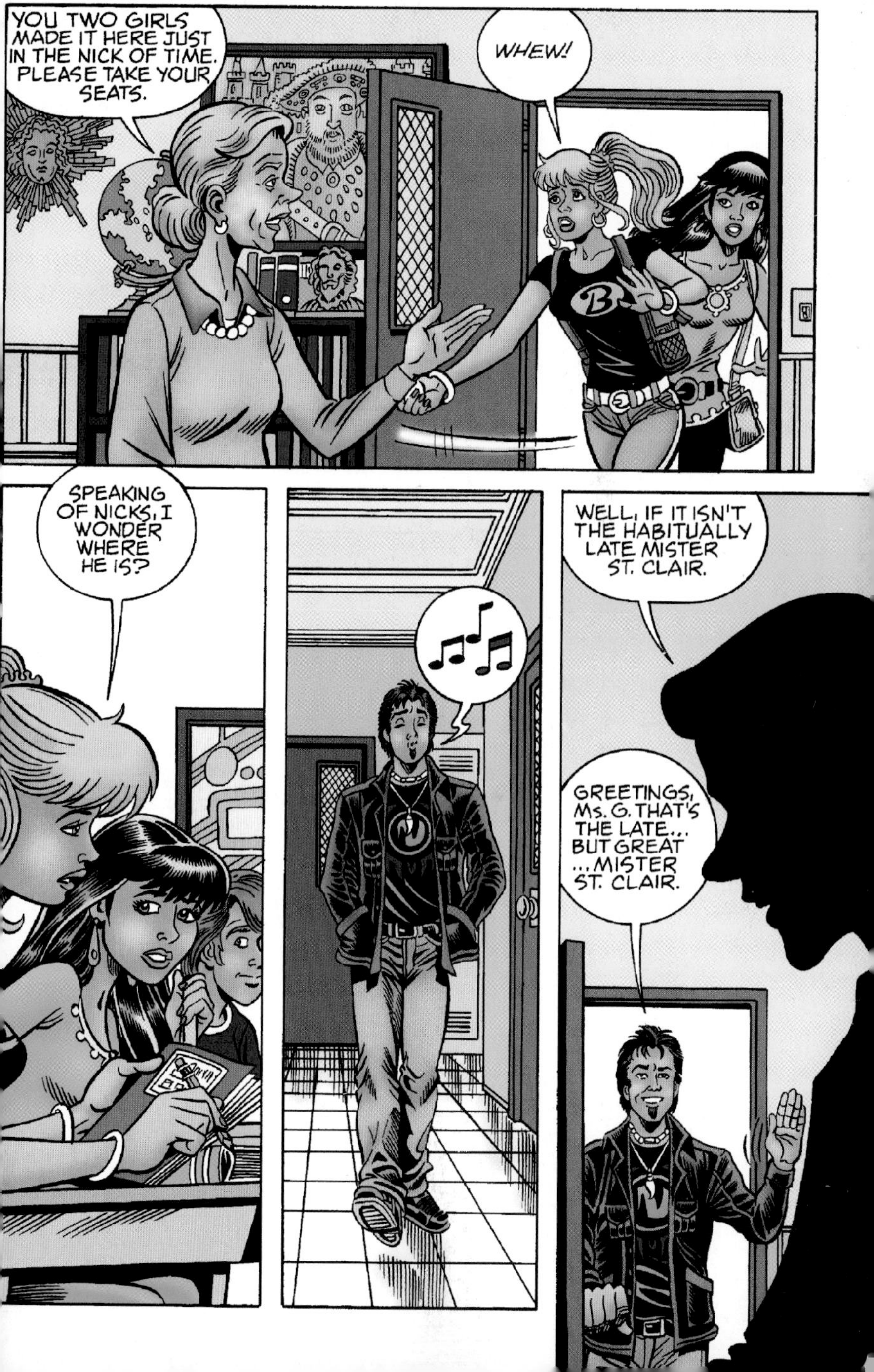
YOU TWO GIRLS MADE IT HERE JUST IN THE NICK OF TIME. PLEASE TAKE YOUR SEATS.
WHEW!
SPEAKING OF NICKS, I WONDER WHERE HE IS?
WELL, IF IT ISN'T THE HABITUALLY LATE MISTER ST. CLAIR.
GREETINGS, Ms. G. THAT'S THE LATE... BUT GREAT ...MISTER ST. CLAIR.

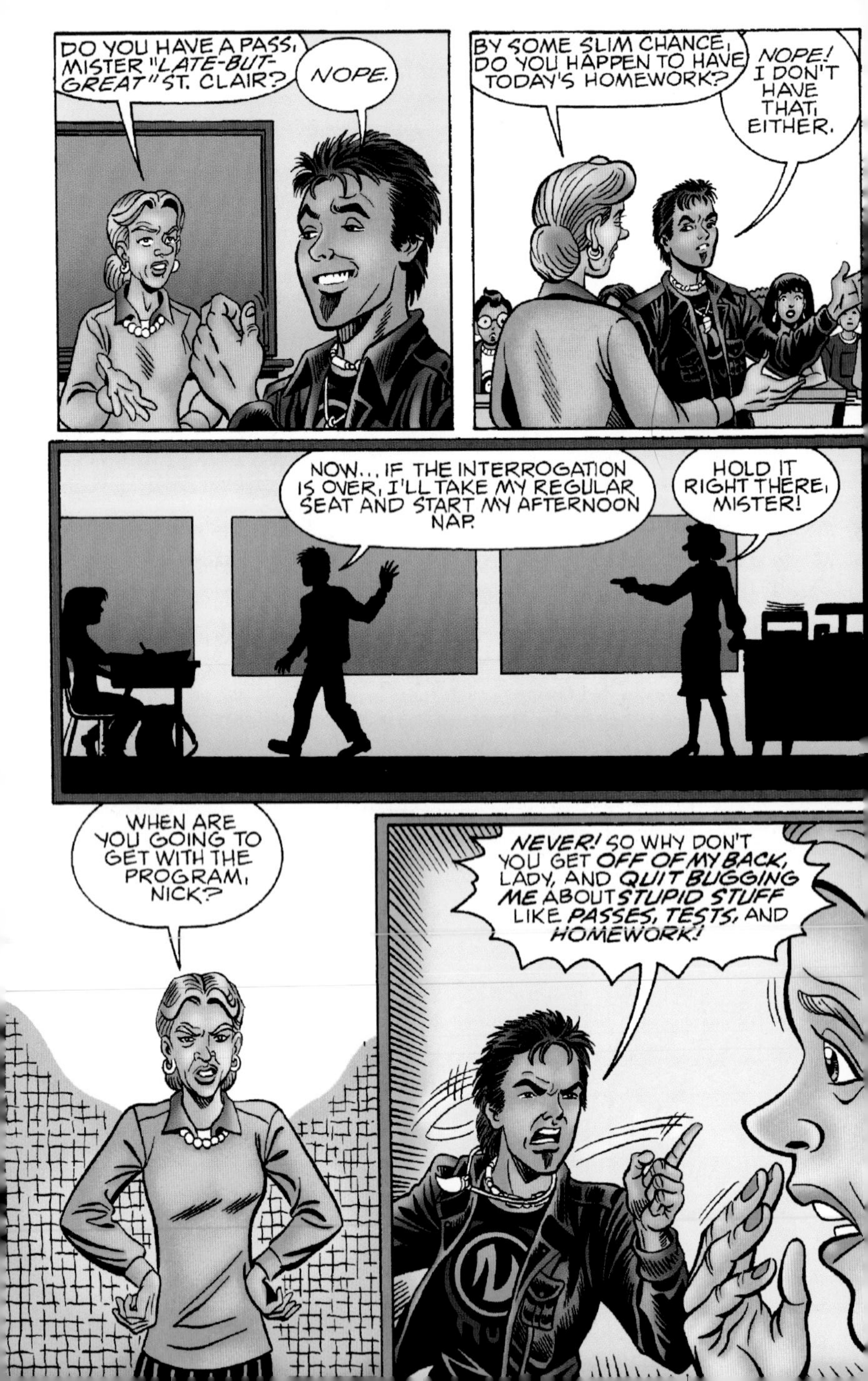
DO YOU HAVE A PASS, MISTER "LATE-BUT-GREAT" ST. CLAIR?
NOPE.
BY SOME SLIM CHANCE, DO YOU HAPPEN TO HAVE TODAY'S HOMEWORK?
NOPE! I DON'T HAVE THAT, EITHER.
NOW... IF THE INTERROGATION IS OVER, I'LL TAKE MY REGULAR SEAT AND START MY AFTERNOON NAP.
HOLD IT RIGHT THERE, MISTER!
WHEN ARE YOU GOING TO GET WITH THE PROGRAM, NICK?
NEVER! SO WHY DON'T YOU GET OFF OF MY BACK, LADY, AND QUIT BUGGING ME ABOUT STUPID STUFF LIKE PASSES, TESTS, AND HOMEWORK!

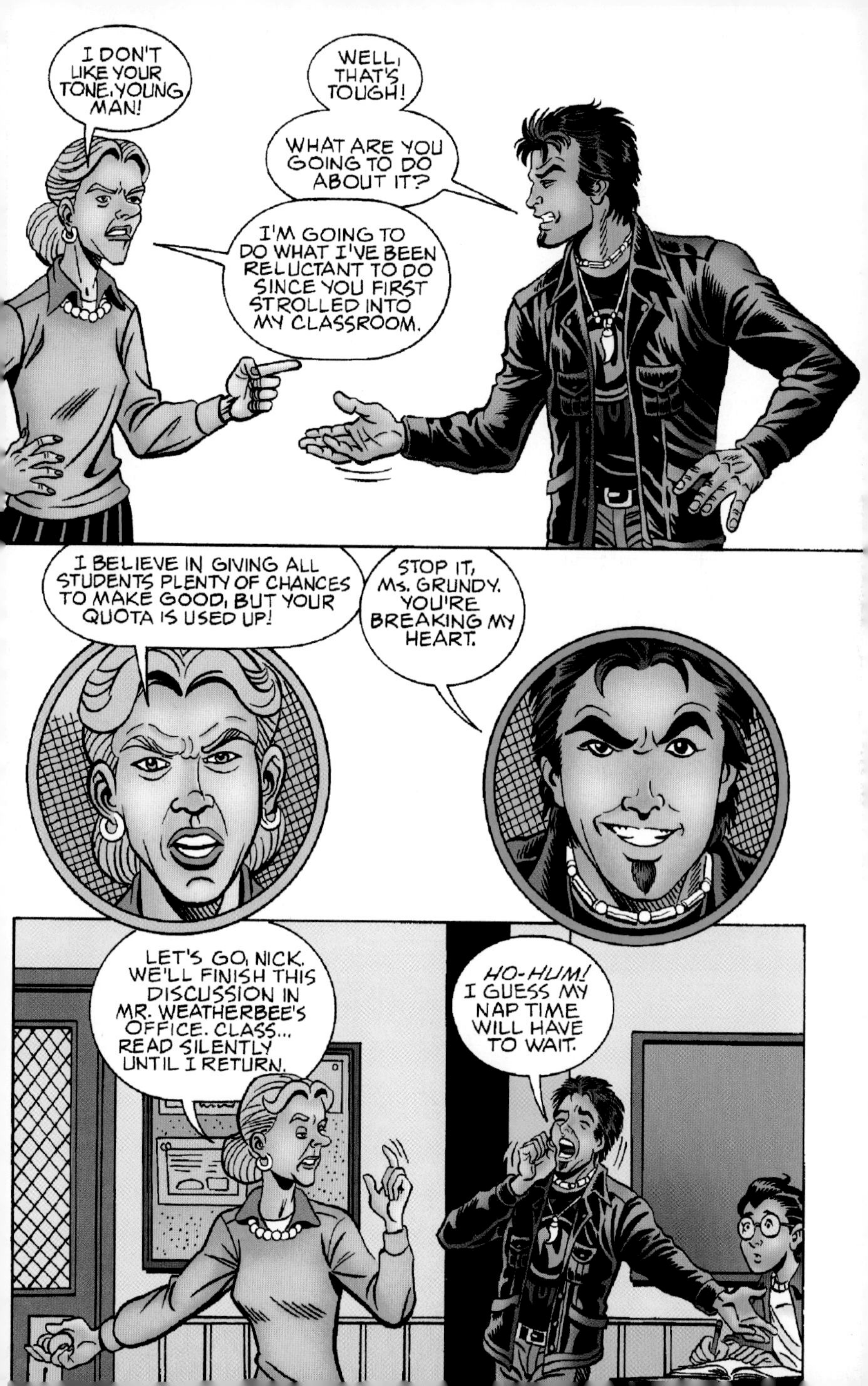
I DON'T LIKE YOUR TONE, YOUNG MAN!
WELL, THAT'S TOUGH!
WHAT ARE YOU GOING TO DO ABOUT IT?
I'M GOING TO DO WHAT I'VE BEEN RELUCTANT TO DO SINCE YOU FIRST STROLLED INTO MY CLASSROOM.
I BELIEVE IN GIVING ALL STUDENTS PLENTY OF CHANCES TO MAKE GOOD, BUT YOUR QUOTA IS USED UP!
STOP IT, Ms. GRUNDY. YOU'RE BREAKING MY HEART.
LET'S GO, NICK. WE'LL FINISH THIS DISCUSSION IN MR. WEATHERBEE'S OFFICE. CLASS... READ SILENTLY UNTIL I RETURN.
HO-HUM! I GUESS MY NAP TIME WILL HAVE TO WAIT.

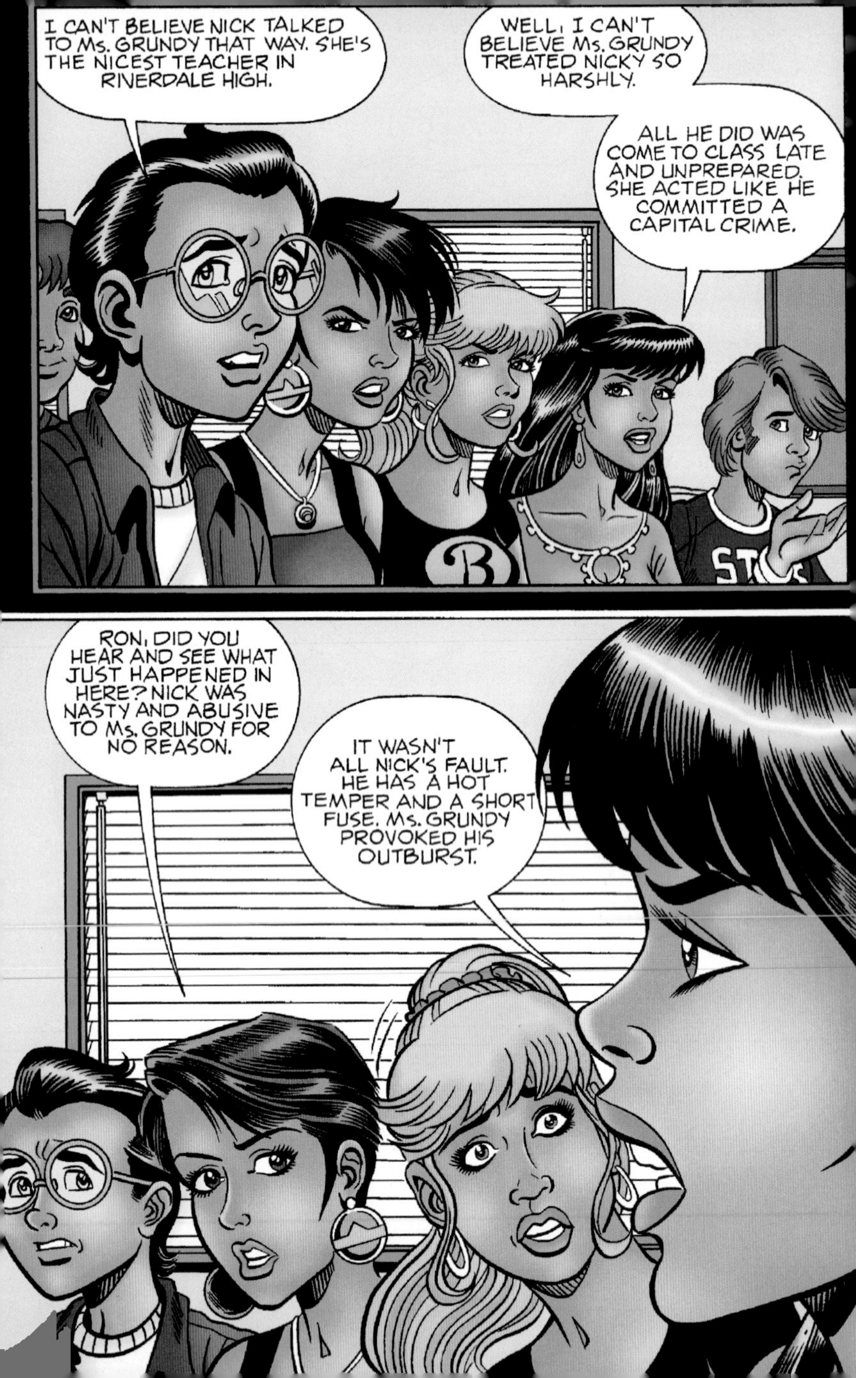
I CAN'T BELIEVE NICK TALKED TO Ms. GRUNDY THAT WAY. SHE'S THE NICEST TEACHER IN RIVERDALE HIGH.
WELL, I CAN'T BELIEVE Ms. GRUNDY TREATED NICKY SO HARSHLY.
ALL HE DID WAS COME TO CLASS LATE AND UNPREPARED. SHE ACTED LIKE HE COMMITTED A CAPITAL CRIME.
RON, DID YOU HEAR AND SEE WHAT JUST HAPPENED IN HERE? NICK WAS NASTY AND ABUSIVE TO Ms. GRUNDY FOR NO REASON.
IT WASN'T ALL NICK'S FAULT. HE HAS A HOT TEMPER AND A SHORT FUSE. Ms. GRUNDY PROVOKED HIS OUTBURST.

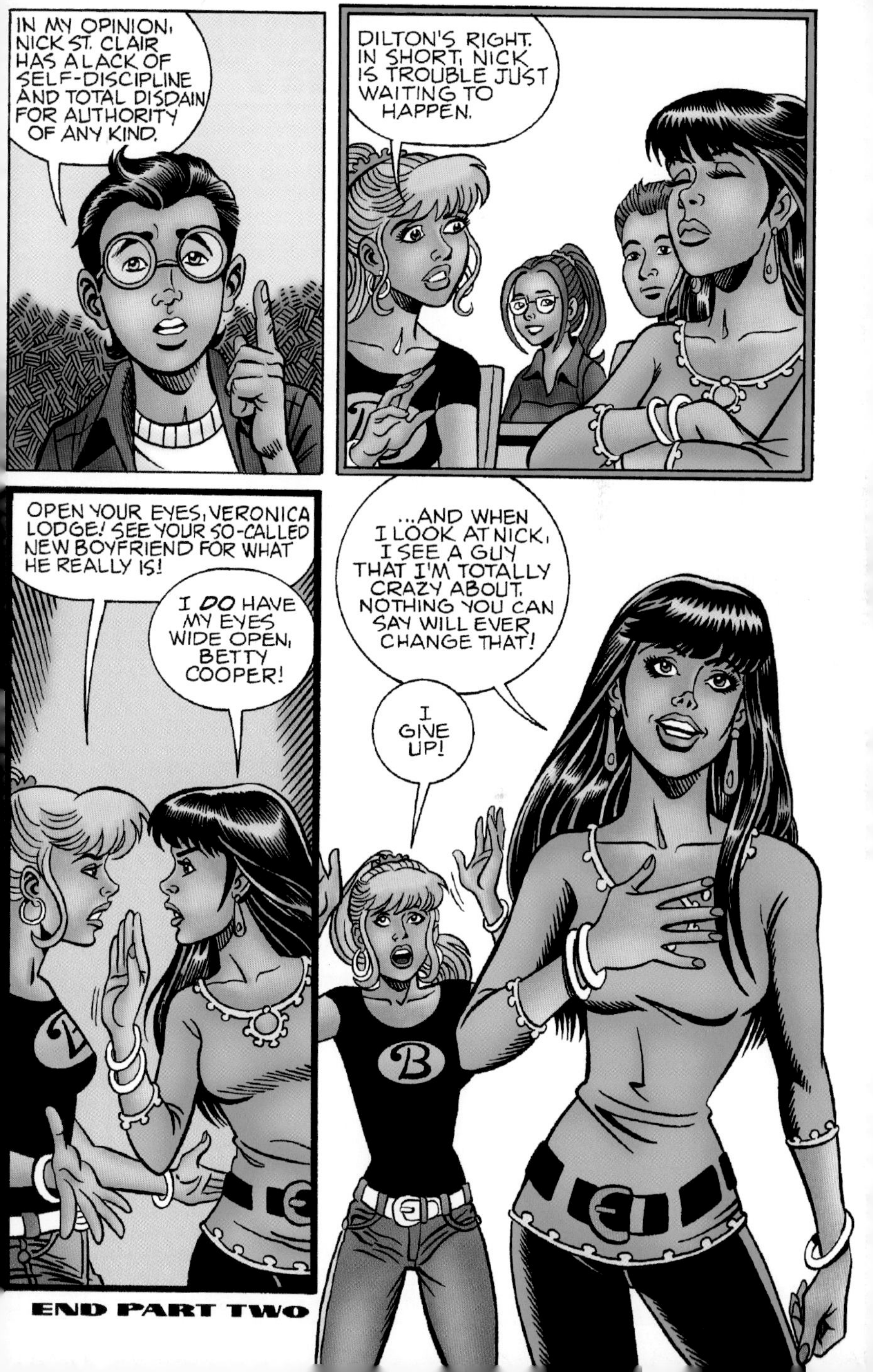
IN MY OPINION, NICK ST. CLAIR HAS A LACK OF SELF-DISCIPLINE AND TOTAL DISDAIN FOR AUTHORITY OF ANY KIND.
DILTON'S RIGHT. IN SHORT, NICK IS TROUBLE JUST WAITING TO HAPPEN.
OPEN YOUR EYES, VERONICA LODGE! SEE YOUR SO-CALLED NEW BOYFRIEND FOR WHAT HE REALLY IS!
I DO HAVE MY EYES WIDE OPEN, BETTY COOPER!
...AND WHEN I LOOK AT NICK, I SEE A GUY THAT I'M TOTALLY CRAZY ABOUT. NOTHING YOU CAN SAY WILL EVER CHANGE THAT!
I GIVE UP!
END PART TWO

BAD BOY TROUBLE! PART THREE

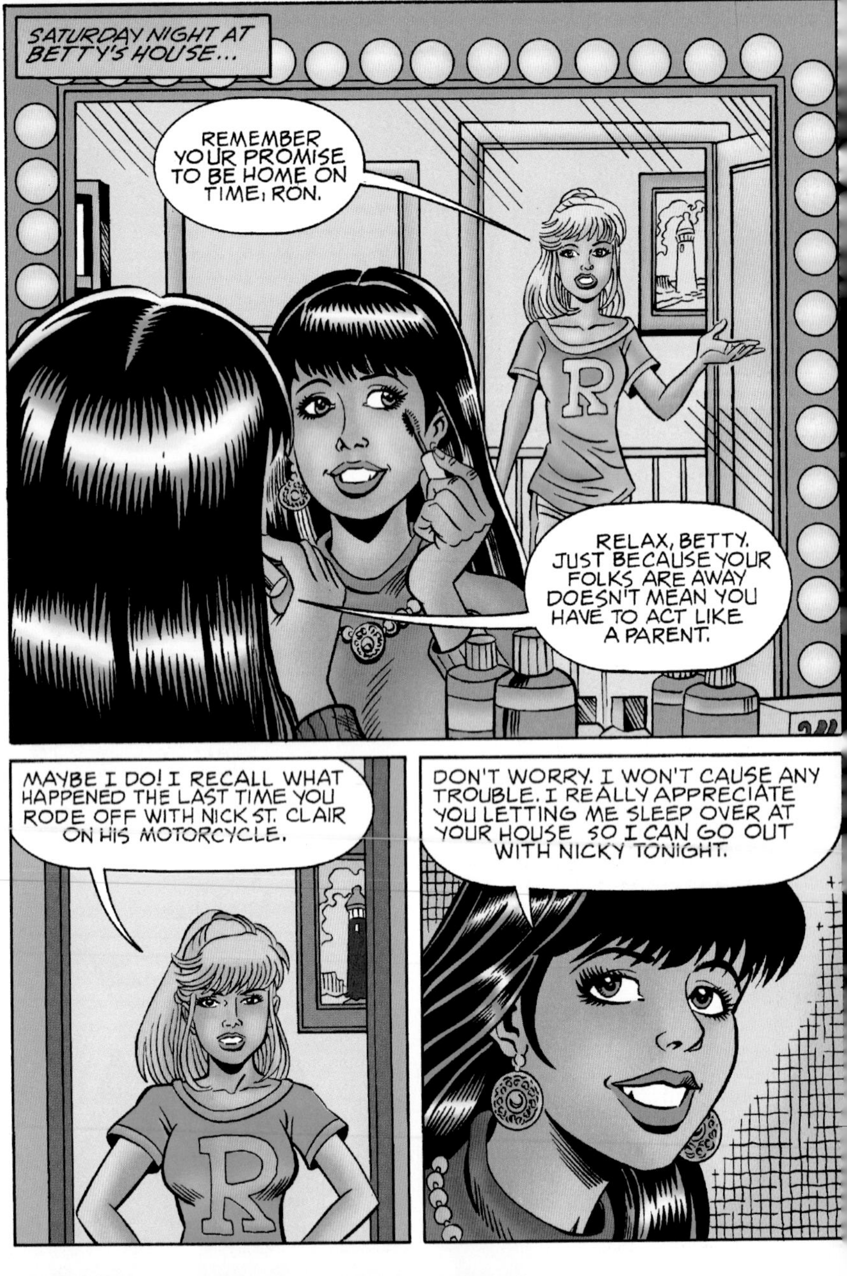
SATURDAY NIGHT AT BETTY'S HOUSE...
REMEMBER YOUR PROMISE TO BE HOME ON TIME, RON.
RELAX, BETTY. JUST BECAUSE YOUR FOLKS ARE AWAY DOESN'T MEAN YOU HAVE TO ACT LIKE A PARENT.
MAYBE I DO! I RECALL WHAT HAPPENED THE LAST TIME YOU RODE OFF WITH NICK ST. CLAIR ON HIS MOTORCYCLE.
DON'T WORRY. I WON'T CAUSE ANY TROUBLE. I REALLY APPRECIATE YOU LETTING ME SLEEP OVER AT YOUR HOUSE SO I CAN GO OUT WITH NICKY TONIGHT.

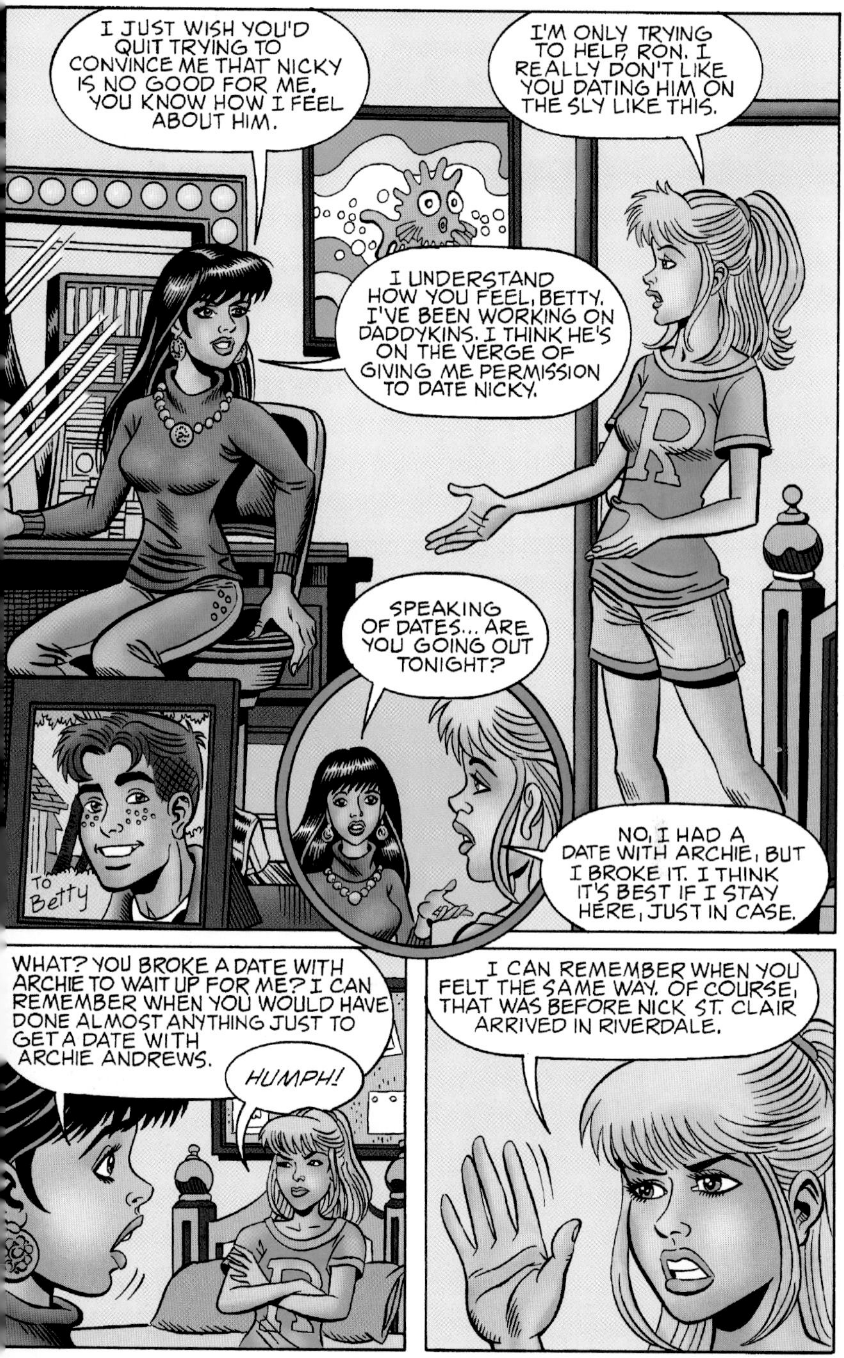
I JUST WISH YOU'D QUIT TRYING TO CONVINCE ME THAT NICKY IS NO GOOD FOR ME. YOU KNOW HOW I FEEL ABOUT HIM.
I'M ONLY TRYING TO HELP, RON. I REALLY DON'T LIKE YOU DATING HIM ON THE SLY LIKE THIS.
I UNDERSTAND HOW YOU FEEL, BETTY. I'VE BEEN WORKING ON DADDYKINS. I THINK HE'S ON THE VERGE OF GIVING ME PERMISSION TO DATE NICKY.
SPEAKING OF DATES... ARE YOU GOING OUT TONIGHT?
NO, I HAD A DATE WITH ARCHIE, BUT I BROKE IT. I THINK IT'S BEST IF I STAY HERE, JUST IN CASE.
To Betty
WHAT? YOU BROKE A DATE WITH ARCHIE TO WAIT UP FOR ME? I CAN REMEMBER WHEN YOU WOULD HAVE DONE ALMOST ANYTHING JUST TO GET A DATE WITH ARCHIE ANDREWS.
HUMPH!
I CAN REMEMBER WHEN YOU FELT THE SAME WAY. OF COURSE, THAT WAS BEFORE NICK ST. CLAIR ARRIVED IN RIVERDALE.

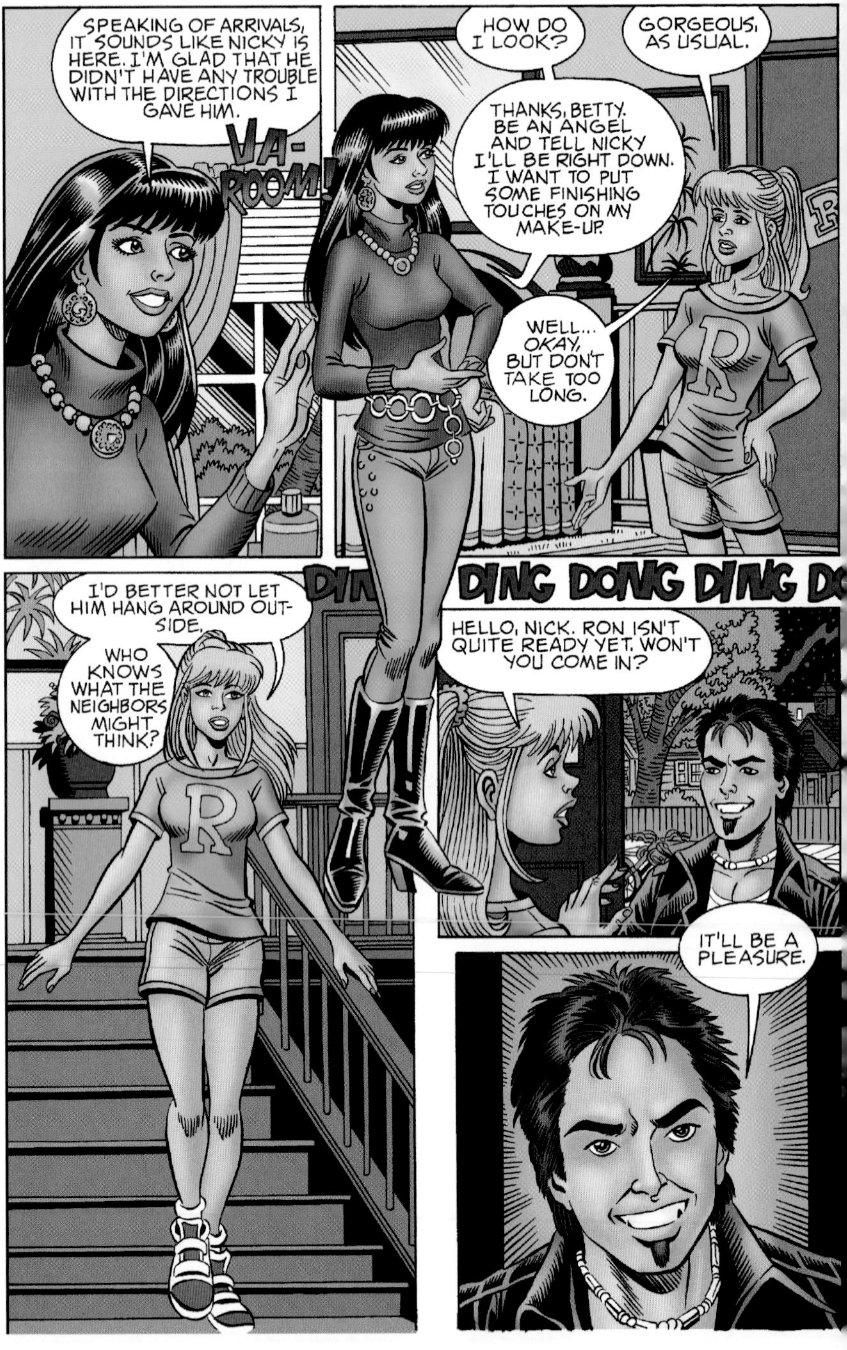
SPEAKING OF ARRIVALS, IT SOUNDS LIKE NICKY IS HERE. I'M GLAD THAT HE DIDN'T HAVE ANY TROUBLE WITH THE DIRECTIONS I GAVE HIM.
VA-ROOM!
HOW DO I LOOK?
GORGEOUS, AS USUAL.
THANKS, BETTY. BE AN ANGEL AND TELL NICKY I'LL BE RIGHT DOWN. I WANT TO PUT SOME FINISHING TOUCHES ON MY MAKE-UP.
WELL... OKAY, BUT DON'T TAKE TOO LONG.
DING DONG DING DONG DING
I'D BETTER NOT LET HIM HANG AROUND OUT-SIDE.
WHO KNOWS WHAT THE NEIGHBORS MIGHT THINK?
HELLO, NICK. RON ISN'T QUITE READY YET. WON'T YOU COME IN?
IT'LL BE A PLEASURE.

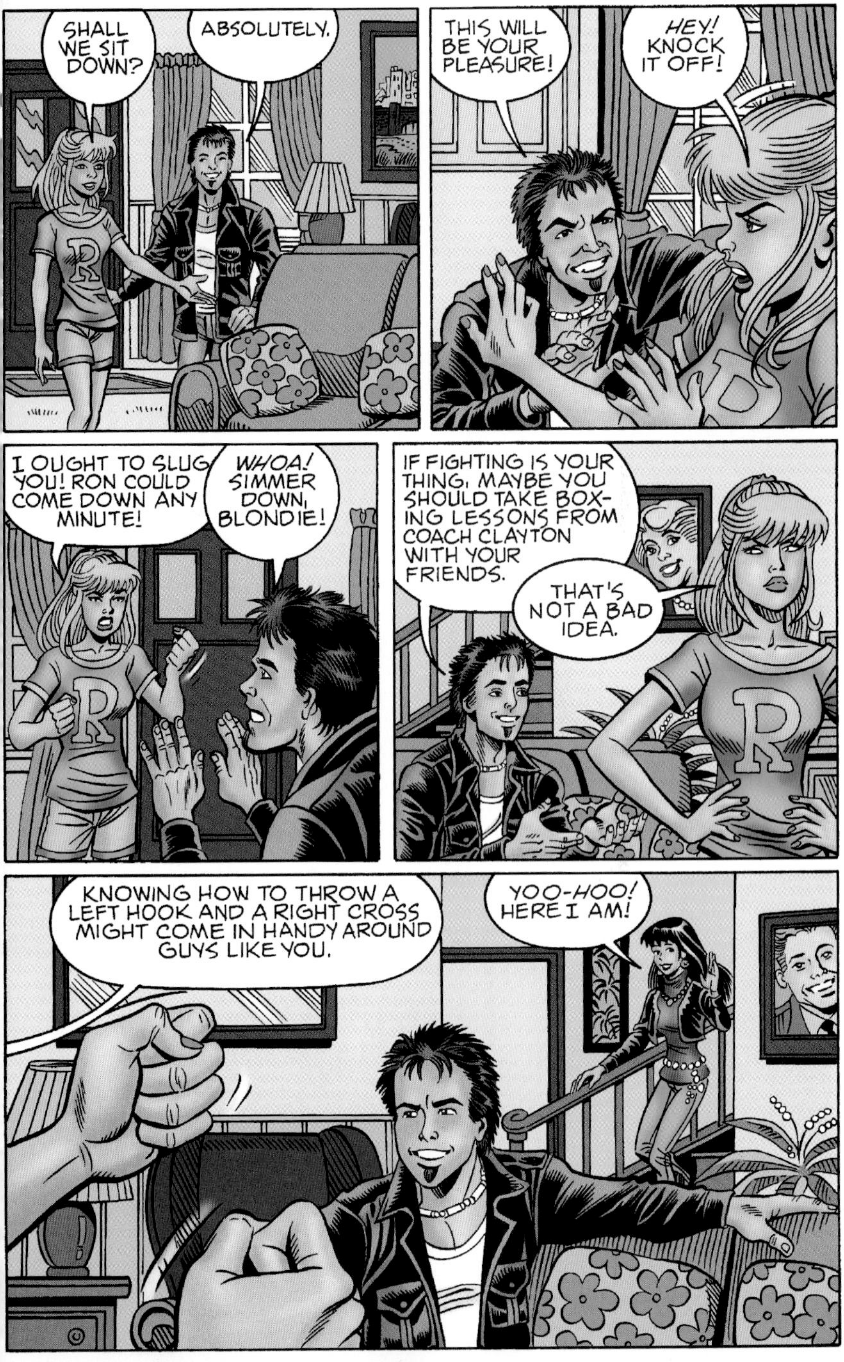
SHALL WE SIT DOWN?
ABSOLUTELY.
THIS WILL BE YOUR PLEASURE!
HEY! KNOCK IT OFF!
I OUGHT TO SLUG YOU! RON COULD COME DOWN ANY MINUTE!
WHOA! SIMMER DOWN, BLONDIE!
IF FIGHTING IS YOUR THING, MAYBE YOU SHOULD TAKE BOXING LESSONS FROM COACH CLAYTON WITH YOUR FRIENDS.
THAT'S NOT A BAD IDEA.
KNOWING HOW TO THROW A LEFT HOOK AND A RIGHT CROSS MIGHT COME IN HANDY AROUND GUYS LIKE YOU.
YOO-HOO! HERE I AM!

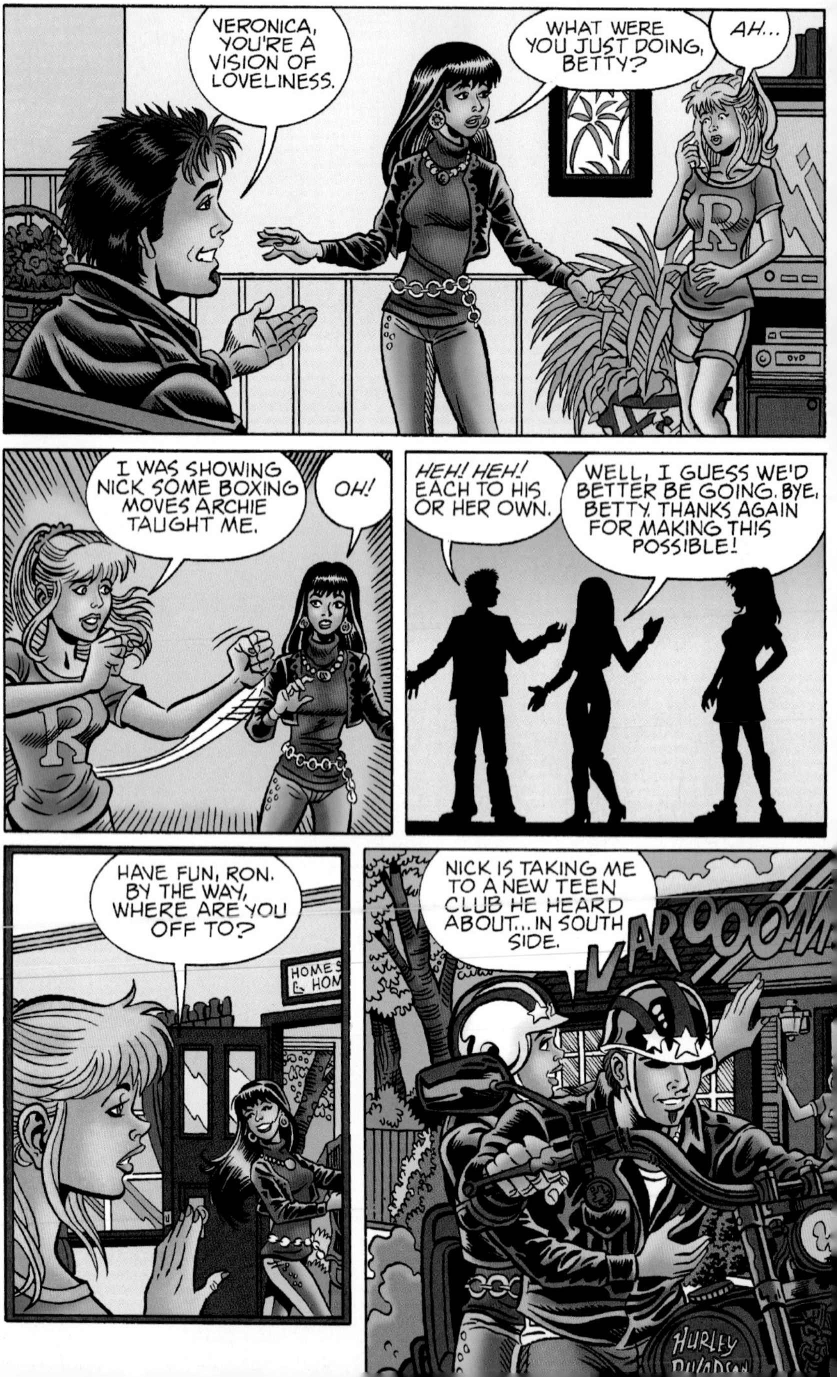

VERONICA, YOU'RE A VISION OF LOVELINESS.
WHAT WERE YOU JUST DOING, BETTY?
AH...
I WAS SHOWING NICK SOME BOXING MOVES ARCHIE TAUGHT ME.
OH!
HEH! HEH! EACH TO HIS OR HER OWN.
WELL, I GUESS WE'D BETTER BE GOING. BYE, BETTY. THANKS AGAIN FOR MAKING THIS POSSIBLE!
HAVE FUN, RON. BY THE WAY, WHERE ARE YOU OFF TO?
NICK IS TAKING ME TO A NEW TEEN CLUB HE HEARD ABOUT... IN SOUTH SIDE.
VAROOOM

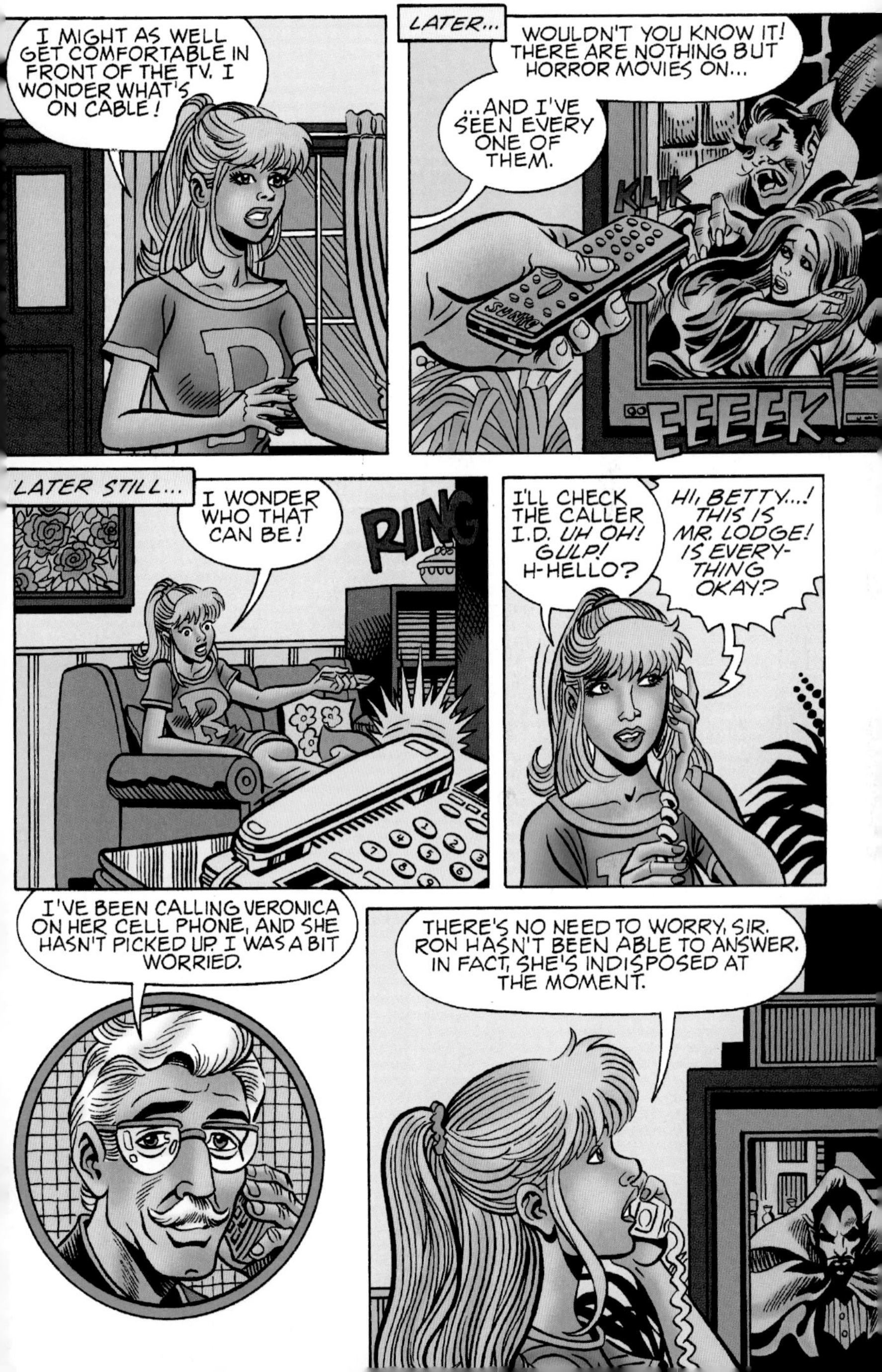
I MIGHT AS WELL GET COMFORTABLE IN FRONT OF THE TV. I WONDER WHAT'S ON CABLE!
LATER...
WOULDN'T YOU KNOW IT! THERE ARE NOTHING BUT HORROR MOVIES ON...
...AND I'VE SEEN EVERY ONE OF THEM.
KLIK
EEEEK!
LATER STILL...
I WONDER WHO THAT CAN BE!
RING
I'LL CHECK THE CALLER I.D. UH OH! GULP! H-HELLO?
HI, BETTY...! THIS IS MR. LODGE! IS EVERY-THING OKAY?
I'VE BEEN CALLING VERONICA ON HER CELL PHONE, AND SHE HASN'T PICKED UP. I WAS A BIT WORRIED.
THERE'S NO NEED TO WORRY, SIR. RON HASN'T BEEN ABLE TO ANSWER. IN FACT, SHE'S INDISPOSED AT THE MOMENT.

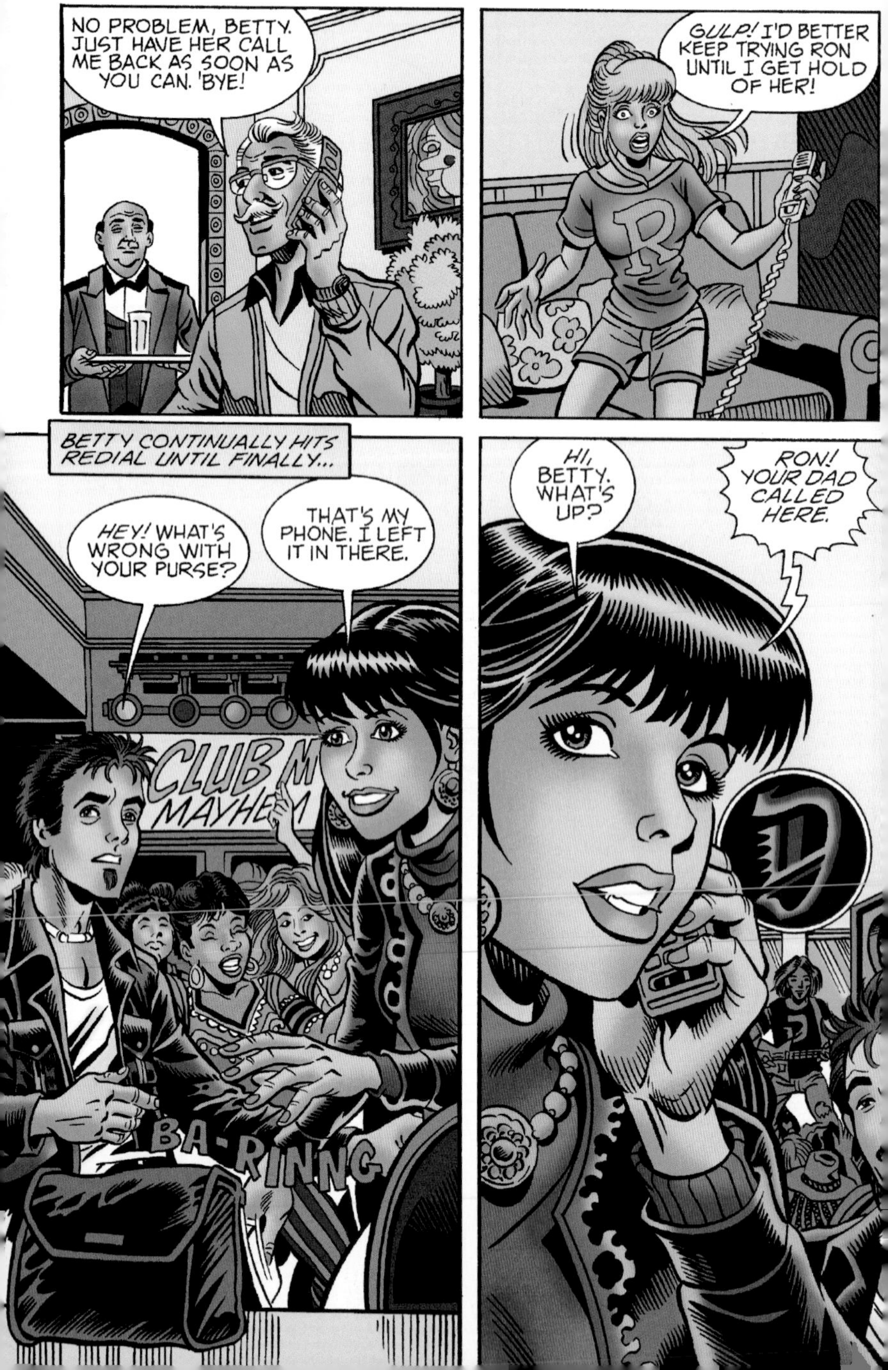
NO PROBLEM, BETTY. JUST HAVE HER CALL ME BACK AS SOON AS YOU CAN. 'BYE!
GULP! I'D BETTER KEEP TRYING RON UNTIL I GET HOLD OF HER!
BETTY CONTINUALLY HITS REDIAL UNTIL FINALLY...
HEY! WHAT'S WRONG WITH YOUR PURSE?
THAT'S MY PHONE. I LEFT IT IN THERE.
CLUB MAYHEM
BA-RINNG
HI, BETTY. WHAT'S UP?
RON! YOUR DAD CALLED HERE.

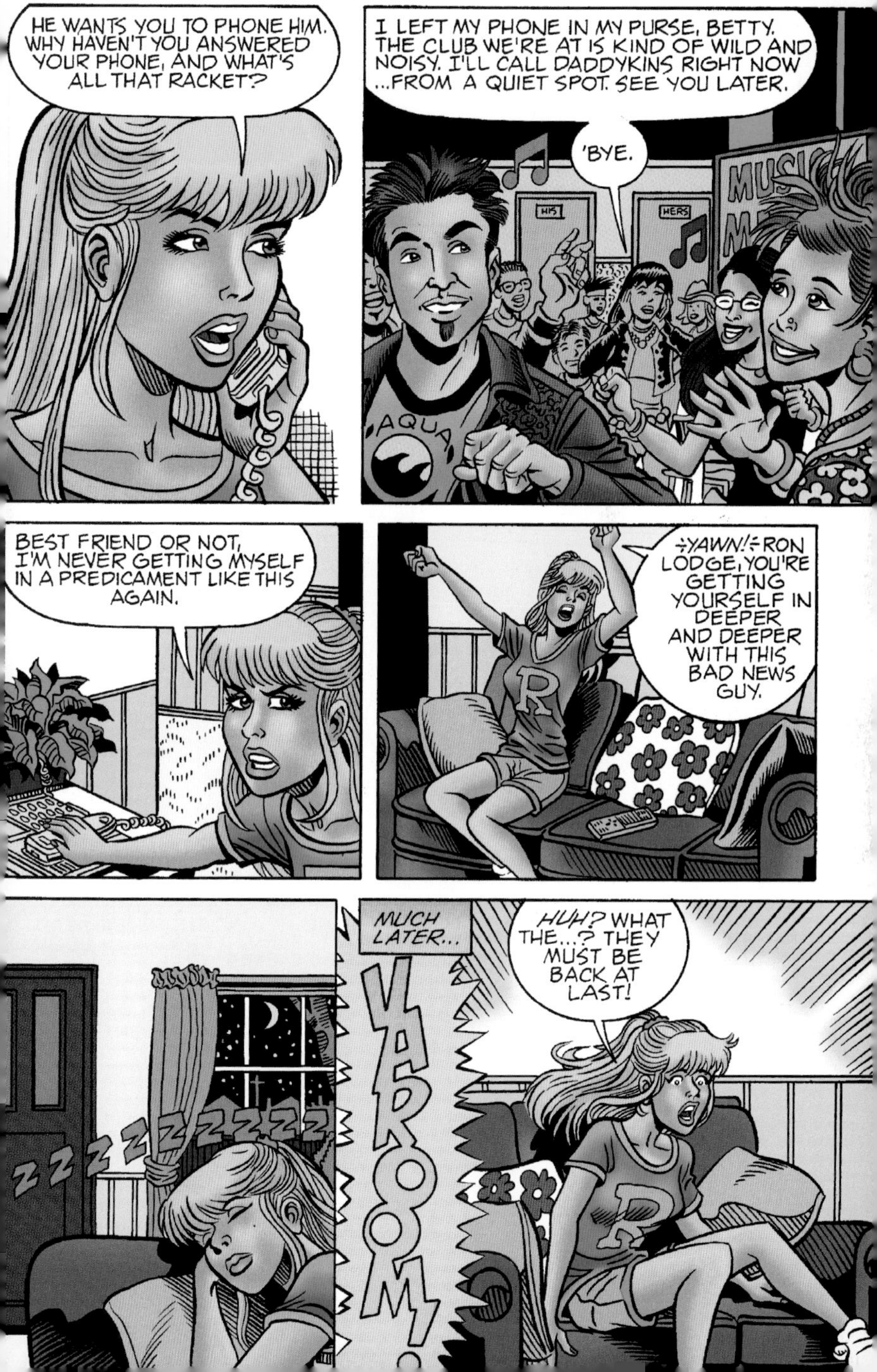
HE WANTS YOU TO PHONE HIM. WHY HAVEN'T YOU ANSWERED YOUR PHONE, AND WHAT'S ALL THAT RACKET?
I LEFT MY PHONE IN MY PURSE, BETTY. THE CLUB WE'RE AT IS KIND OF WILD AND NOISY. I'LL CALL DADDYKINS RIGHT NOW ...FROM A QUIET SPOT. SEE YOU LATER.
'BYE.
HIS
HERS
AQUA
BEST FRIEND OR NOT, I'M NEVER GETTING MYSELF IN A PREDICAMENT LIKE THIS AGAIN.
÷YAWN!÷ RON LODGE, YOU'RE GETTING YOURSELF IN DEEPER AND DEEPER WITH THIS BAD NEWS GUY.
ZZZZZZZZZZ
MUCH LATER...
VAROOOM!
HUH? WHAT THE...? THEY MUST BE BACK AT LAST!

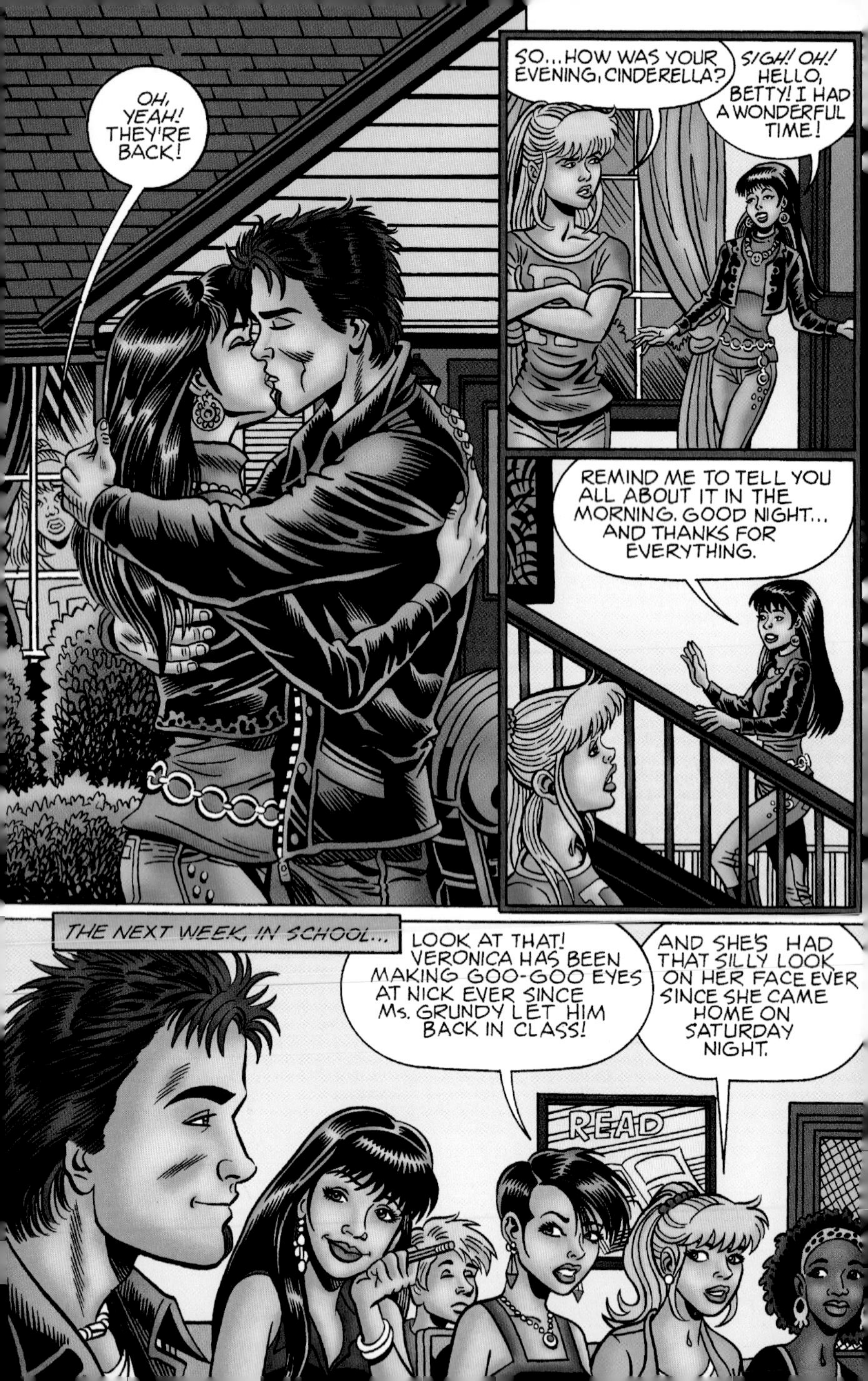
OH, YEAH! THEY'RE BACK!
SO...HOW WAS YOUR EVENING, CINDERELLA?
SIGH! OH! HELLO, BETTY! I HAD A WONDERFUL TIME!
REMIND ME TO TELL YOU ALL ABOUT IT IN THE MORNING. GOOD NIGHT... AND THANKS FOR EVERYTHING.
THE NEXT WEEK, IN SCHOOL...
LOOK AT THAT! VERONICA HAS BEEN MAKING GOO-GOO EYES AT NICK EVER SINCE Ms. GRUNDY LET HIM BACK IN CLASS!
AND SHE'S HAD THAT SILLY LOOK ON HER FACE EVER SINCE SHE CAME HOME ON SATURDAY NIGHT.
READ

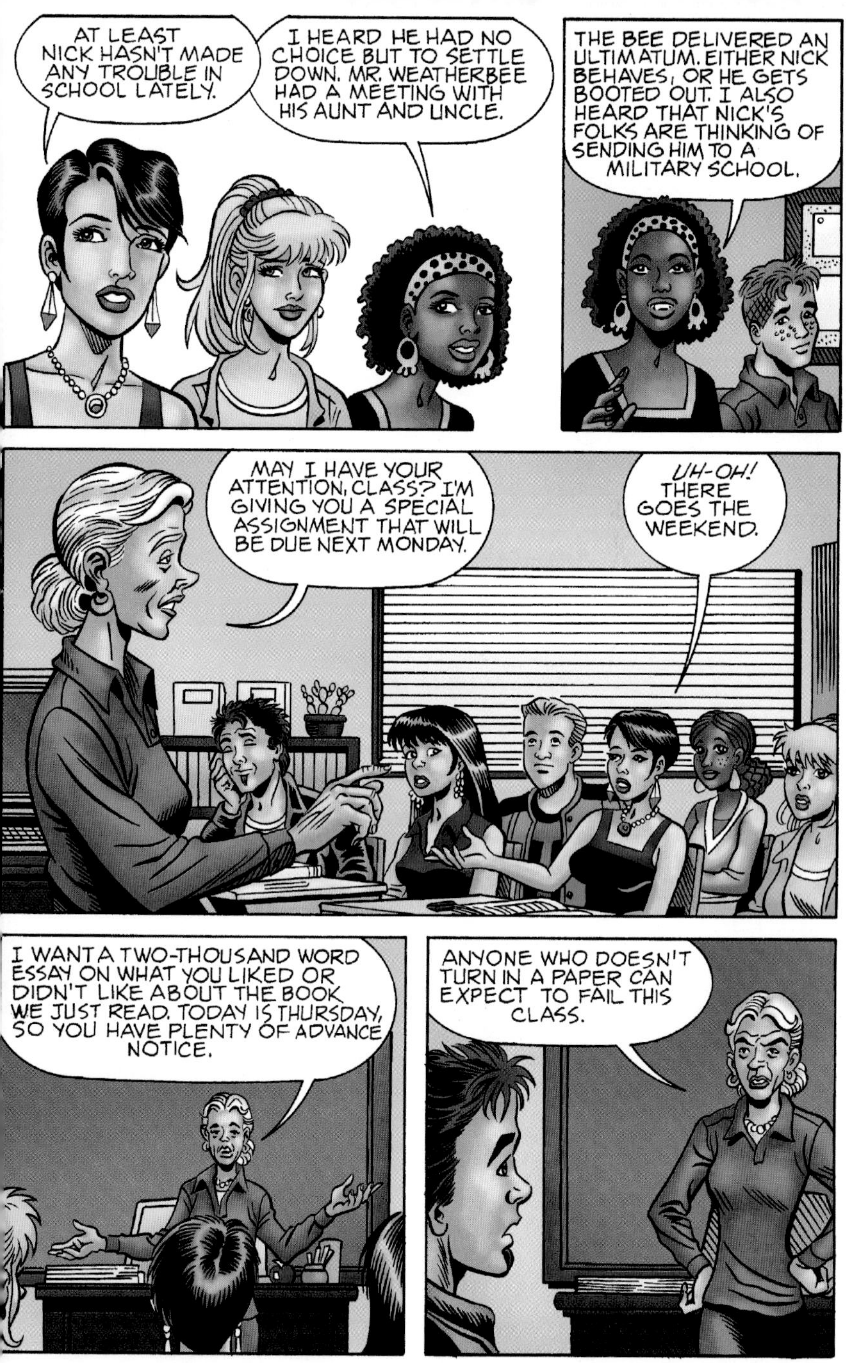
AT LEAST NICK HASN'T MADE ANY TROUBLE IN SCHOOL LATELY.
I HEARD HE HAD NO CHOICE BUT TO SETTLE DOWN. MR. WEATHERBEE HAD A MEETING WITH HIS AUNT AND UNCLE.
THE BEE DELIVERED AN ULTIMATUM. EITHER NICK BEHAVES, OR HE GETS BOOTED OUT. I ALSO HEARD THAT NICK'S FOLKS ARE THINKING OF SENDING HIM TO A MILITARY SCHOOL.
MAY I HAVE YOUR ATTENTION, CLASS? I'M GIVING YOU A SPECIAL ASSIGNMENT THAT WILL BE DUE NEXT MONDAY.
UH-OH! THERE GOES THE WEEKEND.
I WANT A TWO-THOUSAND WORD ESSAY ON WHAT YOU LIKED OR DIDN'T LIKE ABOUT THE BOOK WE JUST READ. TODAY IS THURSDAY, SO YOU HAVE PLENTY OF ADVANCE NOTICE.
ANYONE WHO DOESN'T TURN IN A PAPER CAN EXPECT TO FAIL THIS CLASS.

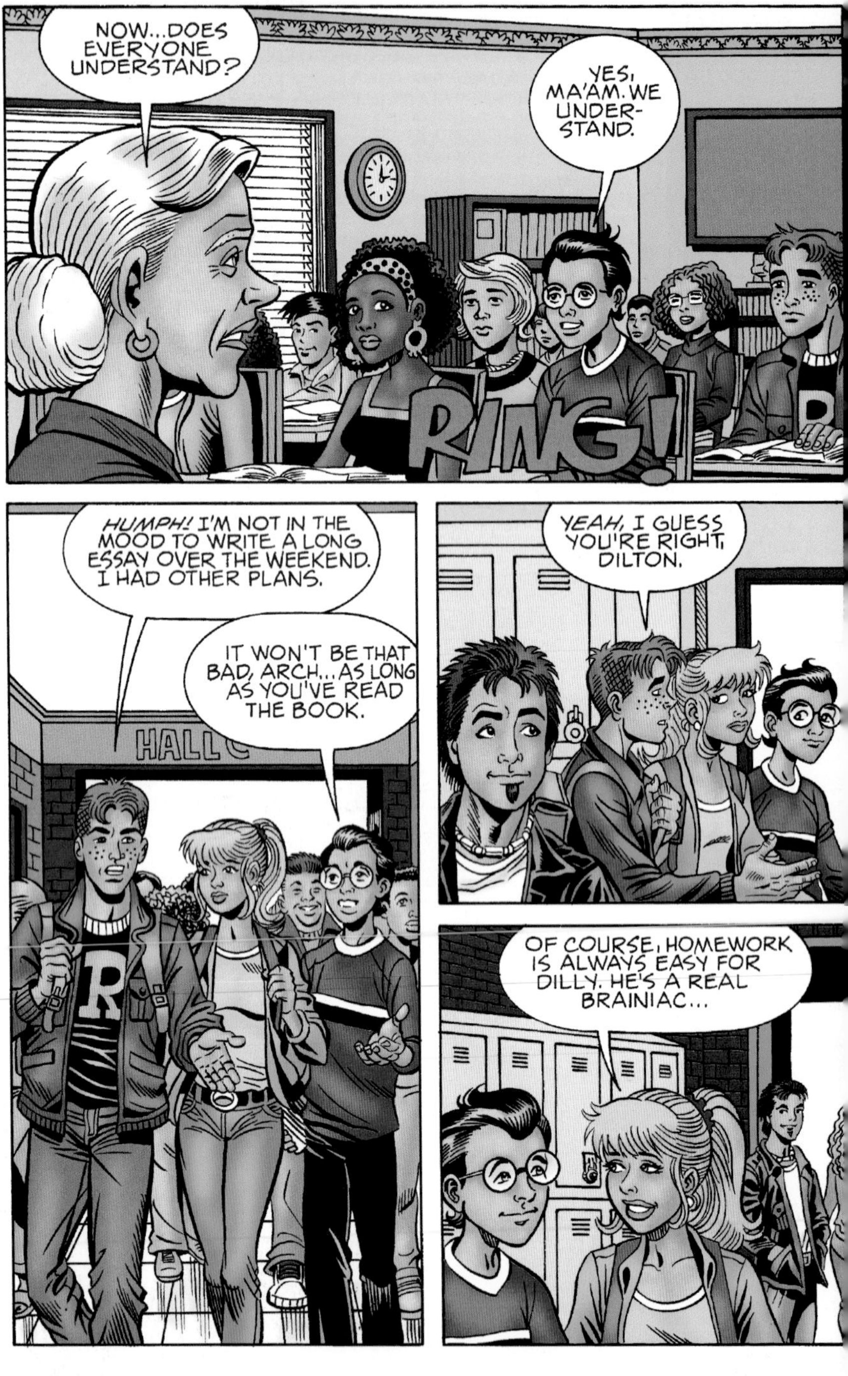
NOW...DOES EVERYONE UNDERSTAND?
YES, MA'AM. WE UNDER-STAND.
RING!
HUMPH! I'M NOT IN THE MOOD TO WRITE A LONG ESSAY OVER THE WEEKEND. I HAD OTHER PLANS.
IT WON'T BE THAT BAD, ARCH...AS LONG AS YOU'VE READ THE BOOK.
HALL
YEAH, I GUESS YOU'RE RIGHT, DILTON.
OF COURSE, HOMEWORK IS ALWAYS EASY FOR DILLY. HE'S A REAL BRAINIAC...

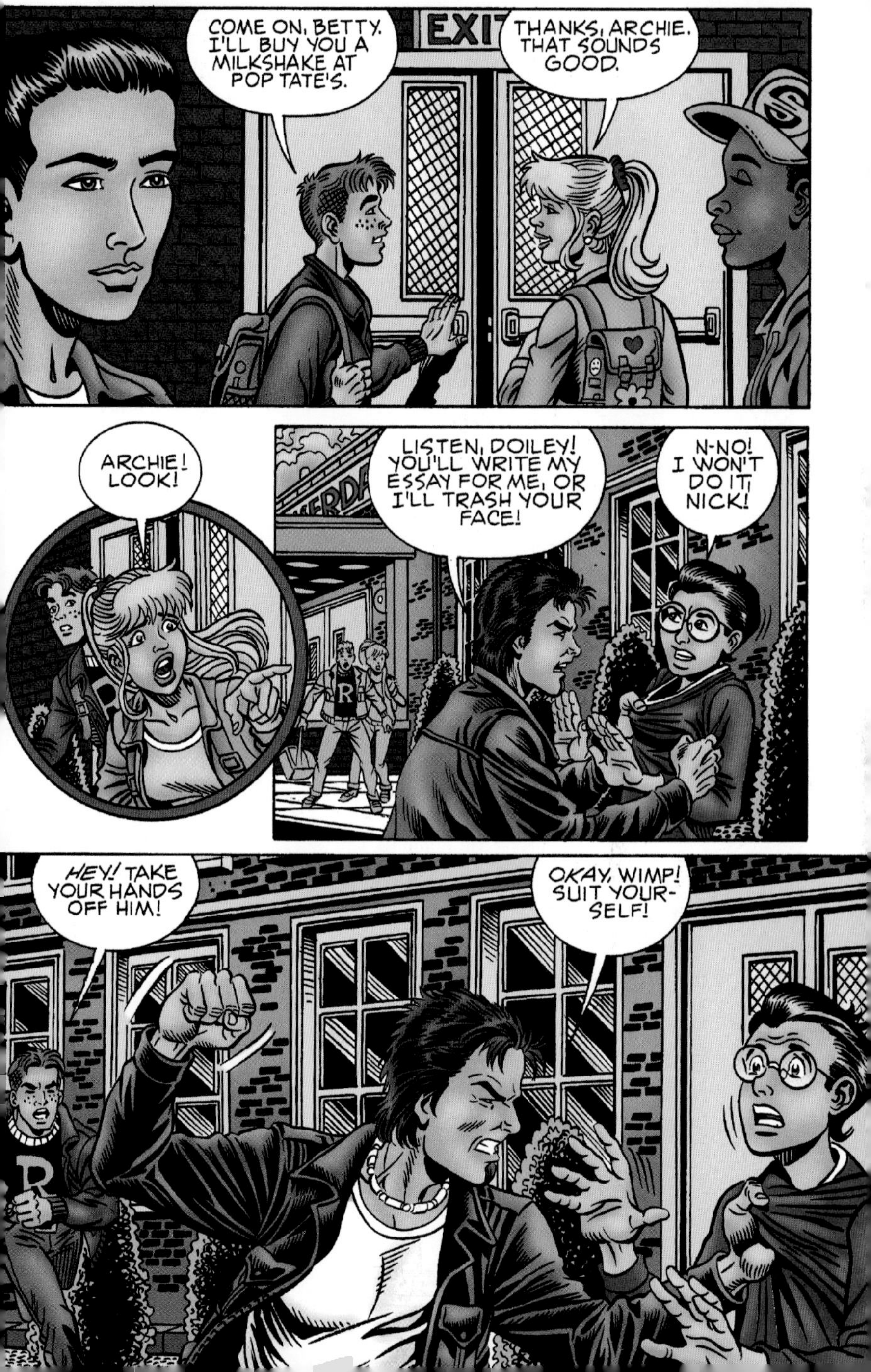

EXIT
COME ON, BETTY. I'LL BUY YOU A MILKSHAKE AT POP TATE'S.
THANKS, ARCHIE. THAT SOUNDS GOOD.
ARCHIE! LOOK!
LISTEN, DOILEY! YOU'LL WRITE MY ESSAY FOR ME, OR I'LL TRASH YOUR FACE!
N-NO! I WON'T DO IT, NICK!
HEY! TAKE YOUR HANDS OFF HIM!
OKAY, WIMP! SUIT YOURSELF!

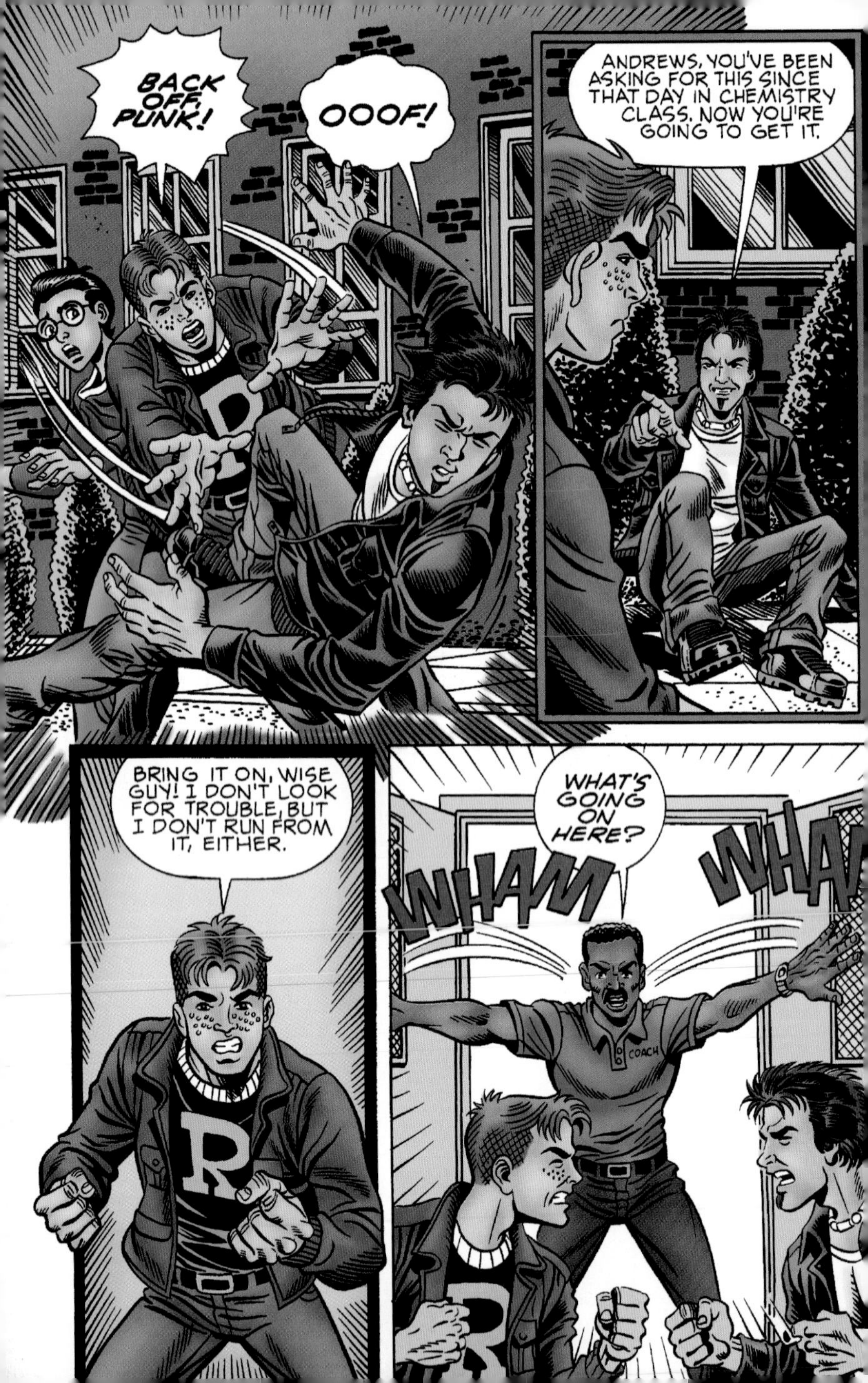
BACK OFF, PUNK!
OOOF!
ANDREWS, YOU'VE BEEN ASKING FOR THIS SINCE THAT DAY IN CHEMISTRY CLASS. NOW YOU'RE GOING TO GET IT.
BRING IT ON, WISE GUY! I DON'T LOOK FOR TROUBLE, BUT I DON'T RUN FROM IT, EITHER.
WHAT'S GOING ON HERE?
WHAM
COACH

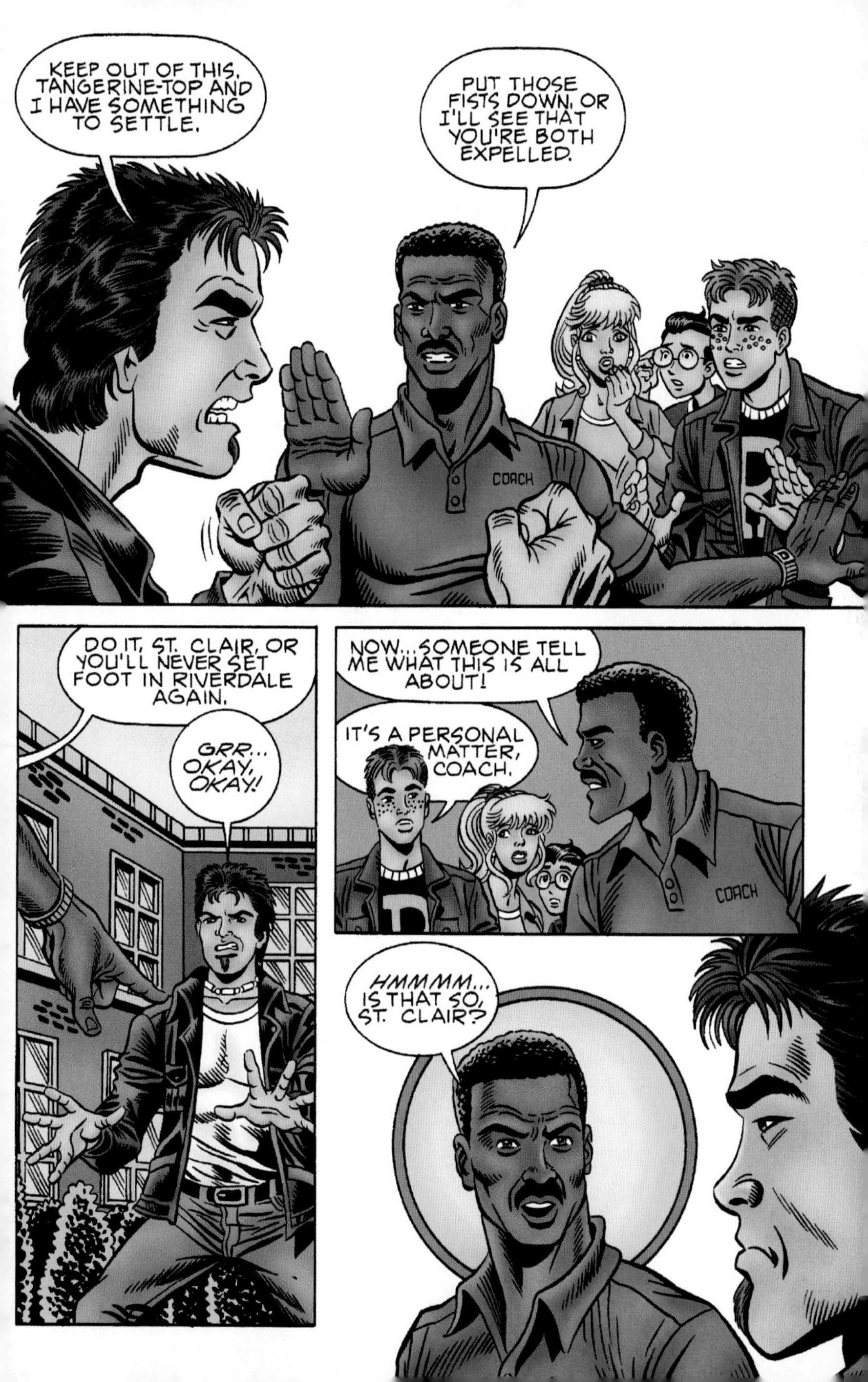

KEEP OUT OF THIS. TANGERINE-TOP AND I HAVE SOMETHING TO SETTLE.
PUT THOSE FISTS DOWN, OR I'LL SEE THAT YOU'RE BOTH EXPELLED.
COACH
DO IT, ST. CLAIR, OR YOU'LL NEVER SET FOOT IN RIVERDALE AGAIN.
GRR... OKAY, OKAY!
NOW...SOMEONE TELL ME WHAT THIS IS ALL ABOUT!
IT'S A PERSONAL MATTER, COACH.
COACH
HMMMM... IS THAT SO, ST. CLAIR?

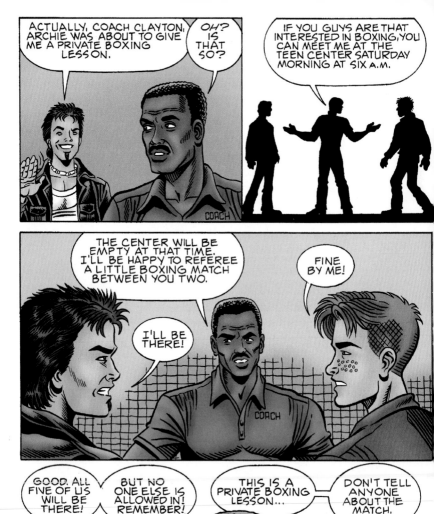

ACTUALLY, COACH CLAYTON, ARCHIE WAS ABOUT TO GIVE ME A PRIVATE BOXING LESSON.

OH? IS THAT SO?

IF YOU GUYS ARE THAT INTERESTED IN BOXING, YOU CAN MEET ME AT THE TEEN CENTER SATURDAY MORNING AT SIX A.M.

THE CENTER WILL BE EMPTY AT THAT TIME. I'LL BE HAPPY TO REFEREE A LITTLE BOXING MATCH BETWEEN YOU TWO.

FINE BY ME!

I'LL BE THERE!

GOOD. ALL FIVE OF US WILL BE THERE!

BUT NO ONE ELSE IS ALLOWED IN! REMEMBER!

THIS IS A PRIVATE BOXING LESSON...

DON'T TELL ANYONE ABOUT THE MATCH.

COACH

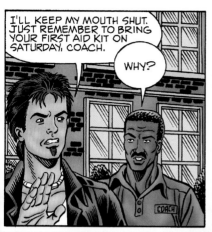

I'LL KEEP MY MOUTH SHUT. JUST REMEMBER TO BRING YOUR FIRST AID KIT ON SATURDAY, COACH.

WHY?

BECAUSE ARCHIE IS GOING TO NEED IT.

EARLY SATURDAY MORNING...

RIVERDALE

RIVERDALE TEEN CENTER DOORS OPEN 8:00 A.M.

INSIDE THE CENTER'S GYM...

I'M READY TO RUMBLE, COACH. WHERE IS RED? DID HE TURN YELLOW?

HERE COMES ARCHIE NOW.

CHAMP

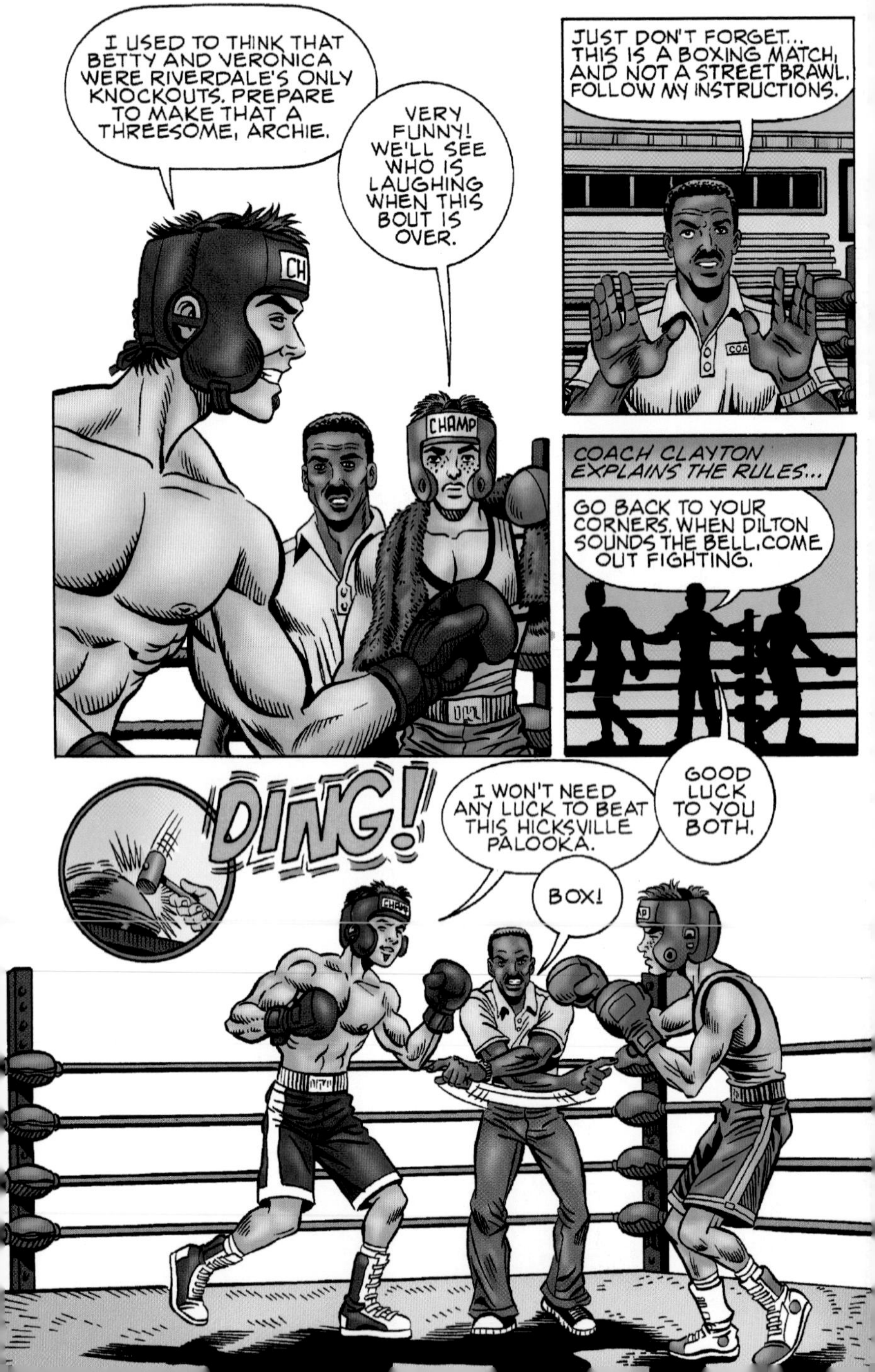
I USED TO THINK THAT BETTY AND VERONICA WERE RIVERDALE'S ONLY KNOCKOUTS. PREPARE TO MAKE THAT A THREESOME, ARCHIE.
VERY FUNNY! WE'LL SEE WHO IS LAUGHING WHEN THIS BOUT IS OVER.
CH
CHAMP
JUST DON'T FORGET... THIS IS A BOXING MATCH, AND NOT A STREET BRAWL. FOLLOW MY INSTRUCTIONS.
COACH CLAYTON EXPLAINS THE RULES...
GO BACK TO YOUR CORNERS. WHEN DILTON SOUNDS THE BELL, COME OUT FIGHTING.
DING!
I WON'T NEED ANY LUCK TO BEAT THIS HICKSVILLE PALOOKA.
GOOD LUCK TO YOU BOTH.
BOX!

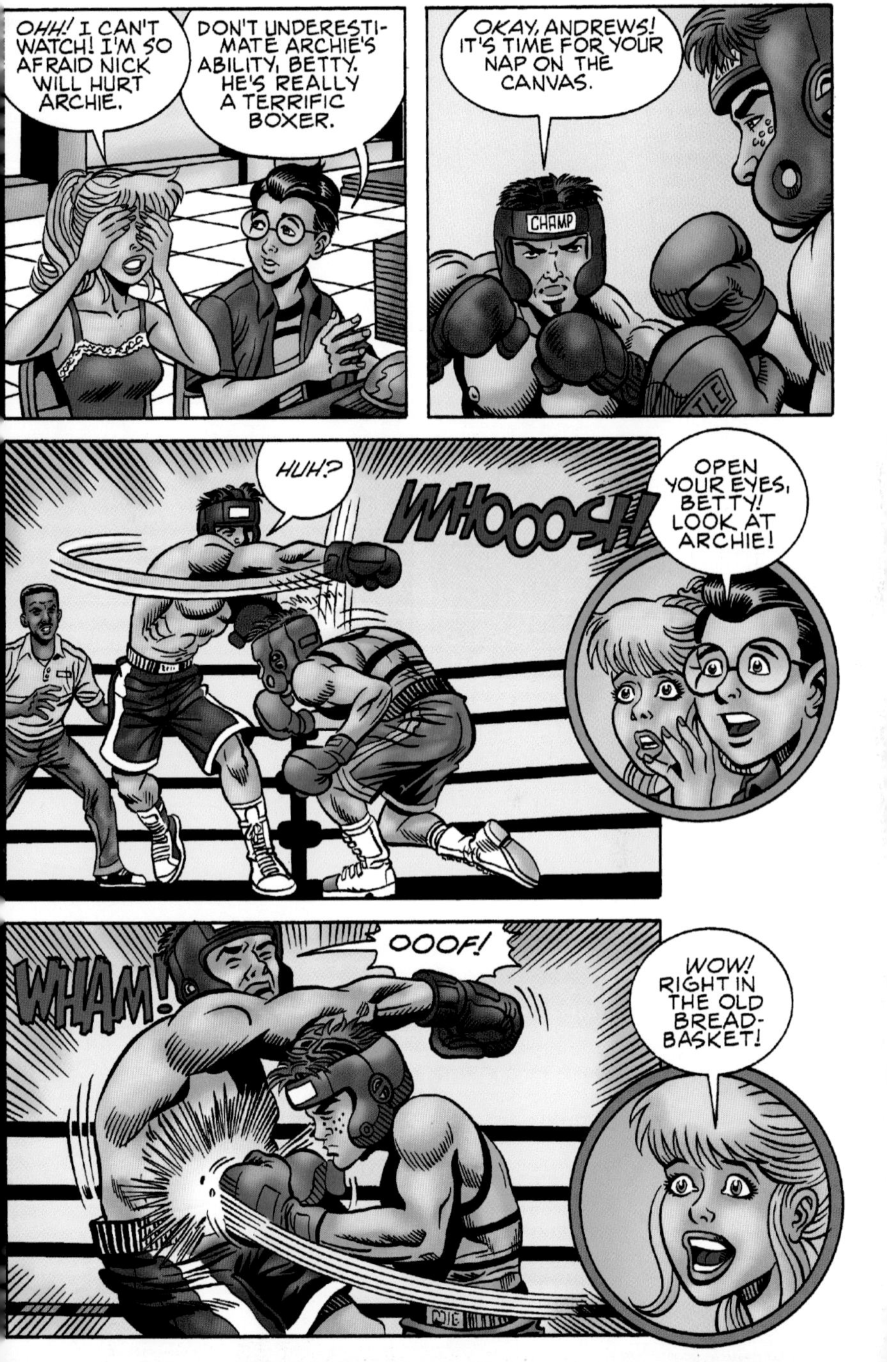
OHH! I CAN'T WATCH! I'M SO AFRAID NICK WILL HURT ARCHIE.
DON'T UNDERESTIMATE ARCHIE'S ABILITY, BETTY. HE'S REALLY A TERRIFIC BOXER.
OKAY, ANDREWS! IT'S TIME FOR YOUR NAP ON THE CANVAS.
CHAMP
HUH?
WHOOOSH!
OPEN YOUR EYES, BETTY! LOOK AT ARCHIE!
WHAM!
OOOF!
WOW! RIGHT IN THE OLD BREAD-BASKET!

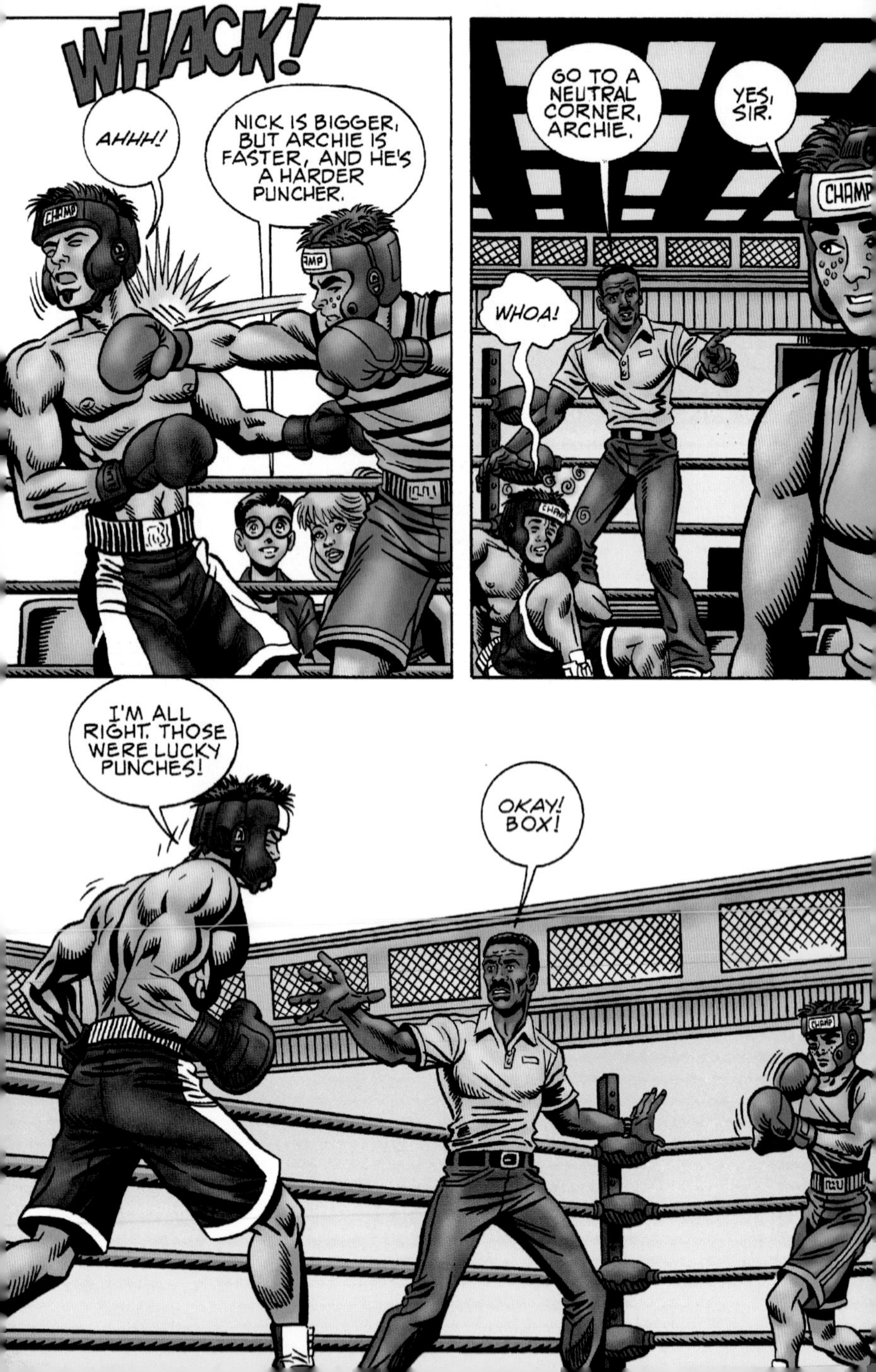
WHACK!
AHHH!
NICK IS BIGGER, BUT ARCHIE IS FASTER, AND HE'S A HARDER PUNCHER.
GO TO A NEUTRAL CORNER, ARCHIE.
YES, SIR.
WHOA!
I'M ALL RIGHT. THOSE WERE LUCKY PUNCHES!
OKAY! BOX!

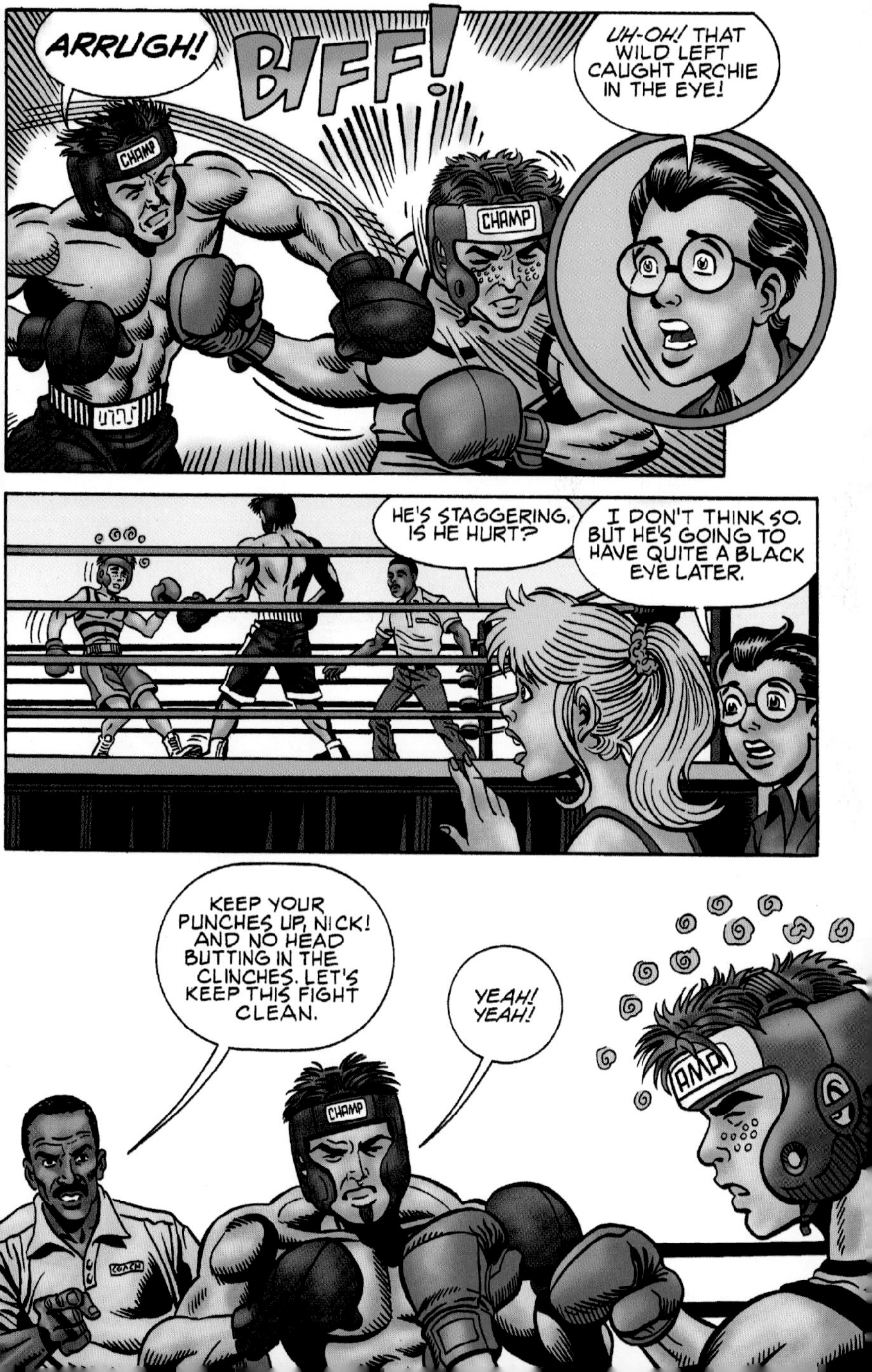
ARRUGH!
BIFF!
UH-OH! THAT WILD LEFT CAUGHT ARCHIE IN THE EYE!
CHAMP
CHAMP
HE'S STAGGERING. IS HE HURT?
I DON'T THINK SO. BUT HE'S GOING TO HAVE QUITE A BLACK EYE LATER.
KEEP YOUR PUNCHES UP, NICK! AND NO HEAD BUTTING IN THE CLINCHES. LET'S KEEP THIS FIGHT CLEAN.
YEAH! YEAH!
CHAMP
AMP
COACH

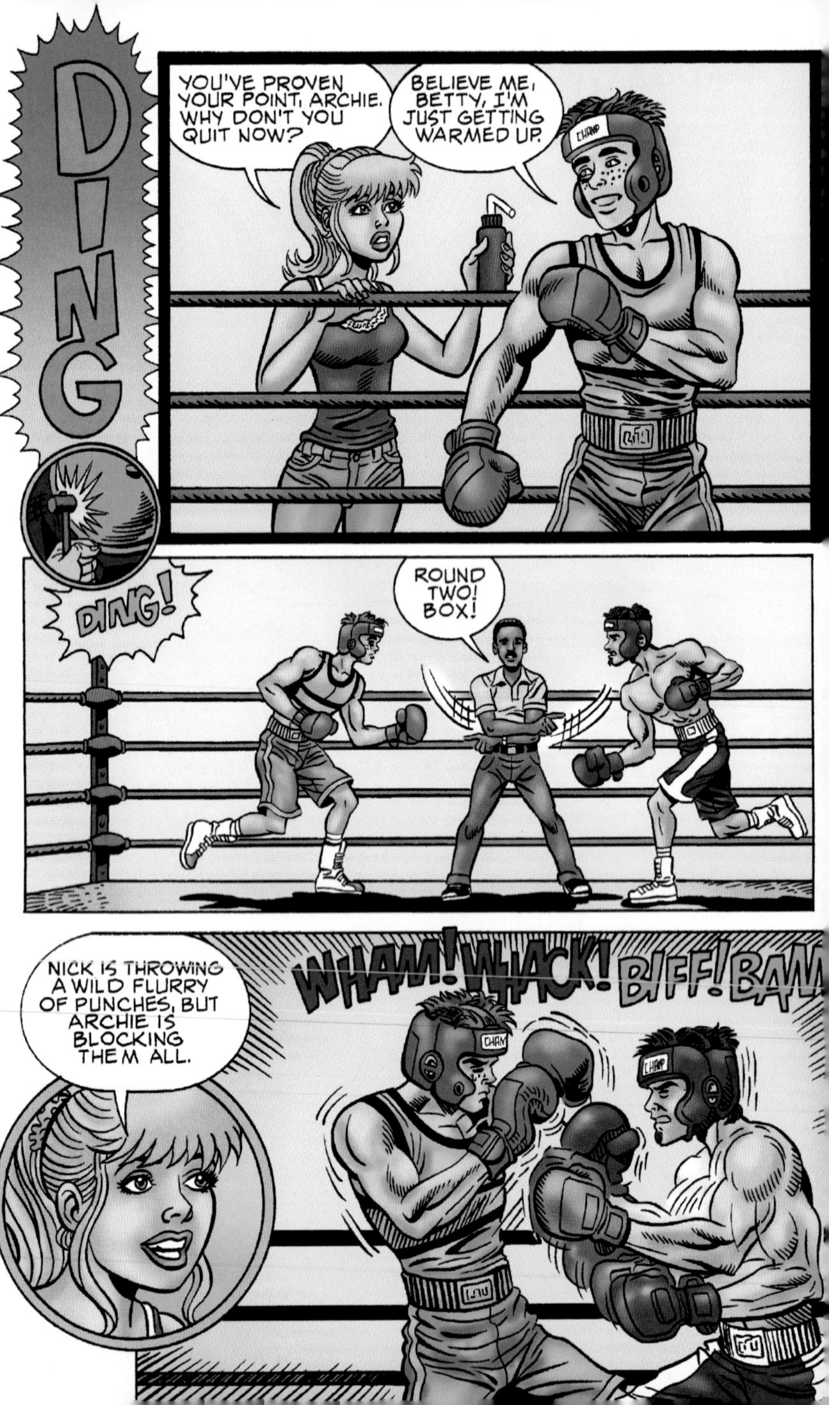
DING
YOU'VE PROVEN YOUR POINT, ARCHIE. WHY DON'T YOU QUIT NOW?
BELIEVE ME, BETTY, I'M JUST GETTING WARMED UP.
CHAMP
DING!
ROUND TWO! BOX!
NICK IS THROWING A WILD FLURRY OF PUNCHES, BUT ARCHIE IS BLOCKING THEM ALL.
WHAM! WHACK! BIFF! BAM
CHAMP
CHAMP

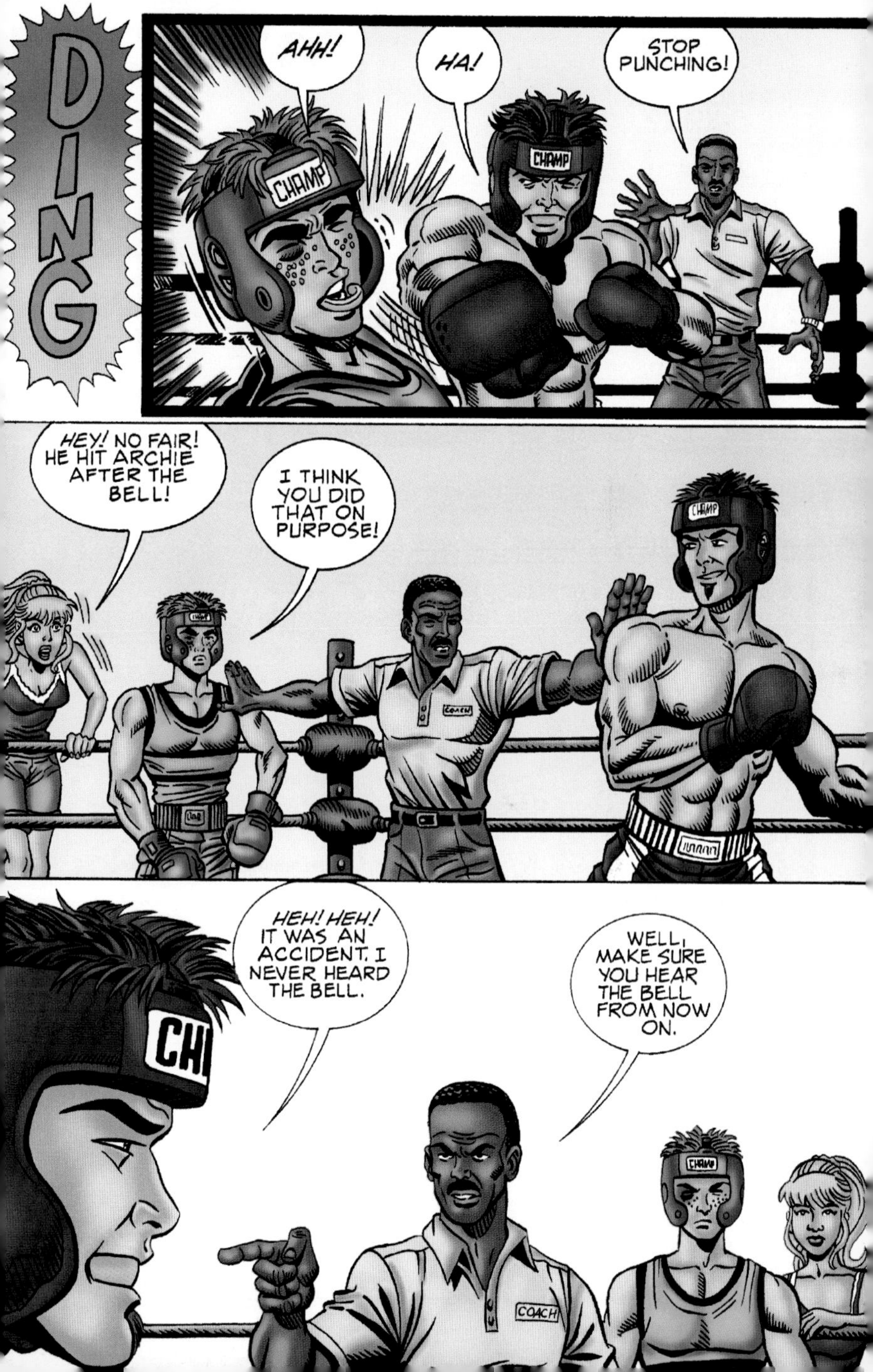
DING
AHH!
HA!
STOP PUNCHING!
CHAMP
CHAMP
HEY! NO FAIR! HE HIT ARCHIE AFTER THE BELL!
I THINK YOU DID THAT ON PURPOSE!
CHAMP
COACH
HEH! HEH! IT WAS AN ACCIDENT. I NEVER HEARD THE BELL.
WELL, MAKE SURE YOU HEAR THE BELL FROM NOW ON.
COACH

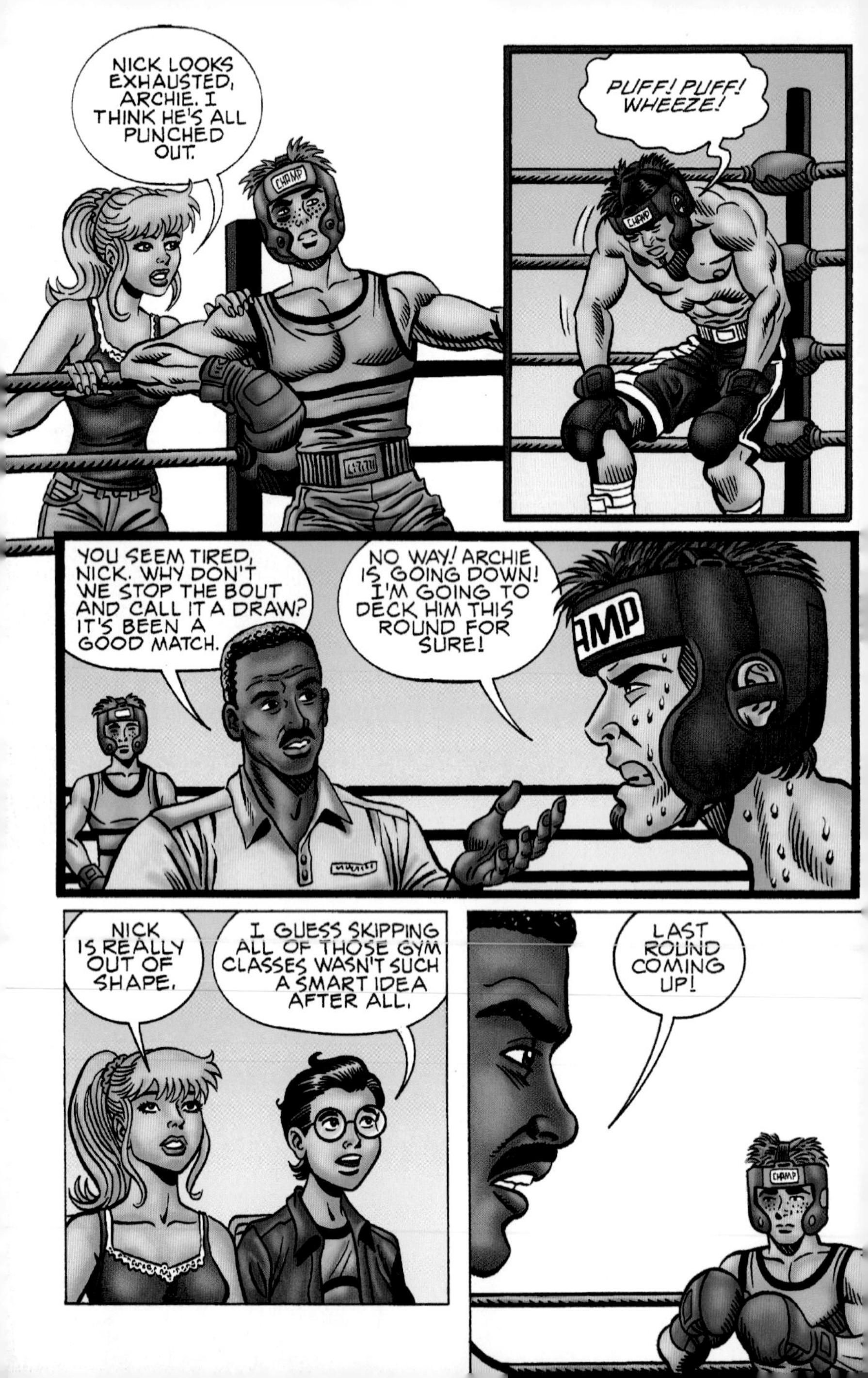
NICK LOOKS EXHAUSTED, ARCHIE. I THINK HE'S ALL PUNCHED OUT.
CHAMP
PUFF! PUFF! WHEEZE!
CHAMP
YOU SEEM TIRED, NICK. WHY DON'T WE STOP THE BOUT AND CALL IT A DRAW? IT'S BEEN A GOOD MATCH.
NO WAY! ARCHIE IS GOING DOWN! I'M GOING TO DECK HIM THIS ROUND FOR SURE!
AMP
NICK IS REALLY OUT OF SHAPE.
I GUESS SKIPPING ALL OF THOSE GYM CLASSES WASN'T SUCH A SMART IDEA AFTER ALL.
LAST ROUND COMING UP!
CHAMP

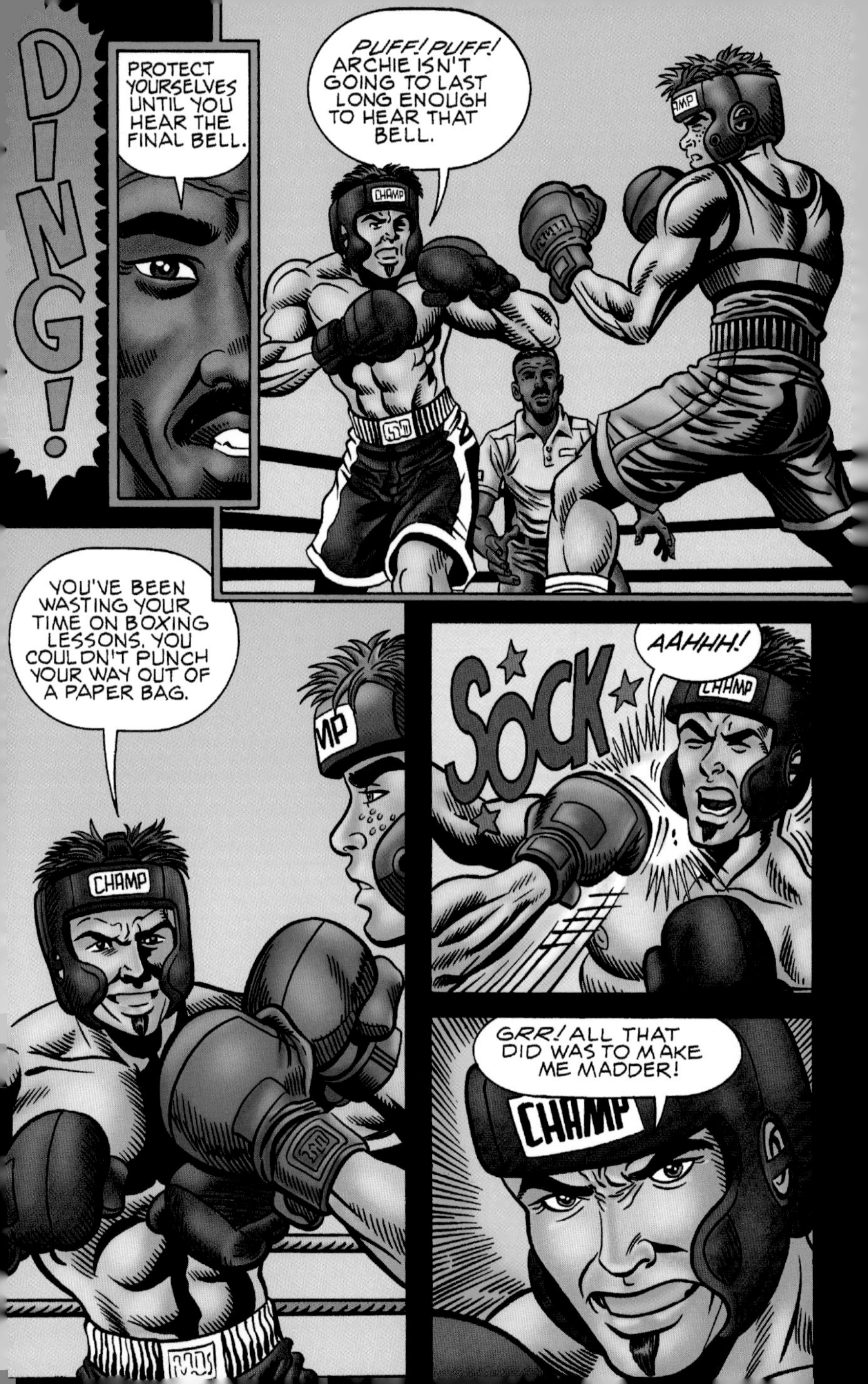
DING!
PROTECT YOURSELVES UNTIL YOU HEAR THE FINAL BELL.
PUFF! PUFF! ARCHIE ISN'T GOING TO LAST LONG ENOUGH TO HEAR THAT BELL.
YOU'VE BEEN WASTING YOUR TIME ON BOXING LESSONS. YOU COULDN'T PUNCH YOUR WAY OUT OF A PAPER BAG.
SOCK
AAHHH!
GRR! ALL THAT DID WAS TO MAKE ME MADDER!

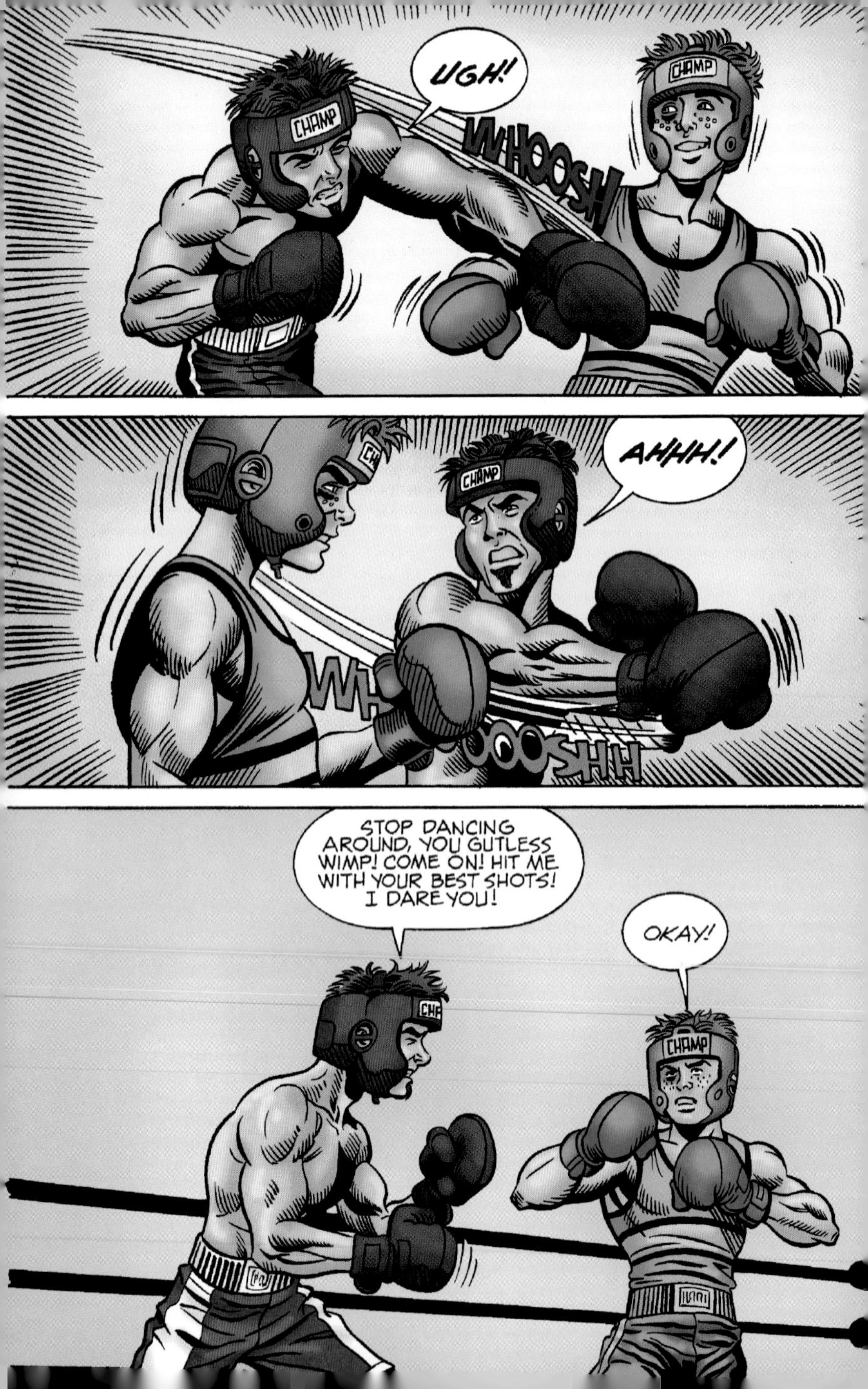
UGH!
WHOOSH!
AHHH!
WHOOOSHH
STOP DANCING AROUND, YOU GUTLESS WIMP! COME ON! HIT ME WITH YOUR BEST SHOTS! I DARE YOU!
OKAY!
CHAMP

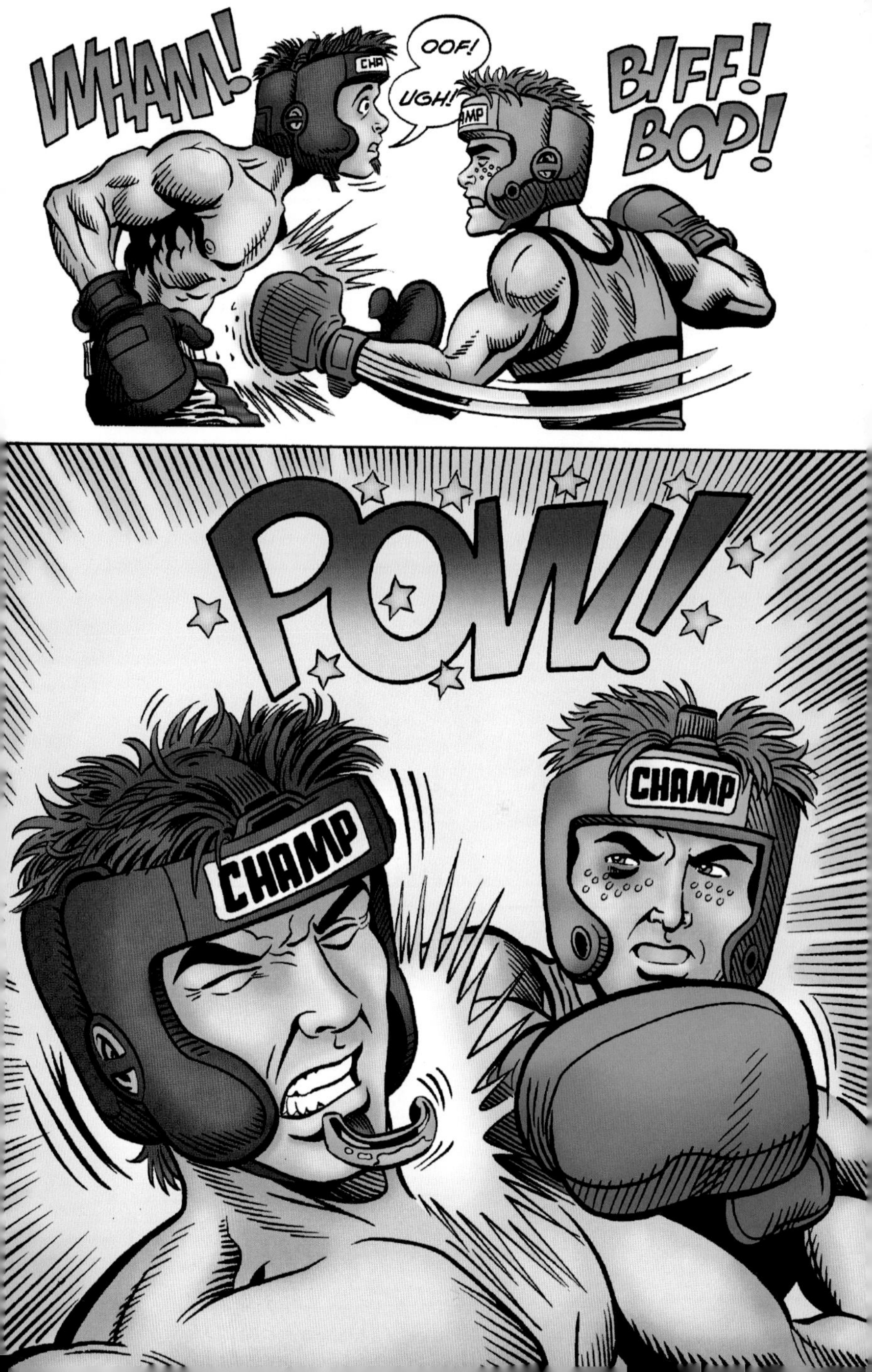
WHAM!
OOF!
UGH!
BIFF!
BOP!
POW!
CHAMP
CHAMP

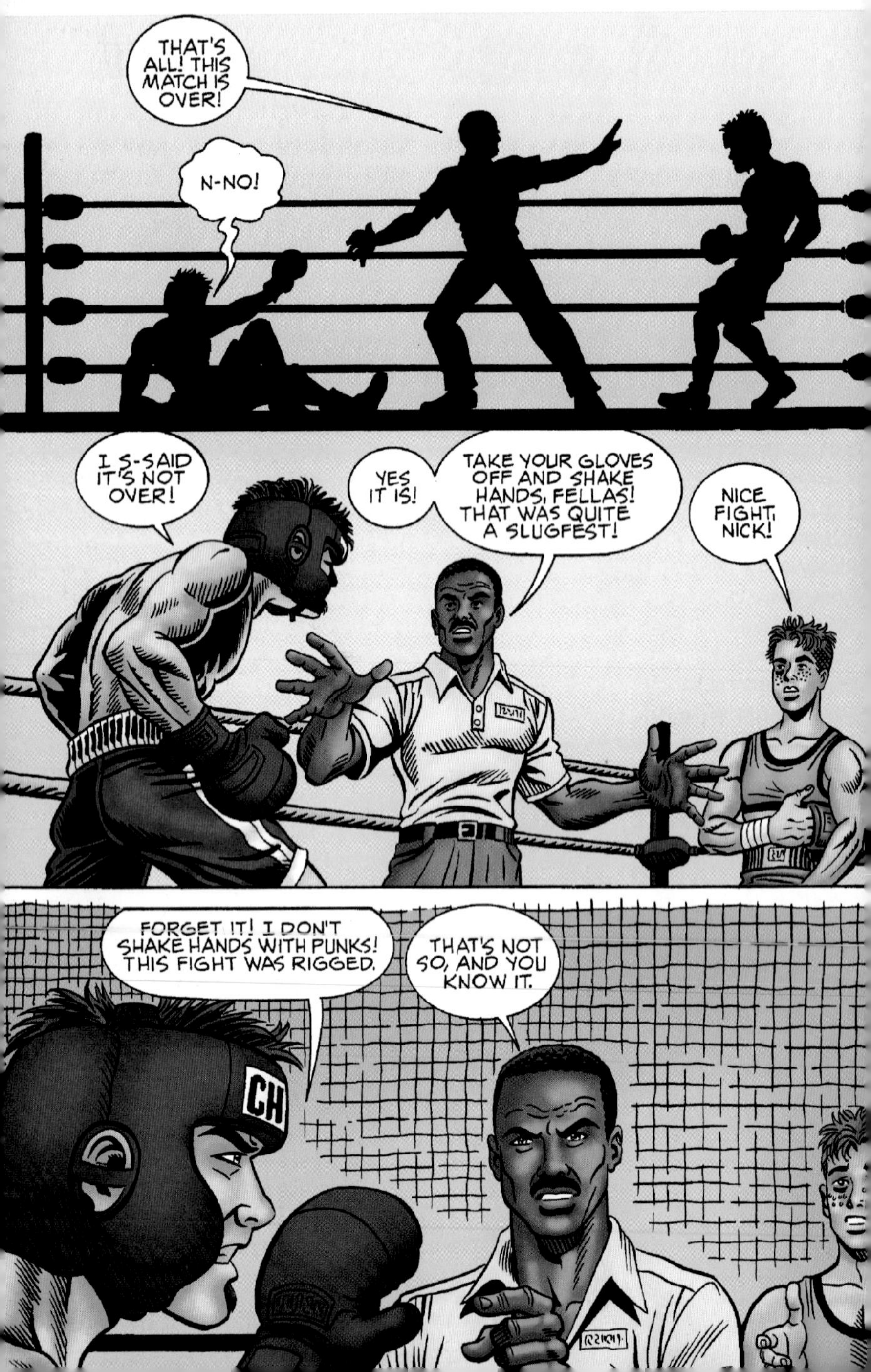
THAT'S ALL! THIS MATCH IS OVER!
N-NO!
I S-SAID IT'S NOT OVER!
YES IT IS!
TAKE YOUR GLOVES OFF AND SHAKE HANDS, FELLAS! THAT WAS QUITE A SLUGFEST!
NICE FIGHT, NICK!
FORGET IT! I DON'T SHAKE HANDS WITH PUNKS! THIS FIGHT WAS RIGGED.
THAT'S NOT SO, AND YOU KNOW IT.
CH

NICK, YOU HAVE THE POTENTIAL TO BE A GOOD BOXER. WHY DON'T YOU JOIN US FOR SOME LESSONS?

I'D BE HAPPY TO WORK OUT WITH YOU.

I WOULDN'T WASTE MY TIME HERE. KEEP YOUR CRUMMY BOXING GEAR. GIVE IT TO ANOTHER DUMB SUCKER.

CHAMP

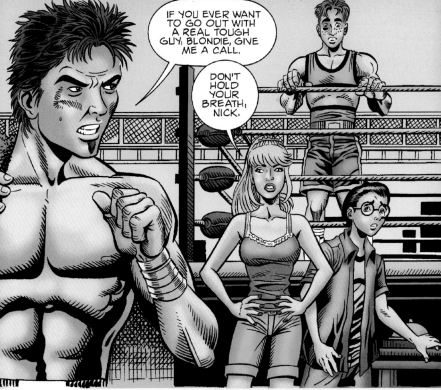

IF YOU EVER WANT TO GO OUT WITH A REAL TOUGH GUY, BLONDIE, GIVE ME A CALL.

DON'T HOLD YOUR BREATH, NICK.

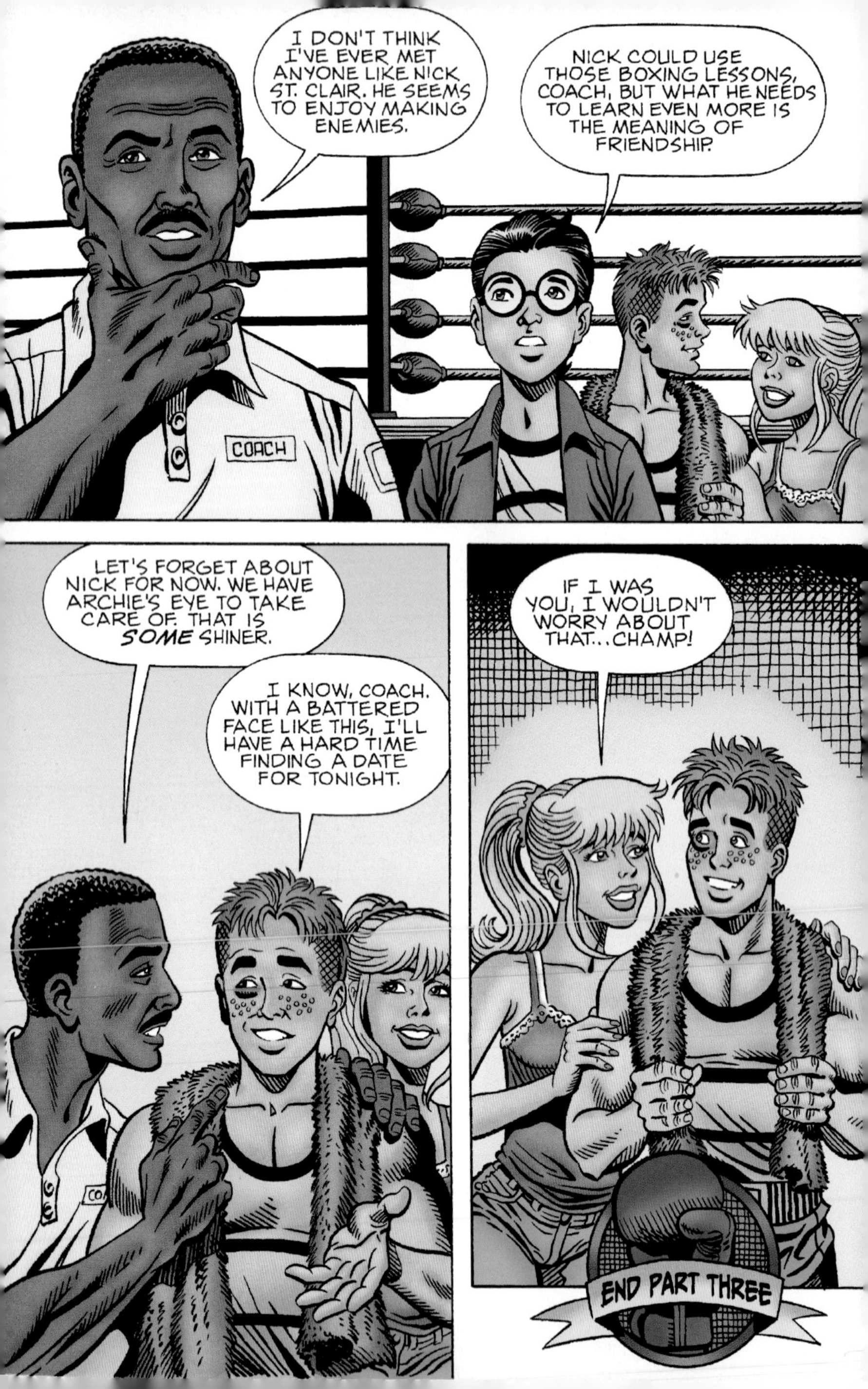
I DON'T THINK I'VE EVER MET ANYONE LIKE NICK ST. CLAIR. HE SEEMS TO ENJOY MAKING ENEMIES.
NICK COULD USE THOSE BOXING LESSONS, COACH, BUT WHAT HE NEEDS TO LEARN EVEN MORE IS THE MEANING OF FRIENDSHIP.
COACH
LET'S FORGET ABOUT NICK FOR NOW. WE HAVE ARCHIE'S EYE TO TAKE CARE OF. THAT IS *SOME* SHINER.
I KNOW, COACH. WITH A BATTERED FACE LIKE THIS, I'LL HAVE A HARD TIME FINDING A DATE FOR TONIGHT.
IF I WAS YOU, I WOULDN'T WORRY ABOUT THAT...CHAMP!
END PART THREE

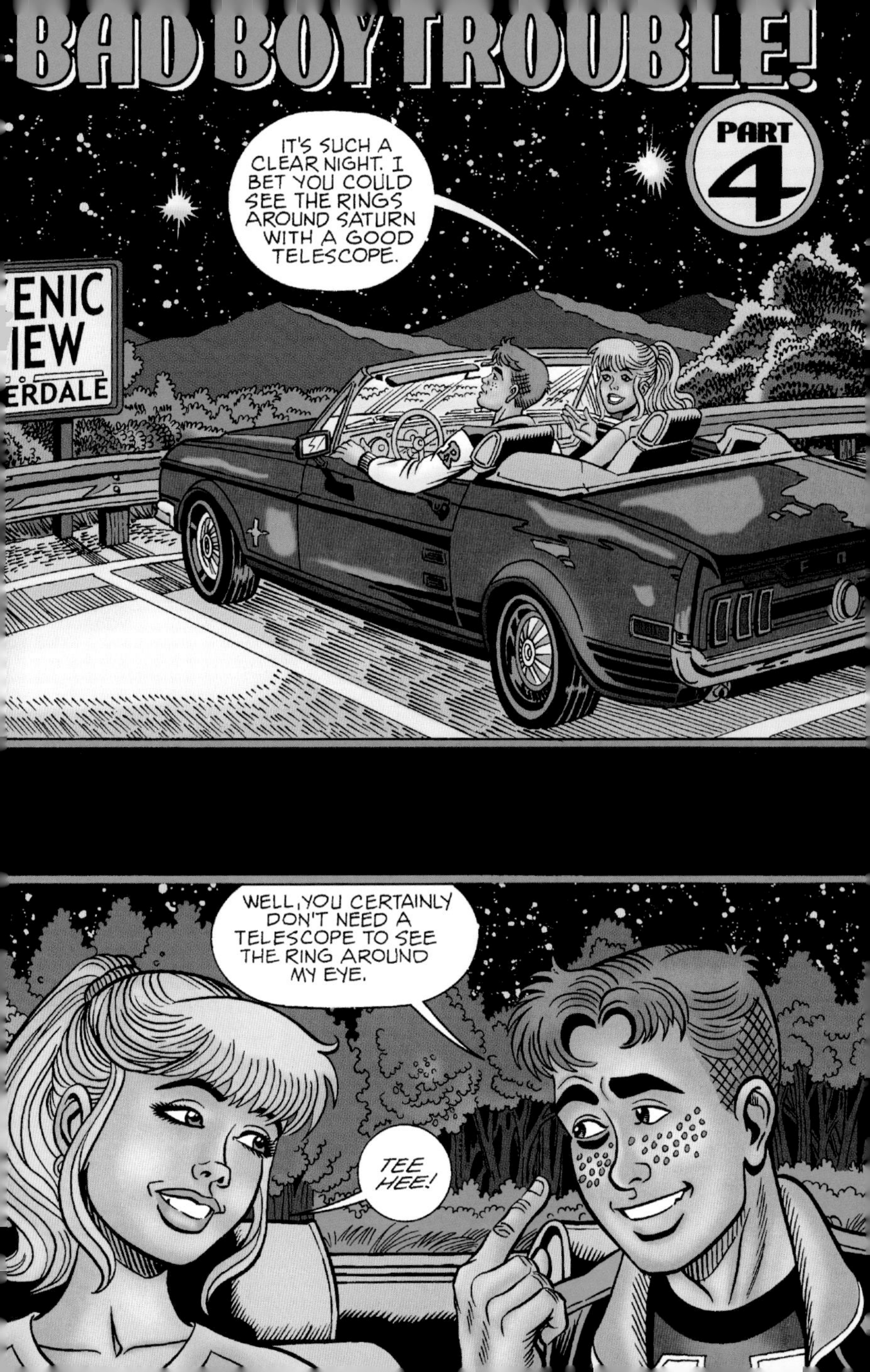
BAD BOY TROUBLE!
PART 4
IT'S SUCH A CLEAR NIGHT. I BET YOU COULD SEE THE RINGS AROUND SATURN WITH A GOOD TELESCOPE.
ENIC
IEW
ERDALE
WELL, YOU CERTAINLY DON'T NEED A TELESCOPE TO SEE THE RING AROUND MY EYE.
TEE HEE!

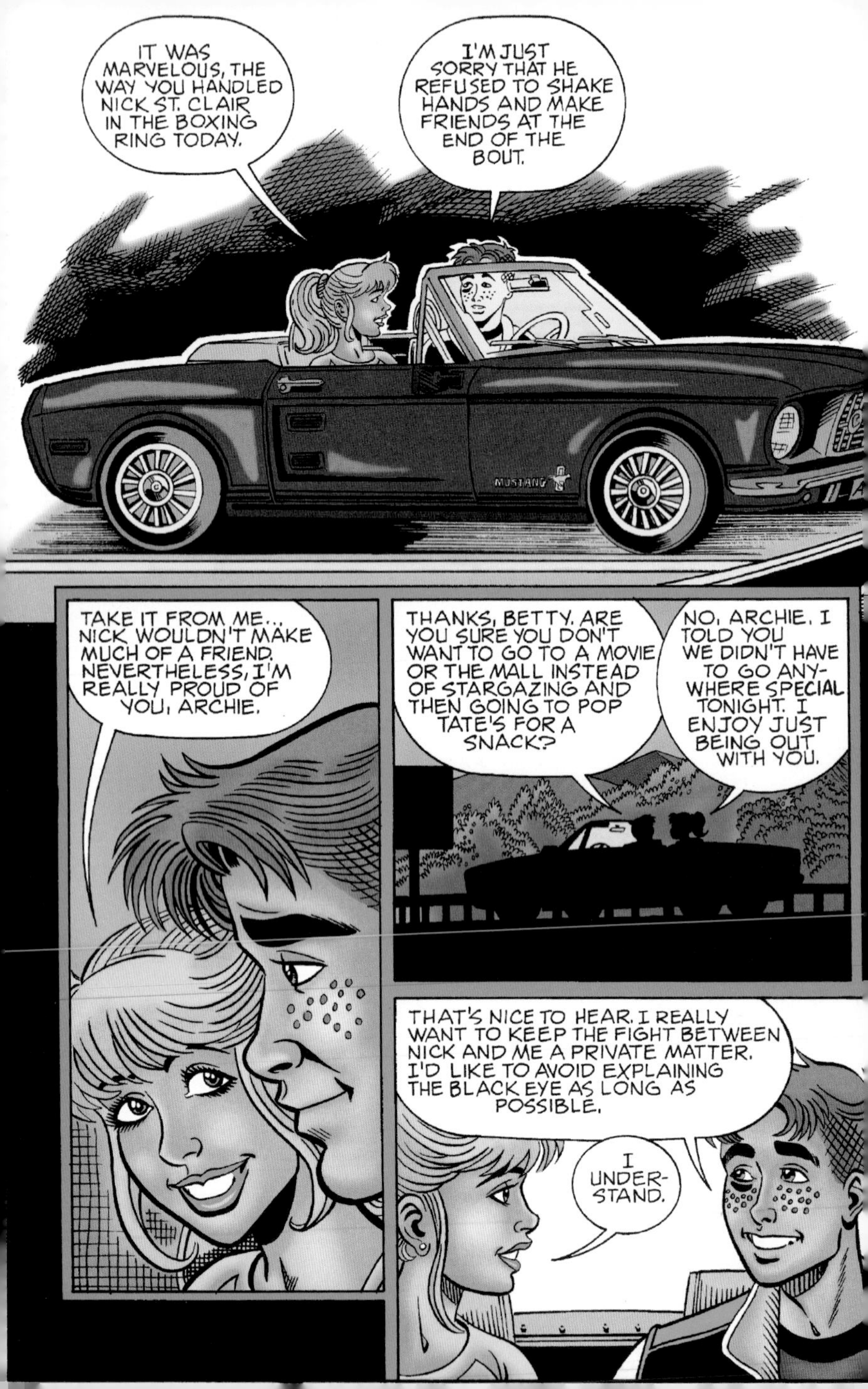
IT WAS MARVELOUS, THE WAY YOU HANDLED NICK ST. CLAIR IN THE BOXING RING TODAY.
I'M JUST SORRY THAT HE REFUSED TO SHAKE HANDS AND MAKE FRIENDS AT THE END OF THE BOUT.
MUSTANG
TAKE IT FROM ME... NICK WOULDN'T MAKE MUCH OF A FRIEND. NEVERTHELESS, I'M REALLY PROUD OF YOU, ARCHIE.
THANKS, BETTY. ARE YOU SURE YOU DON'T WANT TO GO TO A MOVIE OR THE MALL INSTEAD OF STARGAZING AND THEN GOING TO POP TATE'S FOR A SNACK?
NO, ARCHIE. I TOLD YOU WE DIDN'T HAVE TO GO ANYWHERE SPECIAL TONIGHT. I ENJOY JUST BEING OUT WITH YOU.
THAT'S NICE TO HEAR. I REALLY WANT TO KEEP THE FIGHT BETWEEN NICK AND ME A PRIVATE MATTER. I'D LIKE TO AVOID EXPLAINING THE BLACK EYE AS LONG AS POSSIBLE.
I UNDERSTAND.

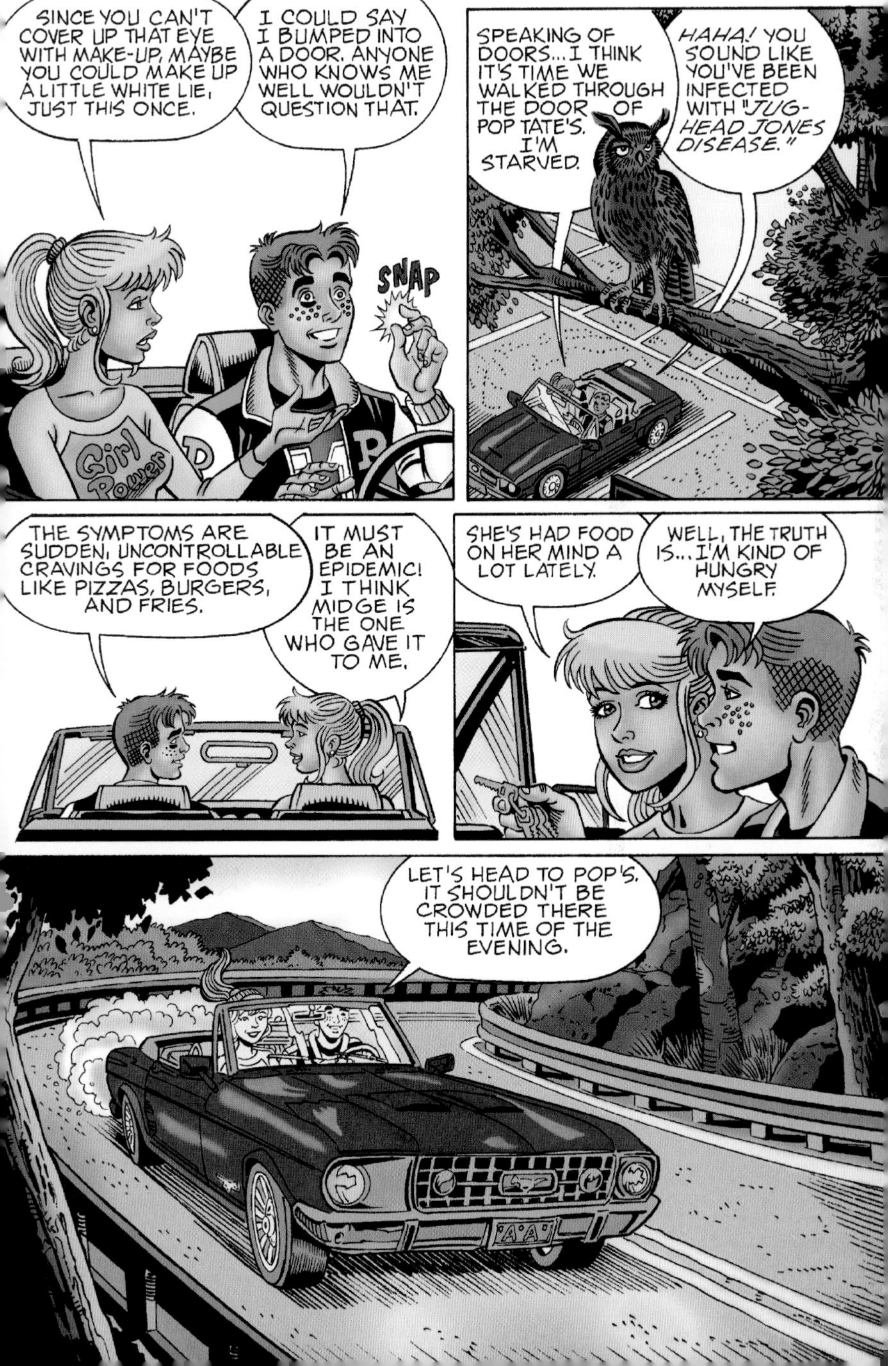
SINCE YOU CAN'T COVER UP THAT EYE WITH MAKE-UP, MAYBE YOU COULD MAKE UP A LITTLE WHITE LIE, JUST THIS ONCE.
I COULD SAY I BUMPED INTO A DOOR. ANYONE WHO KNOWS ME WELL WOULDN'T QUESTION THAT.
SNAP
SPEAKING OF DOORS... I THINK IT'S TIME WE WALKED THROUGH THE DOOR OF POP TATE'S. I'M STARVED.
HAHA! YOU SOUND LIKE YOU'VE BEEN INFECTED WITH *"JUGHEAD JONES DISEASE."*
THE SYMPTOMS ARE SUDDEN, UNCONTROLLABLE CRAVINGS FOR FOODS LIKE PIZZAS, BURGERS, AND FRIES.
IT MUST BE AN EPIDEMIC! I THINK MIDGE IS THE ONE WHO GAVE IT TO ME.
SHE'S HAD FOOD ON HER MIND A LOT LATELY.
WELL, THE TRUTH IS... I'M KIND OF HUNGRY MYSELF.
LET'S HEAD TO POP'S. IT SHOULDN'T BE CROWDED THERE THIS TIME OF THE EVENING.
'A'A'

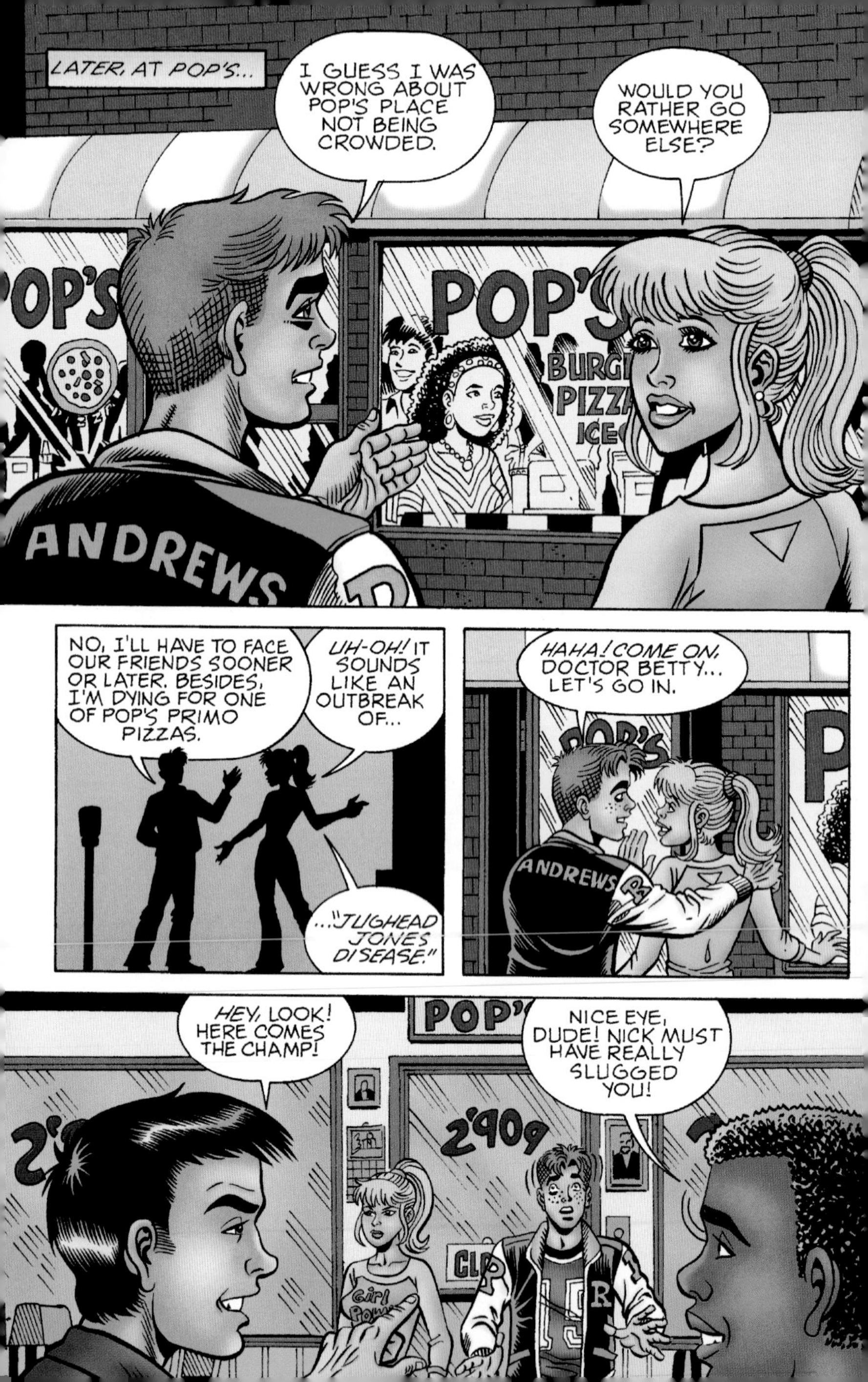
LATER, AT POP'S...
I GUESS I WAS WRONG ABOUT POP'S PLACE NOT BEING CROWDED.
WOULD YOU RATHER GO SOMEWHERE ELSE?
POP'S
ANDREWS
NO, I'LL HAVE TO FACE OUR FRIENDS SOONER OR LATER. BESIDES, I'M DYING FOR ONE OF POP'S PRIMO PIZZAS.
UH-OH! IT SOUNDS LIKE AN OUTBREAK OF...
..."JUGHEAD JONES DISEASE."
HAHA! COME ON, DOCTOR BETTY... LET'S GO IN.
ANDREWS
HEY, LOOK! HERE COMES THE CHAMP!
NICE EYE, DUDE! NICK MUST HAVE REALLY SLUGGED YOU!
POP'S

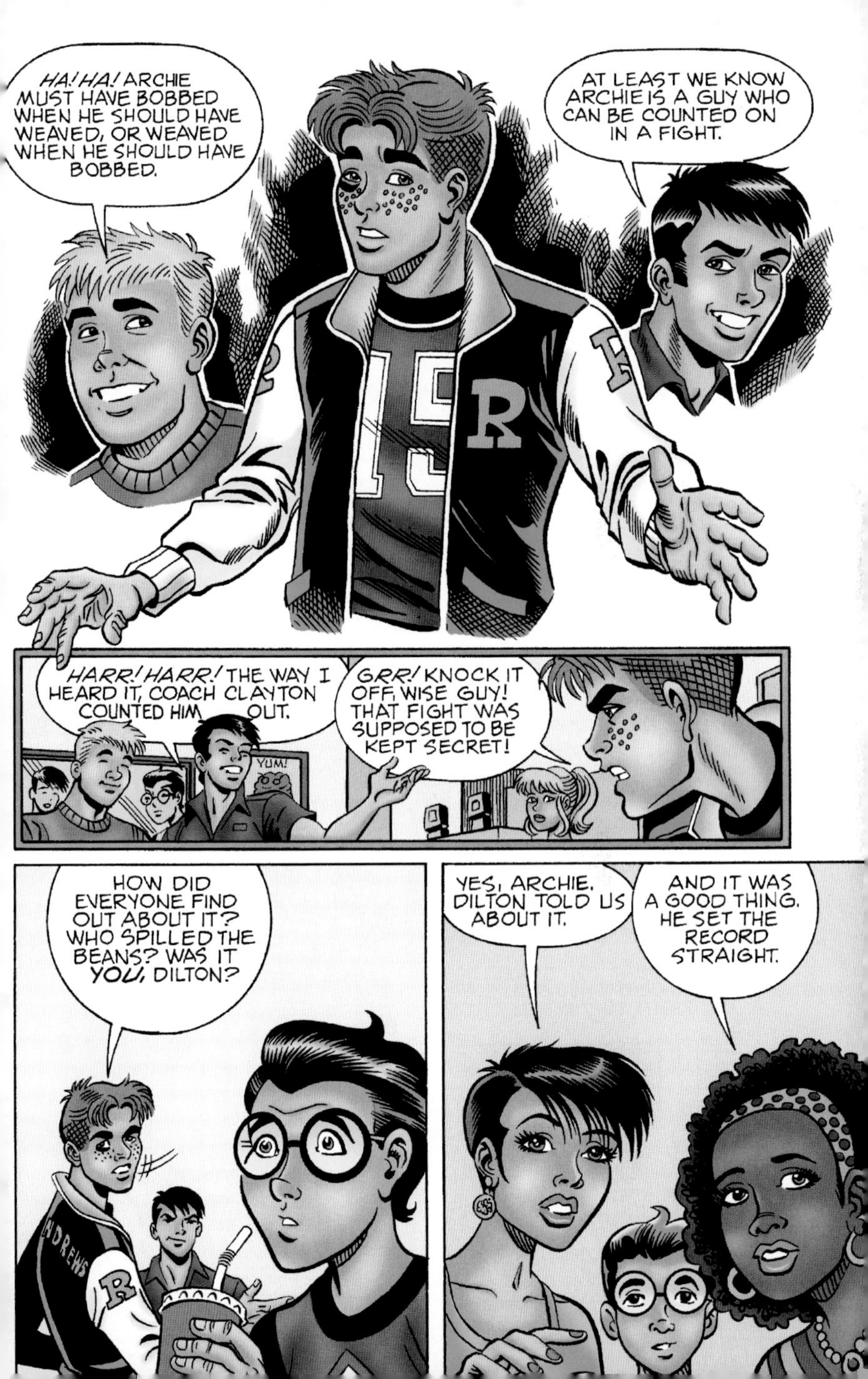
HA! HA! ARCHIE MUST HAVE BOBBED WHEN HE SHOULD HAVE WEAVED, OR WEAVED WHEN HE SHOULD HAVE BOBBED.
AT LEAST WE KNOW ARCHIE IS A GUY WHO CAN BE COUNTED ON IN A FIGHT.
HARR! HARR! THE WAY I HEARD IT, COACH CLAYTON COUNTED HIM OUT.
GRR! KNOCK IT OFF, WISE GUY! THAT FIGHT WAS SUPPOSED TO BE KEPT SECRET!
YUM!
HOW DID EVERYONE FIND OUT ABOUT IT? WHO SPILLED THE BEANS? WAS IT YOU, DILTON?
ANDREWS
YES, ARCHIE. DILTON TOLD US ABOUT IT.
AND IT WAS A GOOD THING. HE SET THE RECORD STRAIGHT.

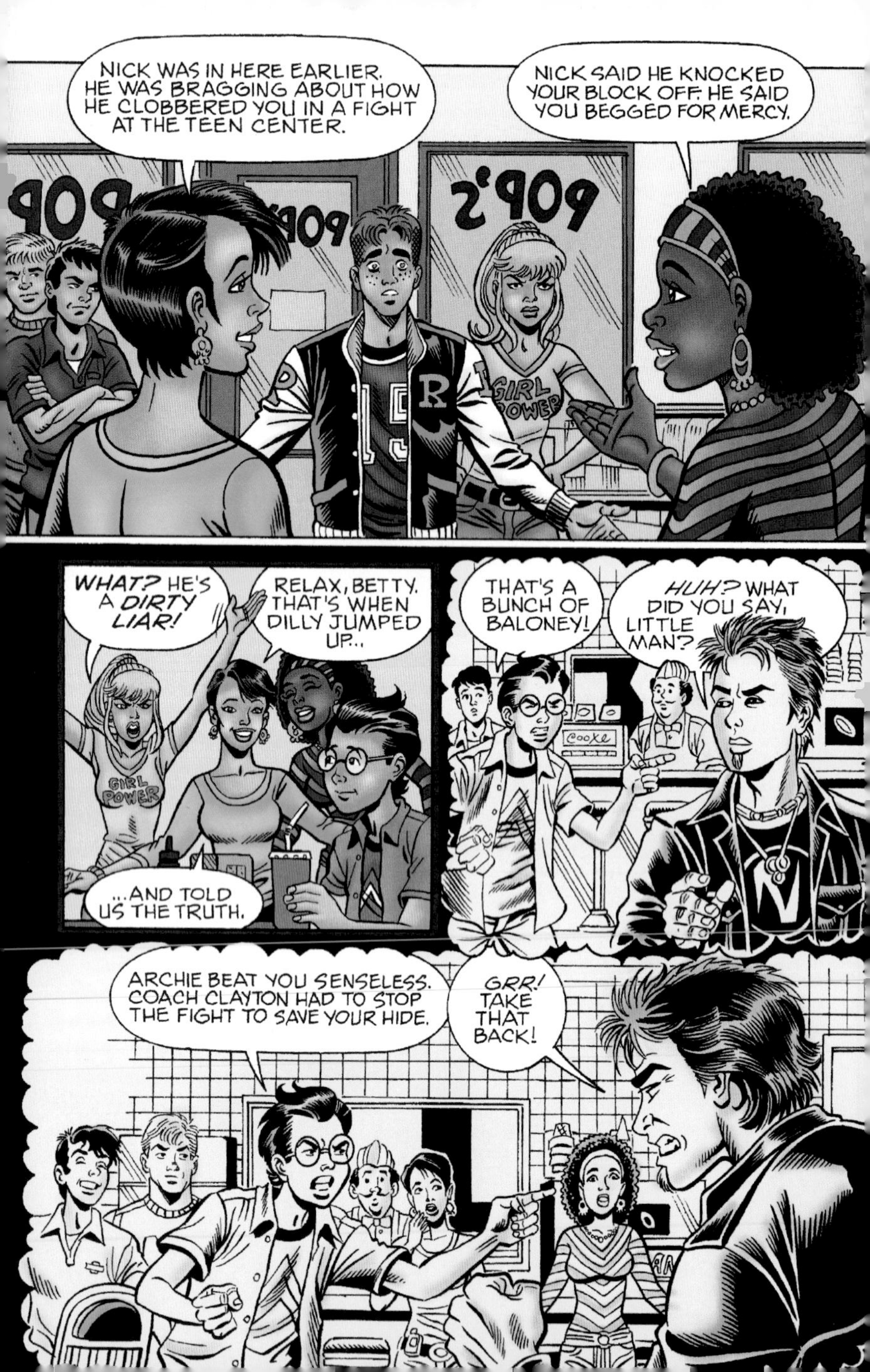
NICK WAS IN HERE EARLIER. HE WAS BRAGGING ABOUT HOW HE CLOBBERED YOU IN A FIGHT AT THE TEEN CENTER.
NICK SAID HE KNOCKED YOUR BLOCK OFF. HE SAID YOU BEGGED FOR MERCY.
POP'S
WHAT? HE'S A DIRTY LIAR!
RELAX, BETTY. THAT'S WHEN DILLY JUMPED UP...
...AND TOLD US THE TRUTH.
THAT'S A BUNCH OF BALONEY!
HUH? WHAT DID YOU SAY, LITTLE MAN?
ARCHIE BEAT YOU SENSELESS. COACH CLAYTON HAD TO STOP THE FIGHT TO SAVE YOUR HIDE.
GRR! TAKE THAT BACK!

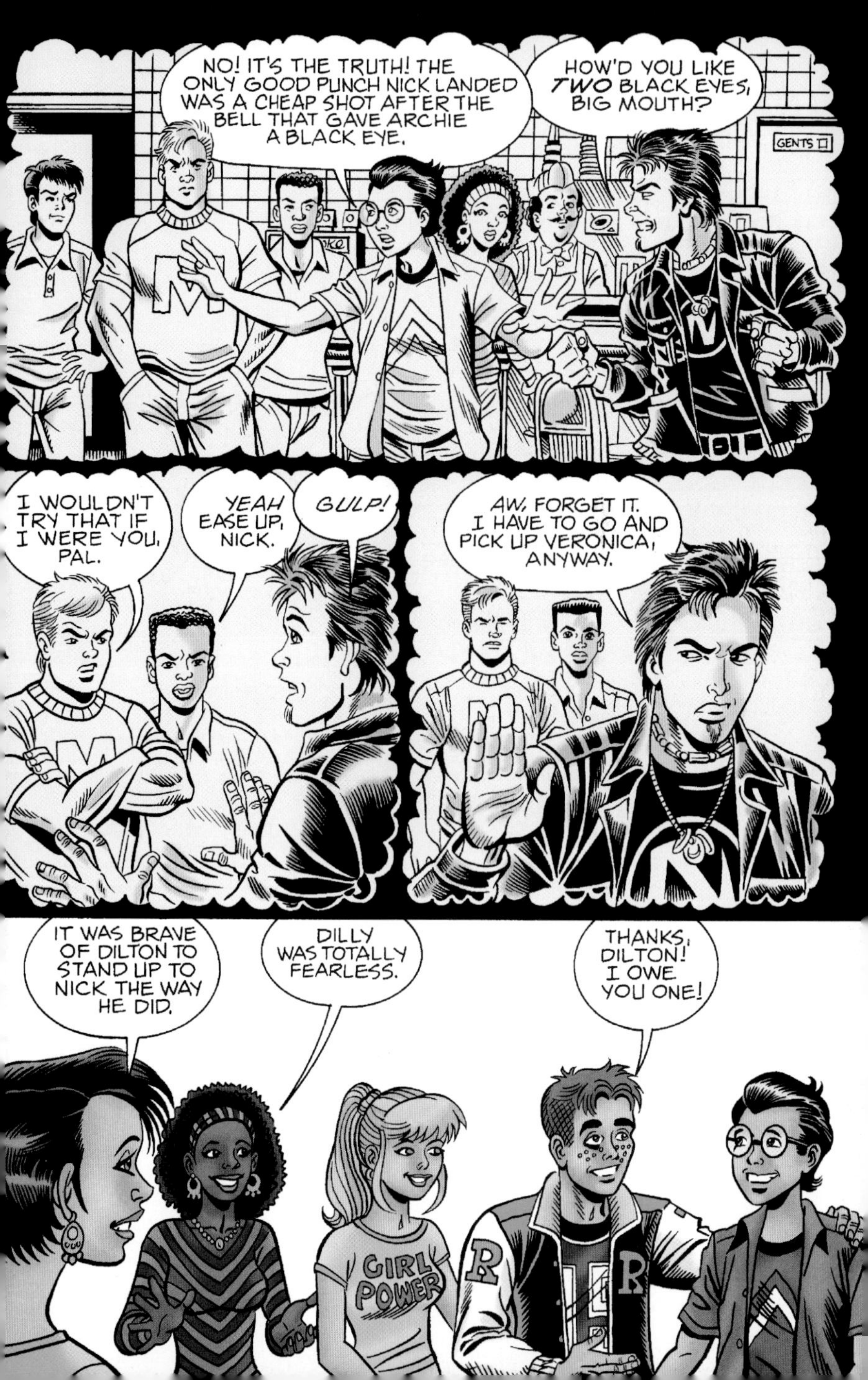
NO! IT'S THE TRUTH! THE ONLY GOOD PUNCH NICK LANDED WAS A CHEAP SHOT AFTER THE BELL THAT GAVE ARCHIE A BLACK EYE.
HOW'D YOU LIKE TWO BLACK EYES, BIG MOUTH?
GENTS
I WOULDN'T TRY THAT IF I WERE YOU, PAL.
YEAH EASE UP, NICK.
GULP!
AW, FORGET IT. I HAVE TO GO AND PICK UP VERONICA, ANYWAY.
IT WAS BRAVE OF DILTON TO STAND UP TO NICK THE WAY HE DID.
DILLY WAS TOTALLY FEARLESS.
THANKS, DILTON! I OWE YOU ONE!
GIRL POWER

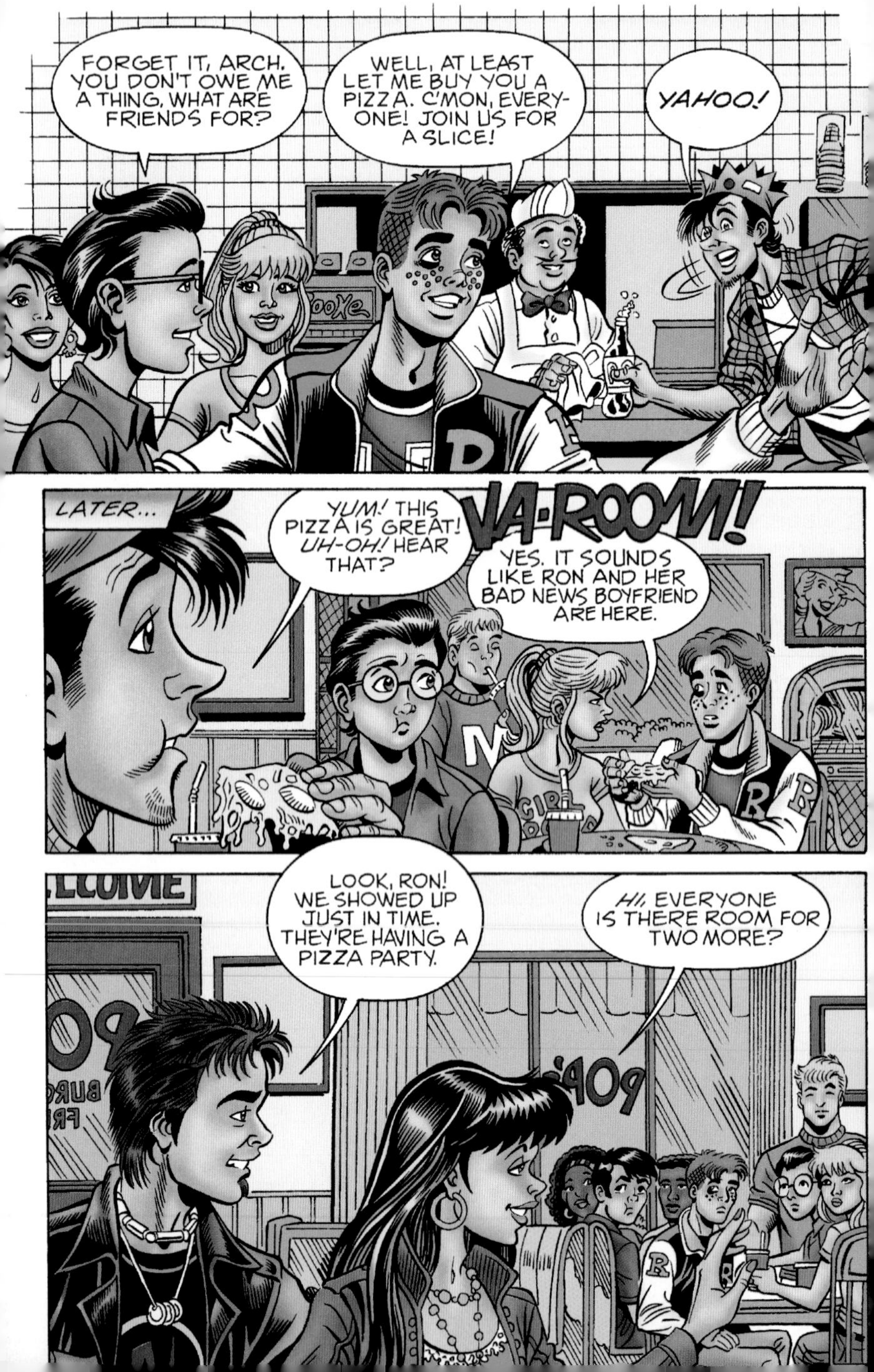
FORGET IT, ARCH. YOU DON'T OWE ME A THING. WHAT ARE FRIENDS FOR?
WELL, AT LEAST LET ME BUY YOU A PIZZA. C'MON, EVERY-ONE! JOIN US FOR A SLICE!
YAHOO!
LATER...
YUM! THIS PIZZA IS GREAT! UH-OH! HEAR THAT?
VA-ROOM!
YES. IT SOUNDS LIKE RON AND HER BAD NEWS BOYFRIEND ARE HERE.
LOOK, RON! WE SHOWED UP JUST IN TIME. THEY'RE HAVING A PIZZA PARTY.
HI, EVERYONE IS THERE ROOM FOR TWO MORE?

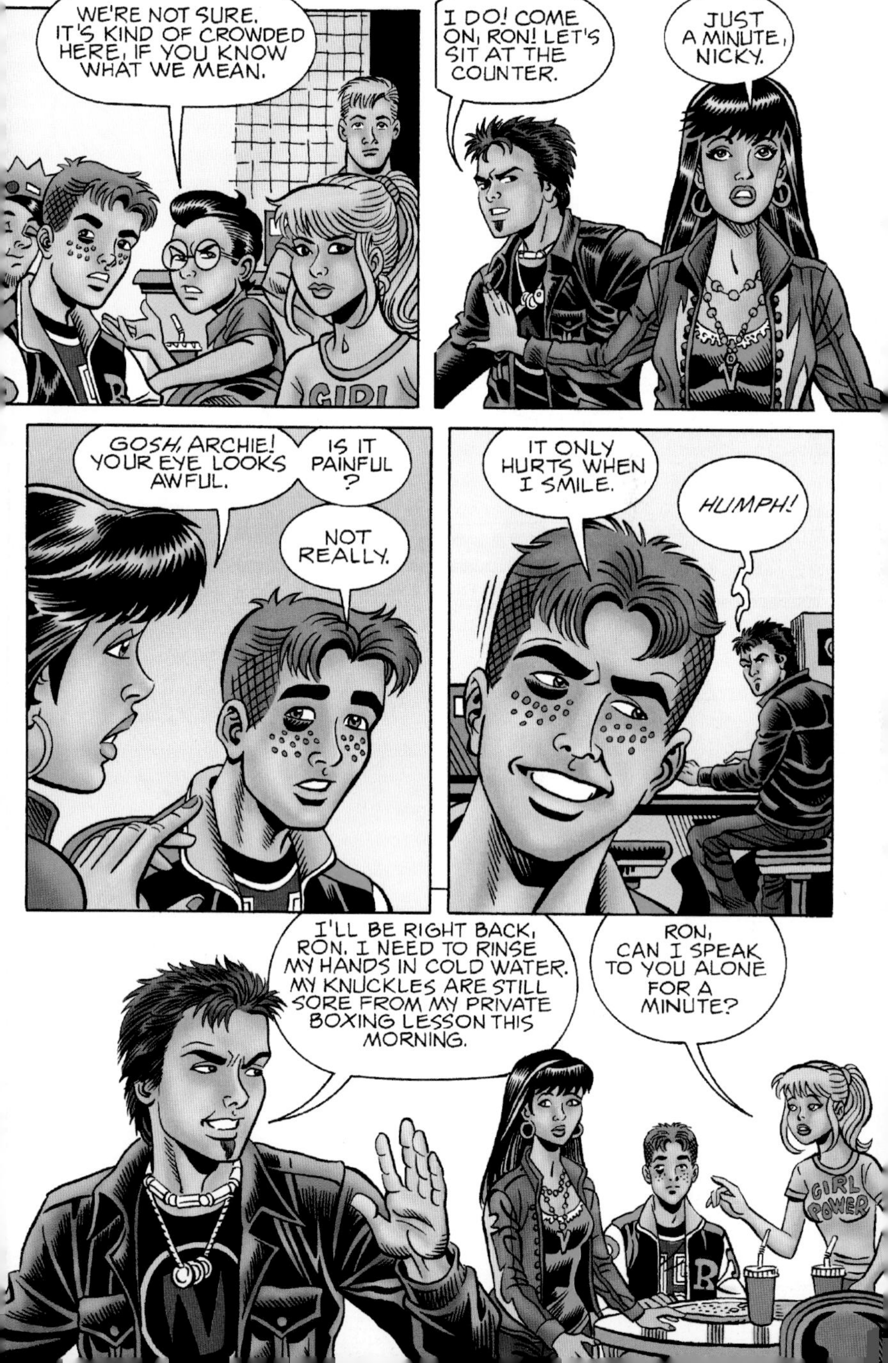
WE'RE NOT SURE. IT'S KIND OF CROWDED HERE, IF YOU KNOW WHAT WE MEAN.
I DO! COME ON, RON! LET'S SIT AT THE COUNTER.
JUST A MINUTE, NICKY.
GOSH, ARCHIE! YOUR EYE LOOKS AWFUL.
IS IT PAINFUL ?
NOT REALLY.
IT ONLY HURTS WHEN I SMILE.
HUMPH!
I'LL BE RIGHT BACK, RON. I NEED TO RINSE MY HANDS IN COLD WATER. MY KNUCKLES ARE STILL SORE FROM MY PRIVATE BOXING LESSON THIS MORNING.
RON, CAN I SPEAK TO YOU ALONE FOR A MINUTE?
GIRL POWER

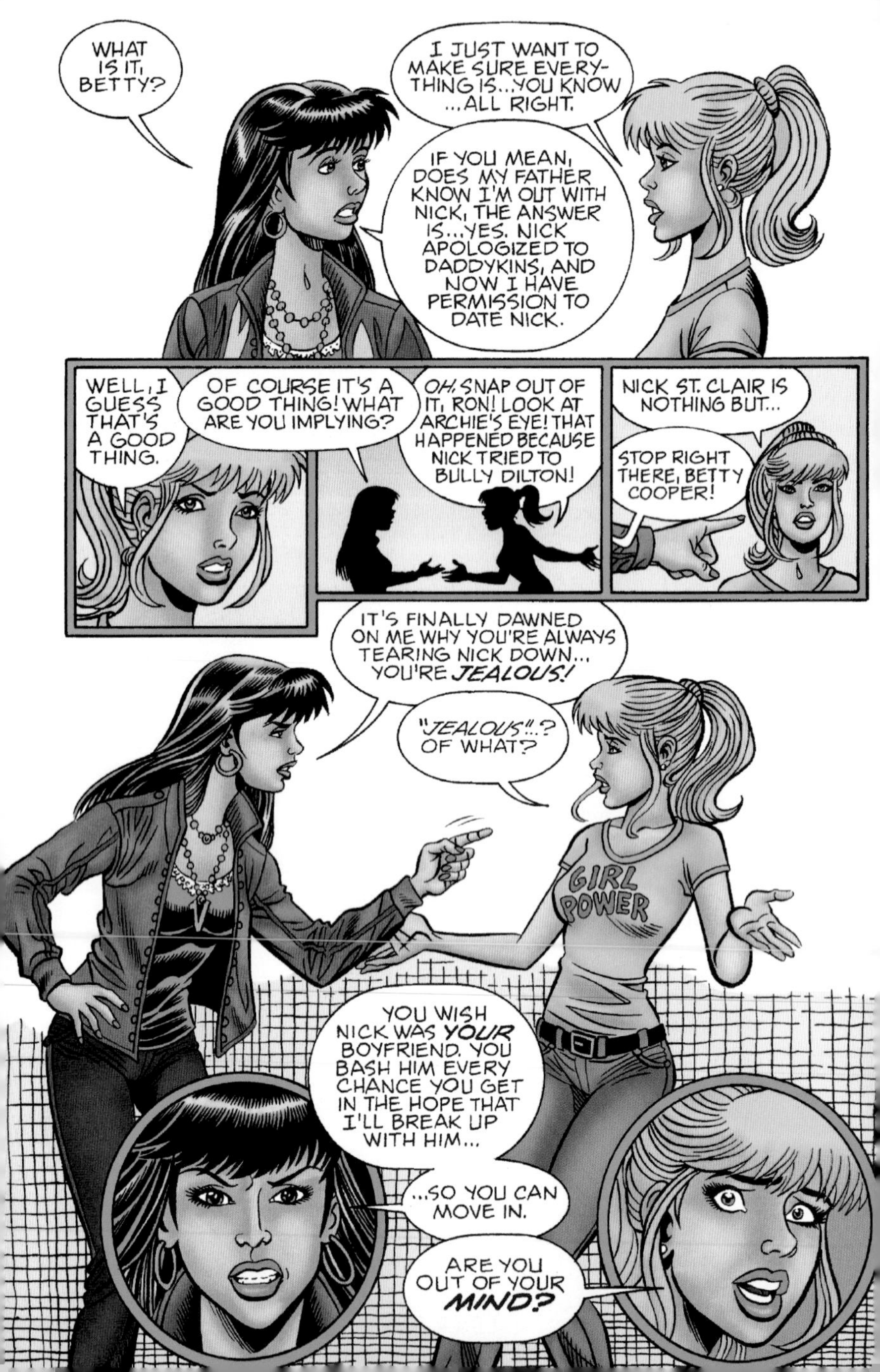
WHAT IS IT, BETTY?
I JUST WANT TO MAKE SURE EVERYTHING IS...YOU KNOW ...ALL RIGHT.
IF YOU MEAN, DOES MY FATHER KNOW I'M OUT WITH NICK, THE ANSWER IS...YES. NICK APOLOGIZED TO DADDYKINS, AND NOW I HAVE PERMISSION TO DATE NICK.
WELL, I GUESS THAT'S A GOOD THING.
OF COURSE IT'S A GOOD THING! WHAT ARE YOU IMPLYING?
OH, SNAP OUT OF IT, RON! LOOK AT ARCHIE'S EYE! THAT HAPPENED BECAUSE NICK TRIED TO BULLY DILTON!
NICK ST. CLAIR IS NOTHING BUT...
STOP RIGHT THERE, BETTY COOPER!
IT'S FINALLY DAWNED ON ME WHY YOU'RE ALWAYS TEARING NICK DOWN... YOU'RE JEALOUS!
"JEALOUS!"..? OF WHAT?
GIRL POWER
YOU WISH NICK WAS YOUR BOYFRIEND. YOU BASH HIM EVERY CHANCE YOU GET IN THE HOPE THAT I'LL BREAK UP WITH HIM...
...SO YOU CAN MOVE IN.
ARE YOU OUT OF YOUR MIND?

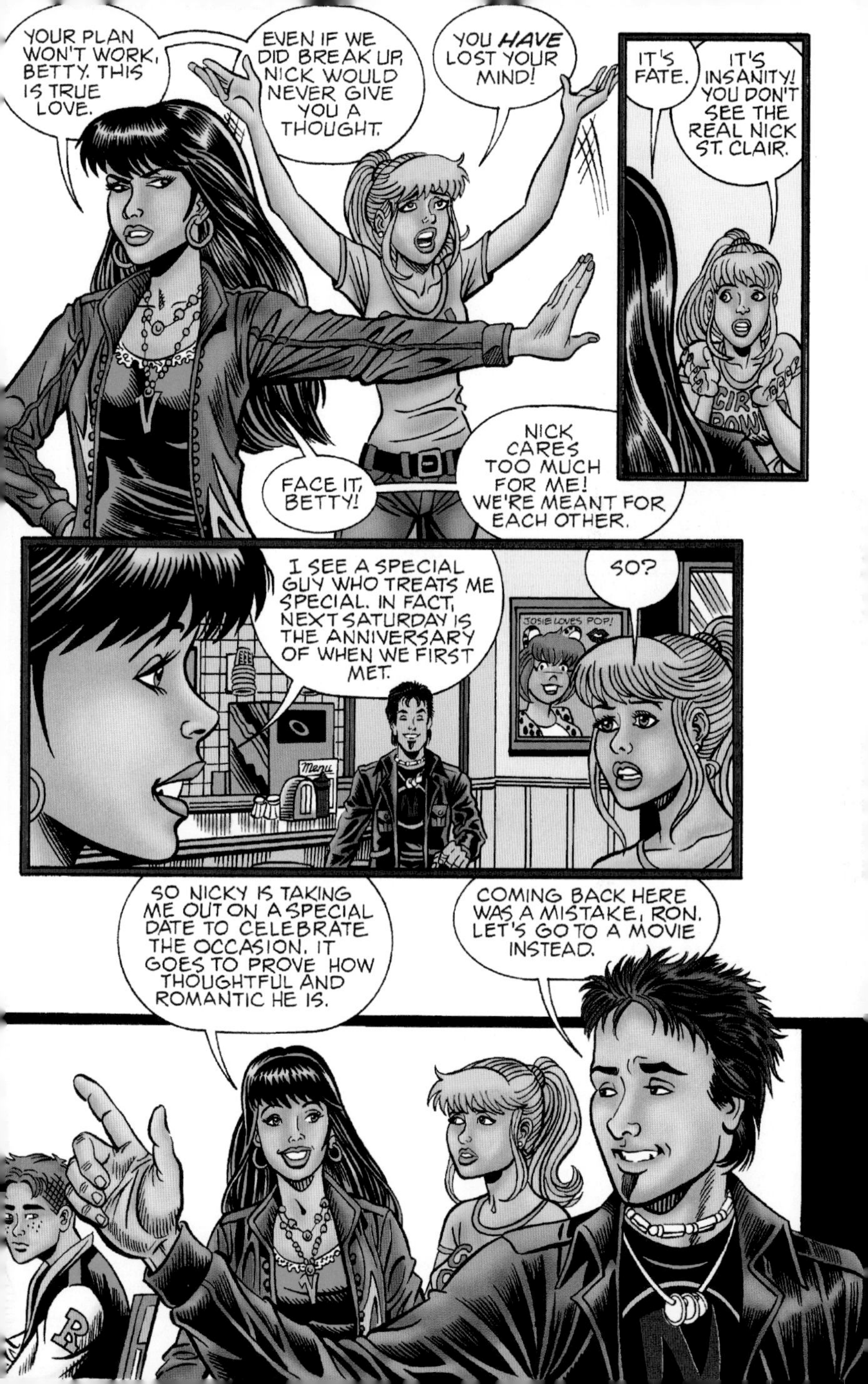
YOUR PLAN WON'T WORK, BETTY. THIS IS TRUE LOVE.
EVEN IF WE DID BREAK UP, NICK WOULD NEVER GIVE YOU A THOUGHT.
YOU *HAVE* LOST YOUR MIND!
IT'S FATE.
IT'S INSANITY! YOU DON'T SEE THE REAL NICK ST. CLAIR.
FACE IT, BETTY!
NICK CARES TOO MUCH FOR ME! WE'RE MEANT FOR EACH OTHER.
I SEE A SPECIAL GUY WHO TREATS ME SPECIAL. IN FACT, NEXT SATURDAY IS THE ANNIVERSARY OF WHEN WE FIRST MET.
SO?
JOSIE LOVES POP!
Menu
SO NICKY IS TAKING ME OUT ON A SPECIAL DATE TO CELEBRATE THE OCCASION. IT GOES TO PROVE HOW THOUGHTFUL AND ROMANTIC HE IS.
COMING BACK HERE WAS A MISTAKE, RON. LET'S GO TO A MOVIE INSTEAD.

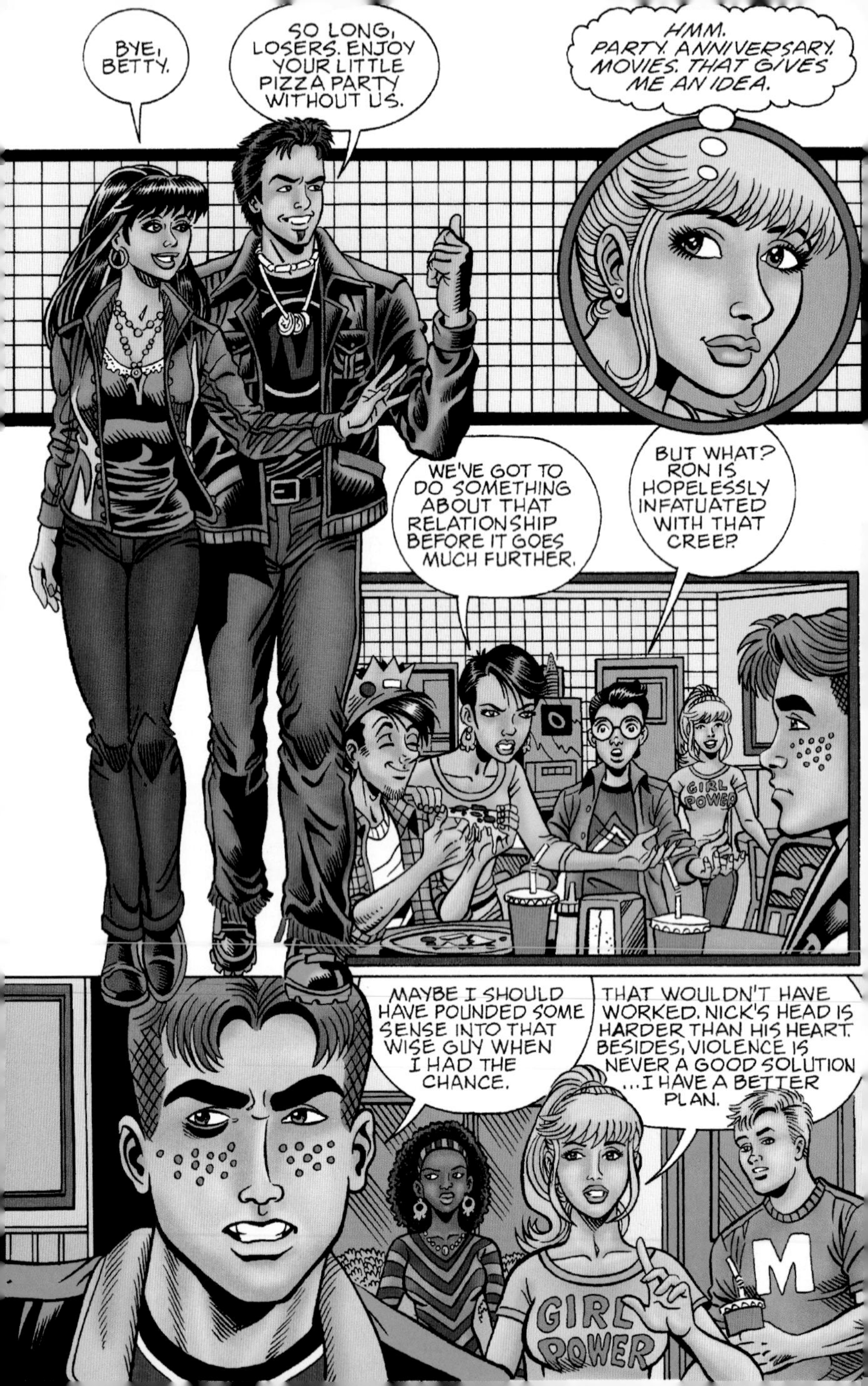
BYE, BETTY.
SO LONG, LOSERS. ENJOY YOUR LITTLE PIZZA PARTY WITHOUT US.
HMM. PARTY. ANNIVERSARY. MOVIES. THAT GIVES ME AN IDEA.
WE'VE GOT TO DO SOMETHING ABOUT THAT RELATIONSHIP BEFORE IT GOES MUCH FURTHER.
BUT WHAT? RON IS HOPELESSLY INFATUATED WITH THAT CREEP.
GIRL POWER
MAYBE I SHOULD HAVE POUNDED SOME SENSE INTO THAT WISE GUY WHEN I HAD THE CHANCE.
THAT WOULDN'T HAVE WORKED. NICK'S HEAD IS HARDER THAN HIS HEART. BESIDES, VIOLENCE IS NEVER A GOOD SOLUTION ...I HAVE A BETTER PLAN.
GIRL POWER
M

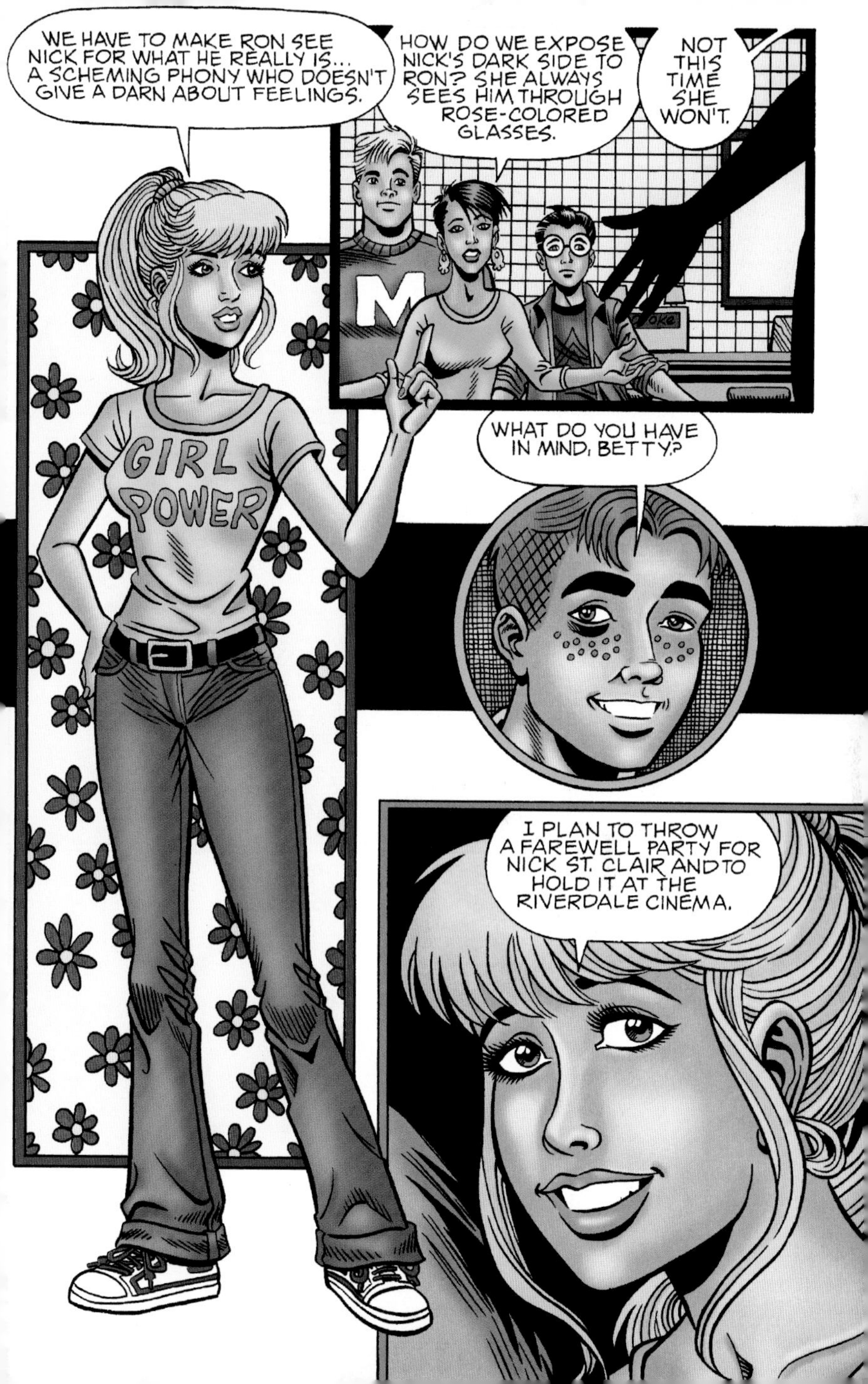
WE HAVE TO MAKE RON SEE NICK FOR WHAT HE REALLY IS... A SCHEMING PHONY WHO DOESN'T GIVE A DARN ABOUT FEELINGS.
HOW DO WE EXPOSE NICK'S DARK SIDE TO RON? SHE ALWAYS SEES HIM THROUGH ROSE-COLORED GLASSES.
NOT THIS TIME SHE WON'T.
WHAT DO YOU HAVE IN MIND, BETTY?
I PLAN TO THROW A FAREWELL PARTY FOR NICK ST. CLAIR AND TO HOLD IT AT THE RIVERDALE CINEMA.

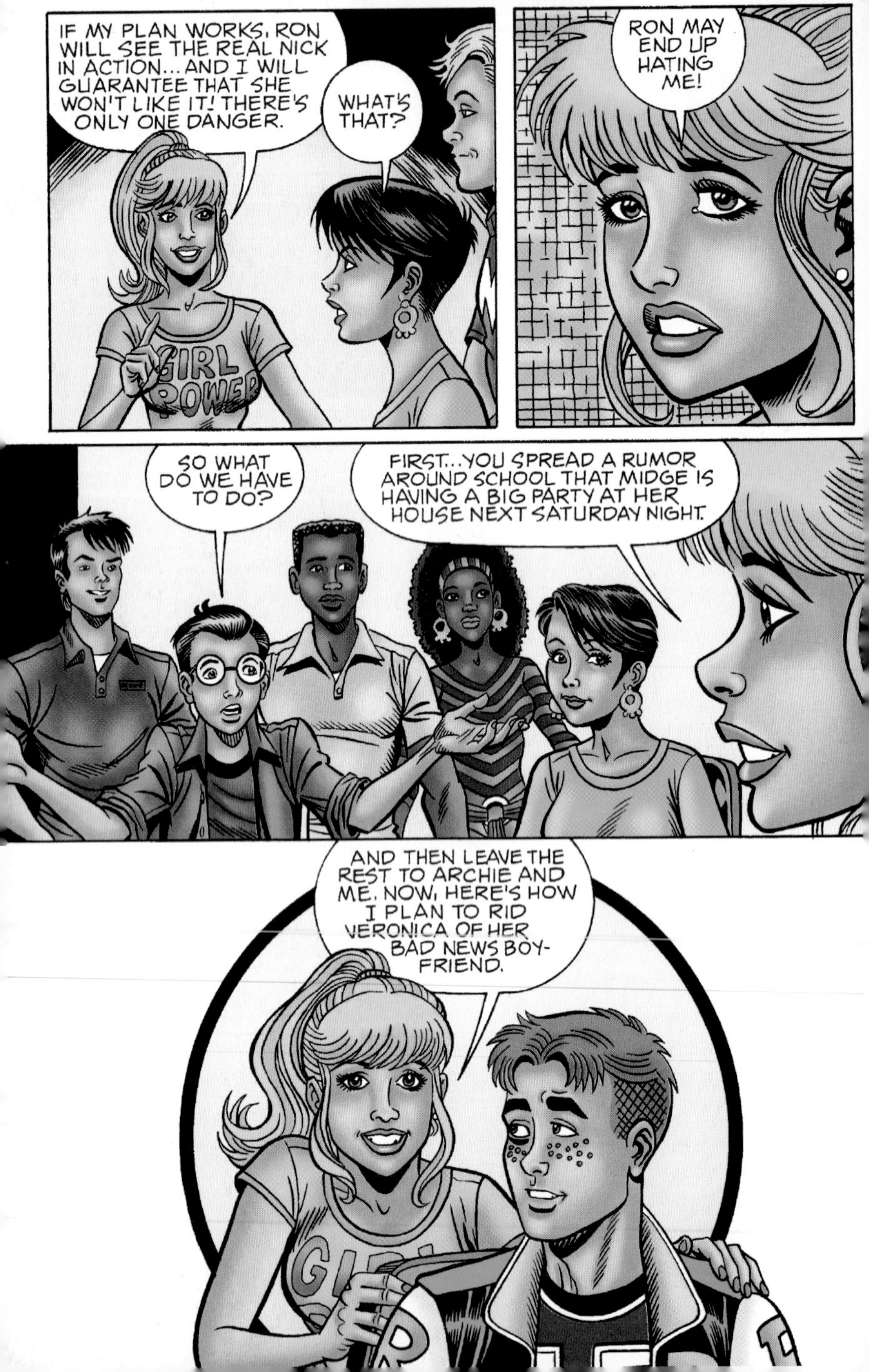
IF MY PLAN WORKS, RON WILL SEE THE REAL NICK IN ACTION... AND I WILL GUARANTEE THAT SHE WON'T LIKE IT! THERE'S ONLY ONE DANGER.
WHAT'S THAT?
RON MAY END UP HATING ME!
SO WHAT DO WE HAVE TO DO?
FIRST...YOU SPREAD A RUMOR AROUND SCHOOL THAT MIDGE IS HAVING A BIG PARTY AT HER HOUSE NEXT SATURDAY NIGHT.
AND THEN LEAVE THE REST TO ARCHIE AND ME. NOW, HERE'S HOW I PLAN TO RID VERONICA OF HER BAD NEWS BOY-FRIEND.
GIRL POWER

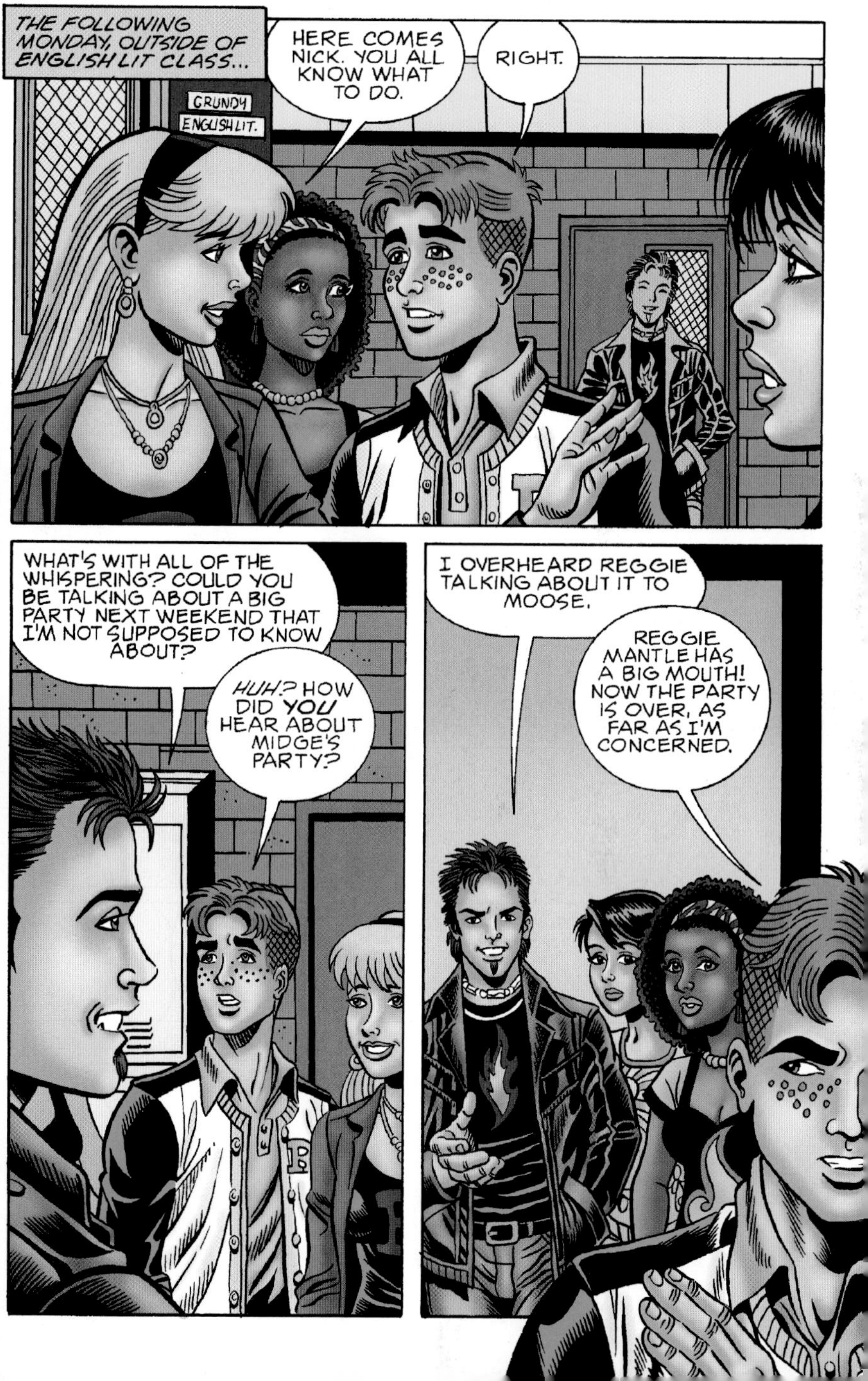
THE FOLLOWING MONDAY, OUTSIDE OF ENGLISH LIT CLASS...
GRUNDY
ENGLISH LIT.
HERE COMES NICK. YOU ALL KNOW WHAT TO DO.
RIGHT.
WHAT'S WITH ALL OF THE WHISPERING? COULD YOU BE TALKING ABOUT A BIG PARTY NEXT WEEKEND THAT I'M NOT SUPPOSED TO KNOW ABOUT?
HUH? HOW DID **YOU** HEAR ABOUT MIDGE'S PARTY?
I OVERHEARD REGGIE TALKING ABOUT IT TO MOOSE.
REGGIE MANTLE HAS A BIG MOUTH! NOW THE PARTY IS OVER, AS FAR AS I'M CONCERNED.

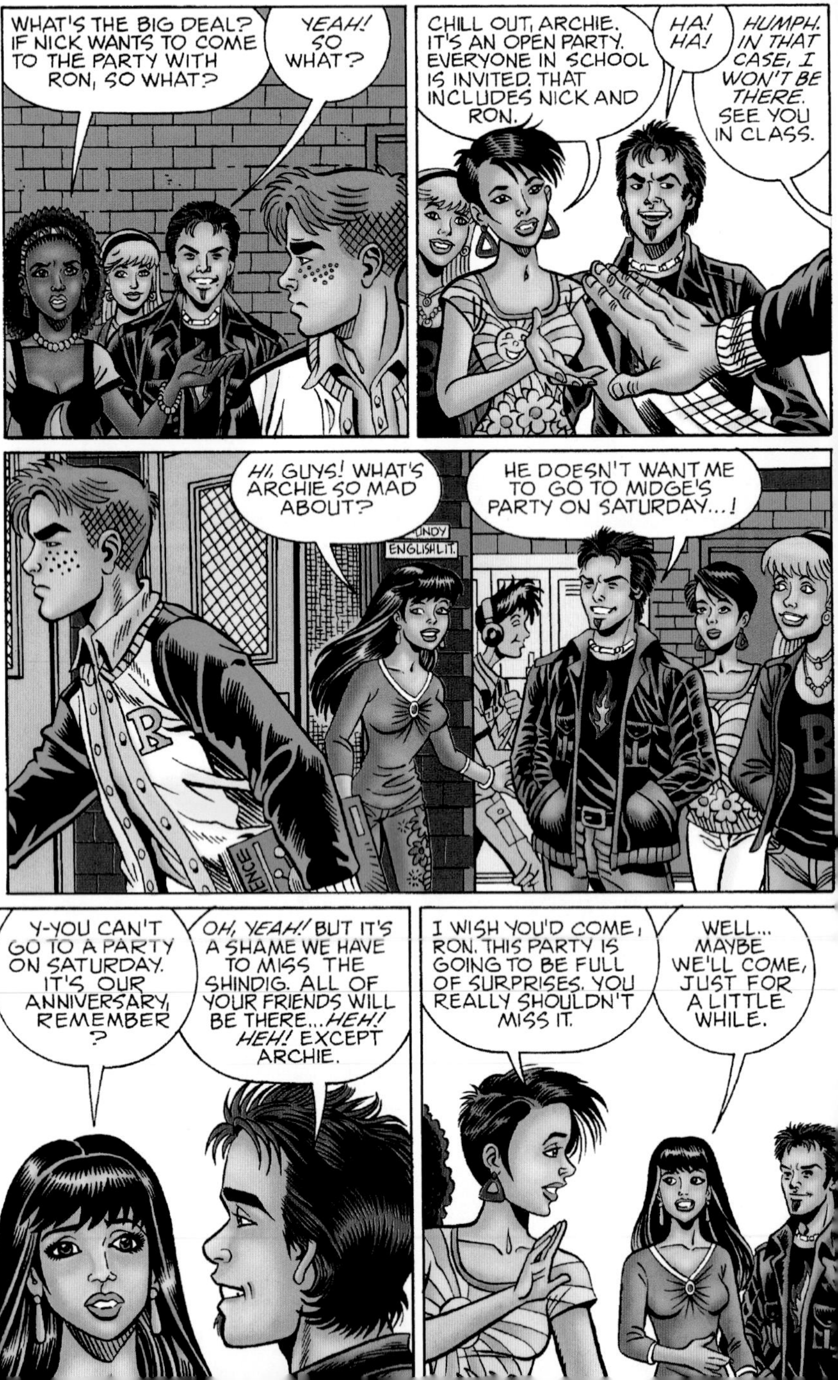
WHAT'S THE BIG DEAL? IF NICK WANTS TO COME TO THE PARTY WITH RON, SO WHAT?
YEAH! SO WHAT?
CHILL OUT, ARCHIE. IT'S AN OPEN PARTY. EVERYONE IN SCHOOL IS INVITED. THAT INCLUDES NICK AND RON.
HA! HA!
HUMPH. IN THAT CASE, I WON'T BE THERE. SEE YOU IN CLASS.
HI, GUYS! WHAT'S ARCHIE SO MAD ABOUT?
HE DOESN'T WANT ME TO GO TO MIDGE'S PARTY ON SATURDAY...!
ENGLISH LIT.
Y-YOU CAN'T GO TO A PARTY ON SATURDAY. IT'S OUR ANNIVERSARY, REMEMBER?
OH, YEAH! BUT IT'S A SHAME WE HAVE TO MISS THE SHINDIG. ALL OF YOUR FRIENDS WILL BE THERE... HEH! HEH! EXCEPT ARCHIE.
I WISH YOU'D COME, RON. THIS PARTY IS GOING TO BE FULL OF SURPRISES. YOU REALLY SHOULDN'T MISS IT.
WELL... MAYBE WE'LL COME, JUST FOR A LITTLE WHILE.

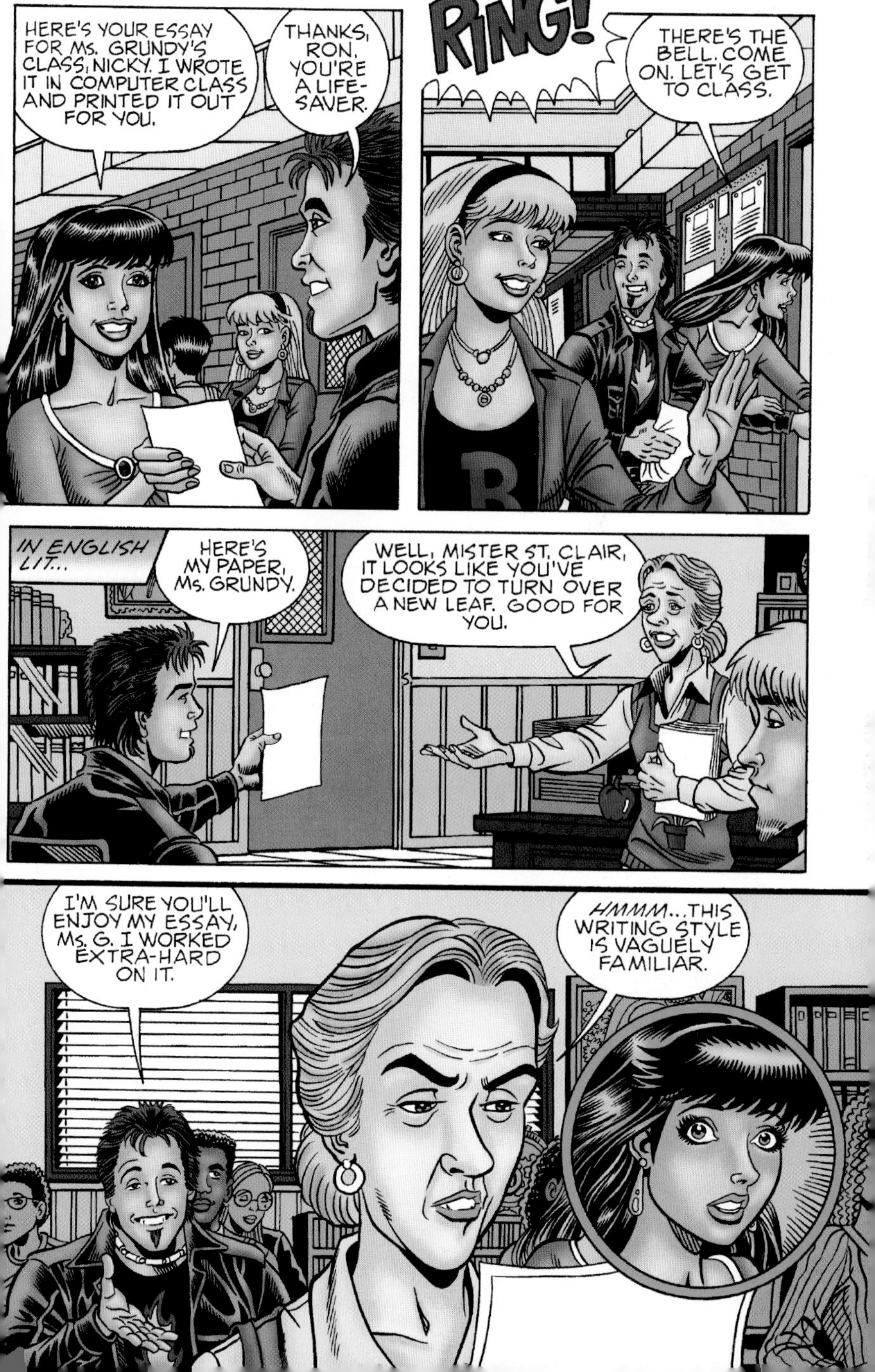
HERE'S YOUR ESSAY FOR Ms. GRUNDY'S CLASS, NICKY. I WROTE IT IN COMPUTER CLASS AND PRINTED IT OUT FOR YOU.
THANKS, RON. YOU'RE A LIFE-SAVER.
RING!
THERE'S THE BELL. COME ON. LET'S GET TO CLASS.
IN ENGLISH LIT...
HERE'S MY PAPER, Ms. GRUNDY.
WELL, MISTER ST. CLAIR, IT LOOKS LIKE YOU'VE DECIDED TO TURN OVER A NEW LEAF. GOOD FOR YOU.
I'M SURE YOU'LL ENJOY MY ESSAY, Ms. G. I WORKED EXTRA-HARD ON IT.
HMMM... THIS WRITING STYLE IS VAGUELY FAMILIAR.

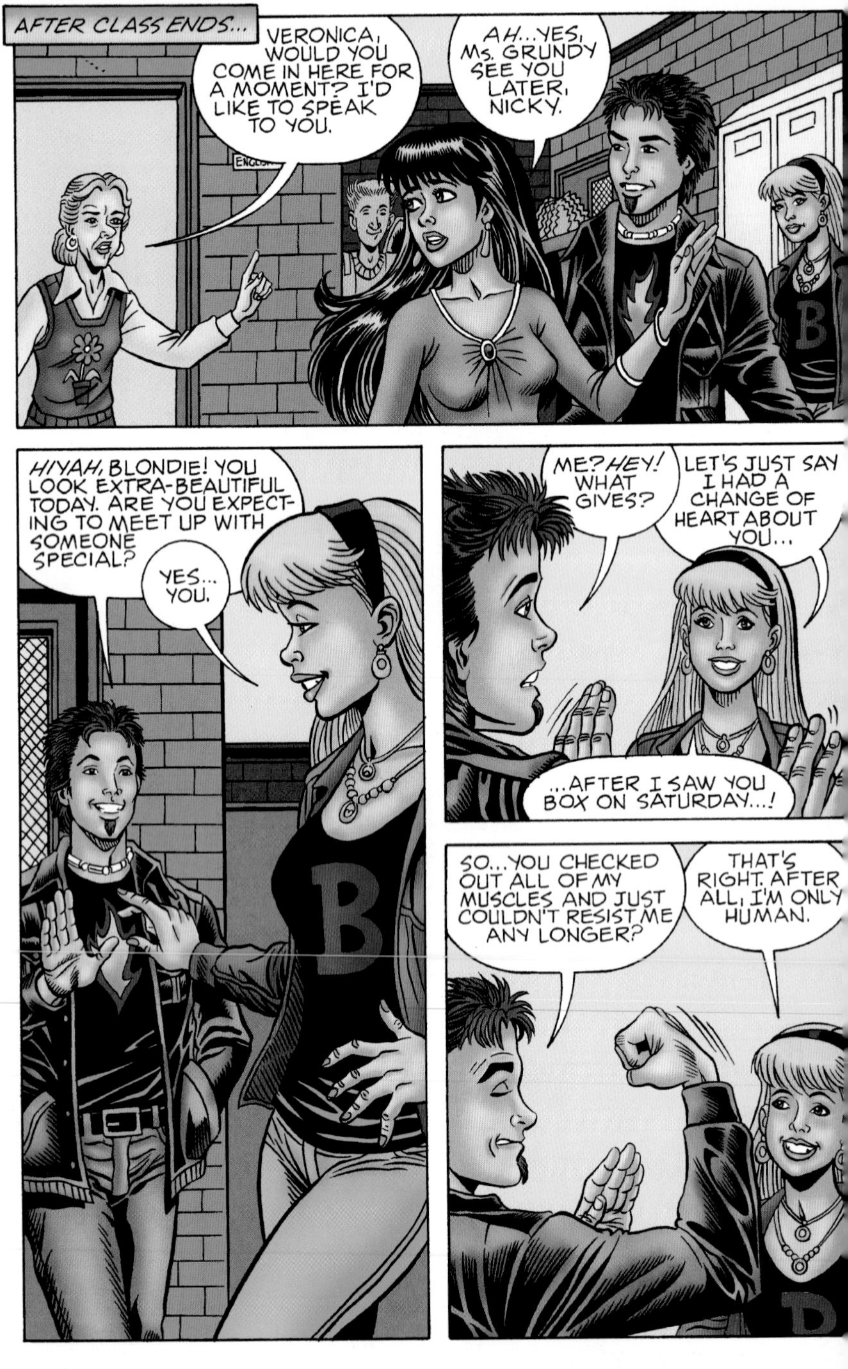
AFTER CLASS ENDS...
VERONICA, WOULD YOU COME IN HERE FOR A MOMENT? I'D LIKE TO SPEAK TO YOU.
AH...YES, Ms. GRUNDY SEE YOU LATER, NICKY.
HIYAH, BLONDIE! YOU LOOK EXTRA-BEAUTIFUL TODAY. ARE YOU EXPECTING TO MEET UP WITH SOMEONE SPECIAL?
YES... YOU.
ME? HEY! WHAT GIVES?
LET'S JUST SAY I HAD A CHANGE OF HEART ABOUT YOU...
...AFTER I SAW YOU BOX ON SATURDAY...!
SO...YOU CHECKED OUT ALL OF MY MUSCLES AND JUST COULDN'T RESIST ME ANY LONGER?
THAT'S RIGHT. AFTER ALL, I'M ONLY HUMAN.

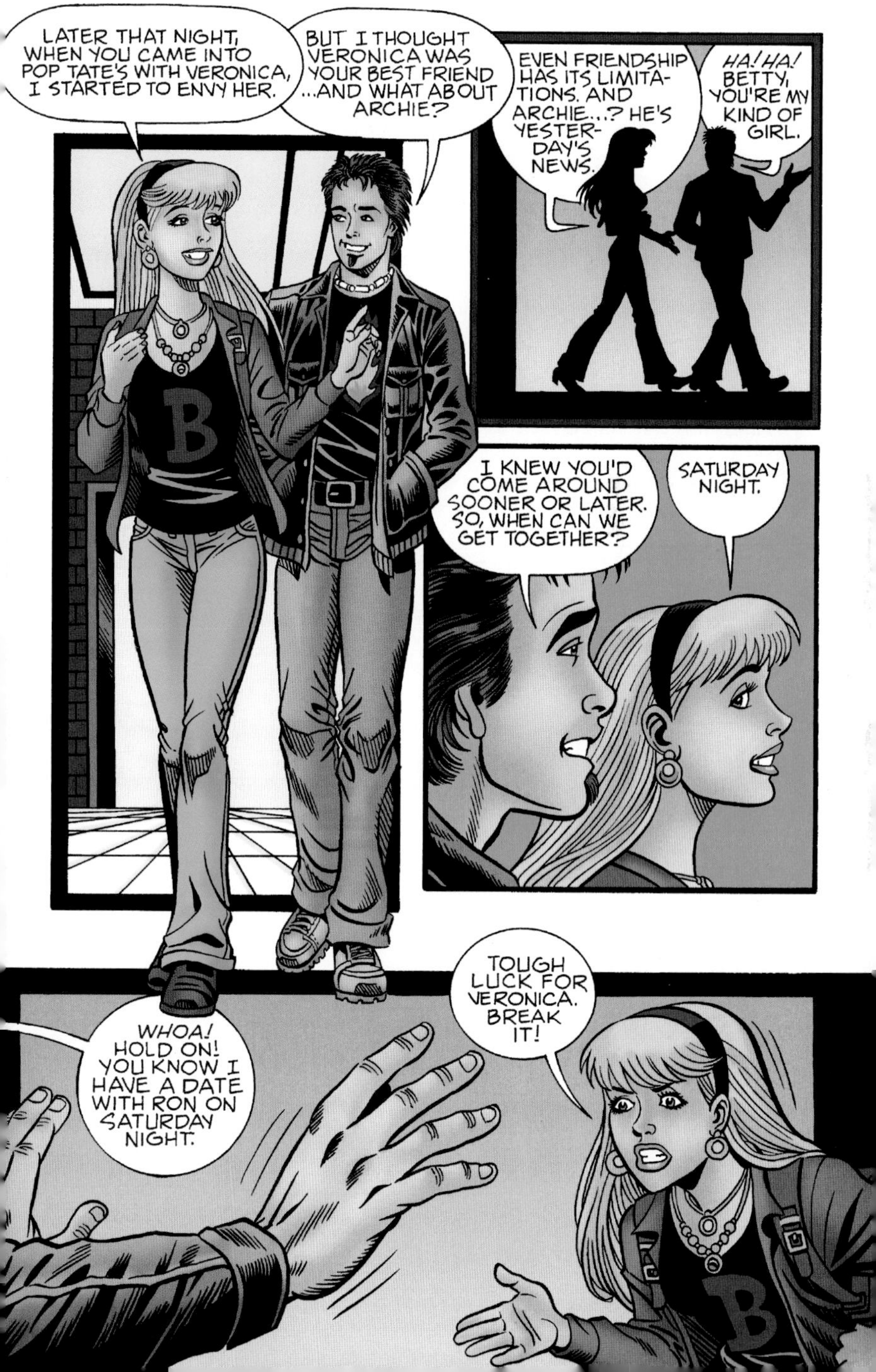
LATER THAT NIGHT, WHEN YOU CAME INTO POP TATE'S WITH VERONICA, I STARTED TO ENVY HER.
BUT I THOUGHT VERONICA WAS YOUR BEST FRIEND ...AND WHAT ABOUT ARCHIE?
EVEN FRIENDSHIP HAS ITS LIMITATIONS. AND ARCHIE...? HE'S YESTERDAY'S NEWS.
HA! HA! BETTY, YOU'RE MY KIND OF GIRL.
I KNEW YOU'D COME AROUND SOONER OR LATER. SO, WHEN CAN WE GET TOGETHER?
SATURDAY NIGHT.
WHOA! HOLD ON! YOU KNOW I HAVE A DATE WITH RON ON SATURDAY NIGHT.
TOUGH LUCK FOR VERONICA. BREAK IT!

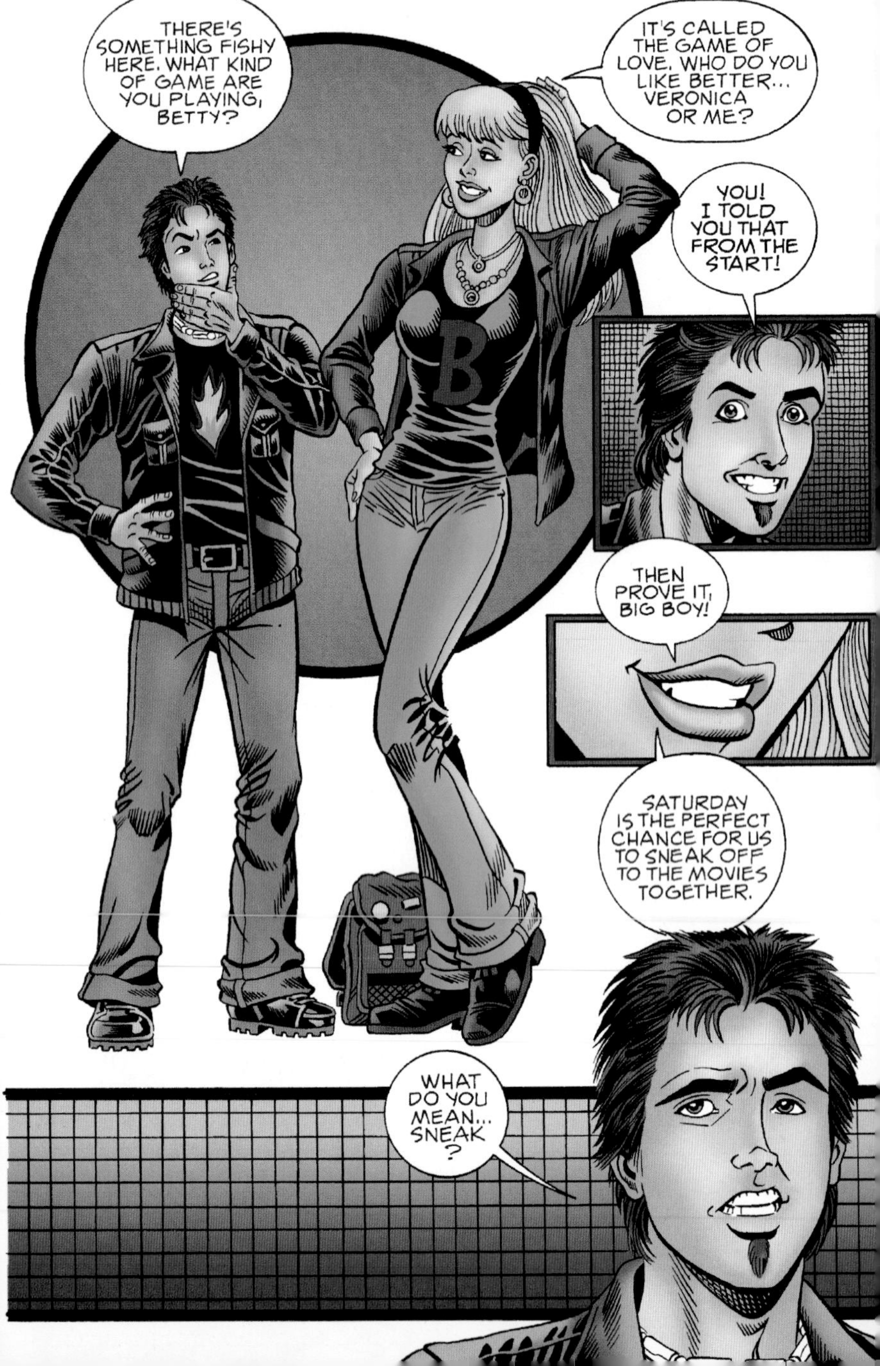
THERE'S SOMETHING FISHY HERE. WHAT KIND OF GAME ARE YOU PLAYING, BETTY?
IT'S CALLED THE GAME OF LOVE. WHO DO YOU LIKE BETTER... VERONICA OR ME?
YOU! I TOLD YOU THAT FROM THE START!
THEN PROVE IT, BIG BOY!
SATURDAY IS THE PERFECT CHANCE FOR US TO SNEAK OFF TO THE MOVIES TOGETHER.
WHAT DO YOU MEAN... SNEAK?

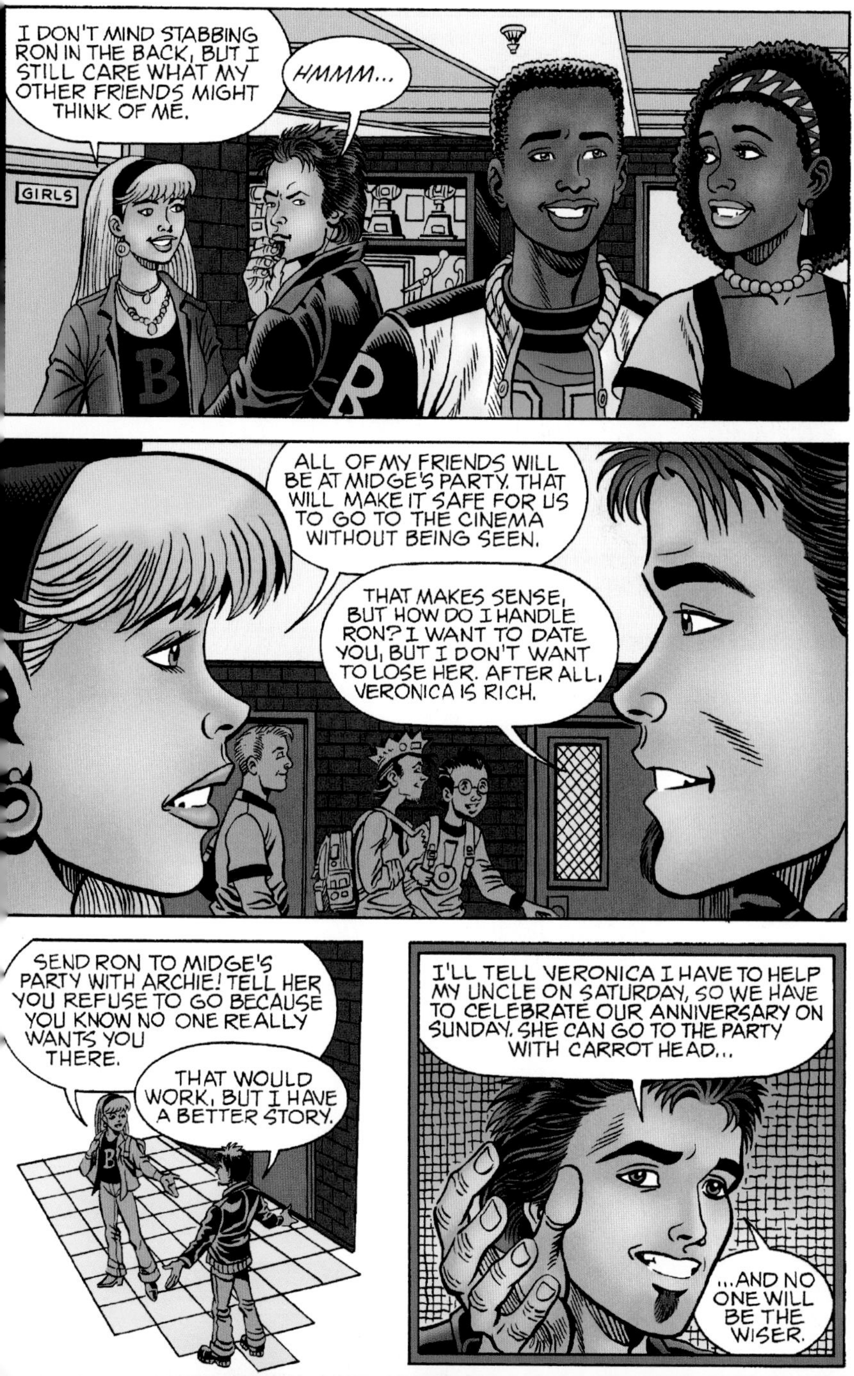
I DON'T MIND STABBING RON IN THE BACK, BUT I STILL CARE WHAT MY OTHER FRIENDS MIGHT THINK OF ME.
HMMM...
GIRLS
ALL OF MY FRIENDS WILL BE AT MIDGE'S PARTY. THAT WILL MAKE IT SAFE FOR US TO GO TO THE CINEMA WITHOUT BEING SEEN.
THAT MAKES SENSE, BUT HOW DO I HANDLE RON? I WANT TO DATE YOU, BUT I DON'T WANT TO LOSE HER. AFTER ALL, VERONICA IS RICH.
SEND RON TO MIDGE'S PARTY WITH ARCHIE! TELL HER YOU REFUSE TO GO BECAUSE YOU KNOW NO ONE REALLY WANTS YOU THERE.
THAT WOULD WORK, BUT I HAVE A BETTER STORY.
I'LL TELL VERONICA I HAVE TO HELP MY UNCLE ON SATURDAY, SO WE HAVE TO CELEBRATE OUR ANNIVERSARY ON SUNDAY. SHE CAN GO TO THE PARTY WITH CARROT HEAD...
...AND NO ONE WILL BE THE WISER.

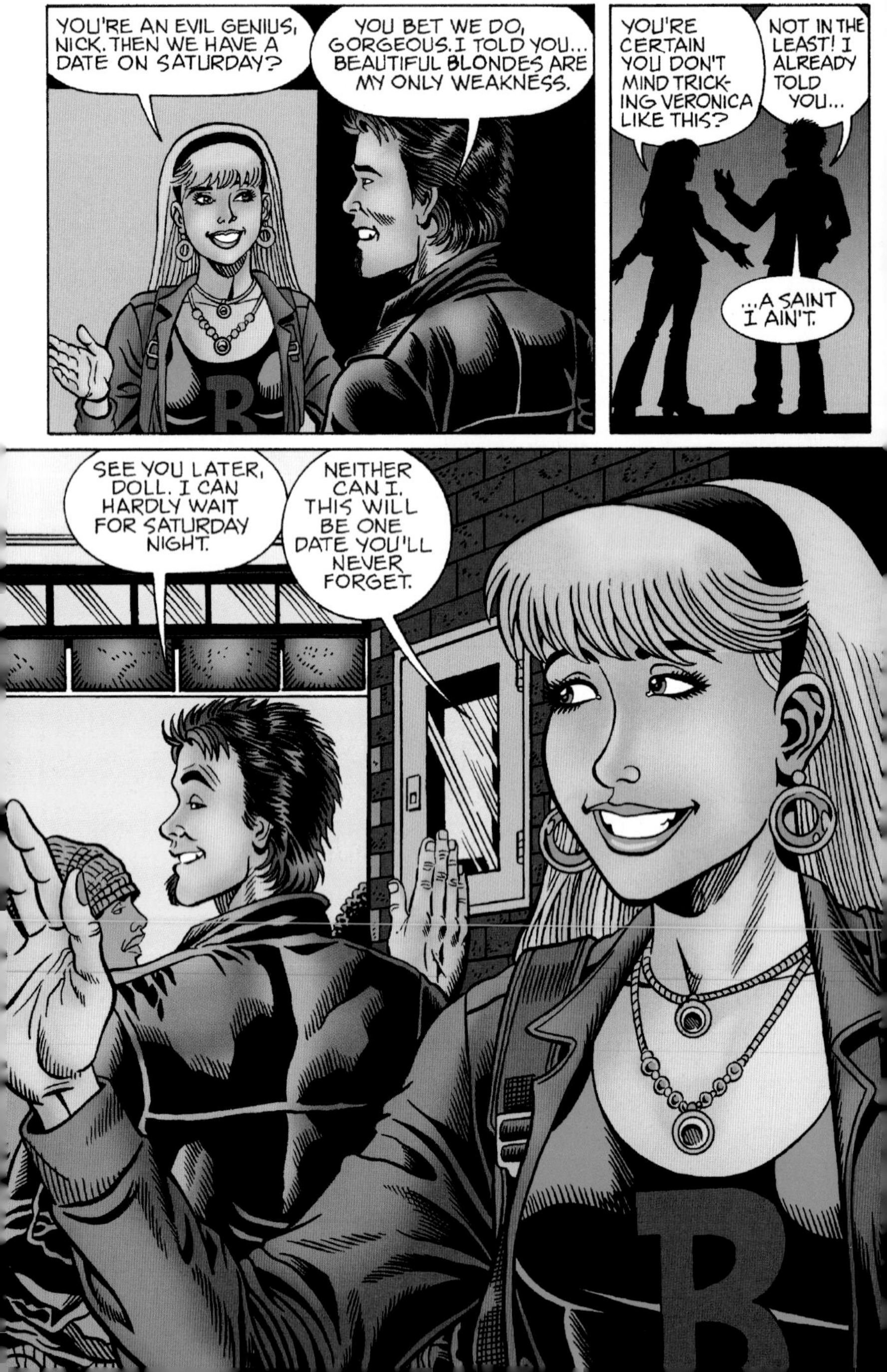
YOU'RE AN EVIL GENIUS, NICK. THEN WE HAVE A DATE ON SATURDAY?
YOU BET WE DO, GORGEOUS. I TOLD YOU... BEAUTIFUL BLONDES ARE MY ONLY WEAKNESS.
YOU'RE CERTAIN YOU DON'T MIND TRICKING VERONICA LIKE THIS?
NOT IN THE LEAST! I ALREADY TOLD YOU...
...A SAINT I AIN'T.
SEE YOU LATER, DOLL. I CAN HARDLY WAIT FOR SATURDAY NIGHT.
NEITHER CAN I. THIS WILL BE ONE DATE YOU'LL NEVER FORGET.

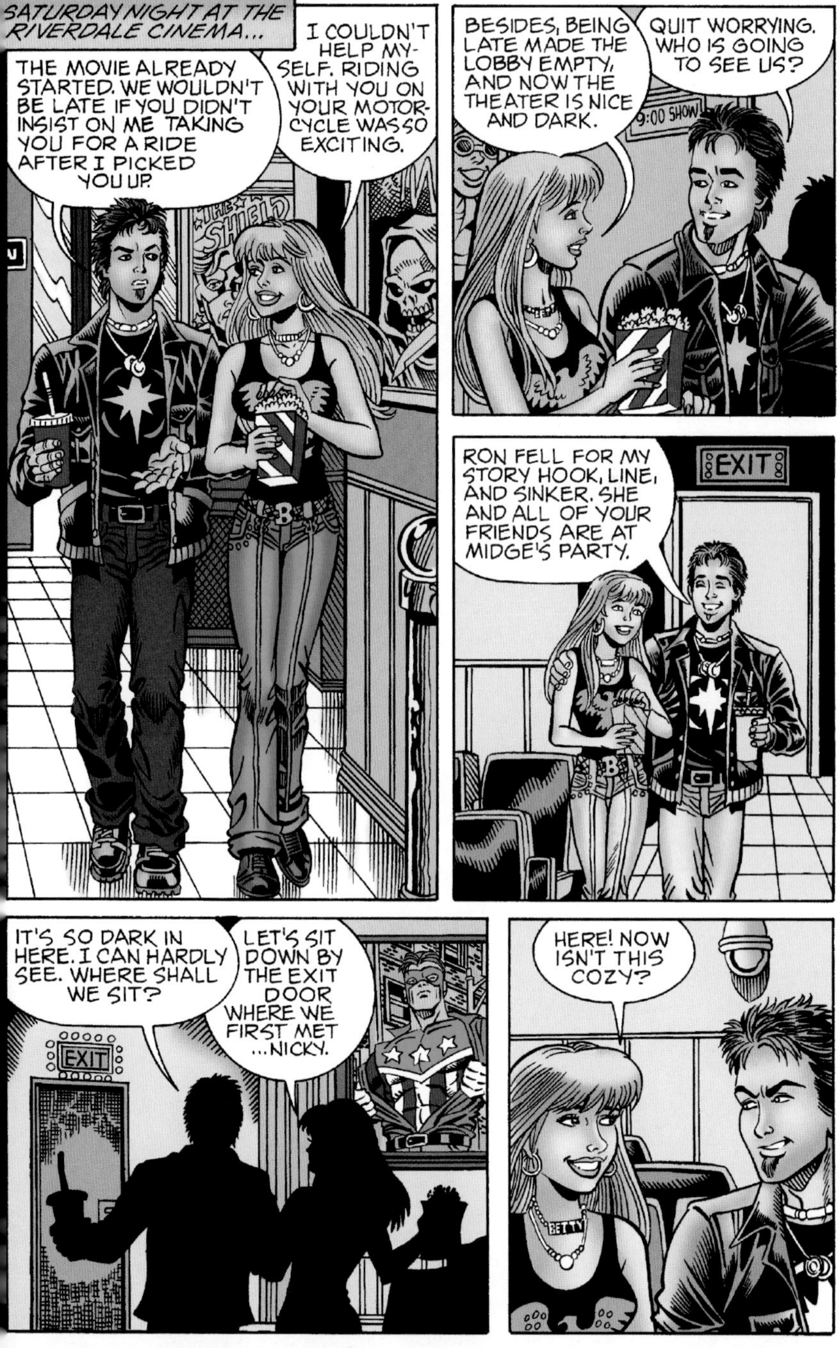
SATURDAY NIGHT AT THE RIVERDALE CINEMA...
THE MOVIE ALREADY STARTED. WE WOULDN'T BE LATE IF YOU DIDN'T INSIST ON ME TAKING YOU FOR A RIDE AFTER I PICKED YOU UP.
I COULDN'T HELP MYSELF. RIDING WITH YOU ON YOUR MOTORCYCLE WAS SO EXCITING.
BESIDES, BEING LATE MADE THE LOBBY EMPTY, AND NOW THE THEATER IS NICE AND DARK.
QUIT WORRYING. WHO IS GOING TO SEE US?
9:00 SHOW
EXIT
RON FELL FOR MY STORY HOOK, LINE, AND SINKER. SHE AND ALL OF YOUR FRIENDS ARE AT MIDGE'S PARTY.
IT'S SO DARK IN HERE. I CAN HARDLY SEE. WHERE SHALL WE SIT?
LET'S SIT DOWN BY THE EXIT DOOR WHERE WE FIRST MET ...NICKY.
EXIT
HERE! NOW ISN'T THIS COZY?
BETTY

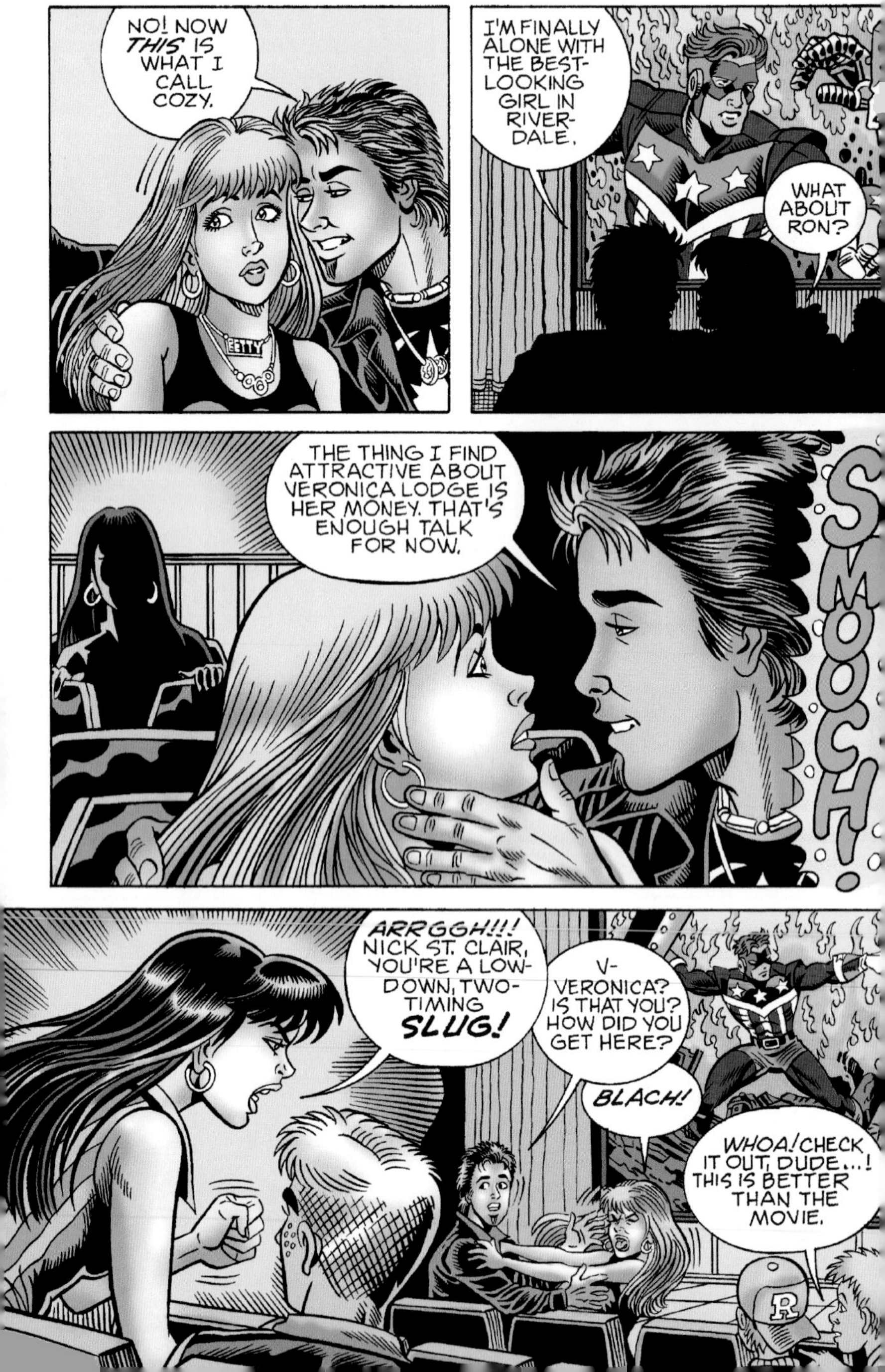

NO! NOW THIS IS WHAT I CALL COZY.
I'M FINALLY ALONE WITH THE BEST-LOOKING GIRL IN RIVERDALE.
WHAT ABOUT RON?
THE THING I FIND ATTRACTIVE ABOUT VERONICA LODGE IS HER MONEY. THAT'S ENOUGH TALK FOR NOW.
SMOOCH!
ARRGGH!!! NICK ST. CLAIR, YOU'RE A LOW-DOWN, TWO-TIMING SLUG!
V-VERONICA? IS THAT YOU? HOW DID YOU GET HERE?
BLACH!
WHOA! CHECK IT OUT, DUDE...! THIS IS BETTER THAN THE MOVIE.

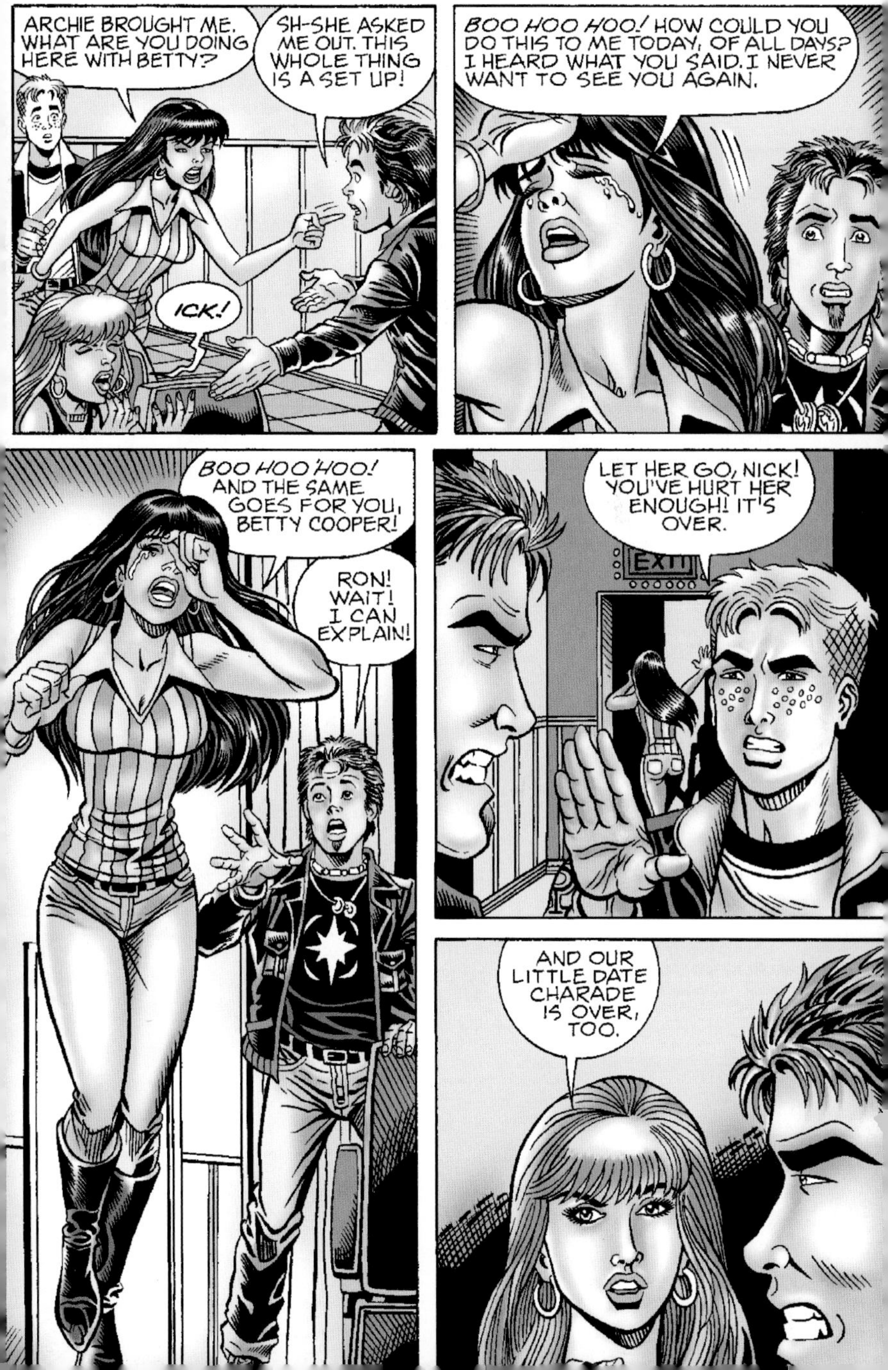
ARCHIE BROUGHT ME. WHAT ARE YOU DOING HERE WITH BETTY?
SH-SHE ASKED ME OUT. THIS WHOLE THING IS A SET UP!
ICK!
BOO HOO HOO! HOW COULD YOU DO THIS TO ME TODAY, OF ALL DAYS? I HEARD WHAT YOU SAID. I NEVER WANT TO SEE YOU AGAIN.
BOO HOO HOO! AND THE SAME GOES FOR YOU, BETTY COOPER!
RON! WAIT! I CAN EXPLAIN!
LET HER GO, NICK! YOU'VE HURT HER ENOUGH! IT'S OVER.
EXIT
AND OUR LITTLE DATE CHARADE IS OVER, TOO.

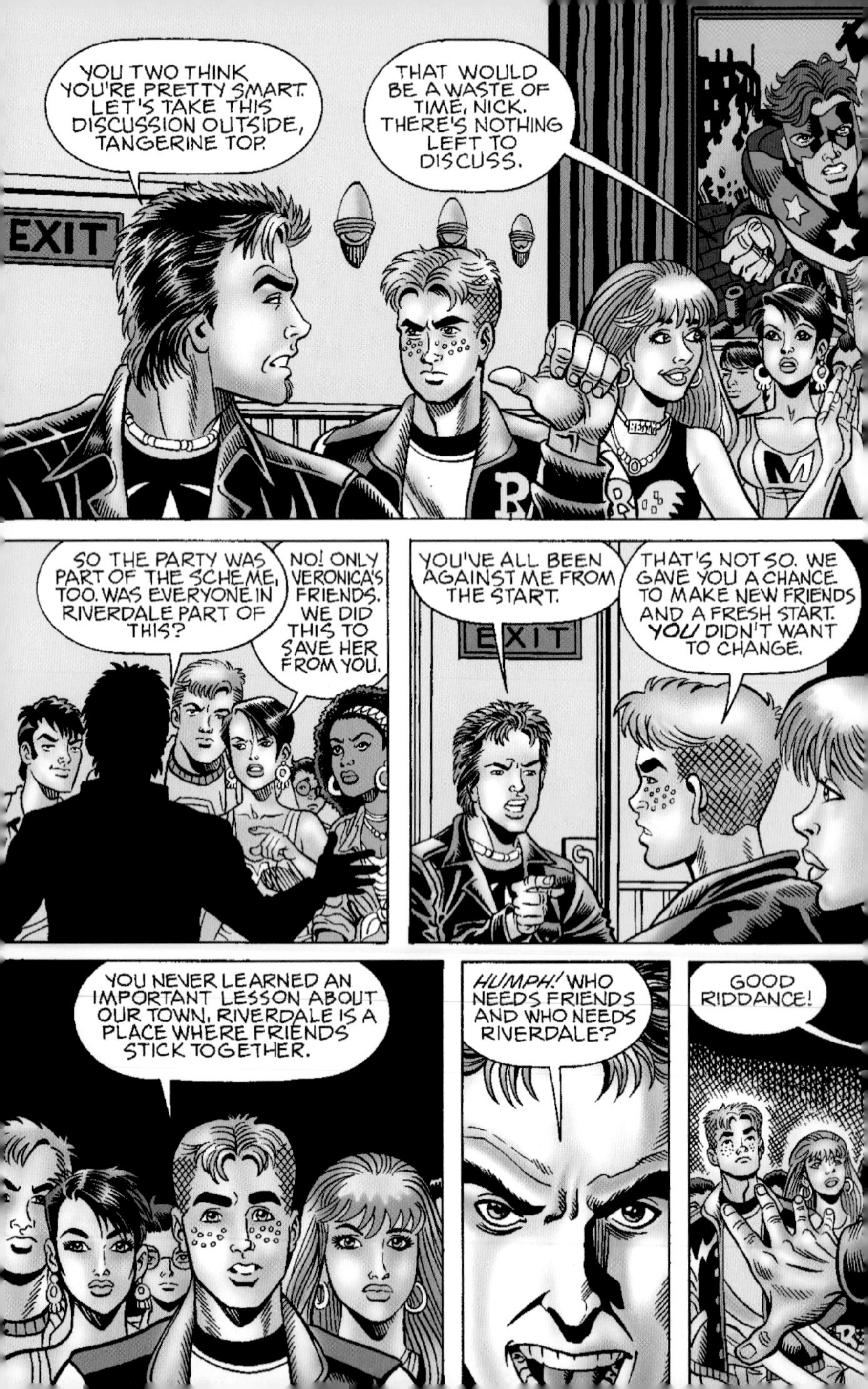
YOU TWO THINK YOU'RE PRETTY SMART. LET'S TAKE THIS DISCUSSION OUTSIDE, TANGERINE TOP.
THAT WOULD BE A WASTE OF TIME, NICK. THERE'S NOTHING LEFT TO DISCUSS.
EXIT
SO THE PARTY WAS PART OF THE SCHEME, TOO. WAS EVERYONE IN RIVERDALE PART OF THIS?
NO! ONLY VERONICA'S FRIENDS. WE DID THIS TO SAVE HER FROM YOU.
YOU'VE ALL BEEN AGAINST ME FROM THE START.
EXIT
THAT'S NOT SO. WE GAVE YOU A CHANCE TO MAKE NEW FRIENDS AND A FRESH START. YOU DIDN'T WANT TO CHANGE.
YOU NEVER LEARNED AN IMPORTANT LESSON ABOUT OUR TOWN. RIVERDALE IS A PLACE WHERE FRIENDS STICK TOGETHER.
HUMPH! WHO NEEDS FRIENDS AND WHO NEEDS RIVERDALE?
GOOD RIDDANCE!

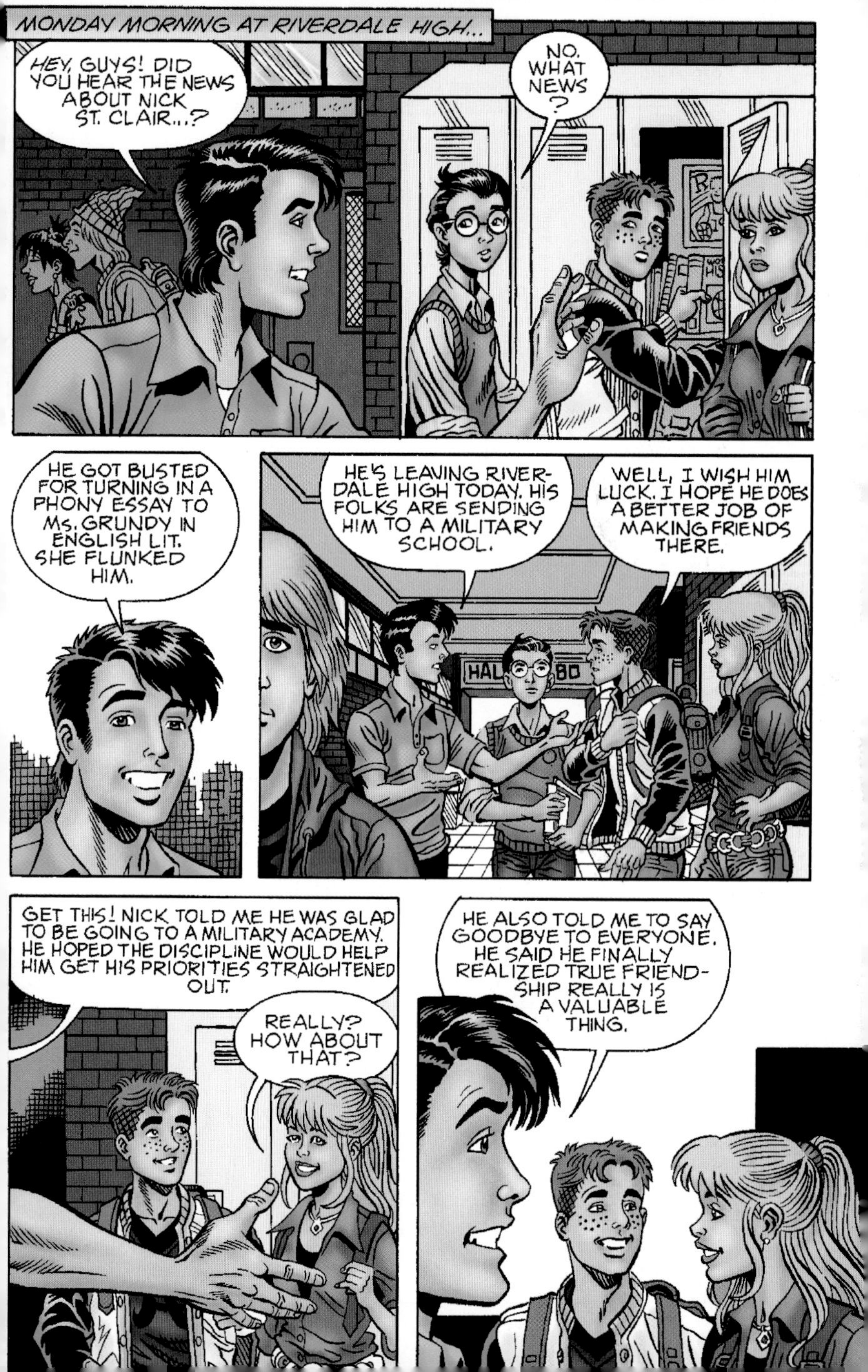
MONDAY MORNING AT RIVERDALE HIGH...
HEY, GUYS! DID YOU HEAR THE NEWS ABOUT NICK ST. CLAIR...?
NO. WHAT NEWS?
HE GOT BUSTED FOR TURNING IN A PHONY ESSAY TO Ms. GRUNDY IN ENGLISH LIT. SHE FLUNKED HIM.
HE'S LEAVING RIVER-DALE HIGH TODAY. HIS FOLKS ARE SENDING HIM TO A MILITARY SCHOOL.
WELL, I WISH HIM LUCK. I HOPE HE DOES A BETTER JOB OF MAKING FRIENDS THERE.
GET THIS! NICK TOLD ME HE WAS GLAD TO BE GOING TO A MILITARY ACADEMY. HE HOPED THE DISCIPLINE WOULD HELP HIM GET HIS PRIORITIES STRAIGHTENED OUT.
REALLY? HOW ABOUT THAT?
HE ALSO TOLD ME TO SAY GOODBYE TO EVERYONE. HE SAID HE FINALLY REALIZED TRUE FRIEND-SHIP REALLY IS A VALUABLE THING.

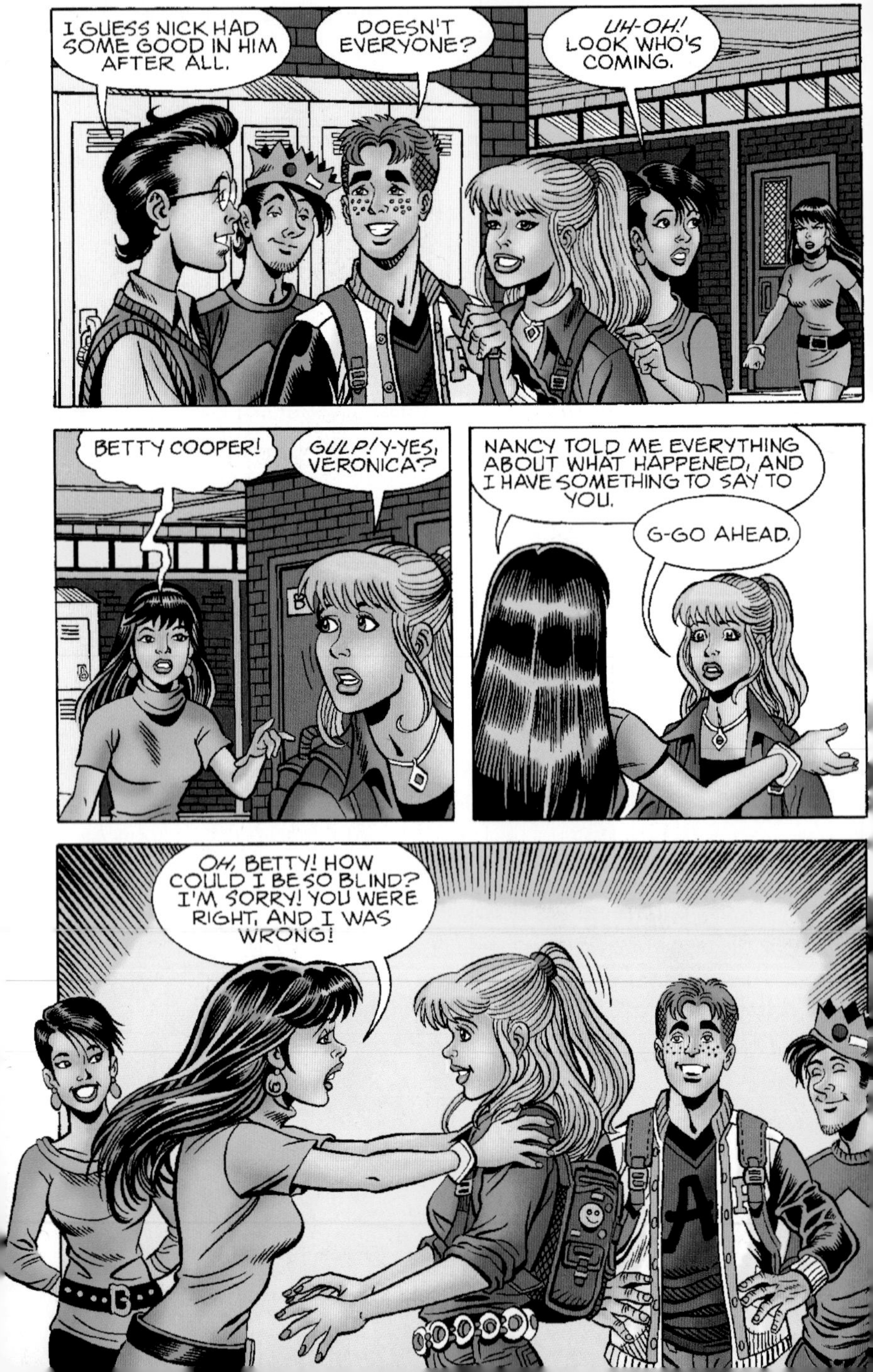
I GUESS NICK HAD SOME GOOD IN HIM AFTER ALL.
DOESN'T EVERYONE?
UH-OH! LOOK WHO'S COMING.
BETTY COOPER!
GULP! Y-YES, VERONICA?
NANCY TOLD ME EVERYTHING ABOUT WHAT HAPPENED, AND I HAVE SOMETHING TO SAY TO YOU.
G-GO AHEAD.
OH, BETTY! HOW COULD I BE SO BLIND? I'M SORRY! YOU WERE RIGHT, AND I WAS WRONG!

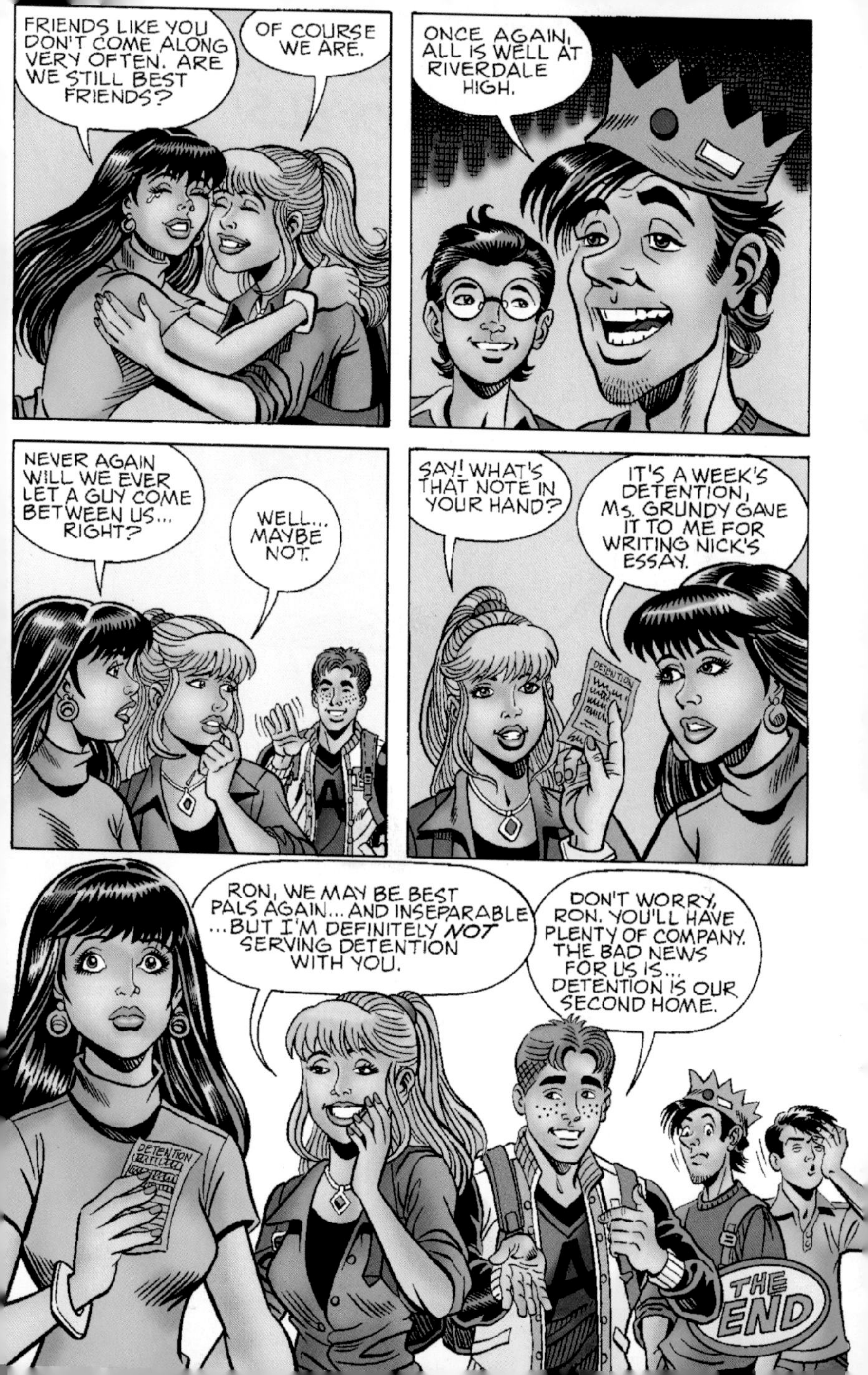
FRIENDS LIKE YOU DON'T COME ALONG VERY OFTEN. ARE WE STILL BEST FRIENDS?
OF COURSE WE ARE.
ONCE AGAIN, ALL IS WELL AT RIVERDALE HIGH.
NEVER AGAIN WILL WE EVER LET A GUY COME BETWEEN US... RIGHT?
WELL... MAYBE NOT.
SAY! WHAT'S THAT NOTE IN YOUR HAND?
IT'S A WEEK'S DETENTION, Ms. GRUNDY GAVE IT TO ME FOR WRITING NICK'S ESSAY.
DETENTION
RON, WE MAY BE BEST PALS AGAIN... AND INSEPARABLE ...BUT I'M DEFINITELY NOT SERVING DETENTION WITH YOU.
DON'T WORRY, RON. YOU'LL HAVE PLENTY OF COMPANY. THE BAD NEWS FOR US IS... DETENTION IS OUR SECOND HOME.
DETENTION
THE END

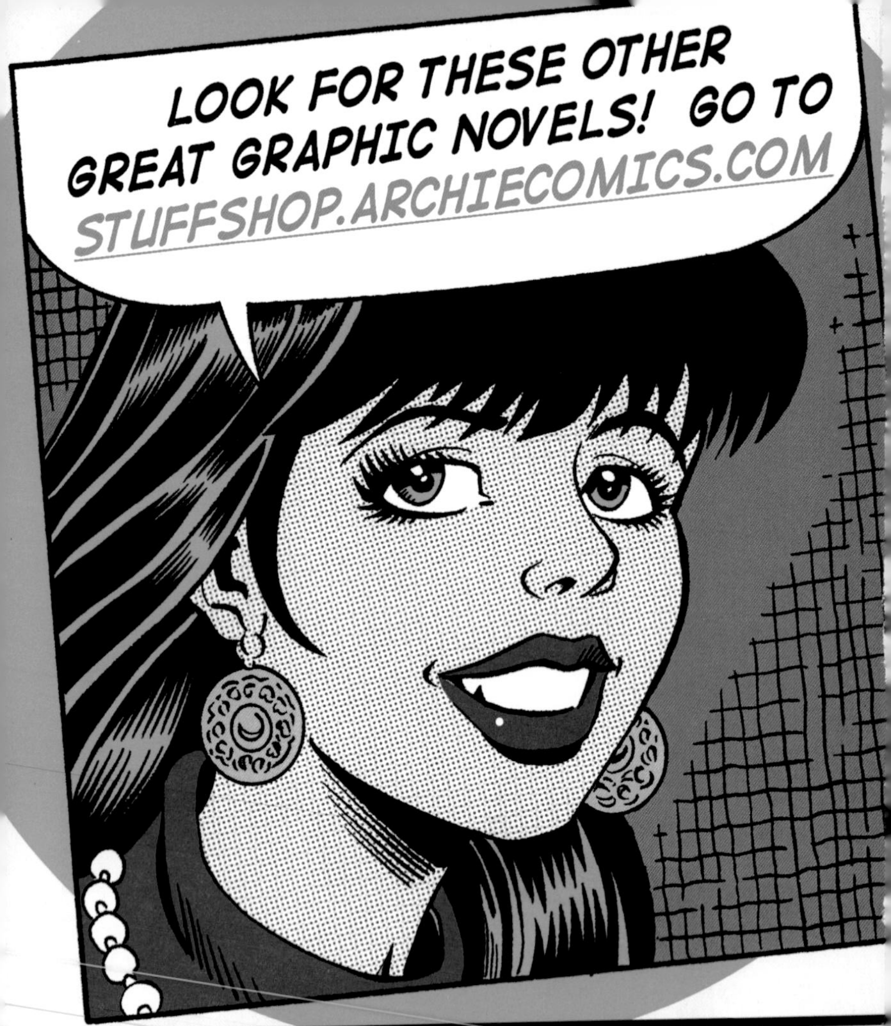
LOOK FOR THESE OTHER GREAT GRAPHIC NOVELS! GO TO STUFFSHOP.ARCHIECOMICS.COM

ARCHIE AMERICANA SERIES

BEST OF THE FORTIES
BEST OF THE FORTIES-BOOK 2
BEST OF THE FIFTIES
BEST OF THE FIFTIES-BOOK 2
BEST OF THE SIXTIES
BEST OF THE SEVENTIES
BEST OF THE EIGHTIES

MORE GREAT GRAPHIC NOVELS

BETTY & VERONICA SUMMER FUN
THE ADVENTURES OF LITTLE ARCHIE
THE BEST OF JOSIE & THE PUSSYCATS
ARCHIE'S CLASSIC CHRISTMAS STORIES
ARCHIE'S CAMP TALES